THE·LAST·SECRET

Also by Mary McGarry Morris

Vanished

A Dangerous Woman

Songs in Ordinary Time

Fiona Range

A Hole in the Universe

The Lost Mother

THE·LAST·SECRET

A Novel

Mary McGarry Morris

Shaye Areheart Books / New York

Copyright © 2009 by Mary McGarry Morris

All rights reserved.
Published in the United States by Shaye Areheart Books, an imprint of the
Crown Publishing Group, a division of Random House, Inc., New York.
www.crownpublishing.com

SHAYE AREHEART BOOKS with colophon is a registered trademark of
Random House, Inc.

Library of Congress Cataloging-in-Publication Data

Morris, Mary McGarry.
The last secret : a novel / Mary McGarry Morris.
p. cm.
1. Adultery—Fiction. 2. Secrecy—Fiction. 3. Psychological fiction.
4. Domestic fiction. I. Title.

PS3563.O874454L37 2009
813'.54—dc22   2008025587
ISBN 978-0-307-45127-9

Printed in the United States of America

Design by Lauren Dong

10 9 8 7 6 5 4 3 2 1

First Edition

To John C. McGarry—

my father,

looking seaward

out at me

THE · LAST · SECRET

They still don't believe her, and why should they, but it's always the same, it is—this same dream, darkness, heat, and the song, the same song, same deafening beat.

Driving. Midnight. Still driving; their beacon through the desert, flashing lights, pink and green neon from the roadhouse roof. Eddie cruises the parking lot. He parks on the farthest side, in shadows. Tired and hungry, she slips after him into the reek of beery dust. It coats the bar top, the windows, the dimly lit jukebox blasting that song "Gimme Some Lovin' " over and over and over again. Their luck's about to change, Eddie says. He feeds quarters into the jukebox, the last of their money—hers, mostly.

Sitting behind them, the only other customer, a skinny man, grimy shirt, loosened tie, jacket bunched up next to his beer mug. His head bobs over the table. Her own face floats in the murky bar mirror, outlined in blinking red Christmas bulbs. This inferno of caged heat pulsates between the sagging ceiling and gritty plank floor. A dream, nothing's real. The blur of overhead fan blades dizzies her.

Elbows sticking to the bar, she sips a rum and Coke; only seventeen, but as long as she keeps sliding the drink back in front of Eddie, the skinny bartender could care. He ignores her, acts like she's not even here. She grabs another cherry, and Eddie winks in the mirror. Their last meal, hamburgers—this morning; "poor man's brunch," Eddie said. Every time the bartender looks away, she grabs more, cherries, olives, slimy little cocktail onions, shoves them into her mouth, swiveling on the stool to hide her ravenous chewing. They have devoured the bowl of pretzels. After warm beer in the car all day, it's rum Eddie wants. The more he drinks the sharper he grows, pale eyes glinting, voice roughening, snagging on her soft parts, moving deep inside, his hard running feet, tingling through her legs and thighs, belly and heart, pounding with the music. She covers her grin. Drinking makes her tired and silly, the least little thing, she's laughing so hard she can't stop. Or crying. Today, mostly crying.

Another quarter, that song again.

Eddie pauses by the table. The man's head jerks up. Laughing, Eddie leans close, back muscles rippling through his damp T-shirt. Blond, tanned, blue eyes, dimples, oh God. Her eyes burn. Eddie's gesturing. The man glances back, and she looks away. Now Eddie's hand is soft on her thigh, one finger stroking flesh high, high between her legs. Her eyes close as his mouth brushes her ear, singing that song, heat in her ear.

She's known him forever, it seems through the haze of longing. But only a summer month before she was a chambermaid at the Clayborne Hotel in Lake George that drizzly day when he drove up in the yellow Mustang, top down, his arm over the back of the seat. "Hey, pretty girl," he called as she dragged along the gravel path in her baggy green uniform, arms loaded with buckets, scrub brushes, and mop. "I've come to rescue you."

It was her last summer of high school. Six years older, he knew so much about life. After Yale, he'd invested the ten-thousand-dollar graduation gift from his wealthy grandfather in an international grain brokerage company. In just three months' time he made a quarter of a million dollars. Then came the sharks who, with a taste of his blood, wanted more. "Bad deals and blind faith," he'd sigh. "A deadly combination." There was a great job in L.A., a friend of his grandfather's. He just had to get there.

Tall with boyish hips, still almost flat-chested, but she drove him crazy, Eddie said. "You're the first one," he whispered in his bleak room, rented by the night. Too busy studying, he'd never had a social life. He liked to turn all the lights on while undressing her.

Eyes closed, her arm over her face, trembling, craving the stasis of sleep while he stroked her feet, traced each bone in her rib cage, murmuring, "There, pretty girl, there, there."

Eleven when her father died. Her mother, by necessity, stern, a schoolteacher who, after having raised her older daughter Carol to a college-educated, newly wed nurse, was bewildered by this younger child's moody volatility.

One day after work Eddie came by to say he was going. L.A. They couldn't hold the job much longer. Did she want to come? Yes or no. Time was running out. He had another one of his terrible headaches.

She called from the road, cringing as her mother demanded to speak with this Eddie she'd never even heard of, much less met. Smiling, he took the phone and apologized for their abrupt departure, but she could rest assured her daughter was in safe hands.

"I love her, Mrs. Trimble. And I'm going to take care of her. Always. I promise. All we want is your blessing."

"My blessing!" her mother shrieked across the line. "My blessing! All you'll get from me is a warrant for your arrest!"

Watching a baseball game at the end of the bar, the bartender hunches close to the snowy black-and-white TV screen. Another quarter. That song again. Eddie's song. Red lights flash on his face. Her stomach lurches, oniony bile searing her throat. Her sweaty thighs stick to the brittle plastic. Eddie's arm falls, heavy on her shoulders. His tongue drags over her ear. She can't believe what he wants.

Turning from the table, the man watches with a wet, imploring grin.

"Like a joke. You'll see. C'mere. Feel. Feel, can you feel that?" Eddie asks, pressing against her leg. "You know where that belongs. You know. You know . . ." His moan burns her ear. "Just a little, that's all, to get us outta here."

"No . . . no," she whispers, curling her neck away from his face. It takes all her effort.

"Look at him." With Eddie's contemptuous gesture, the leering man waves. "Flashing that roll, just begging for it, and us hungry. Come on. L.A., that's all."

"No."

"Just get him outside, that's all I ask."

"No. No, Eddie!"

They'll be doing the drunk a favor, Eddie says, smiling. The man tries to wink back, instead both eyes close. "His money's gonna be a whole lot better spent feeding us than on that."

"I can't. I can't. I can't. I can't." She is crying again.

Eddie shades his eyes. "Jesus Christ! Will you cut that out!" Clenched jaw. Squinting. It's the flashing lights. His headaches scare her.

"I can't help it." She blows her nose in a stiff cocktail napkin. "I'm sorry!"

"Just get him outside."

She shakes her head.

"In my car. Front seat."

"No!"

He squeezes her wrist against his chest. "Tell you what then, I'm walking out that door, and you either come out with the asshole and we're on our way in two minutes, or stay here." He leans close. "For all the fuck I care!" He storms out.

"Eddie!"

The closing door, her flesh ripping from the stool, the grinning man, clutching his suit jacket, staggering her way. "You pretty . . . pretty . . . ," he stammers, reaching for her. "You pretty thing, you . . ."

"No. Don't." Ashamed, she doesn't want the bartender to hear. She gets the door open. "I'm leaving. I have to go. You stay here. Don't come out." She can't pull free. His fingers dig into her arm. "He's out here! Don't." She pushes him. In the parking lot their scuffling feet scrape a dead echo through the desert stillness. She shoves him away. "Go back in! Please!"

"No!" His voice thickens with anger. "I can't wait! I'm gonna fall asleep. We hafta do it now!" As if for inspection he straightens, lifts his chin, stares at her. "I come fast," he promises with the pathetic, earnest dignity born of a lifetime justifying inadequacies. "And I don't slobber around after."

The Mustang's shadowy hump rises from the side of the building. From here the man can't see Eddie crouched in back.

"See, you don't know . . . you don't understand . . . this isn't what you think," she whispers. "This isn't—"

"I know what this is!" the man shouts, his narrow face hatefully contorted. "It's a quick fuck before you go fuck your pimp on my fuckin' twenty bucks."

"No! Please! Listen!" With the press of sweat, his, hers, unwashed, vile, her knees sway. "I have to get out of here!"

"C'mere." He's trying to kiss her mouth. "You sweet . . . sweet . . ."

"Where's your car?"

"He said his car . . ." Gesturing, he teeters.

"No! He's in there. In the back, waiting! C'mon!" She grabs his arm.

"Pervert . . . goddamn pervert." The man staggers against her. " 'Magine . . ."

It seems the longest walk through the heat, jagged and spitting light from the gigantic pink and lime green flower, flashing overhead, obscene against the stars and the high white peel of moon. Nearing the Mustang she senses Eddie's dark coil about to spring. She runs toward the man's car, pulling him with her.

"Hurry!" she hisses as he fumbles in his pocket.

"Oh, Jesus." He peers at the loose keys in his palm. "She can't wait . . . here . . . here, she goes," he mutters, finally unlocking the door. She scrambles inside, pushes down the lock on her side.

"Lock it!" she cries through the trapped heat.

Instead, he is rolling down his window, entreating her thickly to be patient. The Mustang door flies open and Eddie jumps out.

"Close it!" She leans, reaching across him to do it herself.

"Oh, you," the man moans, forcing her head into his lap.

"No!" she groans, hitting him. She sits back. Blood trickles down her chin. His ring, nails, something has cut her lip. "Start the car! Just start the car!"

The man's window darkens. Eddie's hand darts in, opens the door. One knee braced on the seat, he jams the heel of his hand into the man's nose, shoves him against her. "Grab him! Hold him!" Eddie yells, face taut in the dim overhead light as he pins the man down. His struggling, oily head grinds against her chest. His whimpering pleas sicken her.

Through the distant night comes a probing yellow eye, the train's steel and wooden clatter, the hard-beating ruckus of the song:

So glad we made it,
So glad we made it,
You gotta gimme some lovin',
Gimme some lovin' . . .

Breaking free, the man lurches forward, reaches under the seat. A lead pipe. He swings and Eddie knocks it from his hand.

"Asshole! Stupid asshole!" Eddie's eyes widen, his nostrils flare with the grin of gleaming teeth as the pipe splits the man's face in two. The man jerks forward, arms cradling his head. "What'd you do that for?" Eddie keeps demanding in a high, gasping voice, of her, of her, of her as the pipe smashes the man's head until he sags against the steering wheel.

Opening the door, she half falls, half slides, crawling, then running, across the road toward the looming yellow light. Crossing the tracks, she waves her arms and screams into the deafening commotion. "Help me! Help me!" Freight and tank cars roar by, parallel with the roadbed. "Help me! Help me! Help me!" she pants, running with the clattering train. In the gaps between cars, come flashes of headlights, going in the same direction as the train. "Oh, Eddie," she cries, head back, arms pumping as she runs faster than she has ever run. "Eddie!" she sobs, teary phlegm leaking into her bloody mouth.

The caboose hurtles past, distant, fading, Eddie's taillights with it. She stumbles onto the road, back the way she came, the sudden quiet bearing only the platplatplat of her sandals on the macadam, her gasping, wheezy breath, as behind her swells the anxious whine of a car. She dives into the shallow ditch beside the tracks. Eyes closed, she lies curled in cinders. With her cheek to the hard rise of the gully, scrubby brambles snag her arms and legs. The oncoming wheels pulsate in her skull. He slows down, speeds past. She scrambles onto the road, stomach churning with every step. All at once she bends over, vomits, legs splayed, chest heaving, still gagging as headlamps flare high from behind, illuminating the emptiness ahead. The truck slows in a squeal of air and brakes. The driver peers down from his silver cab. "You okay?" he hollers.

"I need a ride!"

"Get in!"

"Oh, Jesus," she cries as the door closes and the big rig rumbles ahead.

"What happened?" the barrel-chested man asks, dead cigar stub clenched between his teeth. "You in trouble?"

"I don't know!"

"What happened?" He taps his chin, the blood.

"There was a fight . . . and my boyfriend . . . oh, God, I'm so scared. Something terrible happened. Oh, God, God, help me, please help me," she sobs.

"He in a convertible? Yellow Mustang? Then slide down, just slide down," the driver says. "Okay," he says when the car whizzes by.

A few miles ahead a cruiser passes, dome light spinning red. The truck driver flips on his radio, keeps glancing in the rearview.

A woman's staticky voice: "Ambulance! Up to the club. Fast, Buddy says."

"Oh, God," she moans into her sticky hands.

"Somebody's hurt." The driver looks at her.

"My boyfriend. Eddie," she sobs. "This guy tried to hit him. With a pipe. And then, oh, God," she gags, retching again.

"Hey, hey, c'mon now," the driver says. "You're all right now. Hey, I got kids myself. How old are you anyways?"

"Seventeen," she bawls at the horror, the shame of it. Her careful upbringing, her hardworking, principled mother.

"What's your name?"

"Nora." She hesitates. "Trimble."

"Where you from, Nora?"

"Massachusetts."

"You run away from home or something?"

"No. I don't know."

"Wanna go back?"

"I don't know. I don't know what to do. Maybe I should go back, go back and help. Oh, God, he's back there. In the car. He's hurt."

"Who? Eddie?"

"Oh my God," she moans, covers her face.

"How old's Eddie?"

"Twenty-three."

"Eddie's a big boy. He'll take care of it. He don't need you."

A whoosh now, like the unsealing of a vault, as the truck slows for the ramp onto the interstate.

CHAPTER·1

One more time now," the photographer says. "Smile, Mrs. Hammond. You, too, Father Grewley. Don't look so grim."

Nora shivers through a taut smile.

"Freezing," Father Grewley says, teeth chattering.

The camera keeps clicking. The pictures are being taken on the front steps. SOJOURN HOUSE says the gold-leafed sign. Last night in his State of the Union address, the president praised, along with others, Nora and the young priest for their work on behalf of battered women. Overseen by the parish and privately funded, the house is staffed by volunteers. Every penny, loaf of bread, beds, linen, even oil for the ancient furnace is donated. They operate without state or federal money because as Father Grewley has just told the *Newsweek* reporter, their mission is "about neighbors helping neighbors." And this way their only guidelines are their own. Nora is the new chairman of the board of directors.

"Oh boy," she sighs as a small blue car pulls up to the curb. The magnetic sign on the opening door says THE FRANKLIN CHRONICLE. Camera in hand, Jimmy Lee tumbles out, running as if to cover a fire.

"Sorry I'm late, Mrs. Hammond," he apologizes, taking his place beside the magazine photographer who looks tempted to turn his camera on his pony-tailed six-foot-seven counterpart.

"That's okay, Jimmy," she calls back. "Do your thing."

"You should have a coat, Mrs. Hammond. It's wicked cold. I could run back and get you one. Or we could go inside maybe." Shoulders

hunched, he begins to shoot. "That's good, that's good. Father Grewley! Look up a little more, that's better, that's better. Good! Great!
Great shot! Traffic was terrible," Jimmy Lee says in the midst of his
legendary balletic routine, crouching, leaning, two steps back, a spin,
forward lunge, camera clicking, flashing, the entire process so
bizarrely awkward that the magazine photographer and interviewer
are trying not to laugh at this clown, this yokel from the local paper.
"Gotta get this right," Jimmy Lee mutters, dropping into a sudden
squat. "Big story! Can't mess this one up, can we now?" he says with a
grin at the magazine people as he jumps up and snaps their picture.
"Bet you don't get many of yourself on the job, now do you? Gimme a
card, JPEG it to you." He runs up to Nora and hugs her. "How's that?
How's that? Feel better? Any warmer now? Okay, good. Gonna run
this now. See you! Bye now!" he calls. He jumps into his car and pulls
away on squealing tires.

"Who was that masked man?" the magazine reporter asks.

"He works for the *Chronicle*," Father Grewley says on their way up
the stairs.

"Can you imagine what those pictures'll look like?" the photographer says.

Father Grewley holds the door for Nora who pauses before stepping inside. "So that you'll know," she says back to them. "Jimmy Lee
works for me." The warm vestibule smells of meat loaf and onions.

"Mrs. Hammond owns the *Chronicle*," Father Grewley informs the
sheepish young men on their way into his office.

In fact, the paper is equally owned by Nora's husband, Kendall
Hammond, and his brother, Oliver, with their cousin Stephen holding
a 10 percent share. Always a family enterprise, it was originally named
the *Hammond Chronicle*, until 1897 when a more civically sensitive
Hammond relative, a woman actually, widow of the late and profligate
Cecil Hammond, Ken and Oliver's great-grandfather, changed the
masthead to the *Franklin Chronicle*.

The reporter is asking Father Grewley about Sojourn House's volunteers. Mostly women, he says. Some men. They usually handle bigger projects, like the new gutters and downspouts they installed last

summer. The furnace cleanout, that's always done by the same man. Tom Hollister. "That's H-o-l-l-i-s-t-e-r," the priest spells. "Now, the new cedar fence, those men're Leo Ross, Jack—"

"That's okay." The reporter closes his notebook. Sojourn House is part of a larger story, he explains. Probably just a sentence or two will even get in.

A rare look of disappointment clouds the priest's face. "Well, maybe one of the guests would talk to you. Get their perspective. You know, to give you a better feel for the place. Alice. Don't you think?" he asks Nora.

Nora doesn't know what to say. The whole point of Sojourn House is anonymity for the women seeking protection here. Not only is Alice one of their newer guests, but the poor thing can barely make eye contact, much less speak to anyone.

"Yeah, well, maybe if there's a follow-up. Sometimes that happens. You know," the reporter says to Nora as if she will understand, being in the same business, after all. Actually, she has nothing to do with news stories anymore. Thanks to her brother-in-law, editing special supplements is what she does now. Reporting was her first job after college. She worked for a small paper on the south shore before being hired by the *Chronicle*. Two years later, she and Ken, the publisher's son, were married. After Chloe's birth she retired, not returning until Drew started middle school. Ken didn't want her to go back to work. In fact, it caused one of their worst disagreements. They certainly didn't need the money, but the children *did* need her at home, Ken insisted; a weak argument now that they were older, especially since she could schedule the job around their activities. He finally understood that she *needed* to work. There was only so much to be done around the house. She'd never been particularly domestic, anyway, didn't enjoy crafts like her friend Robin, and she wanted more than just volunteer work, which, like her status as Ken Hammond's wife, still seems more derivative of his success than hers. Tennis and golf weren't fulfilling the way they were for so many of their friends. Even Robin had stopped playing. Only because of the baby, Lyra, Ken pointed out.

Robin and Bob Gendron's second child was a shock, born when

both parents were in their forties. The two families don't see as much of each other as they once did, but Nora still values her friendship with Robin, secretly envying her looks, joie de vivre, and unflagging energy. Even her unexpected pregnancy seemed a lark. Lately though, life seems to be taking its toll. Poor Robin has her hands full now between Bob's chronic drinking and trying to keep up with a small child and a teenager.

It was Oliver who finally talked his brother into Nora's return to the paper. They needed a supplements editor, and who better? She was smart, unflappable, well respected, and most important, could be trusted. Loyalty matters to Oliver, sometimes to a fault. When it comes to running the paper, Oliver usually prevails.

"This could be such a boost," the young priest says after the magazine reporters leave. Something in his tone irritates her. What? His eagerness, his delight in the attention? Let him have his moment, she reminds herself uneasily. Ken's words; he can't understand her need to always bring people back down to earth. Solid ground. Reality, where life should be lived. The safest place, for her, anyway. Happiness so often trails a long shadow: another of her mother's bracing maxims. She knows Ken's right. He's been after her for years to "stop and smell the roses instead of being such a slave to the clock and other people's rules." And she has been trying, but lately he only seems annoyed. Last Friday, seeing his agitation after a meeting with Oliver, she suggested they hop in the car and drive to New York for the weekend the way they used to. Find a nice hotel room, then wander around the city for two days, just the two of them. "C'mon!" she teased, flipping him the car keys. They landed on the floor. "Why?" he asked with such bewilderment that she felt foolish.

Father Grewley's telephone rings. "Hello!" he answers, beaming at Nora. The calls have been coming in all day, well-wishers, new people wanting to jump aboard. "Wonderful! He is? Yes, of course. We'd be honored! Oh . . . well, actually, they just left." Congressman Linzer's office, he says, hanging up. He laughs. "His assistant said they're going to try and get the reporters back. See if they need coverage of the congressman looking the place over."

"God, he's such a publicity hound!"

"But useful to the cause," Father Grewley laughs.

Like herself, she thinks. A cog. Like the volunteers in the dining room setting the dinner tables. Meat loaf, mashed potatoes, and gravy tonight, the priest announces with the clatter of plates and flatware. He invites her to stay and eat with him and the "guests." Alice would love spending more time with her, he says. Nora's been such a good mentor to her. She wishes she could, she says, squirming. Actually, she can't stand eating here. She'll do anything to help Father Grewley and these unfortunate women. She painted the kitchen walls and helped clean out the verminous cellar, but the thought of actually sitting down and sharing a meal here makes her queasy. Another unsettling truth about herself that demands compensation, longer hours, harder work, and more money.

CHAPTER·2

He's already passed two shelters. The best one is on the other side of the city. Fastidious in appearance, he puts a high price on quality. The irony of his rattish slither close to the buildings isn't lost on him as he tries to avoid the downpour from the roof edges. Crossing the street, he runs. The rain pelts him in blinding sheets. He ducks into a brightly lit drugstore. His shoes squish loudly on his way to the back. His wet clothes are plastered to his trim frame. He aches with humiliation. He can't get into his room. In addition to back rent, the landlady says he owes her $440. The computer's a piece of junk, and she wants her money back. The woman's a bald-faced liar, claiming it's stolen, because her nephew traced the serial numbers. There are no serial numbers. He removed them before he sold it to her. It was working fine until she let her kids play with it. People are always trying to take advantage. Disrespect. There's only so much he can take.

The clerk limps up the aisle. Everyone's got something, some flaw, their price for living. Headaches are his. Some days he can't even get out of bed. A bad hip people can see; a headache, they think he's lying. She wears a red smock. With her silvery hair she looks good in red. Not many do. Seldom wears it himself. He prefers pale blues, greens. And black. He favors black. Put him in a black suit, starched pink shirt, and stand back.

"Can I help you, sir?" She wants him to see the cell phone in her hand.

He's been back here too long. She's uneasy; two convenience store holdups in this area in the last three weeks. He should put her mind at ease, tell her there's too many people in here. Plus the pharmacist up there, peering down from his catwalk. Convenience stores are easier, especially late at night. But he gets off on her edginess. A form of respect. He hates being overlooked, hates to be stared past. Empty people miss the subtleties.

"Trying to find a magazine, that's all." Really, refuge from the rain.

"Which one? There aren't many we don't have."

"Newsweek." He could care.

"Here you go." Hands it over. Sending him on his way.

"Hmm, let's see. Maybe this isn't the one," he stalls, turning pages.

"You're getting it all wet."

"You're the one that gave it to me," he growls, stares hard, until she leaves.

Nobody's fool, that's for sure. Not after all he's been through, but right now, at this very moment, he finds himself on the high end of chance. Pure luck, that's what this is, her picture in this magazine, picked at random, in this drugstore the rain drove him into. He grins. A different last name. He's long ago forgotten the other one. But the face jumps out at him. How many Noras look like that? Strong, thin features, full mouth, deep-set eyes from what he can see. Hard to tell. He studies the picture. He'd almost forgotten. Young and soft, mostly what he remembers. He chuckles. A priest standing next to her. Family owns a newspaper. She wants to give back. They all do nowadays, the rich bitches. Well, give some to him, then. Yeah. Least she can do. Share with those less fortunate. Proud bastard like himself, two nights on a train station bench. Talk about democracy, country's so busy worrying about minorities it's lost sight of real citizens, people like himself. His great-grandfather helped build the transcontinental railroad, two uncles fought in Korea, one met Jack Dempsey once, something like that. Details get fuzzy. Static in the airwaves, voices fading in and out. That's his thing, sensitivities, knowing what's on someone's mind before they say it. So when they do, it's confusing because he's already heard it, feels like that, anyway. The shelter is the last place on earth he wants to go. Sleeping on a cot with drunks and crazies. He folds his arms to hide his shaking hands. His medicine's in his padlocked room. He tucks the magazine down the back of his pants and runs outside into the gale-driven rain. Long way, but his mind's on other things. Opportunity. His future.

Wet hair drips into his eyes. The puddle at his feet is from his clothes. He can't even use the bathroom until he's been evaluated. He sits in the waiting room. The intake counselor is on break. He angles his head to see past the flashing lights that come with the headache. This one's bad. Tension. Stress. Closes his eyes, waits for his name to be called. Eddie Krippendort. The counselor's questions confuse him. Yeah, you try thinking straight when the top of your head's gonna blow, he tells him.

Once, when he was little, his mother smashed the side of his head in, that's what happened. That's how he always tells it. She hated him, but it wasn't his fault, he just shouldn't've been born, she said. Lydia Krippendort, insisting she wasn't his mother, when he knew better. But he let her have her illusions, crazy woman that she was. One day she gave him away. Just like that, to a perfect stranger on a busy street. They locked her up. End of story.

"How old're you, Eddie?"

"Fifty, sixty." He laughs. "Whatever works."

"Any booze, drugs, on you?"

"No, sir."

"Been here before?"

"Once."

"When?"

"Year ago? I forget."

"You on disability?"

"No." Nothing preventing him from getting a job, one doctor wrote. Sociopathic tendencies. Reading upside down, among his many talents. Set fire that night to the back of the doctor's office.

"You work?"

"When I can."

"What do you do?"

"Whatever."

"What was your last job?"

"Vice president of Microsoft."

"Come on, Eddie. I just gotta fill in the blank, that's all I'm doing."

"Sparkle Car Wash on Marquand."

"When?"

"December."

"How long?"

"One fucking day."

Looks over his smudged glasses. What? Like he's offended?

"You know what it feels like, swabbing the back of a car, freezing cold water running down your arms and legs?" He wants to work, hates being broke. When he was younger he always had nice clothes and a car. Things are harder now. Lost a little off his fastball. He doesn't say this, doesn't tell how tired he gets. The headaches come too often. The medicine dulls the edges at least, when he can afford it. The intake counselor is bored, tired, whatever. He could care, Eddie sees. Heard it all so why the hell should he? Over and over, day after day, from the stiffs, the maimed souls, the walking wounded. Losers. Worst of all's being lumped in with them.

"And my headaches, that was the thing." With the cold, they start up again.

"You got a record?"

"Yeah." He laughs. A record. Perfect. That's it exactly. Half a lifetime gone, he'll tell her. And now it's payback time. Time to give back. To the needy. The truly deserving. God's battered children, all the ones who weren't born into the lucky sperm club.

He sits on the edge of the cot, unlacing his wet shoes. He puts on the clothes they gave him, threadbare pants and a ripped T-shirt, until his own are dry. He stretches out on the cot and opens the magazine. Now, with her face, it's coming back, her laugh, the sweet trust of her touch. Before what happened. It wasn't just the drunk, but him, too, going off the deep end. Lucky for her she ran. It might've been her. And now, lucky for him.

Like these pants, time has frayed the seams. Beginnings and endings run together. Even the women, he can't remember. Some, he didn't even like their smell. The headaches do that, heighten his senses. Smell, for instance, and hearing. Certain sounds are startling. Terrifying. He used to love the sound of a train, relentless in all its rackety force, or the drone of a low-flying plane, thrilling him with the possibility of its crashing before his eyes. The same with the quick gasp of a woman's voice. Now it's all dread. Steel sky lowering, walls pushing close.

The next morning is the social worker. Lisa goes over yesterday's form, gives him a list of jobs. The shelter has contacts with businesses needing help.

"Anything there look interesting?"

Three hundred pounds, anyway. He's disgusted by the flap of flesh that melds her chin to her neck. He is repelled by voraciousness, people who gorge themselves, drink too much, especially this one, silver bracelets jangling on thick, spotted wrists, the low V of her neckline crimping the freckled fat of her breasts, sausage into its casing, flaunting her flesh, why? For these miserable souls? He pictures her primping in the morning, leaning close to the mirror, swiveling on that red lipstick, all the while getting wet, thinking of the lucky stiff she'll turn on today. The air thins. Harder to breathe. Her fat cells, she sucks it all in. Pig. Disgusting pig.

"The dishwashing job's cool. Bannerman's, the steak house, they feed their help good." She swallows hard; he imagines her snuffling food off the soiled plates coming into the kitchen to be washed.

" 'Fraid I'm overqualified."

"So's everybody, but it's a stepping-stone. That's what we're doing here. Inch by inch."

"The rubber tree plant," he chuckles. But, of course, she doesn't get it. "Tell you what. Give me the address. I'm heading east soon. A business opportunity." He stands up when she hands him the address she's just written on the shelter letterhead. "This'll be my grubstake," he says, folding the paper into his pocket.

"Yeah, you'll like their steak. I've eaten there before. And the Delmonico potatoes, they're to die for."

"You know what a grubstake is?"

"No. My favorite's the porterhouse. Oooh, and prime rib."

"You like to travel?"

"Nah. Airplane seats." Shaking her head, she spreads her hands to indicate girth. As if he hasn't noticed.

"What about by car? You can get places that way, right?"

"I guess."

"Best way to travel. Take your time. Stop when you want. I used to do that, drive for a living."

"Yeah?"

"Yeah. One time I drove this old couple, L.A. to Boston. Took our time." He shrugs. "Stop when you feel like it. Grand Canyon. Vegas. Eat your way across."

"Sounds like fun."

"Yeah. Go where you want, see what you want to see."

CHAPTER·3

Ten minutes late. When she turns the corner, the car skids. She slows down. This storm isn't supposed to intensify until later, but the dark roads are already slick. Hard to see with the snow falling so fast, sheets of big wet flakes across her headlights. She was supposed to meet Ken in his office at five. Something's wrong, she can feel it. Of the two of them, Ken's always been the more upbeat, but lately he seems depressed, almost remote at times, like a man besieged, hounded, but by what? Work? His family?

A couple of nights ago, Chloe and Drew had been teasing each other all through dinner. She could sense Ken's edginess, but she was enjoying their good-natured banter. The pleasure they found in each other's company, even their occasional annoyance with one another, seemed a joyful contrast to her own teenage years, the sameness of such silent, weary meals that the scrape of a fork against her mother's teeth could set her heart beating faster. "Geeky," Chloe had called her brother's plaid shirt. Drew glared at her a moment, then caught himself as he so often must lately. He laughed and said her tight, low-rise jeans were "slutty."

"That's it, you're done! Leave the table, goddamnit!" Ken roared.

"He was just kidding," Nora said, shocked as Drew stomped upstairs, then slammed his door.

"He didn't mean anything," Chloe snapped at her father, and with that, Ken threw down his napkin and stormed into his study, holing up there for the rest of the evening.

So unlike Ken. He is a chronic optimist, according to gloomy Oliver, which is precisely why the brothers work so well together. Oliver loves the newspaper, but has little patience and less affection for most people. Ken finds tedious the details of running the paper, but he loves people, making him the perfect spokesman for the *Chronicle.* It is Ken who sits on the boards of banks and charities, Ken who cuts ribbons and, from years of groundbreaking ceremonies, has his own display of silver shovels hanging on their garage wall. "Our poster boy," Oliver sniped recently after Ken's picture ran in the paper three days in a row. Uncharacteristically, Ken called him on it, and Oliver's response was a shrug and a snide look. Ken was deeply offended. That alone is cause for alarm. For years the brothers have played off one another's foibles, with Ken rarely letting Oliver cloud his sunny aura. But in these last few days they're barely speaking to one another. At yesterday's editorial staff meeting each sat stonily at opposite ends of the table. It fell to their cousin Stephen to initiate discussion of various topics, which became uncomfortable at times, with Ken the easy target of Stephen's sarcasm.

Once again last night Ken didn't come to bed. He said he'd fallen asleep watching television. This morning when she asked what was wrong, was he still upset with his brother, he turned quickly in the doorway and said it was a lot more complicated than just Oliver. He was backing out of the garage when he called and asked her to meet him tonight at five so they could talk.

"Come on back in. We can talk here," she said, watching his car inch down the driveway, cold sweat rising on her back. They hadn't made love in weeks. Months, really, since there was any real passion between them. Maybe longer. Just middle-age doldrums, her friend Robin said once, assuring her that every couple goes through it, which Nora was relieved to hear. Ken was always the better lover, but for a while now, she's felt his impatience, his eagerness to get it over with, so he could read, watch television, brush his teeth, anything. He blames his back yet somehow manages to play racquetball twice a week. Saturday night after a wonderful dinner out and two bottles of wine with Bibbi and Hank Bond, she locked their bedroom door, telling him how she'd spent the entire evening aching for him, for every inch, every part of him. He wouldn't have to move a muscle, just lie down, she'd take care of every single thing, she promised as she unbuckled his belt. He muttered something. What? He was tired. Well, that's why, she laughed, her tongue in his ear as she unzipped his fly. He moved her hand away. He'd better go down and take some Maalox, his stomach was killing him.

"Drew's still there," he said this morning from his car.

"So? Besides, he's in the shower."

"I can't. I'm running late."

"Well, why in the office, then? Why there?" He usually couldn't wait to get away from the paper. And never stayed until five.

"I have a meeting right after." Had he sighed?

"So, when you come home, then."

"We need to talk."

"Why? What is it, Ken? Tell me. Tell me now." In the silence she could feel it. The old fear. That night, that man, so long ago. So, he knew, he finally knew.

"I'm just not myself."

"You're depressed." Please let that be it. Please, she implored some-one. God.

"Yeah. I guess so. Or something like that."

"Well, that happens, honey. But the trouble is it just never happens to you, so now that it has you don't know how to cope. Right?"

"I don't know," he said softly.

She parks next to his car. Funny, she thinks, hardly any snow on it, but the usually gleaming black sports car is mud-spattered and skirted in road salt. Clothes are piled on the front seat, pale blue cotton sweater, yellow blazer, polo shirts. Summer clothes. Probably cleaned out his locker at the club, to bring them to the cleaners. Ken cares how he looks. Always has. Like his mother. A beautiful woman, Addie, with jet black hair and bright eyes. Their daughter, Chloe, has her grand-mother's dark silken hair and the same gritty laughter that sent men tripping over curbs and bumping into doorways, trying to see the source of that marvelous voice.

Chloe, she thinks, unlocking the back door that leads to the editorial offices. She's in trouble again. That's why Ken's been so preoccupied and troubled. The worst came last year: Chloe and herboyfriend Max Lafferty holding hands in the family room while Max informed them that he and Chloe were getting married. Everything had been figured out, he said, brandishing his spiral notebook of lists. He would finish high school, of course, and then go on to college for his journalism degree. Chloe would work and he would, too, summers and vacations, and the baby would be in day care. They hadn't told his parents yet, but he knew they'd do their best to help. (Mr. Lafferty was a mailman with twin daughters in college.) Plus, Max added, listing the baby as a dependent would look even better on the financial aid applications. Ken was stunned into rare silence.

"What about Chloe?" Nora asked the gangly seventeen-year-old boy Chloe had been dating for less than three months. He didn't even have his license yet. The first time Nora met him he had been on his skateboard.

"We figure she'll go when I'm done," Max answered, a flush of confidence reddening his freckles.

"It'll be my turn." Chloe smiled up at him.

"Well, that's not the way we figure it, Max," Ken said.

"With all due respect, sir—," the gangly boy began.

"No due respect, just get the hell out!" Ken growled.

"Dad!" Chloe cried.

"Mr. Hammond, I don't—"

"She's sixteen, and how the hell old are you?"

"Seventeen, sir."

"Right. So leave, Max. Just leave. I'm taking care of this. Not you."

And so he had. Nora had been the one wanting to wait, so they could handle it sensitively, give Chloe time to talk it through, sort out her feelings, let her get her head on straight so the right decision could be made and she could fully understand the repercussions of her actions. For Ken there was only one decision, and it had already been made. They took her to the clinic and stayed home with her for the two days after, then sped her to the emergency room in the middle of the night when the bleeding wouldn't stop. In the end, as always, it was her father she clung to, her father who always understood her, far more than her mother.

Some daughters have to get far apart from their mothers before they can ever get close, Nora's mother said right before she died. Nora had been trying to apologize not just for her own difficult teenage years but, without actually saying it, her eight-day disappearance with Eddie Hawkins. Eight days of hell, her mother had called it, the night she picked her up at the bus terminal. Eight days Nora would give anything to take back. Especially now. Whenever she's afraid of something happening to Ken or her children, the floodgates go up, with all the old dread and guilt seeping back in.

There was the night last summer when Ken was called down to the police station. Chloe had been brought in along with a lot of her friends from a keg party that had been raided. She was drunk and vomiting, the chief said. "She needs a lawyer," Nora said, starting to dial Stephen's number, but Ken said he'd handle it. The only reason she was vomiting, Ken informed the chief, was because she'd been sick for days with the flu. Even though she reeked of booze and could barely talk, the chief let him take her home. The other parents were called and nothing was ever in the paper. Days later Nora was still angry, shaken. Chloe's losing control like that hit too close to home. But for Ken it was just one of those hot shit things all kids do sooner or later. He thought it was wild the way boys flocked around his Chloe. Her poor grades and his had always been a joke between them. Although lately, with college looming, he's been after her to study more. Last September he promised Chloe her own gold card if she made honor roll.

"Absolutely not!" Nora protested. That would be irresponsible of him. Last month he'd found Chloe smoking a joint in her room. Stubbing it out, he told her there was a time and place for everything. "And this isn't it," he said. "Not on a school night. Not up in your room all by yourself."

Nora sailed into him. "So it's okay? But just don't do it alone, that's what you're saying."

"That's not what I said." His eyes dulled with a familiar weariness.

"Yes it is. In other words, it's okay as a social act, just watch out for the whole bad habit thing."

For the rest of that night Ken was so quiet she accused *him* of sulking, though she's always been the brooder, the grudge holder, the darker spirit. "You're mad at me," she said when she looked up to find him staring at her.

"Actually," he sighed, resting his head back on the chair, "I was just envying you."

"For marrying you, you mean," she laughed. Their oldest joke, but that time he didn't even smile.

"It's your good sense, your values. You always get right straight at things, you know what I mean?" he said with a sigh that even now, weeks later, bothers her.

She opens Ken's office door. The only light comes from the black-shaded lamp on the credenza. Day and night, he usually has every light burning in here. He sits with his hand on his chin. Just thinking, he says, when she asks if he has a headache.

"What's wrong, Ken?" And with his long gaze, she is acutely aware of the tangle of potted vines hanging in the dark window and, beyond the glass, the jagged row of icicles dripping onto the granite sill. "My God, what is it?" She sinks into the chair and unbuttons her coat. His hair is mussed and he's unshaven. "You're scaring me, Ken!" Chloe: she knows by his utter devastation.

"This is so hard." He has to clear his throat.

Though she won't say it now, her mind is made up. Chloe will have to find her own way out of whatever mess she's gotten herself into. This time she'll make her own appointment. Chloe needs to see how this is tearing her father apart. Oh, Kenny! she thinks, with her hand over his, dear carefree Kenny, this is what you get for spoiling our little girl rotten.

"This is so hard," he repeats, wincing. "I've got to tell you this. I've got to. And I don't know how. Jesus, this is the hardest thing I've ever had to do. But then I think you know. I think you know some of it. A little. You must." His hand slips free. "I tried to stop it. I never wanted to hurt you. More than anything else it was that, not wanting to hurt you and Chloe and Drew." His voice cracks. "That's what tears me apart. That's the worst of it—hurting anyone, especially you. Especially you." He blows his nose. "The thing is, it started almost as a joke, really. Innocent, like, 'How come you never invite me to lunch? It's always Bob.' And we were such old friends, it seemed . . . it just seemed funny, you know, so . . . I did. I did. I met her and it just—" He shakes his head, closes his eyes. "Happened," he whispers.

"What are you talking about?" she says, but he's right, isn't he? His agitation these last few weeks, his remoteness. She knows. Of course she knows. Now that she knows she is sure she has known. Known what? That for the last few weeks everything's been a lie? It makes no sense. Nothing does.

"Robin. Robin and me." His hoarseness grates in her ears, sets her teeth dryly on edge. Robin and Bob, their dear old friends, his childhood playmates, and Robin, his teenage steady. His lover.

"You fucked her?" She is as startled as he is by her smooth utterance of a word she hasn't used in over twenty years. He nods, mouth trembling. "How many times?" she asks, and he winces.

"I don't know." He won't look at her.

"Why don't you know?"

"I just don't. Please, Nora, that's not—"

"Not what? Not important? Well, to me it is! What was it, at lunch? Or . . . or after that? Last week, when you missed the staff meeting, was that it? Is that where you were?"

He stares with stricken, unblinking eyes. "Nora, I'm not talking about a few . . . a few times," he says, gasping out *times*. "I'm talking about a relationship we . . . I had."

"A relationship?"

"For four years."

A relationship. All she thinks about, even now, a week later, this pressure building in her head. For four years her husband has been spending every spare moment with Robin Gendron. Where? He doesn't want to, but she insists he tell her. After years of lies, she is entitled to the truth. He owes her that much, at least. But can't she understand that all talking about it does is to keep hurting her, and he doesn't want to do that anymore?

"I have to know so I can get things straight. So I can put things in perspective."

"What? What do you have to know?"

"Everything!" she insists. Everything.

Chloe and Drew leave for school. The minute the door closes she races into the kitchen. She doesn't trust herself near him when the children are home. Under her bathrobe are yesterday's clothes. She fell asleep on the couch and when she woke up at three in the morning, thoughts racing, she didn't dare go up to bed because all she wants to do is hit him. And hurt him, and hit him. Ken hunches over his granola and thinly sliced bananas. For days all she's been able to keep down are saltines and weak tea. He stops eating and puts his hand over hers. "I've told you the truth, Nora. I have."

"You haven't told me where."

He closes his eyes. "Mostly there, at her house."

Shocked, she pulls away. "But what about Drew?" He and Clay were best friends. Drew would be over there all the time. Her mouth falls open, remembering a day last summer. Drew came home with his cheek bruised. Basketball in the face, he said, but after that he stopped hanging out with Clay, stopped going to the Gendrons'. "He knew, didn't he?"

"Of course not," Ken insists. "My God, Nora, give me some credit at least."

Credit! the madwoman raves inside her head. Credit for what? For being duplicitous enough? Sneaky enough? Or for knowing how an affair—excuse me! a *relationship*—should be conducted? And what two people would better know than sweet, generous Robin and dear, fun-loving Ken.

"So where, then? Where did you usually fuck her?" She likes the way the word rolls off her tongue, the power of its vileness and poison. His misery hearing it.

"Nora, please." I'm trying to eat, is what he wants to say as he picks up his spoon. If only he would so she can dump the bowl over his head or throw it through the bay window, an explosion of plants and glass onto the stone patio. Life's wreckage made visible, rubble underfoot, shards for all to see. Instead of this bloodless dying.

"In her bed? In the basement? The car?" Yes, she sees. All those places. Everywhere and all the time. The thrill of it. Teenagers again. "What did you say when the children were there?"

"I told you, they weren't."

"What about Lyra? What is she now, four?"

"Almost."

"She must've been there. Of course she was." She had to have been, throughout. "What does she call you? Ken? Kenny? Uncle Ken?" She remembers something. The club. The Fourth of July cookout? No, Labor Day. The little girl asleep in Ken's arms. So sweet of him, Nora thought, watching his easy tenderness cradling the child. Bob was drunk so Ken drove him home, once again. Ken called to say he'd be late getting home, Bob needed some settling down. She throws back her head and laughs. Yes, all so perfectly orchestrated. "What would you do after you put him in bed, climb in on top of . . . his wife?" She can't bear saying her name anymore. *She, Her, the Bitch.* He knows who she means. And so does she, knows, by the long, dismal sigh that it happened like that, Bob passed out in the next room, down the hall, downstairs, but under the same roof, the three of them, Bob, Robin, and Ken, entwined since childhood, playmates from first grade on. Did he ever wake up? He must have. To go to the bathroom, to vomit, the two of them tensing closer as he staggers down a dark hall-way, she pictures it, their naked clutching, her breath on his hairless chest, every sick detail. There must have been some close calls. There were, weren't there? Weren't there? What was it like to be inside her, having to worry the whole time that Bob might stumble in on his old friend fucking his wife, her long blonde hair hanging down in Ken's face, because that's how she keeps picturing it. Can't stop seeing Robin lean over him in broad daylight, all the lights in the room on so he can admire every naked inch of her tanned body, perfectly toned and muscled from the years of tennis and running, Pilates, weights. Her six-pack abdomen, he actually said that, teasing her, at the club last summer.

"Well, would you? Did you? You must have."

"Don't. Please, Nora."

"Was it more exciting that way?"

"I don't want to do this anymore," he says, rubbing his eyes.

"Oh, you don't? You don't want to? Oh, poor Kenny. Why? Is it too upsetting? Too painful? Does it hurt too much? In here? In here? In here?" she screams, pounding her chest, over and over and over again.

CHAPTER·4

And last but never least, our Hospital Building Committee's esteemed chairman, Kenneth J. Hammond, and his lovely wife, Nora," the faux British voice intones over the loudspeaker.

"Spare me," she whispers, and Ken's jaw clenches. The wide gilt-trimmed doors swing open. Arm in arm they enter the hotel's glittering ballroom, Nora in black silk, hair tightly back from her waxen face, Ken in his tux, pink silk paisley cummerbund and bow tie. Applause quickens as lovable Ken tips an imaginary hat from table to table, his boyish grin, ever the crowd-pleaser. The ice queen smiles, nodding, sore eyes forced wide, stiffly gracious, throat shredded raw from screaming. Even though Ken has assured her Robin and Bob won't be here, her gaze lasers from table to table.

An elderly blonde in a red strapless dress that cuts into her flaccid bosom reaches for Ken's hand. He bends to kiss her bright rouged cheek. A dear old friend of his mother's Nora knows, can't retrieve the name. In these last few days, lobes of memory have been wiped out, bludgeoned by betrayal. Her brain feels bruised. *Nora, you remember Mumma's dear friend, Sissy.* Of course. The Hammonds have a wealth of dear old friends. Of course they do, old family that they are. And Ken, dearest of all, the bastard . . . son of a bitch. Blood seeps hot into her face. Like his father, whose affairs people still recall with an affection usually heard in the play-by-play reminiscences of old college football games. No, that's just another way of letting him off the hook. She has to guard against that, blaming everyone but him. Ken pulls out her chair, with a flourish shakes out her napkin, places it in her lap. Everyone laughs.

Stephen and Donald sit across from them. Stephen blows her a kiss and Donald winks. They ignore Ken. But he pretends not to notice. Donald is an anesthesiologist. He and Stephen have been together longer than she's been married. The Coxes are here too, and the Jerrolds, the Whitemans, the Bonds, the usual fund-raising glitterati. Evvie Cox is chairperson of tonight's Hospital Ball, an especially notable event, being the fiftieth. Evvie looks exhausted. Thin and graying, she's recently had a heart attack. People keep coming to the table to tell her how wonderful she looks, how spectacular the ball is, how brave she is. Jack Cox's eyelids thicken with his second martini. Soon, he'll be arguing with someone, waiter, friend, it won't matter.

Joanne Whiteman's nervous chatter begins. "You look great, Nora. But no tan! How long were you there for?"

"Where?" She's trying to catch the waiter's eyes.

"Anguilla."

"We haven't gone yet. That's Friday."

"I'll bet you can't wait. Hasn't this been the worst winter, so much snow and everyone coming down with that new flu, Taipei or something, I forget the name. But if it weren't for the house, I'd be on the next plane out of here, but they're just starting the wallpaper, and I don't care what anyone says, but I refuse to try and run things in cyberspace. You can't. There's no way. I mean, you know! It's all part of a bigger picture. You need the lighting and the feel of the room and the whole flow—"

What the hell is she talking about? "Excuse me, Jo." She waves. "Waiter!" Does she sound as desperate as she feels? "Waiter!"

Stephen gets up and leans close. "You look gorgeous. As always," he says with a supportive squeeze of her shoulders and a quick glance at Ken before he wanders off. Donald's fat cheeks redden as he watches him go. Abandoned again, she knows how he feels. Stephen, who can never sit still, runs on nerves while Donald is sweet and uncomplaining.

Joanne has Ken's ear now. Her house is one of six on this spring's

Franklin Ladies Historical House Tour. She's in charge of publicity, but with so little money for advertising, she's hoping the *Chronicle* will run a few stories early enough to get the word out. Evvie Cox has just been called out to the welcoming table to verify the identity of some people who've forgotten their tickets.

"As if anyone in their right mind would want to crash this sleepathon," Christine Jerrold whispers, and Nora laughs. Now with her drink, she feels safer. "Do you like my dress?" Christine asks. She is a tall, large-boned woman with short blonde hair who loves golf, excels at it.

"I do." Nora pretends to study it. "Haven't you worn something like it before, though?"

"Yes! *This* dress!" Christine laughs. "I've worn the same one to every single Hospital Ball since 'ninety-nine. It's my little protest."

"That's great, Chris. That's really great." She smiles. Third year in a row, this same conversation. Her eyes sting. She needs more eyedrops.

The Bonds have been talking over their shoulders to friends at the next table. As they turn back, Nora watches Ken's face brighten, the grin, the twinkling eyes. Bibbi and Hank Bond are Ken's idea of a great couple. Hank has a boat, his own plane, and of course he golfs, plays some racquetball, loves to party, holds his liquor almost as well as Bibbi. Their small perfect teeth gleam in the frame of their deep tans. With their husky voices, short black hair, perky little noses, they might be brother and sister. Cousins, anyway. Maybe they are, she thinks. Maybe that's why these people's blood runs so thin. So shallow. All the years of social incest. Some problem with their daughter, she can't remember what, but that's what happens. Bibbi leans across Hank. "Kenny," she says, with a consoling pat on his arm. "Thank you," she adds. And with the quick stab of his glance at Nora, another piece of the puzzle moves into place.

So, they knew, not only knew, but probably covered many times for their sweet Kenny, collaborating with Robin, scheming with him. Her hands writhe in her lap. Her fingers attack one another, picking nails, stripping bits of cuticle until they are raw and sore. Yes. Probably went out together, the two couples. Bibbi would think herself brave, a foil in the name of love. Yes. All those hot afternoons Ken appeared in Nora's office, was suddenly there, loosening his tie, telling her how Hank had just called to invite them out to the boat for drinks and dinner, last minute, but what the heck. She always had to remind him of the same thing—her seasickness, assuring him he should go ahead. She'd do fine here without him. Are you sure now? he'd ask, the boyish concern barely concealing delight.

"It's this heat. I'm just no good in this heat," he'd sigh.

"It's not the heat, Kenny, now be honest," she'd laugh. "You're just not good much after noontime."

"I know, but don't tell Ollie," he'd say in a waggish whisper, peeking into the corridor for escape.

She stares at him now, her jaw set. Torn from her moorings, she can't help herself. She's been swept off her feet by so powerful a force that there's no fighting it, nothing to hold on to. Nothing fixed. No one to trust. Every event, every memory, every conversation, however innocuous, demands examination, each word and detail culled, dissected in the harsh light of this new terrible knowledge—that for the past four years her husband has been sleeping with another woman. And he will not have it called an affair, refusing to allow her that small security, however painful. Why? Does that make it seem tawdry, beneath him? Does its connotation of brevity and superficiality taint what he and the bitch have shared? While on the other hand, does calling it a relationship invest it with depth and connection? Caring? Love? Around the table mouths open and close, laughing, talking, drinking, smiling. *Boring Nora, always way too serious, well, she finally got her comeuppance, and this soundless screaming, can't they hear the madwoman? Of course they can. They're just pretending, being polite. Mustn't spoil their evening. Their ball. All the expensive dresses. Their delight in one another. Stupid to have come. She doesn't belong here. Never has. Never will.*

This morning Drew asked to spend the weekend at his friend Billy's house. He didn't say so, but he wants to escape the bedlam of slamming doors, the sudden tears, Ken's sorrow, her flights into the bathroom, where she runs the shower to drown out the moaning.

Drew's request triggered another memory, the last time he spent the weekend at Billy's. Just this past December. Ken had driven up to Burlington that Friday for a conference of New England newspaper publishers. He called early that evening to say there was a blizzard and rather than risk a treacherous drive back, he'd get a room and leave first thing the next morning. Of course, she said. Good idea. No problem. She should have gone online and checked the weather up in Vermont. Probably still could. She'd need the date. December's telephone bill. He probably drove up there with *her,* the two of them laughing in anticipation of a night together without excuses, making a joke of not having to sneak in, God knows when, and pretend that he'd fallen asleep on the couch, watching television. Thinking back, she is shocked at her blindness.

The glittering din, all these smiling faces, talking at once, the gold and black themed ballroom teeming with people who know that Ken and Robin Gendron . . . what? How do they put it? Slept together? Had an affair? Not for four years—no, four years is more than that. Four years is commitment. It's love. That's what Ken means by *relationship.*

"Smile!" Jimmy Lee has them all pushing their chairs closer to fit in the picture. "You're not smiling, Mrs. Hammond!" Jimmy says from behind his camera.

She tries.

"Better than that, Mrs. Hammond! You look like you've just lost your best friend," he chides.

Joanne Whiteman glances at Bibbi Bond, who draws a deep breath, ticks her square red nails on the rim of her plate.

The adultery support group, Nora thinks, flashing a wider smile. After the picture, Ken excuses himself and, with frail Evvie on his arm, goes off in search of other ball committee members, Jimmy Lee in their wake, bags of equipment slung from his black leather coat. As the *Chronicle*'s front man, Ken is their Kiwanian, their Elk, their Rotarian, their chamber of commerce vice president, their hospital board treasurer, their Boy Scouts board member, their greater Franklin Ecumenical Executive Council member. Ken attends luncheons and ribbon cuttings, while behind his locked door, Oliver pores over text, and Stephen manages finances. A perfect weave of temperaments.

"Hi, hon. How're you doing?" Bibbi slips into Ken's chair, squeezing her hand with a solicitous smile.

"Fine. Just fine." She pulls her hand away.

"That was a great picture of you in *Newsweek*." Bibbi says Letitia Crane wants her to help out at Sojourn House.

"Really?" She's unable to look away from Bibbi's smooth, round face, the bright-eyed, clawing little animal. Robin Gendron's best friend and also prep school classmate of Ken's. The same sympathetic expression he must have sought out when he needed someone to talk to, to share their secret with, so, of course, he would have chosen this bubble of insincerity. Oh, the intrigue of it all, and Bibbi's delight these last four years.

The orchestra is playing "Some Enchanted Evening" as the first few couples begin to dance. The last dishes are being cleared by waitresses in ruffly black aprons. But Donald continues to eat. Free of Stephen's monitoring eyes, he's cutting the prime rib Joanne just passed his way. Nora's plate is gone. She can't remember if she ate anything. Sweat leaks down her ribs, skinny getting skinnier. Her diamonds feel jagged against her throat.

"I've thought about helping out," Bibbi says between fluttery finger waves and lightning-flash smiles at passing dancers, sweeping by as they reach out to touch the treasured woman. "But I don't think I've quite got the stomach for it. Some things I'd rather not know." She cringes. "I admire you, though, Nora. Honestly, all that you do there."

"I don't do anything." Buoyed by the dreamy quality of her voice, she lifts her empty glass, and their waitress returns with another gin and tonic. "I just provide them with the Hammond family name and see to it they get all the publicity they need. What I am," she declares between pensive sips, "is Father Grewley's shill . . . his shield of social importance . . . if you'll allow the alliteration!" Her laughter is too sudden, and ragged.

Bibbi glances at Donald, busily scraping the last morsels of au jus–soaked gratiné before Stephen's return. She leans close. "Nora."

"What? What is it, Bibbi? What do you want to say? I don't think this is quite the right place though for . . . for what? What would you call it, Bibbi? What? What game is this? What—"

"It's not a game," Bibbi says in a low, urgent voice. "And I know how you feel."

Nora bursts into deep liberating laughter. It is all very, very funny. She keeps wiping tears from her eyes. Not only funny but ridiculous. After all, what does tough-ass Nora Trimble expect? Nothing changes. No one changes. "We just get to be better liars!" She explodes with wheezy laughter. She looks around. Some remarkable observation has just been made, though in the next bewildering moment it is lost.

"Nora, come outside with me," Bibbi whispers. "Please."

Around them heads are turning. Hank rises to stand with his hands on the back of her chair. "Okay, okay, now. Just take it easy, dear heart," he says.

"What? What did he call me?" More laughter. She tilts her head back and smiles up at him. "Dear heart! Dear heart!" Tears run from the corners of her eyes: this pride of lions guarding its kill.

"Nora," Hank says sternly, face reddening. "Don't do this."

She wants to pour her drink down her throat in one long gulp but, under their reproachful stares, allows herself only neat sips. This is how Oliver drinks, she is thinking. All day long, these little sips, how he gets through his life. *Oh, Oliver. Help me. Someone help me.*

"I'll get Kenner." Hank steps briskly away.

Kenner. Their ridiculous nicknames. Nor, they tried calling her, until she nipped that in the bud. *My name is Nora, plain and simple, Nora!* Did she just say that? Should have if she didn't.

"Get Evvie!" Jack Cox looks up and calls. "Get fucking Evvie," he mutters.

"Poor Evvie," Bibbi sighs, sitting back, as if by willing the burden of greater threat onto Jack, Nora may snap to.

"Is that what you said?" she asks, aware that her voice has thinned with the gin and is probably lost now in the hard beat of the song "Jump" that the band starts to play. Only a few couples dance. Most stand around clapping. Robin and Ken always danced the fast numbers together, while she and Bob watched, laughing. "Is that what you've been saying, all this time? Poor Nora?" she says louder, so Bibbi can hear. Hands on her knees, she leans forward. "Poor Nora! Poor, poor Nora! The poor dear fucking heart!"

Roused from his feed, Donald lumbers to her side, napkin dangling from his enormous collar. It's all right, he tells her. Everything is going to be all right.

In the cold, shocked silence she wets her lips, smiles. She sits very, very still, smiling shyly up at Ken who makes his way toward her. Table by table, eyes drop as he passes. "Come on, Nora." He slips the napkin from her lap, recoiling at the dots of blood from her torn cuticles. Bibbi passes him Nora's beaded purse.

"Thank you," she says, before turning to go. "You're both so good at this."

Bibbi and Hank smile wanly. Ken holds her close through the chandeliered sparkle of the lobby, then out to the parking lot where a fine snow sifts over the cars. Inside, he sits for a moment staring into the fan of darkness the wipers make on the white windshield.

"I'm so sorry, Nora." He rubs his face. "I can't stand to see you hurt. You know that. I don't know why . . . I don't know what happened . . . I don't know why I told you," he moans, his voice thick with anguish.

"You don't know why you told me!" She springs, slapping him, punching his head. "That's all you're sorry for, isn't it? That's all you care about, damn it! Isn't it? Admit it! Admit it! Admit it!" she cries, pummeling his hunched back as he sobs with his hands over his head. "Oh my God!" she gasps, shrinking back, as the two visions merge, him, that man sagging over the wheel. "Oh my God . . . oh my God," she whispers, sinking against the door. "Take me home. Just take me home."

CHAPTER·5

In the murky twilight Lisa almost looks pretty. Or is it the intimacy of these last few days together? Hardest to overlook at first was the wide neck and thin carroty hair exposing patches of pink scalp, but now it's her mouth he's most aware of, ropy and wet with constant babble. Her sisters are attractive enough. She showed him their pictures the first night of their trip. They favor their mother while she's cursed with her father's broad back and short legs, poor thing, Eddie thinks with more disgust than pity. Her exuberance reminds him of a neglected dog. Roused by his slightest attention, she's all over him. Worse, when she drinks. Her eyes bulge and spittle sprays the air with her startlingly deep laughter.

She loved Vegas. It was her third trip there, but this one was the most fun, she said. The other times all she and her mother did was play the slots and blackjack, which Eddie refused to do. "Come on, please!" she teased, trying to tug him back into the casino. His eyes burned with rage. It took every ounce of self-control not to slap her. She'd just lost $120. A hundred and twenty when he still had such a long way to go.

"No!" he growled, leaning close. "You'll just blow the rest of it."

"So what? I don't care. Come on, I want to. Please," she begged, pursing her red lips in a garish pout and pulling on him.

"Get your fucking hand off me."

Her head snapped back, eyes so suddenly thick with tears, that for a second he thought he'd hit her. She turned, pushing through a crowd of old ladies wearing name tags and red straw hats, getting off the elevator.

"Lisa! Wait! I'm sorry."

To make it up to her, they took in a late show, Céline Dion. "I love you, Céline," Lisa shrieked during the applause, whooping and stamping her feet at their table in the back row. They were both drunk, her a lot, him just enough to have made penitential love to her in their cheap motel room with its cigarette-stenchy, light-and-air-stifling maroon drapes.

"She's my favorite singer. It's like she becomes transported. Did you notice that, how it's almost, like, religious," she shouts over the air-conditioning and Céline's new CD that she'd bought for him. Paid cash, as she has for everything so far. No bills when she gets home, he reminds her whenever she takes out a credit card. To pass like vapor, leaving no trail, steers every decision, each unlikely route on the map. Out of her sight, he shreds every receipt. She admires his caution about money and is touched by his shame at not having any of his own right now. His concern for her well-being has eased her early fears. She can tell him anything, she confided last night.

She is talking, still talking. Louder, now, to be heard over the music. Please, he thinks, soon, needing, aching to close his eyes, but can't. Not yet.

"You know what I mean, like the way she's actually feeling it, becoming the music?"

Eyes fixed on the road, he nods.

"We should turn off soon, huh?" She sighs.

The brown, dusty landscape of rocks and wind-stunted trees depresses him. Like her talking, endless, unpunctuated by anything memorable. She's only got two more vacation days left. She could call in sick: in her inflection a suggestion, which he ignores. But then again, she hates doing that. Leaving them short-handed.

"When my father retired, he had two hundred and twenty-six sick days. Can you imagine? His whole time working, he only got sick once. A hernia, and four days after the operation he went in to work."

"Huh!"

"Yeah. He's quite a guy. I think you'd like him. Did I tell you about his trains?"

He nods, but she continues anyway. "The whole basement's set up with tracks and tunnels. Mountains even. You won't believe it when you see it." Leaning, she rips the Velcro flap on the soft nylon cooler between her bare feet. Another irritation, always taking off her shoes. He hates the sight of her thick toes, the purple painted nails, grotesque the way the little toe curls over the one next to it. Her stubby fingers paw noisily through the ice then, hold up a dripping can. "There's another root beer. Last one, want it?"

"No, that's okay." He squints, trying to read the sign in the distance. His eyes are terrible. Along with everything else, his glasses are lost in the locked room.

She pops open the can and he tries not to glance in the mirror. As she sips, her full upper lip curls over the rim. Suddenly, this enrages him. The indignities he must endure, watching, seeing his own sniveling self with this beast. They better start heading back, she says again. There's a staff meeting first thing Monday and her boss is counting on her to have the monthly report ready.

"Liam. He's the one I told you about, the folk singer. Just the nicest guy, but the shelter, his heart's not in it. Sad really when you think of it. I mean, forty-two years old and his wife, she just got sick of the whole hippie thing and left. And you can't really blame her. I mean, two little girls, just the cutest things . . ."

He tries to tune her out. Out of the blue, she'll start talking about Liam. "Hey," he interrupts. "Sounds like your boss's got a thing for you."

"Actually, he did try and kiss me once. At a retirement party, but I told him, not with a married guy. No way." She looks out the side window, grinning, reliving the pathetic moment.

"What if I said, you've just spent the last five days sleeping with a married man?"

"Are you serious?"

"Maybe." The quiver of her lip fills him with fleeting exhilaration.

And then he's irritated again. Gullible people are weak. Weakness annoys him. Bile seeps into his mouth.

"Well, are you or aren't you?" she demands, though, he can tell, she doesn't believe him.

"Why?" He laughs. "What difference does it make? You had a good time, right?"

"Well, I wouldn't've come, for one thing." Her large face flushes, mottled and red as the purse clutched to her belly.

Oh yes, you would've, he thinks. "Actually, my wife died. But that was a long time ago."

"Oh, I'm so sorry. What happened?"

"She was murdered."

"Oh my God! By who? Who did it?"

"Don't know. They never caught him."

"That's so awful. It must be such a terrible feeling."

"No. Actually, she wasn't a very nice person."

"You're kidding, aren't you?" She scratches the dry bumpy skin on her freckled arm.

"She treated me like shit. But I put up with it. That's the way I am." Helen. Not really his wife, but she let him stay with her. No guilt, remembering it now, just regret that he wasn't more patient. Stupid of him. He let his temper get the best of him. But then so did she. "She couldn't handle her liquor," he sighs.

For the next few minutes neither one speaks. Lisa stares out the side window, still gripping her arm. He hasn't really thought much about Texas or Helen, and it is with increasing bitterness that he must now. Her first mistake was the lie, claiming to be a wealthy widow, when she was really divorced and on the dole. Half the time her alimony checks never came. Withered, bleached old bitch, her K-Y Jelly tube under the bed, holding out her arms through the camphored darkness one night, then shrieking the next for him to get the hell out, he was nothing but a leech, a loser. And what was she, no class, no taste, desperate not to be old. Edward, she announced at the condo pool to the lizard-skinned crones asleep on their frayed lounges, with their mouths sagging open, anesthetized by their lunchtime gin, yes, *Edwahd,* who would be taking her to Mexico as soon as his boat was repainted.

Lisa reaches into her paper bag. "Want some?" Cheese and peanut butter crackers. Her way of breaking the ice. She peels open the crinkly red cellophane strip.

"No thanks." Her uneasiness both amuses him and sets him on edge.

"You hardly ever eat."

"I don't eat to eat, just when I'm hungry."

The smell of peanut butter fills the car. He peers at the sign. EXIT TOLOPOS. One mile ahead. Cracker crumbs dot the wide black swath of her pant legs.

"Are you mad at me?" She touches his arm, and he can barely breathe.

"Course not."

"How come you're so quiet then? I mean, the whole trip, it's been great, we've had so much to talk about. Right from the start I had this feeling . . . like, we knew each other, you know what I mean? And now I feel . . . I don't know, kind of funny, like . . . ."

"Like I've changed?" It's a struggle not to smile. They're all the same. A man, any man, plain and simple, that's what they want. Worse they're treated, hungrier they get. Pathetic.

"Yeah, like something's wrong. Like, really wrong."

"I'm tired, that's all. Just kind of tired." To keep her calm he pats her leg, forces himself to leave his hand there. She's big, and he's not as quick as he used to be.

"Let me drive, then."

"I'm okay."

"I wasn't trying to make you mad before. What I said back there. You know that, right?"

Barely listening, he nods, turns on the directional.

"Tolopos. Are you just turning off? Are we heading back?" she asks with some disappointment. She doesn't want the fairy tale to end.

"I don't know. Just sounds kind of . . . intriguing. Don't you think?"

"Yeah it does, doesn't it?" The prospect of his improving mood delights her. "Tol-oh-pos," she says. "Tol-oh-pos, like an Indian tribe or some kind of rock band. I'll have to tell Liam. He writes all his own stuff. Tol-oh-pos, Tol-oh-pos, Tol-oh-pos," she sings, strumming an imaginary guitar, or maybe a banjo, to judge from her now accelerating rendition. "Tol-oh-pos!" She laughs, continues to strum.

Here, the road narrows.

"Look out!" she yells, pointing to the pregnant beagle waddling across the road. "Don't!" she screams and covers her face.

He gets close as he can, at the last minute jams on the brakes.

"That's not funny," she says.

"Who's laughing?"

She turns away and looks out the side window.

Same four small houses: one-story, flat roofs but now in each scrubby front yard there is a large satellite dish. This last one, his grandmother's. Where they sent him when his mother got sick. Four kids in that cramped box, him the fifth. With their own litter already jammed into one bedroom, his aunt and uncle stuck him in with Grandma Vernile. Now it's Alzheimer's, but then they said hardening of the arteries, dementia, causing her to sleep enough through the day to wail all night long while he cowered under her musty house dresses, the head of the cot jammed into the closet, the only way they could fit him in. Because it was Vernile's house, they had to do the best they could, until things got better: meaning, her death. His aunt and uncle would inherit the house, a foregone conclusion with the other daughter so long ago judged incompetent, Lydia, the one who would not be his mother.

The boy could share the room with his grandmother, the caseworker said, but with him in there, they couldn't use the outside lock to prevent her night-roaming. "Just lay there," his uncle said, pushing aside the hanging clothes. "And don't get her riled up." If she tried to get out he was supposed to wake them up. One night she did, during a violent electrical storm. He told them, but as usual they didn't believe him. *Hard to with a born liar, plain and simple,* his aunt complained to the caseworker. *Everything about him's twisted, opposite what it should*

be. But what good's the truth when no one cares. Next day, the sheriff's deputy brought Vernile home, carried her into the house, so dehydrated she kept passing out. The deputy wanted to take her to the
hospital, but his aunt refused. Last thing her mother would want, she
said. That's when they crammed him in with the cousins, least that's
how he remembers it. A few nights later, Vernile escaped again. Took a
few days, but they finally found her body, down by the gulch. Nobody
had to tell him they'd left the door unlocked. Even the cousins knew.
Big relief, as it turned out, for everyone, the whole family. Except for
him. Him, they sent back. "Just plain mean," she said, his aunt, when
the caseworker came to pick him up. "Ice in his veins. Not an ounce of
feeling for anyone but himself." Real kind lady, Aunt Tina.

He continues down Lowes Road until it forks to the left along this
rutted trail to the gulch.

"Where are you going?" she asks, uneasily. With every jounce, the
flap of her chin jiggles up and down. She peers out the window.
"What's down here?"

"I don't know. Let's see."

"It's getting dark."

The sky through the stunted trees is a sooty gray, the quarter moon,
dull as if cut from a cloud. There used to be a clearing where his uncle
dumped brush and trash, but he can't find it. POSTED. Signs nailed
to the trees. NO DUMPING. All about the environment now. Preserve
the pristine landscape, yeah, for the fat cats. One good thing, probably
nobody comes here anymore. Even better. He smiles and pulls off
the road, cuts the engine. Head back, he puts his arm over the top of
her seat.

"Let's go Eddie, please? I don't like it here."

"It's me you don't like. Admit it." He laughs.

"No!" She looks at him. "When I said that before, about our
age difference, I didn't mean that, the way it came out. I meant it as a
compliment."

Now he remembers. She had said that he didn't seem thirty years
older than she was. In fact, he seemed more like someone her own age.
Younger even, in a lot of ways.

"I did, really."

"Well, thank you. I wasn't sure where you were going with it, that's all."

His softer tone pleases her.

"This has been the greatest vacation I ever had." She sighs and rests her head against his arm. "And I know what you said about . . . about taking it slow and all, but I really, really—"

He strikes, that big, soft gullet, flappy under his fingers, squeezing before she can say it, before she makes him feel more worthless. Her arms flail, her legs thrash up and down. Worst, though, is the gagging. Finally, when her bulbous eyes freeze with deadening shock, he pulls her out onto the ground, drags her by the ankles, as far into the bushy growth as he can manage. He works quickly, removing any easy means of identity, clothes and jewelry, spits on the fingers to get the rings off. The second pierced earring's stuck in the lobe. He rips it out. A week, a week with the car should get him close enough, he thinks, running around gathering fallen branches to cover her with, then armloads of rubbly brush. New plates: always easy. Then, far enough away, a Goodwill bin for these clothes and the rest in her suitcase. That way, no suspicions raised. Better than a Dumpster. Pockets jingling with jewelry, brushes himself off, climbs back into the car. In the purse, almost eleven hundred cash, his now, finally on his way, past the dun-colored house. They never should have done that, put a little boy in with a crazy lady. A string of pale smoke shimmers up from the stovepipe. He kept waiting for the call to come, or a letter, or his case-worker to walk into his classroom with the good news: now, with the spare room they wanted him back.

Such is life. This silence a relief. A blessing. Like this, he thinks, later in the day, driving through waves of cold rain thickening to sleet, moments when he feels the pure magnetism of his destiny. Pulling him closer. His spirit soars. So near is he that his throat constricts and tears well in his eyes. It used to be money he desired, and women, or at least the release they provided. But now it is far less clear. A place, he thinks. Yes, someplace where he will belong. Where he can feel finally safe in his own skin.

The president commended her and her priest for their faith-based initiatives. He thinks about this as the huge double rigs bear down, but he refuses to yield. It's true. No matter what happens, he must have faith, in himself and in all that awaits him. The journey may be painful, even demeaning at times, but as long as he persists, it will end well. That's all he's ever wanted. Not even happiness, but peace.

CHAPTER · 6

The beginning of the week has been spent preparing for their trip. Not packing, for that would make too real what she's not sure she can do. Instead, she concentrates on leaving no loose ends at home, at work, no detail overlooked. Order is paramount now, more than ever in this new fragile existence. In the past year the paper has published five supplements, *Holiday, Garden, Automotive, Downtown Franklin,* and *Entertainment,* each filled with advertising. Six this year with the new *Medical* supplement. Her assistant is Hilda Baxter, recently widowed mother of three adult children, who is now plowing all her energies, ideas, and wisdom into her job. Of the many applicants Nora interviewed, Hilda was the only one who had never worked before. What impressed her most was Hilda's fierce determination to finally have a career, and her confident warmth. But lately, her hovering gets on Nora's nerves. Always watching, listening, she senses something's wrong, clearly wants to help, but isn't sure how.

Seven thirty at night and Nora is still in her office, doing nothing, staring. Folders and papers cover her desk. With the tap at the opening door, she grabs a folder.

"Now you're running on downtime," Hilda says, peering in. "This is when people make their most mistakes."

"I'm almost finished," she says dully, eyes shaded. "Go ahead. I'll see you tomorrow."

"I feel guilty leaving you here," Hilda says, stepping into the office.

"Well, don't." She looks up, as rankled by the intrusion as by the concern in Hilda's round, earnest face. She is a nurturer, but one compelled to fill every space, emotional and physical. Her once spare outer office is now lush with jungly plants. Clippings of her favorite sayings are taped to the walls. On her desk she keeps a basket of seasonal sachets made from her own herbs to give to people. Every Monday she brings in a new coffee cake she's baked. She thumbtacked crepe paper pumpkins on the doors for Halloween and glittery snowflakes for Christmas. What Nora has enjoyed as Hilda's motherly touch now feels suffocating and manipulative, a way of taking control. "One more to go, then I'm done," she says, picking up another folder.

"I already did that one." Hilda angles around the side of the desk for a better look. "Chiropractors. That's done!" She seizes the folder. "Now, you just pack up, missy, and head for—"

"Give me that!" Nora snaps, and Hilda recoils, face red, suddenly awkward, comical looking in her pin-striped gray suit, her need to look professional, trying to fit into a man's world, trying to belong, after all those years of aprons. *Oh God, how pathetic, because that's what happened, so blinded by my own self-importance that I never saw what was going on, instead was flattered by Robin's attention, touched by all her fussing, cherry pie because it was my favorite, hand-painted clay pots, her own sweetly scented soaps, when it was never about me. Never.*

"I'm sorry," Hilda gasps. "I didn't mean—"

"No, I know. I know you didn't. It's me, I'm just . . . tired." Oh God, oh God, she thinks, hating herself even more.

"Then let me help!" Hilda cries, touching her shoulder.

Nora can only stare up at her. How? but can't ask. Because in order to take she would have to give. And the giving, like every intimacy, is far too much of a risk. Especially now. "I'm almost done," she says.

She stares at the closing door, knees jammed painfully up into the desk edge, drawing deep, measured breaths, counts on each to twenty. Doesn't move. Listening for footsteps, presses humming, electricity crackling through cables, endless reams of paper being readied for print, the pulse beat of a manageable life, where problems can be solved and decisions made unhindered by malice or despair. If you do A and B, C inevitably follows. All she has left of stability.

She doesn't want to leave this desk. Doesn't want to go to Anguilla tomorrow. Doesn't want to be alone with Ken. Not now. If she stops, she will come apart. Better to keep busy, keep moving. That's how she's gotten through this week, almost every waking hour spent here. Chloe is just getting over the flu. Drew has been moody and short-tempered, but she clings to this grueling schedule, leaving by seven, not getting home until nine or ten at night. Slow down, Ken warns, before she ends up sick like Chloe and won't be able to go on the trip. But she knows he's grateful to be out from under the crush of her misery. It's pure survival. Work keeps her afloat. It's all she has, the only time in the day she doesn't hear the screaming, that rage in her head, her own mad wail.

She takes the back stairs, instead of the elevator. She doesn't dare talk to anyone right now. A smile, a pat on the back, and she'll come undone. On her right is the composing room where printers are working on tomorrow's edition, but the door is closed. Next is the brightly lit newsroom, though there are only three reporters at their desks, one flipping through a magazine, one typing, one asleep, tilted back in his chair. As she hurries past, the reporter stops typing and calls to her, but she pretends not to have heard.

"Hey, Nora!" he calls from the doorway. "I didn't know you were still here. This guy called and I said you already left. I'm sorry."

"That's okay. I'm sure he'll call back."

"Probably. He said it was important. I tried to get his name, but all he said was Ed."

"God. Ed Martino. He's already changed his layout three times this week," she calls in her rush to the door.

The disorientation of these past few weeks involves all her senses. Everything seems filmy, blurred, as if looking through water-smeared glasses. As she walks to her car she feels the breakdown starting, parts shifting, details fading. She scans the empty lot, for a moment can't recognize the name on the parking sign. NORA T. HAMMOND. Nothing to do with her. Words, letters, her weary brain struggles to process. It takes both cold, trembling hands to fit the key into the ignition.

Two more errands left. Busywork, keep the gears turning. Checks needing Father Grewley's signature and her proposal for the *Medical* supplement for Oliver to consider while she's gone. Neither stop is necessary, but reasons enough not to go straight home. Thinking is the killer. Even now on this short drive to St. Paul's rectory, the analysis begins, sifting through the dregs of once-mundane facts and events for more lies, more betrayals. This sickening need to know everything is destroying her. And yet, how can she not? Behind every truth lurks a darker truth. Behind the simplest reality, betrayal. The black pearl bracelet last Mother's Day, pink and white roses on her birthday, the red silk robe on Valentine's Day, what were they? Guilty counterparts to the gifts he probably chose with greater care and delight for Robin? Beautiful Robin who loved jewelry and flowers and pretty things in a way Nora never had.

On impulse she pulls into Kay McBride's driveway. If asked she would have said that she and Kay have been friendly for years, though Kay considers Nora her closest friend. She doesn't deserve a friend like Kay. All the time she's spent with Robin and Bob, instead of with Kay who wasn't part of a couple, such a waste. Kay is everything Nora is not, easygoing, good-natured, honest about her feelings. Maybe that's it. With Kay she always feels a little guilty. False, for not being half the person Kay thinks she is. Nora's life has always seemed so easy in comparison. Kay's husband died of kidney failure a few years after they were married, leaving Kay with a six-month-old baby and a pittance for insurance. Kay got her broker's license, and Nora was one of her first clients. They met when she and Ken began looking for a bigger house. Nora was pregnant for the third time and their three-bedroom Cape wasn't going to be big enough. Or at least that's what she told Kay. In truth, Ken never liked the neighborhood. He wanted to live where he'd grown up, on the north side of town, nearer the club, where most of the homes couldn't even be seen from the road. With

Kay's help they found the house they still have, bright, airy, and as it turned out with Nora's miscarriage, bigger than they would need.

The only light is on upstairs, but she keeps ringing the bell.

"Nora!" Kay says, throwing open the door, still putting on her robe. "What're you doing here? Shouldn't you be packing?"

"I've been meaning to call you. All your messages . . . it's just been . . . crazy!" And suddenly she's in Kay's arms, sobbing. She can barely speak.

"Poor kid. Oh, you poor kid. Here. C'mere. Come sit down."

Kay leads her into the small den. The love seat creaks under them.

"What's wrong?" Kay asks, and Nora can only shake her head. "Tell me. Just say it."

"It's Ken," Nora cries.

"What? What about him?" Kay looks stricken.

"He's been having an affair. With Robin," she gasps, and Kay sighs. Instead of shock there is only relief in Kay's eyes. "You knew. You did, didn't you?"

"I did. Yes." Kay's arm stiffens against her shoulder.

"How long have you known?"

"I'm not sure."

"Who told you?"

"I don't remember. Someone in the office, I think."

With that, Nora sits forward. "And you never told me. You never said anything."

"Well, I . . . God, Nora. I mean, at first I didn't want to believe it. And then I . . . I couldn't bear the thought of hurting you."

"But I am hurt. You have no idea how hurt I am. The pain I'm in."

"Oh, Nora, I—"

"But the worst of it's knowing that you were in on it, too." She jumps up, heading for the door.

"No! No, Nora!" Kay follows her, barefoot, into the cold, down the walk. Kay grabs her arm and holds on, almost pinning her back against the car. "I never saw them together. Never once! But I told Ken. I told him what a shithead he was. How disgusting I thought it all was. And you know what he said to me? Do you want to know?"

She already does: that he loved Robin and couldn't help himself.

"He said I should tell you, then. If I really believed it was true, if I was that disgusted, then maybe I should do something about it."

"So why didn't you?" Her voice sounds small, far away.

"Because . . . because some things are just . . . just too hard. And I wasn't about to do his dirty work. That would've made it too easy for him."

"But you did. Everyone did. It *was* all so easy for him. Don't you see?"

"I know, and I know why you're saying it, Nora. Because if you put all the blame on him, then you'll hate him. You'll hate him too much for anything to be salvaged. But don't push *me* away. Or anyone else. I'm sure I'm not the only one, the only one who . . . who tried. This is when you need your friends, Nora. Now more than ever."

A relationship. Clearly more than an affair. More than sex. A relationship, a union of emotional depth. Humiliation, Kay obviously thinks. But no—it's the utter rejection. She's always loved Ken, loved him exactly as he was, and for being everything she was not. He had brought security into her life and a lightness of being she'd never known. Before Ken she'd always felt alone. With him at her side she didn't have to be so guarded anymore. She could let down her defenses, breathe, laugh at herself. He made her feel complete, but now what is she? What's left? As she drives, pressure builds in her skull. She wants to save her marriage, doesn't she? Yes. She just doesn't want to be with him. Doesn't want to go home. Doesn't want to go to Anguilla. Even thinking of him makes her skin crawl. Kay's right—she doesn't want to hate him, but she needs to do something, hurt him. Hit him. Over and over again. Not even for the pain he'd feel, but to release this ache in her chest. In her throat, her brain. Just to be able to think clearly again. Or maybe not to think. A sudden jerk of the wheel, accelerator to the floor, and this out-of-control life stops hurting. But Chloe and Drew. Her children. They haven't done anything wrong. She blinks, forces her eyes onto the narrow, winding road.

St. Paul's serves the poorer neighborhoods of Franklin. Father Grewley started Sojourn House five years ago in an abandoned tenement. At first the bulk of the work, cooking and cleaning up, was done by the young priest himself and a few parishioners. Recently, Sojourn House has been relocated in an unused school building, whose twenty-odd rooms serve as clinic, counseling rooms, offices, resource center, and temporary shelter for the abused women and their children needing to get their lives back on track. With enough publicity and the right connections, Sojourn House has become a very chic charity, supported by local businesses and industry. Among their fund-raising events are wine-tasting parties, art auctions, golf tournaments, the highlights of Franklin's social season. Because of all the media attention some people think she actually works at Sojourn House. Congressman Linzer's office has sent her a framed commendation. From the White House has come another, unframed; and everywhere she goes people take time to congratulate her.

"I think that's wonderful, feeding those poor souls," said the supermarket checkout lady.

"Thank you."

"There should be more people like you in this world, Mrs. Hammond," whispered the reference librarian.

"Thank you."

"You're all so kind. We're all so good, so kind and good. Thank you, thank you thank you, thank you! Thank you?" she shouts as the car jolts over the potholes that mark the change of neighborhoods, past crowded tenements. "For fucking what?" she yells, laughing. With the slightest acceleration the car flies along the dirty snow-banked streets, past the three-deckers and their first-floor pizza places and pawn shops, still brightly lit. Here, even the barber shops stay open late, sanctuaries where men can linger instead of going home to pain and failure. For the first time in her life, she understands. She turns up the radio until throbbing music fills the car.

"A relationship!" she cries over the drumbeat. "Oh my God, my God. Oh my God!" she moans. She's never been a good enough mother, or good enough wife, or good enough lover, or good enough daughter, or good enough sister, or good enough friend. Never good enough. No matter where she goes, what she does, always an aloneness, that breathless, uncontainable need to flee, her flesh crawling with this same revulsion and panic. "Don't," she warned Ken when he first laid his hand on her stomach, beneath tightly grasped sheets of her dark, dark bedroom, needing time, that was all, time to take a deep breath, to relax, to dare feel anything, with even his breath at her flesh unbearable.

"Close your eyes and make believe I'm somebody else," he whispered once. Somebody exciting. Somebody who's crazy about you . . . Eddie's face she saw. And no matter how hard she tried to make it Ken's face, it was still Eddie, with every gasp, full of him, his voice, touch, smell, so heavy with yearning she could barely keep her eyes open, even in the hard light of day, nights later, cringing in the glare of the hot pink and green light flaring over the man's sagging back as he sank across her legs, pinning her against the seat, with Eddie, running around to her side, police coming, train coming. Coming. "Wake up, honey." Ken was shaking her. "Wake up, you're having a bad dream, that's all."

In front of the small rectory, she turns off the engine, wets her finger, and rubs away smeared eyeliner. The minute she steps into the brisk night air, heels scraping the gritty brick walk, she can think clearly again. She rings the doorbell, takes deep breaths as she waits, noting the scroll of newspaper frozen into the front lawn, and she knows why she's come here so late at night to deliver three paltry checks she's already held for days and as easily could have mailed. She needs help.

The door squeals open and the slight young priest with round, rimless glasses and thinning hair smiles out at her. "Mrs. Hammond! Nora. What a surprise." He wears a baggy blue sweater over his black pants. And soft leather Indian moccasins, beaded like a child's.

"I have these checks," she says, fumbling them from her briefcase. One flutters to the floor and she and the priest almost bump heads as they bend to get it. "They came to the paper. Ken and I are leaving tomorrow."

"Oh. Thank you. But you didn't have to come out so late. I could have—"

"No!" she interrupts. "I wanted to. Besides, I . . . I was out, I mean, out this way anyway." With her faltering voice he peers over his glasses.

"Well, come on in, then. Come inside." He steps back. From the parlor doorway to the right comes the violet wash from a television screen and voices, then laughter. "Father Connelly and I were just watching a movie," he explains.

She sees the old priest's stocking feet draw back as if to stand up. "I can't, but thanks. I'm running late," she calls as she starts back down the steps.

"You have a good trip now," Father Grewley calls, waving the checks.

Thank God. Thank God, she thinks, shocked at how close she came again to losing it. Her face flushes at the thought of pouring out her misery to the wide-eyed young priest. He's heard more than his share of troubles in his ministry, but not from Nora Hammond. She is supposed to be strong. Control is the key. She has to take charge of her pain and confusion and wrestle it into manageable shape. No one else can do that for her. The first time she went to pieces at home, Ken suggested a counselor. He has the name and telephone number of a good one. But she can't. Not now. Not yet. It would be like trying to tweeze out dirt and grit from an oozing wound.

"So, what do we do? What do you want? What're our choices?" he said, trying to hide his annoyance, when she refused. "Or do we just keep on like this?"

It isn't the smooth passage that he expected. He doesn't know what he wants except for her to move step by step through some mad formula that begins with betrayal and debasement, and hopefully, logically, if the proper methods are utilized, will end with . . . with what? Happiness? Coexistence? He has no idea how many choices she has. So many, she can barely keep them straight. There is murder and suicide and slashing and nervous breakdowns and arson and anonymous letters, the gouging with her own ragged nails of Robin Gendron's flawless glowing cheeks from her darkly lashed blue eyes to her delicate dimpled chin.

She turns down Fairway Road, past the club, up the slight rise, then the long, winding driveway to FairWinds, Oliver's home. She drives slowly, careful to keep to the middle. Once covered with white marble chips so that on a moonlit night the driveway meandered along the dark hillside like a pale river, now it is rutted and stone-humped. The Hammonds built this three-story brick manor with its oak-paneled hallways and high-ceilinged rooms at the turn of the century. It was here that Ken brought her to meet his parents and Oliver, newly married and quickly divorced, who had temporarily moved back to Fair-Winds. At first glance she thought Oliver was Ken's uncle, like their mother, calling him Kenny. Ten years older than Ken, he still seems more avuncular than brotherly. Oliver lives here alone, the lovely old living room, its deep windows overlooking the town, now, for all intents and purposes, his bedroom. It contains no bed, but a huge leather recliner that adjusts into twelve different positions (all but the missionary, Ken likes to joke) and Oliver's clothes, the few he has. She hopes Annette Roseman isn't visiting, though she's only run into her here a few times. For years the remote, elegant woman has been Oliver's companion. Annette and her disabled son live in town with her mother, who was one of old Mrs. Hammond's housekeepers. No one knows if Annette has ever been married or who the father of her son is, though few suspect Oliver. The boy, a young man now, is too dark, his features favoring his mother's race. Ken said Annette's baby was born in New York City when she was in college. Her return to Franklin coincided with Oliver's return to FairWinds. Annette is a highly regarded portrait artist, whose commissions run into the thousands.

Nora parks under the portico. She looks to make sure the front room light is on before she climbs the wide granite steps. It takes four rings of the bell before Oliver finally appears behind the etched door glass.

"What is it?" he says, running his fingers through his unruly hair. His baggy eyes are heavy with sleep. Though his tie is still on, his white shirt is unbuttoned to the waist and his unbuckled belt dangles from his rumpled suit pants. Apologizing, she follows him through the drafty, unlit foyer into the spacious living room. On the narrow credenza to the left of the door are stacked laundry boxes, torn open whenever he needs a fresh shirt. Under the credenza, on the plank base between two ornately carved mahogany pedestals, sags a large green trash bag filled with soiled shirts. The smell is always the same here, stale: stale clothes, stale furnishings, stale flesh. The only light in the long room comes from the pitted brass floor lamp next to Oliver's chair. Its pleated silk shade is yellow with cigar smoke. Ashes salt its base. Oliver's cast-off black socks lie strewn in front of his chair like a tidal deposit of seaweed.

"The layouts. I should have just left them on your desk!" she shouts over the classical music. "I didn't realize how late it was."

"It's all right. It's okay," he sighs, sinking his huge body down into his chair. With a touch of a button, the back tilts, the seat glides forward, and the padded footrest lifts his bare feet. He aims his remote at the old stereo system, lowering the volume. His chair rises from a sea of dropped newspapers and books, musical CDs, coffee cups, three black wingtip shoes, and across the marble coffee table his suit coat, carefully folded. In this cavernous house, this corner is all he needs anymore. Upstairs, his childhood bedroom contains all the books and games of his youth. She is overcome now with a companionable sadness. This is what becomes of the unloved. Bare feet. Musty clutter. Fatigue that seeps from the pores into cloth, plaster, wood.

"What time are you leaving?"

"It's a seven thirty flight. We're getting picked up at five. We land in San Juan at ten thir—"

"So, show me what you've got," he interrupts. It is a habit both brothers share, asking a question, then growing bored with the answer. Ken's suggests a certain boyish distraction, while Oliver only seems rude. At first, it took her a long time to warm up to Oliver. But now his brusqueness is also his saving grace. Always to the point, he never leads anyone on.

"I thought a piece by each of the hospital's board members. Pictures of the newest units, labs, whatever." She stands over him, handing down the sample layouts. "I thought something from a nurse, say, and a lab technician, a housekeeper, EMT, all the different viewpoints on—"

"Kenny's doing good, huh?" He looks up over the smudged half glasses perched on the tip of his nose.

"What do you mean?" she says sharply.

"Just that." He shrugs. "We had lunch. He seemed a hell of a lot more engaged, I thought. That's all." He shuffles through the papers. "He had me worried there for a while."

"How's that?" She passes him more sheets.

"Oh, I don't know. For a while there he just wasn't tuned in, you know?"

"What do you think was wrong?"

"Ah, who the hell knows. Probably the same cobwebs, same treadmill we all get stuck on." He glances up, frowning, rolling his hand. "Where's the ads? You gonna run this on love or something?"

"They're just mock-ups." She gives him four more. "I mean, nobody's even gone out yet."

He looks over her proposed ads, nodding, muttering. "Cheap bastards," he says when he comes to the companies he doubts will buy space. He reaches beside his chair and brings up a bottle of scotch and a glass, cloudy with amber rings. He fills the glass, sips it warm, no ice. He asks about her dates for getting the supplement in on time, then raises his glass. "It's your ball. Run with it."

"You sure now?" She's not surprised. The trick is to answer Oliver's questions before he asks them, then tunes you out.

"Sure I'm sure." He reaches down for another glass and pours it half full. "Bon voyage!"

"Bon voyage!" The long burning drink makes her eyes water and her nose run.

Oliver is telling her about today's phone call, complaining about the recent *Chronicle* photo of state senator Bob Gallewski. In it, Gallewski, with tumbler in hand, looked dazed, thick-featured, open-mouthed, and if not intoxicated, certainly slow-witted. His campaign manager, Abby Rust, is demanding they run a better one. " 'But, Abby,'

I said, 'if I do that, next thing I'll be running photo retractions on the bake-sale ladies and the Eagle Scouts.' " At the thought of it, Oliver laughs, refills his glass. "Before and after editions."

"You've got to admit it's a dirty trick," Nora says as she moves about, kicking socks into a pile, lining up shoes by the door, stacking weeks of newspapers and magazines. "It's like another kind of power you have over someone." She hangs his suit coat over the back of a chair. "One nobody can really call you on, it's so insidious."

"As conscience of the people." He hoists his glass. "However self-appointed." Then takes a drink.

"What if it was me? Suppose Ken and I were in a messy divorce, what would you do?" She is stacking his CDs on the cluttered table next to him.

"What I usually do in domestic matters." His eyes lift slowly to hers. "Nothing. Nothing at all."

"Ollie," she begins, then catches herself. He despises conversations like this. Get too personal and he'll walk away. The hell with it. She can't keep up the façade. This pretense of a normal life is destroying her. It takes too much energy. More than she needs to talk, she wants Oliver's help, though hasn't the slightest idea what form that might take. Not financial and certainly not emotional, for that is beyond Oliver's ken. What she wants is to stop hurting.

"You knew all about it, didn't you?"

"What do you mean?"

"You know what I mean. Don't—"

"For a couple years now. All right?"

She shakes her head, not knowing whether to laugh or cry, though seems to be doing both. "A couple years. Great! That's just great. I guess everyone knew, huh? Probably even Chloe and Drew. Everyone but me. But I guess that's how an affair works, doesn't it? Excuse me, a relationship. That's what he calls it. Not an affair, no, that would be too, too, what? Cheap? Trashy? Low class? God knows, Ken's not that, is he?"

"What do you want me to do, Nora?" He hasn't moved, his features lost in shadows, his voice cold, almost angry.

"Oh, nothing! Nothing. Just thought we should get it out there. You know, be perfectly honest with one another. I mean, isn't that what we've always done?" Though their honesty has always been about work, she realizes. She knows as little about him as he does about her. Of course his first loyalty would be to his brother.

"Why're you mad at me? What'd you want me to do? Break up your family?"

"No." She's crying again. "It's just . . . I'm so hurt. I feel so alone."

"But you're still together, right?"

"Barely."

"What do you think, I just sat idly by? Of course I didn't. I tried. I did the best I could."

"What? What did you do?"

He takes another long drink. "I told him what an asshole he was. What a loser. I told him you were the best thing that ever happened to him and I wasn't going to be party to anything that would destroy that."

"Party to anything, what do you mean?"

"Just that."

For days this conversation replays in her head. All she can conclude is that Oliver regards her as some kind of crutch for Ken. Take away the crutch, his brother goes down. And maybe it's true. Maybe that's what did it, what's still keeping them together. Her strength, something Robin lacks. That's what Oliver was trying to tell her.

CHAPTER · 7

Saturday, 5 a.m.: Chloe is staying at her friend Jesse's house. Drew will be at Johnny Hale's while they're in Anguilla. The limo has been idling out front for fifteen minutes.

"What's the holdup?" Ken calls up from the front hall.

She can hear voices, the door opening, then closing as the driver carries their luggage down to the car.

"Nora! C'mon!" Ken calls.

Down in the driveway the trunk bangs shut. Fully dressed, hair blown dry, makeup on, she sits on the edge of the bed, staring at the deep molding around the two-over-two panels on the door painted Luster Pearl. Two years ago this room was done over. How important the color seemed then; after all, it was their bedroom. The cut-glass doorknob glitters as it turns.

"Jesus, Nora. We're going to be late." He gestures back over his shoulder. "Why're you just sitting there?"

Imagine that, she thinks, looking at him fresh and trim, pressed khakis, lavender Polo shirt, so eager, ready for a good time. As always. Just another vacation, winter getaway, that's all. Recharge the batteries. As if nothing has ever happened. Walk out that door and they'll be the same two people they've always been. Ken's good at that, better in his role than she's ever been in hers. Theater, that's what this is, living theater.

"Nora?"

"I'm not going."

"What do you mean? What're you talking about?" He lifts his hands in astonishment.

"Nothing. Because what on earth would we talk about?"

"We'll . . . we'll relax. Get away from . . . everything."

"Can you do that? Really? Because I can't. I don't know how. I keep trying, but I can't. I can't sit beside you on a plane, or on a beach, or in a hotel room, or a restaurant. I can't."

"What do you mean you can't?" He's trying to sound understanding, but she sees the utter panic in his eyes.

"I can't pretend."

"I don't want you to pretend. That's not what this is."

"What is it, then?"

"We need to get away."

"Why? What good will it do?" She stares up into his lean, boyish face. "I can't. Not now."

"What, then? You won't talk to a counselor." He leans close, voice faint with the one thing she hasn't heard before, fear. "What're we going to do? We've got to do something."

"Then *you* talk to me, Ken. *You* listen to me. Answer my questions. Even if they hurt. Answer them! I can't do this in front of someone. You know I can't. It's . . . it's too damn degrading." And with that he turns and walks downstairs. Certain he's leaving without her, she watches from the window. He speaks to the driver who laughs. They remove the suitcases and golf clubs from the trunk. As he tips the amused driver, she imagines the repartee. *Women, always changing their minds at the drop of a hat.* Corny, but not from Ken. Part of his charm, to be so hip yet endearingly old-fashioned. And then, as if from high on the helm of his wrecked ship, he gives his departing rescuer a brisk salute.

Her sense of time is skewed. It's like losing a basic faculty, taste, smell, touch; everything seems unremarkable. A week has passed and yet there's not a day she can recall.

"You feel all right, Mom?" Chloe asks from the half-opened door.

"I'm . . . I'm just . . ." Nora struggles to open her eyes. She took a sleeping pill at bedtime and for the first time in weeks has slept through the night. "What time is it?"

"Quarter of eight. I was gonna leave, but I figured I better check."

"Quarter of eight! What're you doing here? Damn it, Chloe, you're late again." Squinting, she sits up on her elbows. "You know what Mr. Brown said. One more tardy slip and you'll be—"

"It's Sunday."

"Oh." Her eyes close heavily.

"Want me to open the drapes?" Without waiting for an answer, Chloe opens the ivory panels and stands looking down into the front yard. Nora turns from the sudden glare. How like her father. Bring in the light, get on with life. Her daughter can't bear dissension in the house. "It's beautiful out!" From anyone else this bright insistence would ring false, but Chloe needs cheeriness, demands it. "It snowed. All night long. It just stopped." She leans over the low sill. "Hey. Somebody's down there. I'll go see what he wants." She hurries from the room. The doorbell is ringing.

Nora wonders if Ken is downstairs. Though they still go to bed in the same room, by morning he's gone, having slept most of the night in the guest room, on top of the spread, covered with an afghan. Probably so as not to alarm the children. For a week now they've barely spoken. Her last-minute refusal to go to Anguilla shocked him. The tables have turned. Now *he* has a reason to be angry, a reason to sulk for long hours in his study, a reason to avoid her. Suddenly, he is offended, the one aggrieved. And she doesn't care. There is no energy left for scenes or confrontations. This silent morass is a relief for Chloe and Drew. At least on some level life can seem a little more normal. In the past she and Ken seldom argued about anything, which was not for lack of trying on her part. Some conflicts need to be worked out, and it's only natural with children, especially teenagers. But with the slightest turmoil Kenny would disappear. "Not my bag," he'd say. Lightheartedness, his dispensation, a free spirit not to be sullied.

Nora slips into her robe as she looks out the window. Whoever it was is gone. The tire tracks in the new snow are from the street. The snow in front of the garage doors lies undisturbed. Ken must still be here. As she passes the guest room she notes the closed door. He usually leaves before the children realize he's slept in there, but apparently, in his rejection, he doesn't care. On her way downstairs she knows by the fizzy popping sounds from the den that Drew is playing *Band of Brothers.* Video games are allowed only on weekends, no more than two hours, whether all in one day or however he wants to break it up. As a result he is usually up first thing Saturday morning before anyone else. That way no one knows how long he's been at it. So Nora has had to set an additional rule. No games before 7 a.m. She stands in the doorway. The dark wooden blinds are still closed. The only light comes from the wide screen, flickering and harsh, making Drew seem not just small on the hassock but caught in the cross fire. As the screen explodes with gunfire, jagged light rips orangey red gashes across his splotchy face. His thumbs jig over the controls. Always harder to reach than Chloe, he has been unusually quiet these last few weeks. It's all right, she wants to say, but can't lie to him. If only she could pretend, like Ken. Parallel lives. The public face veiling the private agony. Secrets, sad to have to keep them at such a young age, sadder when you can't do anything about them. Ken used to be so sensitive when it came to his children's feelings. He couldn't bear seeing them hurt. Hadn't their humiliation even occurred to him? Especially Drew's. Clay Gendron was his best friend. She puts her hand on Drew's shoulder and kisses the top of his damp head. He smells of perspiration. If she doesn't remind him, he won't shower. Sometimes he has to be ordered to take one. Soon, she'll be wondering why he takes so many.

"How about some pancakes?" she asks, wearied by the deadness in her own voice.

"I'm good." He leans a little with the remote as he maneuvers a tank down a narrow city street.

He dislikes sports but loves math and computers. Ken has stopped asking him to play tennis or racquetball with him. He spends too much time in the house, Ken complains. "Look at him, how un-healthy he looks." Drew has her pale coloring and lately his face, even the back of his neck, is mottled with angry-looking acne. Last Christ-mas she told him she would call a dermatologist. But then she had to cancel the appointment. Something came up. What? What could have been more important than helping Drew feel better about himself? That's the difference between the two children. Chloe would have pestered her until she made another appointment, while Drew is con-tent to be left alone. First thing Monday she will call Dr. Rosen.

"I'm going to make some anyway. So, when you're ready."

"I already ate."

In the kitchen Chloe slouches over the center island, sipping coffee and watching the small television on the counter.

"For godsakes, Chloe. Cartoons?" she makes herself say, trying to care, trying to snag some emotion that will pull her back into the old life.

"The Simpsons. They're not cartoons."

"Oh?" Nora assembles the pancake ingredients on the counter. Even if no one eats them, she needs to do this, ritual, the grounding of ordinary things. Ken wants her to accept his confession, talk to a ther-apist, and get on with life. What he doesn't want is fallout. She has to get back on her feet, but her way. According to her needs, for once, her timetable, not his. Nothing is more important than her children, and for their sake she needs to put the pieces back together. She can't keep falling apart. Her influence as a member of the Hammond family on behalf of Sojourn House is finally making a difference. One of the Boston television news anchors wants to come out and interview Fa-ther Grewley as part of a weeklong spotlight on domestic violence. Now, more than ever before, she enjoys her work at the paper. Until Ken's bombshell flattened her, she'd loved her life, considered herself blessed, not just with material goods but with the opportunity to help people. The Hammond name can open practically any door, and as many wallets. She is just beginning to realize her role in this. Not many people want to turn Ken Hammond's wife down, fewer still, the powerful Oliver Hammond's sister-in-law. Having finally found a way to make a difference and help those less fortunate, she can't dribble it away in self-pity.

"I'm not hungry," Chloe warns over *The Simpsons'* chatter as Nora breaks two eggs into the dry ingredients.

"I know." Streaks of yoke yellow the batter as she stirs, the same color as Homer Simpson's face. Chloe never thinks she's hungry, and yet she has the best appetite in the family. "Who was that at the door?" Now, vanilla extract, a pinch of cinanamon. Upstairs a door opens and closes: Ken on his way into the bathroom.

"Some guy, he was looking for a street." Something that Homer Simpson does makes Chloe laugh.

"What street?" She glances over at her daughter. Such a beautiful girl. So natural in her warmth, everything Nora ever envied in her own peers, growing up. Amazing that she is hers, in spite of all the trouble and worry. Now more than ever, Nora is determined that this lovely child not grow up like Robin Gendron, pampered and expecting everything to be given to her. Even someone else's husband.

"Clayborne. He said he didn't know if it was Clayborne Street or Road or Lane. Just that it was Clayborne something."

The spoon sinks into the bowl. Nora stares, blankly. Doesn't know what to do, how to get it out. If she touches it, she'll get batter on her fingers. Ken is coming down the stairs.

" 'Not around here,' I told him. Least I never heard of it," Chloe says.

"Heard of what?" Ken asks, coming into the kitchen. He kisses Chloe's cheek then takes his grapefruit, mango, and peach juice from the refrigerator. The health food store blends a fresh batch for him every few days.

"Clayborne Street," Chloe says. "Some guy. He said he'd just keep driving around. Sooner or later he'd find it."

"Well, that's one way of doing it." Ken drinks his juice. "Or get a GPS."

"What did he look like?" she asks.

Chloe looks up from the television. "Actually, kinda cute. For an old guy, that is." She grins, anticipating her father's question.

"How old was he?" he asks.

"Umm, same as you, I guess."

Kenny hoists the glass. "Thank you very much!"

"He had these really, like, amazing eyes. All pale and blue, like, looking into light."

Nora lights the burner, sprays oil on the griddle. She removes a small ladle from the stone pitcher and tries to flip the fallen spoon from the bowl into the sink. It misses, lands on the counter spattering the backsplash with batter. She squeezes out the sponge and scrubs the tiles clean.

"Mom, the griddle, it's smoking!" Chloe makes the practiced climb onto the counter to unscrew the smoke detector before it goes off.

"I got it!" Ken grabs an oven mitt and moves the griddle off the burners. "No harm, no foul."

"Mom," Chloe says. "Your hands . . . they're shaking."

"My stomach. It's a little shaky. That's all."

"Then sit down. Here," Ken insists over her protests until she has no choice but to sit in the chair he has pulled out. "Chloe, get your mum some crackers or juice or something." He stands behind her, kneading her shoulders. "It's okay. It's okay," he keeps saying, his chest like a wall against the back of her head. "We're gonna take good care of you, don't you worry."

CHAPTER · 8

Nora is waiting to see Oliver. Throughout the day people have been hurrying in and out of his office. Ken was the last one in. They can't sit on the CraneCopley story much longer, not with the grand jury meeting. Until a few years ago the company was still a small, local operation specializing in electronic equipment for home and commercial security. Now, with fear and paranoia such big business, their sensitive surveillance equipment protects government buildings, famous landmarks, huge shopping malls, and most airports. The double *C* with an eyeball in its center is a globally recognized logo. Crane is from Lyndell Crane. Copley just sounded prestigious, according to Lyndie.

He and Ken have been friends for years. Lyndie's wife, Letitia, is a Sojourn House board member. A plain, forceful woman, she wields her reputation as the no-nonsense daughter of a school janitor so effectively that her often cruel frankness is considered endearing, refreshing. A breath of fresh air, people like to say. Nora has always found her irritating, but useful. When Letitia Crane asks for contributions, donors, fearing her caustic tongue, have a hard time saying no. For the greater good to be realized many distasteful people have to be not merely endured, but stroked, Nora is learning.

She hasn't been told the details, but she does know that Lyndie Crane stands accused of rigging government contracts, as well as financial mismanagement. Oliver's door opens and Ken emerges, shaking his head. He looks drained.

"Unbelievable," he says, gesturing for her to follow him into his office. "I mean, what was he thinking?" he says when she closes the door. "He had everything. What more did he need? I don't get it." That he seems so personally affronted annoys her in the way imbroglios involving Ken and their friends always have. More so, now. Most of their crises seem so shallow that she long ago gave up trying to empathize. But this, as Ken is pointing out, is far different. Crane-Copley employs 350 workers locally, not to mention another 1,200 across the country. Late last night she heard him on the phone trying to talk Oliver into not "piling on Lyndie."

"Essentially what he did was steal from his own people. That's the bottom line here," Ken fumes, pacing back and forth. "Like that layoff last week."

"What layoff?" So leveled by her own pain she's hardly been aware of anyone else's. War, terror bombings, plane crashes, a disastrous stock market, these occur in a dimension beyond her own.

"Seventy-eight people, and that's just the first of . . ."

She stops listening. Her brain fizzes with connections. Everything is personal. There are no coincidences. The man at the door asking for Clayborne Lane. Her world has been weakened. She feels vulnerable, naïve, as it occurs to her that Bob Gendron works for CraneCopley. When he couldn't find a job anywhere, given his many terminations, Ken asked Lyndie to "take the poor bugger on." Now she's remembering Ken's weary explanation for another late-night arrival, a year or so ago. He'd been at some banquet or board meeting with Lyndie and as much as he wanted to come straight home when it was over, he had to get Lyndie alone so he could ask him if he'd help Bob. The poor guy was desperate. He and Robin were living just about at poverty level. Bob hadn't worked in four months and his drinking was worse than ever. Why didn't Robin work, she asked. Wouldn't that help? Put food on the table, anyway.

"Lyra's only two," he said incredulously.

"So? A lot of women with two-year-olds work. Especially when they have to. When they have no other choice," she added.

"You didn't," he said with that defensiveness she learned long ago to overlook. After all, he and Robin were as close as brother and sister, everyone knew that.

"I had a choice, didn't I? Thanks to you, Kenny," she added with such genuine tenderness that his quick retort confused her.

"Well, Robin doesn't have a Kenny, now, does she?" he said.

So another piece fits into place: Robin *did* have a Kenny, just not enough of him.

Ken is complaining that their story is far more sensational than it needs to be and Oliver refuses to tone it down.

"So did Bob Gendron get laid off, too?" she interrupts.

Ken looks confused. There is the slightest flush at his throat, in the soft flesh she used to love to kiss, right under his jaw.

"He works there, right? CraneCopley? You got him the job?"

"Oh. That's right. No, I think he's still there. One of the lucky ones. So far, anyway." So smooth, so natural, his commingling of deceit and truth, insignificant tributaries trickling into one vast river.

"Because of you, Ken." Because of the paper, she wants to add.

"This has nothing to do with"—here, the slightest hesitation—"them."

Of course it does. One way or another, like all the lies so convoluted, yet densely linked, the original motive is lost, indiscernible. Does he think he can get from one side to the other without getting wet, without disturbing, not just surface water, but the muck and stones, the slimy swaying reeds? She has hit a nerve. Again. But in his mind, the fault is hers; another setback. Last night, for the first time in weeks, they slept in the same bed until morning. And now his glance tells her that once again she is endangering everything he's trying to make right between them. Tonight, he will be curt, shrouded in the wounded air that is so hard on the children. They want to know what's going on, but can't bear asking.

She has told him that she is willing to try, but on her terms, however slowly, warily, that may go. Honesty has to underlie every word and deed, every waking moment. If only she could demand an honest accounting of his thoughts. Now, for instance, his eyes are cold, unreadable, only the slightest twitch of his lower lip betraying him. Torment.

Pain. Grief, she thinks, startled, for a moment, almost pitying him for the irony of his criticism of Lyndell Crane. For what had *Ken* been thinking? Hadn't he also had everything a man could want? What more had he needed? she wonders on her way down to Oliver's office.

Oliver's smile breaks into a yawn as she comes through the door.

"Why do you do that?" she teases. "You always yawn when you see me."

"No I don't."

"Yes, you do. I'm always afraid you're bored before I've even opened my mouth."

His laughter ensures the pretense that their last conversation never took place. That he enjoys her company was apparent early in their relationship. There are still times, though, when she considers him the most disagreeable person she has ever known. But warts and all, she likes him, if only just for liking her so much. His enormous desk is covered with papers, but in such neat piles she is always struck by the careful order of his work compared to the disarray of his personal life.

"Maybe it's a warning. But if so, you're the only one who notices."

It's true, and though it's taken a while, she can finally read most of Oliver's signals. He doesn't ask her to sit down. He never does. She says she knows how busy he is right now with the CraneCopley story, but she needs to know if he's had a chance to look at the *Medical* supplement layout yet. He hasn't. She tries to hide her disappointment. And her impatience. This constant motion has overtaken her life. Staying busy, keeping sane. She'll let him get back to work, she says, moving toward the door. But, she adds, she'd really like his opinion.

"Okay."

"So you'll let me know, then?"

"What's to know?" He holds up his hands. "Family. My first priority. After that's the paper."

"Thank you." They're talking about two different things. Or maybe not. Conscious of his intense stare, she smiles brightly.

■   ■   ■

I'm sorry to have to call you in like this, Mrs. Hammond, but I don't know what else to do. Drew and I have had countless meetings. But all to no avail." As he speaks, Mr. Carteil arranges Drew's World History tests for Nora to see. Three D's, the essay questions unanswered. "And now he doesn't hand in the term paper. Doesn't even bother."

Red-faced, Drew looks down. His big sneakers scrape under the conference table.

"I've given him every chance." His white-haired teacher sighs. "You know I have, don't you, Drew?" he asks in exasperation.

Drew clears his throat. His head hangs lower.

"Answer Mr. Carteil," she says.

"Yes, sir."

"Then why? What *is* the problem?"

Drew shrugs.

"Something's wrong, isn't it? A good student like you doesn't just wake up one day and decide to quit trying. Does he?"

Drew shakes his head.

"Drew," she warns, almost in question, his sullenness more shocking than the failing grade.

"No, sir."

"Then what is it?" Mr. Carteil asks as gently as frustration allows. Demanding, but a teacher of extraordinary kindness, he is a legend at the high school. He is well past retirement age, but every year the school board unanimously approves the extension on his contract.

"I don't know," Drew mumbles, hunching his head into his shoulders.

Nora watches guiltily. She should have sent him to Billington Academy where Ken and Oliver went, instead of insisting on a public school education, a more realistic world, her argument then. At least away at prep school he would be spared the turmoil of this more disturbing reality, his home life.

"Well, if you don't know, Drew, who on earth does? This work is your responsibility. No one else's. I was very pleased when I saw your name on my class list. You were excellent in freshman history, the kind of student a teacher needs in his class. Not just interested, not just bright, but excited by the work. Thrilled to be learning." The old man's shrewd eyes shift between mother and student. "Is it me, Drew? Maybe you'd be better off with another teacher. Mrs. Leeman's got a smaller class, maybe it'd be more to your pace. You—"

"No," Drew interrupts.

"What, then?" he asks hopefully.

"I'll just drop it, that's all."

"But it'll be an incomplete, it's so late in the term."

Drew nods miserably. Mr. Carteil sighs. Before they leave, he offers Drew one more chance. If he turns in the term paper and gets an A on it, Mr. Carteil will let him make up one of the tests.

"Oh, Mr. Carteil, that's so kind of you." She is touched by the old man's sensitivity.

But the prospect seems to deflate Drew even more. Their ride home is painful. No matter what she says he stares out his side window. She tells him how much she loves him, what a good boy he's always been, what a wonderful son, and that she understands his unhappiness and blames herself.

"It's not your fault," he says dully.

Uncertain how much he actually knows, she tries to be careful.

"Sometimes even the happiest families have . . . difficulties, honey, and now . . . now, we're going through it."

"What?" Drew's head spins around. "A bad patch?" he says, stinging her with the old family joke: Ken's blithe dismissal of trouble, no matter its gravity, never more than that, just a bit of a bad patch.

"All the turmoil, Drew. I've been so wrapped up in my own problems I'm afraid I haven't taken your feelings into account." She drives even slower. "I guess I was hoping you didn't care. Or notice what was going on. But of course you did, and that was selfish of me." Suddenly blurry-eyed, she has to pull over. "I'm sorry. Oh," she says, fumbling in her purse for tissues. "I don't want to be doing this. Crying like this. It's not fair to you, and I'm so, so sorry." She covers her face with her hands. This is exactly what she doesn't want, to give in to her own pain again. "You're such a good boy. You are, and I've just been such a mess lately."

"That's okay. It's okay, Mum." He puts his hand on her arm.

"It's not okay." She blows her nose and takes a deep breath. "Because we have to talk. That's the important thing. To be honest. To be able to tell one another the truth. I don't know what's going on with you. But that's my fault, not yours. Drew?" His struggle to contain himself is tearing her apart. His chest heaves in and out, his head bobs as he rubs his fist against his mouth. "Say it. Please. Please, baby," she gasps, reaching for him. His arms and back are alarmingly bony as he leans toward her.

"Mum," he cries, his newly deep voice cracking. "Don't get divorced. Please?" he sobs, tears and phlegm leaking down his cheeks and neck.

"No! No. Of course not," she says, truly stunned, and for the first time realizing that in all her misery and anger she has never considered divorce. Not even as a threat.

"Clay said you're going to." He looks at her. She has forgotten those enormous tears, how as a little boy they would pour from his eyes. Ignoring her tissue, he wipes his face on his sleeves. "He said it'd probably take a while, but you would."

"Oh, really? And how would Clay know?" she says, trying to hide her old irritation with Clay. A hyper child who has grown into a near-manic adolescent, yet he and Drew have always been buddies.

"He wants it to happen. He hates his father. He thinks Dad's great. He said we'd be stepbrothers."

She stops breathing. "What did you say?"

"Nothing."

"That's why, isn't it? You and Clay, you hardly ever—"

"I don't know." He shrugs. "We're into different stuff now, that's all."

Always the better athlete, Clay makes every team he tries out for. Until now, that never seemed to matter. Drew enjoyed not having to compete and still being able to hang out with the jocks who liked his quirky humor. Always such a good boy. Such a fine young man. Kind and sensitive. She blames herself for his moodiness these last few weeks, his bleak refuge in the den every day, the computer for solace.

"Your dad and I are trying to get through . . . to get past this. He's a wonderful man. You know that, right?" Her loyalty to Ken is all but destroyed, but the worst thing now is to turn him against his father.

Drew barely nods. The mask slips back over his face. His mother's son, she thinks. Afraid to ask for help.

"He is. He really is. And that makes it even more painful," she tries to explain. "When something like this happens in a family, everyone's affected, not just Dad and me, but you and Chloe. You're going along just fine—or at least you think you are"—here, she regrets her mirthless little laugh—"and then all of a sudden the ground shifts and nothing feels safe anymore."

He is chewing his thumbnail. She's lost him. Damn, she should have let him talk. Selfish to go on like this, trying to make herself feel better. "Drew? Is that how it feels?"

"I guess."

"I know. You're sick of this, aren't you?" Leaning, she kisses his damp, bristly cheek. "That's okay. We can talk later." She starts the car and pulls into the slow-moving traffic. "Just don't keep your feelings all bottled up. Your pain," she says, straining over the wheel to see around the corner. "And your anger."

"That's what Mrs. Gendron said."

"What?"

"That I should talk to Dad, and if I couldn't, then I should feel free to call her."

She can barely grip the steering wheel. Uncomfortable as Drew is, the words spill out of him. His first inkling came late last summer. He had slept over at Clay's house, only Clay forgot to tell his mother he was there. Early the next morning, really early, like four thirty or five, he heard his father's voice. Thinking he'd come to pick him up, Drew started down the hallway just as his father and Mrs. Gendron came out of her bedroom together. Mr. Gendron wasn't home; away on a business trip, Drew assumed. Or maybe in rehab, never a secret in the Gendron household. After that, no one ever said anything. But from then on, Mrs. Gendron seemed nervous around him, uneasy, always asking, "What's wrong? What're you thinking about, Drew? You're worried about something, aren't you? I can tell." Pestering him with questions, Drew recalls, as if she wanted it out in the open but needed him to do it.

"There were a couple other times," he says, but as much as Nora has wanted details, she doesn't want them from him, her son. "And then this one day I'm in the kitchen waiting for Clay. As usual," Drew adds, and Nora glances at him. Like his mother, Clay is always late. "Mrs. Gendron was cooking and feeding Lyra, and he still wasn't there, so I said I better go. 'Wait!' she goes, and she shuts off the stove, then she sits down with me and Lyra. She said she wanted me to know that sometimes things happen between people that maybe no one wanted to happen, but then when they do, people have to try and help one another. And it was weird, the whole time I'm like, what the hell's she telling me this for? And Lyra, she keeps banging her Barbie doll on my arm, tryna get me to laugh, and it's like, all of a sudden I know, I know what she's talking about. 'I better go,' I said. And then she holds my face, like this," he says, hands cupped at his cheeks. "And she says how she loves me like her own son, that's how close we've always been. Both families."

"What did you say?" She can barely get the words out.

"Nothing. I was like . . . freaked. I took off. I went home. And I never went back. It's all just . . . just so fucked up!" He punches the dashboard so hard it leaves a dent in the pale blue leather. "Why? Why's it have to be so fucked up?" he groans. "I don't get it! I just don't get it!"

She drops Drew off at home and tells him she'll be right back. As she drives, she thinks of that day at the beach years ago. The two women, in memory so much younger then, their backs to the hot wind, kneeling, squatting on the square blue canvas, its corners weighted with smooth, flat sea rocks, while they passed out sandwiches to the three children. Robin's peanut butter and Fluff, marshmallow spread a delicacy forbidden in Nora's kitchen. Nora had packed plums, grapes, yogurt, individual bags of Goldfish crackers, organic lemonade pouches.

A brilliant day. The dazzling heat that had driven them to the water's edge, undiminished by the steady wind from the land. They shouted to be heard over the crashing foam-curdled waves, the wind's whine. Voices swelled around them, up and down the beach, children laughing, screaming, mothers calling, each part of something for which she had no name but deeply felt, an inner stillness, a pure moment, a riotous communion on the edge, the very edge of the earth. And for one so seldom trusting happiness, it seemed a kind of rapture, as she watched Chloe, Drew, and Clay run into the surf, hurling themselves headfirst into the churning tide, then surfacing, staggering against one another, sand streaming down their backs and legs, wet hair plastered in dark clumps over their brows and ears as the tide surged in. Squinting under the straw weave of her hat brim, she dug her fingers in the coarse wet sand, the water seeping instantly into each channel as they plunged into the waves again and again. With Nora as sentinel, Robin leaned back on her elbows, her face tanning so easily compared with Nora's pale white skin. Then lifeguards in orange trunks began patrolling the beach, buoys in hand, blowing their whistles. The surf was too rough. Chloe and Clay came running out of the water, but Nora couldn't see Drew. The waves were higher, breaking closer together.

"Where's Drew?" she screamed.

"He was just with us!" Chloe shouted, looking back in fear.

As Nora ran in, sand was being sucked out from under her feet. When she was chest deep, she saw the flail of white sticks, his skinny arms, fighting the wind-driven waves, struggling to get back in. He was eleven. Only eleven, she remembers thinking, a speck in the vastness, the deafening, watery tumult. Never a strong swimmer, she dove against the wave, pulling herself as best she could toward him, getting closer, fighting the current. He was trying, but she could see the terror on his face as the riptide carried him away. Her arms beat against the surge. Faster. Legs kicking. Trying to scream his name, only swallowing more water, then, feeling herself being borne away. Her chest ached, she was tired. Salt stung her eyes. Something snagged her neck, the loop of an arm, and she fought back, thrashing to push free of whatever was dragging her away from her child.

"It's all right! They've got him! They're bringing him in!" Robin screamed against her cheek. "Stay with me!"

"No!" Nora tried again to pull away. Robin wasn't taking them back in, but out, even farther from the beach.

"Don't fight me. I'll get us in," Robin gasped, pleading. "Trust me!"

And she did. On her back, with her face against Robin's slick, wet flesh, she let herself be dragged with the clawing tide until they were no longer swimming against it, but free enough of the current to float in on the incoming tide. Hands reached out, people entreating them to stand, as they sat in the shallow waves and coursing sand, panting and sobbing in each other's embrace.

Another memory to be retrofitted. Held up to the light. Dissected. Four years ago. Had the affair begun? And if so, why did Robin save her?

Even as she turns onto Dellmere Drive she is warning herself not to do this. Pull into a driveway, go home. The image of Robin Gendron's hands on her son's face keeps her from turning.

A remarkable woman. Sweet. Caring. Gentle. Not a mean bone in her body, her own words about Robin. It was only natural for the two families to stay so close through the years, given Ken, Robin, and Bob's lifelong friendship. Nora had welcomed their easy warmth, their affection and gentle humor with one another. She was always the moodier one, more reserved, questioning other people's motives, though never theirs, because they were genuinely good people, especially Robin, quick to laugh and lend a hand. Until Bob's worsening alcoholism these last few years, the two couples had gone out together at least once or twice a month. One spring vacation the two families had spent the week in Disney World in adjoining suites. Other vacations, in the Caribbean. Belize. Long weekends in New York City, Quebec, Montreal. Ski trips in Vermont. Some, she suspected, Ken picked up the tab for. But it didn't matter. They were all so close. So close, she'd even thrown a baby shower for Robin, who burst into tears, with forty whooping women yelling surprise as she came through the door with her pasta machine, thinking she was there to teach Nora how to make fettuccine. Still sobbing minutes afterward, with everyone crowded around, she had to be consoled, hugged and kissed, assured that she most certainly did deserve all this trouble and attention. My Lord, who more than her, always caring, always giving.

A phone call, Robin would insist; that's all and she'd be over. If someone was sick, a missed ride, whatever Nora needed, Robin was there. At first she'd felt swamped by Robin's attention. That's just the way she is, Ken would assure her. And it was true. Kindness, love came naturally to her. Nora used to marvel at the acuity of Robin's sense for a person's pain. How many dinner parties and events had they driven home from with Robin's voice in the backseat filled with concern for "that poor Henderson woman. Her younger sister's schizophrenic, and the family wants to keep her institutionalized, but Jeannie thinks she should be given a chance—"

"Jeannie?" Nora and Ken cried in equal astonishment. Jean Henderson, or "the viper" as she was more commonly known, so cutting and cruel that before they were eighteen, every one of her children had left home, never to return.

"How'd she happen to share that bit of information with you?" Nora asked.

"I don't know. We just got talking, and next thing I knew . . ."

And so it went. Always and everywhere. In spite of her mounting troubles. Or perhaps because of them; over time, her own pain, sculpting, giving depth to her beauty. Because she had no secrets, kept no part of herself private, or so she would have you believe, Bob's drinking and increasing volatility, his erratic employment, their strained finances, their run-down house, it was all there in the tapestry's intricate weave. Her suffering, a brilliant artistry, so submerging herself in another's life that the normal delineation blurs; from her own vulnerability creating an instant emotional communion. Too wounded to be envied, she is the perfect friend. Women admire her; men want to protect her.

The pretty mailbox hangs on its crooked post, clipped more than a few times by Bob's alcohol-fueled swerves into the driveway. Robin painted the climbing blue morning glories herself, hidden among the leaves her signature robin bird. Crafts. Quilting. Dinner parties, she can do it all, sublimely unhindered by her husband's failings, unshamed by his disruptions, unembarrassed by peeling paint, the missing glass in the storm door, the doorbell protruding from a frayed white wire. Less evidence of a failed life than bravely borne wounds, her domestic stigmata. Nora bangs the brass door knocker, pineapple, pitted symbol of welcome. Its dull strike brings fear. Her heart races, her thoughts colliding in bursts so that when the door finally opens, she hears herself hiss, "A malignancy. That's what you are. All you've ever been. Destructive and selfish . . ."

"I'm so sorry," Robin gasps. "I'm so sorry. Please. Please," she cries, holding out her arms as if .this might be healing enough. Without makeup and with her long hair pulled back, she looks tired, but younger. "Please come in, Nora." She opens the door all the way. "I beg you. Please. What happened, it was so—"

"No! Not what happened! What *you* did, that's what's so disgusting!"

"I know that. Of course I know that," Robin weeps.

"And don't you ever again speak to my son. Do you hear me?"

"I—"

"Saying you love him like a son, how twisted are you?"

"But I do," she sobs. "And I love you, Nora. That's the hardest part. Losing all of you."

"No. The hardest part's not getting what you want. What you've wanted all along."

"That's not true! Oh, God. Oh, please. Please, Nora. You have no idea," she calls after her down the path. "I'm so miserable. I'm so unhappy I just want to die. Do you hear me? That's all I want!" she screams. "That's all I want anymore. To die. To be dead! Done with it all!"

"Mommy!" a child shrieks. Robin is slumped, sitting in the doorway, sobbing, berating herself for all the world to see. Lyra stands there, arms around her mother's head.

Nora yanks down on the seat belt, tethered now, anchored and safe. She stares back at the weeping little girl as she starts the car, her safe, sensible Volvo, then drives slowly away, and bursts into tears. Another child's pain—the last thing on earth she wants.

CHAPTER · 9

The meeting ends late. Two board members were upset to find their names omitted from the Sojourn House stationery. Father Grewley spent most of the time trying to placate them. Such a minor point, but the young priest kept saying they needed "to make it right." Every time Nora attempted to move the agenda along, he'd drift back to it again. Easy enough to order new stationery, he supposed. Yes, at an additional cost of eight hundred dollars, the equivalent of a week's worth of groceries, she pointed out, to no avail. Father Grewley can't bear offending anyone, so he is insisting on paying for the printing himself. "Ridiculous," Nora murmurs as the slighted members pass her on their way outside.

"No, no," Father Grewley says. "It's my fault. I should have checked the copy. It's only right. They do so much."

"But that's really all they care about, about their . . . their credentials. Like belonging to the right club. It's not about helping people."

"But people do get helped, in spite of the motivation." He smiles. "Flattery, vanity, guilt, whatever works."

She opens her checkbook, scribbles the amount. Eight hundred dollars. "You're right." She holds out the check. "Whatever works." Hammond money. It never really mattered, now even less. If anything, it seems like a genetic flaw thinning each generation's moral fiber. She'd gladly give it away, every penny of it, just to be happy again. And to see her children strong.

"No, I didn't mean you, Nora."

"I know. But I want to. Please."

She hurries to her car. For all his wide-eyed naïveté, the young priest knows exactly what he is doing. She admires that. It is his mission to craft human weakness to a higher purpose. If only he could do the same with her. Confronting Robin last week brought a brief surge of confidence, a fleeting sense of control, but then her anger turned to guilt, which makes no sense at all. Seeing Robin's pain gave little satisfaction. Hurting her has only made Nora feel worse. Maybe there is no answer beyond forgiveness. It's all Ken seems to want, but she feels empty, with nothing left to give. Going through the motions takes all her energy.

Seven o'clock. Too late to start cooking dinner now. There is a pan of leftover lasagna, enough for Chloe and Drew, anyway. As she drives, she calls home.

"Mom!" Chloe answers. "Where've you been? I've been calling you!"

"A meeting. My phone was off, but Chloe, listen. In the fridge, on the bottom shelf, there's—"

"Mom." Chloe's muffled voice. "There's someone here. He said he's an old friend of yours."

"Who?" She turns onto the highway. "What's his name?"

"Ed Hawkins. But the weird thing is, he's the same one, that guy. The one that was looking for that street before."

She sees him through the door glass. He is sitting at her table watching Chloe take plates from the cupboard. He stands up when Nora comes into the kitchen. For a moment she's surprised that he's older. He's thinner, not as tall as she remembers. There is a silvery blondness to his thinning hair and his eyes, the same pale blue but with a bright transparency she finds hard to look at.

"Nora! It's you! After all this time." His arms spring wide, expecting what, she wonders for a queasy moment: an embrace, a kiss? She shrinks back. He offers his hand.

She can barely touch it. "I'll finish the table," she tells Chloe.

His gaze holds, in full measure of her distress. He smiles. "I was just telling your beautiful daughter how much she reminds me of you. Same age as then, right?"

"Yeah, seventeen. Same as my mother!" Chloe answers, clearly enjoying being part of her mother's reunion with an old friend. She is unrolling place mats onto the table. "So'd you guys go to the same college?"

"More of a summer thing," he says, and Chloe smirks, eyebrows raised. "We worked together," he adds.

A lie. He'd hung around the hotel a lot, particularly the golf course, but he never held a job there.

"So what're you doing here?" she asks, for Chloe's sake, straining to sound unconcerned.

"I didn't know what happened. I always wondered." He'd been in D.C. recently, on business, and what does he pick up but *Newsweek*. There's an article he's interested in, faith-based charities. Doesn't know why, but he kept looking at this one picture. "Took me a minute. Same face, same first name. Nora!"

Hands trembling, she slides the lasagna pan onto the oven rack. She tells Chloe she'd better get started on her homework. But she only has a little left, Chloe protests. "Then go finish it," Nora says. Like her father, Chloe loves company. "Now, please."

"Okay!" Chloe is annoyed.

Smiling, Eddie watches her flounce through the swinging door. "Looks like you."

"No."

"Reminds me of you."

"Why did you come here?"

"Now, that's not very welcoming."

"You have a reason, what is it?"

"No! No reason." He laughs. "I was in the area. Thought I'd stop in, say hello." He is unfolding a newspaper. "Pretty impressive. Family paper." He turns the page, reads the masthead: OLIVER P. HAMMOND, PUBLISHER. KENNETH L. HAMMOND, ASSOCIATE PUBLISHER.

"What do you want?" She already knows. Money.

"You've turned into a very skeptical person, Nora."

"I'd like you to leave, please."

"Please! So, it's a request, it's up to me."

"It's not a request. I'm telling you, I want you to leave! Now!"

"Nora," he chides, holding up his hands. "I thought you'd be happy to see me. I'm all right. See! Aren't you relieved? It was all so crazy that night, so confusing." He grins and his dimples deepen with an intimate sweetness that turns her stomach. "I was so worried about you. All this time I been wondering, did some psycho pick her up? Does she even know what happened? Does she care?"

"So you refuse to leave, is that what's going on here?" She comes around the counter nearer the phone.

"No, I just . . . actually, I'm a little hurt. I just wanted to set your mind at ease, that's all." He picks up a stack of photographs from the counter and riffles through them. They were taken on Chloe's junior class trip to New York City. "Good-looking kids. Think the world's their oyster, that nothing bad's ever going to happen to them." He chuckles. "Good thing they don't know," he sighs, grinning at the picture of Chloe pulling herself up the ladder from the hotel pool. She is wearing a skimpy bikini that Nora said not to bring. Suggestive enough on a beach, but definitely inappropriate on a class trip, especially in such close quarters as an indoor pool. "Now you've even got bikini rules?" Chloe laughed. "That's right!" Nora snapped back, troubled by the echo of her own mother's stridency.

"Like us," he continues. "We didn't know, did we?"

There was no us, no we, she almost says, *but that's what he wants.* She snatches the picture from him. "I'm really very busy."

"Go ahead, don't let me hold you up." He pulls out a stool. "I'll just sit here while you do whatever it is you do."

"My husband'll be home any minute."

"Great! Unless . . . he doesn't know about us." He laughs softly.

She takes the head of lettuce Chloe laid out and begins to tear the leaves into the salad spinner in the bar sink.

"So what happened? Where'd you go? I always wondered."

She turns the water on high. Fill in the blanks and maybe he'll leave. "I got a ride." She speaks so quietly he has to lean forward.

"What about me? Did you ever think, 'Oh, poor Eddie. I should've stayed and helped him out a little'?" He wrings his hands, that same way, slender fingers writhing through one another.

"I was upset." She stares at him.

"Yeah!" Like himself, he means.

"I was very young."

"That's your excuse?" he asks in disbelief.

"Excuse?" Floating romaine leaves brim over the spinner into the sink.

"For letting me take the fall. Twenty years I been in."

Her knees sag. "I don't know what you mean."

"Never gave you up, though. Gentleman to the end, I'm proud of that. 'So who is she? What's her name?' they kept asking. 'I don't know,' I said. 'I don't know.'" He shrugs. "Just kept playing dumb. 'Some chick,' I said. 'Some chick by the side of the road, thumbing a ride, next thing I know some guy's passed out in his car.' 'No,' they go. 'Try dead.'"

Water, the only sound, it keeps running.

"He didn't die." She can barely breathe.

"Really?" Again, his amusement. "That what you wanna hear?" He jams the faucet down, shutting off the water. The sudden silence stunning, like the jolt of an electrical shock. "That what you been telling yourself all these years?" He slips a business card from his breast pocket, scribbles on the back. "My cell." He slides off the stool.

She doesn't pick it up until he is gone.

HARMONY LTD.
P.O. BOX 0367
NEW YORK CITY
NEW YORK

▪   ▪   ▪

A week has passed. Eddie hasn't been back, so he's probably gone for good. He couldn't rattle her the way he wanted. Random, that's all, a blip on the screen. She doesn't believe the man died or that Eddie went to jail. There's no denying the violence of that night, the pipe, blood pouring from the man's face. Ugly, but not murder. Couldn't have been. No. Impossible. He would have told the police she'd been there, too. He never would have protected her all these years, serving a prison sentence in noble silence. Not the type. No. Just a down-on-his-luck loser working a newfound connection.

The shock of seeing him, though, has been an antidote. Injecting one poison into her system to fight another, rousing her from malaise. As in a fever, at its hallucinatory pitch the phantom has slipped from one nightmare into another. The past is dead. Only family matters, her marriage. Now, with perspective, she will be well again. She calls up the back stairs to Chloe. What's taking so long? School starts in twenty minutes. Nora sits at the table with her toast. Stirring his coffee, Ken says he heard the shower go off an hour ago.

"Probably still trying to get the stripes out," he says, and she can almost smile. Chloe sprayed green stripes into her hair for last Friday's varsity basketball game.

"I know. Poor kid," Nora says. Days later, and the stripes still show, even after countless shampooings.

"I'll ask Oliver, maybe Nana's wig's still up in the attic." His grandmother Geraldine Hammond's singed blonde wig is part of family lore. A candle set it on fire one night at a dinner party. After snipping away the burned strands she continued wearing it. Hammondian frugality, Oliver calls it in justification of his own dated wardrobe.

"Don't. Don't even mention a wig. That'll be the next thing, driving around to wig shops." Laughing with him again feels good. A relief. The way things used to be here.

"Outfit us all. The whole family, bewigged, bothered, and bewildered," Ken croons, making her laugh even more. His hand slides over hers. "You look good," he says, and she tries to hold her eyes level with his, but can't. "Are you okay?"

"All right. I guess." Again, ice in her voice; can't help it. Stay on safe ground. So much easier talking about the children.

"Here, Mom." Chloe runs into the kitchen, listing under the weight of her bulging backpack slung over one shoulder. "Can you sign this? I am so wicked late." She holds out a pen and folded paper. "My ride's waiting. That line," she adds in a faltering voice as Nora reads. "The bottom one."

"It's your progress report."

"I know and it sucks and I'm sorry, and I'm really gonna try, but right now you have to sign it so I can bring it back. Please? Please, Mom? Please?" she begs, rocking back and forth on wedged heels.

"One D and three C minuses." Nora pushes it across the table to Ken.

"What's this all about?" he says. "What're you thinking? What do you want, to end up in some two-bit junior college somewhere?"

"If she's lucky," Nora says.

"I know," Chloe groans, pleading for release.

Nora asks how long she's had the progress report. A week, Chloe admits, but she forgot about it. She did. And that's the truth. Nora refuses to sign it until Chloe discusses the poor grades with them and explains how she plans to raise them.

"I can't now, Mom! So just sign it, please! I'm gonna be late and I've already got three tardies."

"Apparently you're going to have to get another one," Nora says, scraping butter onto her cold toast.

"But then I'll get detention!" Chloe cries.

"That's not my problem now, is it?"

"Dad! Please! Will you sign it? Please? It's just the progress report, and I'm trying so much harder now. I swear. I am! I've got the whole rest of the term."

Ken looks at Nora. "What's the harm? Gotta sign it, sooner or later." He clicks open his pen with a stern look at Chloe. "But just so you'll know, your mother's right. This has got to be discussed. Whatever's going on here has got to change."

"I know. I know. Please, Dad." Chloe glances at her watch. "Now Max is gonna be late too."

Scribbling his name, Ken winces. "Max?" he and Nora say in unison. "What the hell?" Ken says.

"He's just giving me a ride, that's all." Chloe snatches up the paper. "Jeez!" she cries with the closing door.

"Was that a slam?" Nora asks, seething.

"One one thousandth of a decibel shy." Ken finishes his coffee. "But I'll tell you something, in my house that progress report would've called for a celebration."

"Ken!"

"I know. Just trying to keep things in perspective, that's all." He stands up to leave. "Goddamn Max Lafferty, that's what really pisses me off."

Nora isn't the first woman to wake up one morning to find her life tipped upside down, which seems to be Kay's theme with this second tale of adultery. Now it's Kay's older sister in Dallas. Married thirty-five years. One day she's hanging up her husband's pants and she finds it. In his pocket. Nora squirms with annoyance. Kay means well, but trivializing what Nora's going through makes her feel worse. *Adultery, no big deal, it happens:* the message here.

Kay continues cutting her asparagus. She and Nora are having lunch at Leanna's, which is halfway between the real estate office and the *Chronicle*. "So Ruthie looks at it, you know, trying to figure, toss it, or is it something Don needs? But damn, if it isn't some kind of condo receipt. Long story short: dear old Donnie's got himself a girlfriend half his age, and he's keeping her in fine style. Big, beautiful condo, parking fees you wouldn't believe, while my sister, well, you know Ruthie, she's so damn frugal she'll only buy a car every ten years. And then they have to be used."

"Poor Ruth." Nora last saw her a few years ago. Pretty, lively like Kay. Beyond Don's brogue she barely recalls the man. "What'd she do?"

"Had herself a messy little nervous breakdown. Two weeks on sui-cide watch in a mental hospital, and now with the Lexapro and coun-seling, she's better. Well, the knives are back in the block, anyway," Kay says bitterly. "My nieces are having a tough time. Thirty and thirty-two, but they still won't speak to their father. In some ways, I think it's worse for the kids when they're older."

Nora agrees, says she's heard that. Now Kay expects to hear how Chloe and Drew are bearing up. But that's where she draws the line. Her children won't be fodder for gossip. No matter how loyal a friend Kay is, it's human nature to tell more than one intends, to be a story's pivot person, the only one who can fill in all the blanks.

"Oh. Before I forget, the Sanders Gallery is showing Annette Rose-man next week," she says to change the subject.

Kay holds up her hands. "Yes! I've been meaning to tell you! I saw her last week. At the symphony, with a very nice-looking man who, by the way, was not Oliver Hammond."

Nora shrugs. "That's the arrangement. She has her life. He has his, and it works."

Kay is staring at her. "Tell me something. You and Ken, you never suspected anything? Not even once?"

"Honestly? No. He enjoyed women, their company. He always did. I knew that." She shrugs. "Just the way he was. Why? Why're you looking at me like that?" Kay obviously wants the salacious details.

"I'm worried about you. You can't just let it out. Even a little, can you?" Kay says.

"And do what? Have my own messy little breakdown?"

"I don't know, maybe. If you need to."

"Well, guess what, Kay. I am. Only it's all in here," she says, tapping her chest as Kay looks up.

"Hey, Nora, how're you doing?" the slender man says, then turns quickly to Kay. "Sorry. I'm Ed. Ed Hawkins. Nice to meet you," he says, shaking Kay's hand. "Thought I'd grab a quick lunch, but all the tables are full."

Nora glances out the window. There's still a waiting line. Please, sit with them then, Kay insists; they're almost done, but he might as well.

Thanking her, Eddie pulls out the chair between them. The women at the next table smile watching him, and he grins at their attention. He's wearing an elegant dark suit and white shirt with trefoil onyx cuff links, his silk tie pale as his eyes. This is his second try here for lunch, he says. He came with a client Monday but same thing, an hour wait, and who has that kind of time to waste in the middle of the workday? Kay agrees. They don't take reservations so the trick is to come early, eleven fifteen, like they did, she tells him. Next time, he'll know, he says with a glance at Nora. Thoughts racing, she still hasn't spoken. What does he want? Coincidence, or did he follow her here?

The sole meunière is very good, Kay is saying, or if he wants something quick, any one of the salad grills.

"Quick is good." He leans close to Kay, touches her arm. "Then I could still eat with you ladies and not get the heave-ho."

Kay gestures for the waitress, who takes his order. Caesar salad with grilled chicken and a glass of soda water, one slice lemon, one lime. He asks if they'd like another glass of wine.

"No, thank you." Her first words.

"I think I will." Kay laughs. "It's been a long week." Kay isn't missing a thing here, Nora knows, her own coldness, Eddie's push to keep the conversation going. He asks Kay what line of work she's in.

"Real estate. Mostly residential." She finishes her wine.

"You're kidding! I wish I'd known. All week I've been out looking at properties. We need a couple acres, six or seven at least. Part of a consortium. Mixed-use housing, that's our specialty. The whole spectrum, luxury, middle class, right down to low rent. Subsidized. With the right connections. Faith-based, if we can." He smiles at Nora.

"Sounds like quite an undertaking," Kay says.

"It is. That's why when I saw *Newsweek,* the article that mentioned Sojourn House, I figured what the hell, what've I got to lose, I'll look up my old friend Nora while I'm here and maybe she can steer me in the right direction."

"Well, if she can't," Kay says, watching Nora, "I don't know who can."

"It's not looking good, Kay." He sips his soda water. "I seem to be striking out here. Big-time." His eyes settle on Nora with cold mocking light. Bitter, somehow, as if there has been an actual business proposal that she has spurned.

"Excuse me," Kay says, putting her napkin on the table. "I'll be right back." She heads toward the stairs, down to the restrooms.

"So, how're you doing?" he asks, grinning at Nora.

The waitress delivers his salad. The minute she leaves, Nora leans over the table. "What is it? Why're you here? What do you want?"

"Help." He smiles. "A helping hand, that's all. To make up for lost time. Chances I never had. Opportunity."

"So this is about money, then, isn't it?" She is almost relieved.

"It's been a long time. How do you put a price on that? On time? I don't know," he sighs. "You tell me."

"So how much? How much do you want?"

His laughter is sad, regretful. "You don't get it, do you? But then, why should you? Nice family. Nice town. Nice life. Hey! Maybe if I hadn't been so worried, driving back and forth tryna find you, maybe I'd'a gotten away, too."

Kay is chatting her way back through the crowded dining room. Eddie stands and pulls out her chair.

"Thank you." Kay smiles up at him, then at Nora, her quizzical gaze seeking direction. "A gentleman, how very refreshing."

Nora has just closed her office door when the phone rings.

"What was that all about?" Kay asks on the other end. "I feel like I just got sucked into a tornado or something."

"I'm not really sure," Nora says, trying to steady herself on the half-truth. "I haven't seen him in years, and now he shows up, acting like . . . well, you heard him, like I'm some vital part of his networking plan."

"I know. Vague, wasn't it?"

"I'll say."

"How'd you know him?"

"I'm not even sure."

"Well. Be careful. There's so many scams around," Kay says.

"I know. And strange people."

"I'd put him more in the hungry category, you know what I mean?"

"I don't know, maybe. Anyway, I better get started here."

"He is nice-looking, though, you have to admit that," Kay allows in a low purr. "Those eyes, they go right through you. I wouldn't mind showing him a parcel or two."

For Nora the rest of the afternoon drags. Hard to concentrate. Her thoughts wheel between Eddie Hawkins's intensity and Kay's nonchalance. She feels stranded again.

Annette's thick dabs of oil give her subjects not just texture but a depth that is sensual yet still precise with certain details. The paintings are beautiful. Maybe her best work, Nora thinks as Stephen and Donald come through the door on the other side of the gallery. She notices that Stephen and Ken merely nod at each other. Stephen wanders off, leaving Donald to talk to Ken, who keeps glancing past him.

"Look at that. The roses," Christine McGuire says to Bibbi Bond and Nora. They are admiring a portrait of two barefoot girls in gauzy blue dresses, sitting on a stone bench. Behind the girls is a latticed arbor and, interestingly, Nora thinks, not the usual profusion of roses but a single arched vine. "The thorns, they look so sharp. You can even see dew on the petals, little beads."

"She's got such an eye," Bibbi says, tilting her head this way and that. For years Bibbi has been a docent at the MFA.

"And still, other details, they're kind of hazy. Like, unfocused," Christine says.

"Impressionistic realism," Bibbi declares with covetous authority. "It's her way of controlling the viewer's perspective. Taking you from the glint on the roses to the light in the girls' eyes."

Nora slips away from the women. She has lost sight of Ken. Strange for so small a place. Probably in the men's room or outside having a cigarette. In the past he was a social smoker, one or two with a drink, but he never wanted the children to know. Lately, though, he has started smoking at home, not in the house, but outside in the driveway or on one of his nighttime walks, which he says help him sleep better. In the morning, she sees him through the window, cigarette already lit as he backs out of the garage.

In the far corner, his back against the wall, Oliver is talking to three men. He is often waylaid like this when he goes anywhere, because he is so rarely seen in public. Rumpled and wild-haired as ever, but at least he's making the effort. Only Annette's show has been able to lure him from his hermetic existence. And then, right before Nora and Ken left to pick him up, Oliver called to say they should go on without him. His back was acting up and he didn't see how he could be on his feet all night. He asked Nora if she'd be sure and tell Annette what happened.

No, she told him. Absolutely not. Not only was it his responsibility, but it was unfair of him to ask her.

"It's getting worse," Ken said when she got off the phone.

"What?"

"The agoraphobia," Ken said, and she was stunned. She'd never thought of it as a psychological condition, just another of her brother-in-law's quirks.

"Who told you that? Oliver?"

"Nobody," Ken said quickly. "Pretty obvious, though, don't you think?"

Once again, she realizes how little credit she gives Ken, especially lately. His sensitivity was what had first attracted her to him. For all his party boy bonhomie, he cares how people feel. Cares deeply. Sometimes too deeply, she thinks with the dull ache swelling in her chest. Cared how Robin felt, but not about her, his own wife. His own children. No! No, she can't keep doing this. Get tough, take charge, be strong, she is constantly reminding herself lately.

They were going out the door when Oliver called back. Could they pick him up? He'd just taken three ibuprofen.

"Yeah, and two quick Johnnies and a cologne shower," Ken muttered when his brother Oliver climbed into the back of the car, the reek of florid booze forcing them to open the windows. The entire ride, he and Ken never spoke to each other.

The crowded gallery is growing noisy. Nora has to step closer to hear what Annette is saying. "Thank you for getting Ollie here. Did you have to hog-tie him?" Annette smiles over her glass of wine, the same deep ruby as her lipstick and long dress. She continues to grow even more beautiful in her maturity. Handsome, with the fine laugh lines around her eyes and mouth, the dramatic streaks of white through her black hair, and her keen-eyed scrutiny.

Oliver seems to be holding up well, they agree. He's still here, at least. Nora tells Annette how stunning her paintings are. They remind her of the portraits Annette did a few years ago of Chloe and Drew.

"You captured something. In each one of them. Their . . . trueness. Such an amazing skill. It must be so hard. Or do you look at someone and just know?"

"Sometimes," Annette says, throwing her head back with the sure, haughty confidence Nora finds fascinating, yet so bewildering when it comes to her relationship with Oliver. "It's quicker with children, they're so much more open."

"What about Oliver? Has he ever sat for you?" she asks too quickly, embarrassed by the feint of the old reporter in her.

"God, no. Oliver? Someone else's vision of him? That'd be like losing the last vestige of control."

"I never thought of it that way. But . . . well, maybe you'd know," she blurts. "Is everything okay with Oliver? Lately, he just doesn't . . . I don't know, I mean, he and Ken . . ." The words trail off.

Annette stares at her. "I probably shouldn't say this, Nora. It's not my place. But I know them too well, the brothers. And no matter what happens, neither one really wants to be free. Of the other, I mean."

"Well, that's not such a bad thing, I guess."

"No. Not unless you're caught in the middle," Annette says, then smiles past her with the gallery owner's bustling approach. "Speaking of portraits, Nora, I'd love to do yours. Would you ever let me?"

"Oh. I don't know. I guess so." She is bewildered, but with the owner hovering can't very well ask Annette what she meant by being caught in the middle. "I'd trust your vision. Sure!"

"People always think you're so reserved, don't they? Maybe even unapproachable. But I see vulnerability and depth," Annette says, her eyes taking Nora's. "And you won't be used. By anyone, will you?"

"So I'd be a challenge, then." Lighthearted as she tries to sound, a tremulous neediness hangs in the air. Its voice, hers, pleading, *Help me! Please!*

Annette smiles. "I would hope so," she says, and Nora's face smarts. Acutely conscious of all the voices and laughter in the room, she feels stranded again, and foolish. Roland apologizes for interrupting, but the writer for *American Arts* is here and wants to meet her. He leads Annette through the buzz of admiring patrons.

Nora wanders into the next gallery. In here are Annette's smaller paintings. Floral compositions, small landscapes Nora pretends to study while she wonders who Annette thinks is caught. Herself? Nora? Or Stephen? Yes, it must be, their cousin with his token share in the paper, 10 percent to Oliver's and Ken's shares, forty-five each. She moves on to the serving table. She dips a broccoli floret in the gummy white dressing, then a celery stalk, carrot sticks. She's hungry. Chloe and Drew are at friends' houses. She'll find Ken and suggest they stop at Braddock's Grille after the show. They both like it there and it'll be dark and just noisy enough to fill in those painful silences, when each knows exactly what the other is thinking. Even if it's only small talk, at least it'll be a start. Better than this constant strain. This man she thought she knew. Like living with a stranger, but worse than that. The insurmountable problem here is that each knows the other too well and, in the knowing, has fouled all common ground.

Of the three this next gallery is the smallest. A few people mill by the door, none of them Ken. She returns to the main gallery but can't see him.

"Excuse me," she says quietly to the elderly man leaving the bathroom. "I'm looking for my husband. Would he be in there?"

"Hardly, my dear," the man says, with a twinkle of amusement. "It's a one-horse stall."

"Nora!" Claudia Trekkle says, brushing cheeks. "I was just at So-journ House, the other day. It was my first time, and oh my God, I couldn't get over it! All those poor women and their sad little children, I don't know, it just got to me. What is going on in this world? I blame the Internet, and all this freedom of speech, and everyone doing their own—"

"Excuse me, Claudia. I'll be right back." She hurries toward the entrance. With the opening door, she spots Ken outside, on the sidewalk. His back to her, he's talking on his cell phone. "I know. I know," she hears him say. "I know how it feels. Believe me, I know."

Afterward, she won't remember which came first, the slap or throwing his cell phone into the road. He runs to get it. "Go to hell!" she says as he grabs her arm, trying to steer her down the street to their car. "Just go to hell, the two of you! I don't care anymore."

"Get in the car!" he demands. "Get in the car and listen to me."

"No!" She struggles to pull free.

"Is this what you want, a scene? A public scene?"

"Yes!" She laughs. "Yes, I do! And that way everyone will know what a—"

His hand clamps over her mouth. Two couples come out of the gallery. They turn in the opposite direction. Nora slumps against him. She feels numb. Numb and cold. Her teeth chatter as she gets into the car. Deadness. All of it.

Listen, he says as he drives. Will she at least listen? It was Bob on the phone. Bob Gendron. "Something happened, but I couldn't understand him. I don't know if he's drunk or—"

"Stop lying to me!" She hits his arm. "It wasn't Bob, it was her. It was, wasn't it?"

He can't even look at her.

"Did you call her?"

He sighs. "I had to. She left this hysterical message." He speaks over Nora's bitter laughter. "There was a fight. Between Drew and Clay, and it sounds like our guy got the worst of it."

Ken had turned off his cell phone in the gallery. When he checked his messages he saw Robin's three calls. He called her back and she said she was at the emergency room. Clay and Drew had been at the same party, and there'd been a fight. The gallery was only a few blocks from Franklin Memorial. How badly hurt is he, she asks. Ken's not sure, but from the way he's driving she's imagining the worst. He speeds into the doctor's parking lot and pulls into a reserved space. The attendant shoots out of his booth and tells them they have to park behind the hospital in the visitors' lot.

"I'm calling security!" he warns in a high-pitched, accented voice as he stalks Ken and Nora through the emergency room doors into the crowded waiting room.

Robin hurries toward them. Behind them, the attendant squeals into his walkie-talkie, calling for backup, a security guard.

"How is he?" Ken asks.

"Good. He's good. The doctor's with him," Robin says.

"I better go move the car. I'll be right back," Ken says, and, as he hurries outside, Nora knows he can't face this meeting between them.

"We're in the wrong place," she says, weak with the irony of her words.

The waiting room is filled with haggard-looking people, none more so than Nora. She feels drained, pinched with distress, while Robin's every word and gesture is a flourish of feelings, warmth, sympathy. Even in gray sweats, no makeup, and her hair tied back in a frazzled pony tail, her girlish prettiness glows. Lyra kneels on the floor, in Cinderella pajamas and pink bunny slippers, coloring on paper a nurse has given her. Unaffected by their last meeting, she smiles up at Nora, a familiar face in this sea of stress and pain. A toddler wails as his mother struggles to hold an ice pack on his forehead. An old man with his hand wrapped in a bloody towel stares dazedly at the floor. His fly is open. At the nurses' station a tearful young girl is trying to translate for the two frantic Spanish-speaking women with her. One is searching through her purse for pill bottles while the other holds her belly, moaning.

"Drew's okay, but he's got a mild concussion. A black eye and contusions on his face. A cut. Here," Robin says, touching her cheekbone. "The right side. And a broken tooth. Well, chipped anyway. This one."

She points to her eyetooth. "He's already been X-rayed. They're just stitching him up. I wanted to stay, but he didn't want me to. Just as well, because then I could be here to tell you."

Nora starts down the hall. Robin scoops up Lyra and hurries along-side Nora through two sets of double doors, down the harshly lit corridor into a treatment ward.

"Shh, Lyrrie, shh," Robin whispers as Lyra complains about leaving crayons behind. She begins to cry. Her crumpled drawing hangs from her fist over Robin's shoulder. Way past her bedtime, poor little thing, Nora thinks, imagining the child being snatched up from a sound sleep: any opportunity to see Ken. "In there." Robin points to one of the drawn blue curtains.

"Drew!" Nora gasps, seeing his battered face. He raises his hand and she holds it with both her own. On the other side of the bed, the doctor is still working on him. Almost done, she says.

"Won't hardly show," she murmurs, snipping the black thread.

Nora's knees sag. She closes her eyes and takes a deep breath.

"I'm okay," Drew says in a gurgly-sounding voice.

"He's going to be fine," the doctor says. She is peeling off her surgical gloves when Ken hurries into the room. As she writes out postcare instructions, she begins to explain them to Robin, who still has Lyra on her hip.

"That's his mother," Robin says.

Nora nods, trying to listen, then hands the forms off to Ken. He is asking the doctor about the concussion.

Nora leans close to Drew who is shivering now. All she wants is to hold him and make everything better. "What happened?"

He shakes his head, and she asks again. "Later," he says, teeth chattering.

"Tell me now," she says, pulling the sheet to his chin.

"Please, Mom?"

"Drew."

"I know," the doctor says, turning back to Nora. "Quite a lot, don't you think, for just tripping in the driveway. Plus the bruised back and the fractured rib." She looks over her square glasses at them. "And the knuckles scraped raw." The surgical tools in the steel tray she's holding rattle as she opens the curtain. "If it were my son, I'd file a police report. Somebody did that. Somebody who wanted to hurt him, and hurt him bad." She closes the curtain behind her.

Robin buries her face in Lyra's hair.

"Who are you crying for?" Nora asks quietly.

"Don't. Please, don't," Ken begs her.

"Tell me you're crying for him, for my son."

"Mom," Drew gasps.

"No, because you're not," Nora says. This surge of bitter power is like inhaling pure oxygen. "It's all about you, Robin. As always."

"Don't make Mommy cry again. Please, Auntie Nor. She loves you," Lyra says, clutching her mother's neck with both arms.

Ken covers his mouth and looks away.

"Why don't you wait outside?" Nora says. "I'll help Drew with his things." She can't bear to be near them, and she is ashamed. Ashamed of her rage and her fear, ashamed that it has come to this, their children's pain. They had been good and decent people, two good and decent families, and now look at them. Especially herself, wanting, more than anything else, to hurt them the way they've hurt her. She helps Drew put on his shirt. Neither one speaks. His sneakers smell rancid as she puts them on his feet. He needs new ones, she thinks, tying them. The only way he can get off the bed is to hold on to her. He gives a painful yelp as he tries to straighten up. Even in the wheelchair he hunches over.

"Maybe we should call the police," she says, looking at his battered face.

"No! I hit him first."

"Why?" Then shakes her head. She knows why.

"We were outside Bradley's house and Clay came up to me and he goes, 'What, do you send your mommy out to fight your battles, Drewie?' And he was drunk, really, really drunk, but I hit him."

She feels sick to her stomach. It's over. The all-consuming anger and suspicion, the blame and the bitterness, it's all too destructive. Which does she want more, punishment and revenge, or peace for her children?

Driving home, they listen in silence as Drew tells them the rest. Friends of both boys tried to separate them, but not before Clay pounded Drew's head into the cement block patio.

"I shouldn't've hit him. I should've just walked away," Drew says, and they both nod. Their unspoken agreement, always: as long as he is honest, it won't be brought up again. At least not to him. Listening now makes Nora realize how open he used to be with them. And how shut down he's become. The Gendrons arrived in two different cars, Drew says. Mr. Gendron brought Clay home but not before Clay yelled at his father and kept trying to hit him. "In front of everyone," Drew says, then looks out the window at passing homes, most in darkness now. Families asleep. Safe.

Ken helps Drew up to his room. The only way he can climb the stairs is to place both feet on each step. Nora checks the phone messages. Five, she sees by the red light blinking on the answering machine. The first call is from Jean Greer, Bradley's mother, saying Drew is hurt, but he doesn't want her to call an ambulance or bring him to the hospital, and she doesn't know what to do. She says one of the boys has already called the Gendrons on his cell phone. She'll try and call Robin. Even in this, Nora's thoughts are a swirl of suspicions and fears clouding the moment. Had Jean mentioned the Gendrons because of the affair linking the two families or because of Clay? The next two calls are from Robin: Drew is hurt and she is on her way to the Greers'. Nora erases them both. She hits the button for the next call, annoyed to hear Chloe's little-girl voice, whispery and cute: Suzanna had asked her and some other girls to sleep over, so she was going to, if it was okay with them. Suzanna who? Nora wonders. Chloe left here, saying she was going to the movies with her friends Leah and Jen. Typical Chloe, no last name, no number. She dials Chloe's cell phone. "Damn," she mutters, hearing it ring upstairs. And now it's too late to call Leah or Jen, and there's no number showing on the caller ID.

One more message. It's him. She keeps hitting the volume button to turn it down.

"Nora. It's me, Eddie. Sorry I haven't gotten back to you about our fair-housing conversation. Hate to leave you hanging like that, wondering where the hell's Eddie. Well, fret no more. Eddie's here, and he's near." Her fists clench with his burst of laughter. "Seriously, though, we need to talk. I'll give you a buzz first thing Monday."

"Ken?" She needs him, not to tell him about Eddie but to be nearby. He isn't in the house. She looks out the kitchen window, expecting to see him in the driveway, having a cigarette. A light snow has begun to fall. His car is running. He sits behind the wheel, smoking and talking on the phone.

Robin. Of course, she realizes with a bolt of foolish amazement. Every night he goes out there, and she's the last person he talks to. The last voice in his day, hers. Emotionally, they're still connected. The truth feels strangely calming. She finally understands. Her marriage is over.

She has just crawled under the covers when he comes in and sits on the edge of the bed. And to everything else that means betrayal, add now, the stench of cigarettes.

"I didn't know about you . . . going there. To their house," he says with his back to her.

With her arms over her head, she lies perfectly still. He clears his throat, coughs. The bed creaks as he turns.

"What do you want me to say?" she asks.

"We have to do something."

"I know." Tears leak from the corners of her eyes into her hair.

"It can't keep on like this."

Eyes shut, she holds out her arms. "Hold me, just hold me, please?"

He does. He lies down and holds her until they are both asleep and she is young again, and that song keeps playing, throbbing in her chest, and the harder she tries to wake up the deeper she sinks into the dream.

■ ■ ■

Nine in the morning. The doorbell rings. Clay Gendron and his father. Clay wants to apologize, not just to Drew but to the entire family, his father says. Bleary-eyed and shaky, Bob Gendron is in almost as bad shape as his son. The smell of booze breath fouls the front hall. Clay keeps swallowing hard and touching his throat, as if he's afraid of vomiting. Taking deep breaths, he rocks back and forth on his heels.

Because Ken doesn't seem the least bit surprised to see them here, Nora realizes Robin told him on the phone last night that Clay would be over. Friends since third grade, Bob stands a head over Ken. An exceptional high school athlete, he was a starting linebacker in college. Varsity all four years. He stayed in great shape for a long time after that, with tennis and racquetball, until drinking consumed everything, his health, jobs, friendships, family.

"At least he's not a violent drunk," Ken used to say, as if that somehow made it better.

"No, just vicious," Nora finally said after one miserable night out with Robin and Bob, who was finishing his third martini when their entrées arrived. Even though Robin quietly asked him not to, he ordered another one. Excusing herself to go to the ladies' room, she circled around into the bar and canceled the drink.

"Bitch!" Bob said when she returned.

"Stop it," she whispered, head down, mortified, eyes bright with tears.

Bob kept it up. Who the hell did she think she was, fucking-miss-high-and-mighty counting his drinks when every night she couldn't get to the wine bottle fast enough.

Cut it out, Ken said quietly. Robin cared about him, that's why she canceled it. The only reason. Usually, that would be enough for Bob to sink into one of his wounded, sullen silences. But not that night.

"Who the fuck asked you?" he bellowed thickly, and everyone around them looked up. "Fucking piece of shit, think you're better than me, well think again, Kenny-boy. You got nothing and you know it, don't you? Because it's all Ollie, right? All Ollie, all the time. Well, you better hold on tight to big brother's fucking coattails—"

"Shut up, Bob," Nora snapped, trying to keep her voice down. "Just shut up. You're pathetic. How can you say that to your best friend? And your wife? Can't you see what you're doing? To everyone!"

It would be their last night out together. From then on, Nora refused to go anywhere with them as long as Bob was still drinking.

After that she began to sense what an intruder she'd been in their friendship, the old intimacies always having to be explained to her. With her outburst, the chemistry had changed, the rupture drawing them even closer, the three of them, further from her, the threat.

"I'm sorry. I'm so sorry," Robin apologized her way out of the busy dining room that night.

And here now, the son, sent by his mother to do the same.

"Sorry." Clay stares down at the floor. "I'm sorry. I really am."

"It could've been a lot worse, Clay," Ken says. "You could've done some serious damage, banging his head like that."

"I know." Clay's voice breaks. He wipes his nose with the back of his hand. Like a little boy, Nora can't help thinking, even though she's irritated with Ken for trying to downplay Drew's injuries. More than anything, though, she is disgusted with Bob Gendron, the sight of him repulsive, dark pouches under his eyes, the bloom of purplish veins in his unshaven cheeks, and the bloat of sagging belly. Look, she wants to say, look what you've done, your son, the spawn of your weakness.

Above them the stairs and railing creak as Drew hobbles down. He didn't want Clay sent up to his room. In the daylight he looks much worse than he did last night. The right side of his face is swollen, black with bruises and dried blood. His lips are split and puffed up.

"Oh," Clay groans, seeing him.

"What." Drew braces himself against the balustrade.

"Jesus." Clay holds his mouth. "I'm . . . I'm gonna be sick!"

Opening the bathroom door, Nora flicks on the exhaust fan as he drops to his knees, gripping the pale green toilet bowl. She notes with pity and disgust his soiled bare feet in rubber sandals, his ripped

T-shirt. Probably the same clothes he wore pummeling Drew, then slept in.

"Been a rough night, I'm afraid," Bob says, almost resignedly, over his son's retching.

"For everyone," Nora says, and he nods meekly.

"Yeah. How ya doin'?" he asks Drew.

"Okay." Drew winces with his quick and painful shrug.

"You don't look okay," Bob says, peering at his face. "One hurtin' dude, aren't you?"

"Probably looks worse than it is," Drew says, trying to stand straighter, and it's all Nora can do to keep from hugging him. He sounds as if he's talking through a mouthful of hot mush.

The toilet flushes a few more times before Clay finally emerges, wiping his mouth with a handful of tissues. He has more color in his cheeks now. His unscathed cheeks. Taller than Drew, he is broad-chested, thick-necked like his father.

"I'm sorry." He holds out his hand, and Drew looks at it. "You don't have to," Clay says, dropping the hand to his side. "I don't blame you. I feel like such a jerk. I coulda really hurt you and I—"

"You did really hurt him," Nora interrupts quietly. Both fathers stare with her unsporting comment, but she doesn't care. This was an ugly act of violence and she won't have it glossed over to salve the boy's guilt. They are the adults here, the parents. If they don't speak the truth, who will? "He has a concussion, a fractured rib, a broken tooth—"

"I know!" Clay breaks in, sobbing now. "I know what I did, and I feel real bad about it. I do, Drew. I mean that."

Ken steps forward and for a sickening moment she is sure from his stricken gaze that he is going to embrace Clay. Instead, he puts his arm around his own son. "Why don't you shake his hand?" he asks gently.

Drew just stands there, looking so slight and miserable next to the men and the bigger boy that she feels like screaming at Ken, Leave him alone, why're you doing this?

"Please," Clay says through tears, again offering his hand.

"Go ahead," Ken urges.

Instead, Drew turns and makes his painful climb back up the stairs.

"Aw, he'll get over it," Ken says with a pat on Clay's shoulder.

"Get over what?" Nora asks.

"Kids," he says with a look of panic: *surely she won't make another scene.* "You know what I mean."

"No. I don't."

"Better get home now," Bob says, opening the door.

"I'm sorry," Clay mumbles.

"It's okay," Ken says, following them out to their car.

She's still standing there when he comes back in.

"Don't look at me like that," he snaps.

"Do you know what the fight was about?"

"You really want to tell me, don't you?" he whispers, his face close at hers.

"Your son's up there beaten to a pulp, and you act like it's nothing. No big deal."

"No. It's a mess. Everything. All of it," he growls, flinging his arm out. "You think I don't know that? You think I want this? Any of it? Do you? Do you?" he demands with a frightening bitterness.

Coldness. Resentment. It's the first time she's ever felt that from him. In all their years together. She has to be careful. Can't push too hard. Can't keep pressuring, piling on the guilt, or there'll be nothing left.

CHAPTER·10

Sunlight streams through her office window. It is beautiful outside, cold but clear, the cloudless sky a blinding blue. She keeps yawning. Last night she and Ken stayed up long after the children had gone to bed, but now that she thinks of it, she did most of the talking. Whenever she brought up Robin's treachery, he defended her, at one point even calling her "a victim of circumstance." Nothing is Robin's fault. Or his. He's the one who betrayed his wife and his best friend but can't or won't say why. Finally, she asked what *she* might have done differently—something, anything that might have prevented the affair. Nothing, he said, sounding surprised. She didn't ask the obvious next question: what might *he* have done differently, because hearing his chipper "nothing" a second time would have been too painful. So she held back, allowing him the lead, in the end both agreeing that they loved their children and for their sake would make every effort to treat one another with respect. As much as she knew she should, she couldn't say the words, she admitted, couldn't say she loved him. Not right now, she said, trying not to cry. At least not in the same way. Sighing, Ken squeezed her hand until it hurt, and in his long pause, she waited, needing him to say it, that he loved her, always had, always would. Instead, he said he understood.

She will go to counseling with him. If the marriage is worth saving, it's the least they can do, she thinks he said. Or did she say it, in desperation, anything, to make herself feel better? Worth saving, she keeps thinking. What, like a TV or car, fix it or get a new one? Tinker with it, see how long they can keep it running? And why *the* marriage? Isn't it *their* marriage? Maddening, all this dissection and second-guessing. But she's trying hard not to keep bringing things up. They have to move on. She's more than entitled to her anger and pain, Ken admitted. But as long as they were being honest about their feelings, then she has to know that the recrimination only wears him down, day after day, grinding away at him. Guilt isn't his strong suit: he actually said that last night. What is your strong suit then, she yearned to ask, was still wondering, hours later, as he snored next to her, telling herself she should be grateful. Yes. Be grateful for that snoring, for the mess, for the pain; she'd read that once, Dear Abby, Dear someone, be grateful he is still here. Grateful she has a husband. A man. Anyone. Grateful she isn't alone.

She is proofing ad layouts when the phone rings, startling her. Hilda's not supposed to put any calls through until she's done.

"What?" she answers distractedly, still reading.

"You don't have an appointment, do you?" Hilda asks in a hushed tone.

"No."

"That's what I thought. Someone's here, though. A Mr. Hawkins? He says he's got an appointment—" His voice in the background. "Nine thirty, he says."

"No, he—" she starts to say, then tells Hilda to send him in. *The nerve, thinking he can just barge in here like this.* Hands folded to keep them from shaking, she stares at the opening door.

"Sorry I'm late," he says, unbuttoning his suit coat and settling into the chair across from her desk like a celebrity about to be interviewed. Almost condescending, as he straightens his tie, smiles.

"Late for what?"

"I hate to keep anyone waiting."

"I wasn't."

"Yes you were."

"We don't have an appointment."

"I know."

"I don't even want you here."

"I know," he says with a note of surprise. "But some things are un-avoidable, aren't they?"

"What do you mean?" She struggles not to lose her temper. He en-joys this, catching her off guard, toying with her.

"Well." He thinks a moment. "Death. Isn't that the most ob-vious one?"

"And taxes." Said with a nod and sweat on her chest as she stares at him.

He draws back, blinking a few times, and she remembers both his dismissive contempt and her eagerness, once, for his approval. "So trite of you, Nora. I'm surprised."

"Why? What did you expect?"

"Oh. I don't know. That teenage girl? The one I used to know. Whatever happened to her?"

"A few weeks. That's all that was."

"Longer than that. I've spent twenty-six years with her. That's a long time. Long and lonesome." He rubs his eyes, then peers out with a sudden thought. "He died. I told you that, right? Took him a while, but like I said, unavoidable." He grins. "You were trying to protect me. But nobody'd believe me. And you weren't there! You could've told them. The guy was a pervert. A drunken pervert, trying to molest a young girl. I did pretty well, though. Held my own, but then, Jesus, Mary, and Joseph, what do they do but push the widow in, in this god-damn rickety wheelchair, you should've seen it. 'My Phil's gone,' " he cries in quivering falsetto. " 'My poor Phillie. Because of him,' she says, pointing at me. 'And now there's no one to take care of me.' "

She can hardly breathe. He fills the room, depleting the air, his studied elegance, the drape of his suit, the fine silk shirt, the tilt of his smooth head, all calculated. Waiting.

"So off I went. In chains." In agonizing detail, he describes his trip to the state prison, the shackles rubbing his wrists and ankles raw, the terror, and his constant faith that she would return and free him from the nightmarish injustice. "All those years, day after day, I kept think-ing, she'll come. She's too decent, too good a person not to."

"Well, I didn't know, did I?"

"You knew."

"No. Not that he died." She can hardly get the words out.

He chuckles. "But now you do. So. It's not too late."

"Not too late for what?"

"I told you before." He picks up the pictures of Chloe and Drew, studying them in the hinged sterling frame. "A chance. That's all I want."

Her mind races. Within minutes, she could get her hands on fifteen thousand dollars, money her mother left her.

"A chance to do what?" she asks carefully. He might take less.

He sets the pictures down, facing him. "It's like, you know, when you cut your fingernails and you flush the pieces down the toilet, I think about that. I like that feeling. Parts of me, like, floating into streams and rivers, the ocean. Feeding something. Fish maybe, then people. Like, something organic. Life. The ongoing process. You know what I mean? Some kind of cycle."

His intensity makes her shiver.

"Regeneration!" he says suddenly. "That's what I mean!"

"If it's money you want——," she begins, then jumps as he pounds the desk.

"You don't get it, do you, goddamnit! It's way past that now. Way, way past. I want a life, that's what I want." His voice softens. "What you have."

"But how can I do that? I don't understand."

"Be my friend," he whispers, straining over the desk. "Just be my friend."

"And then what?" She can't breathe.

"Well. I don't know, do I?" He twiddles his thumbs and looks around. "A job! That's a pretty good start. Place like this, must be something I can do here."

"No. I can't do that. But money, that would help, right?"

"What's that supposed to mean?"

"I can give you money."

"What do you mean, *give* me money?" he sneers.

"A loan. That's what I meant."

"You're kidding, right?"

"To help you get on your feet."

"Get on my feet!" he roars, his arm sweeping clear her desk, galleys, papers, books, her marble pen set, the children's pictures, the antique glass paperweight that was her mother's, radiating wobbly light as it rolls across the floor. "Who the hell do you think you are?" he rages. Standing now, he reaches across the desk as her phone rings.

Nora grabs it before he can.

"What's going on in there?" Hilda asks. "That man, are you all right?"

"Yes." She fixes him with her stare, daring him to take another step. "Something fell. By mistake. Mr. Hawkins . . . he'll be out in a minute."

With that, Eddie sits back down. He covers his eyes.

"You don't sound right," Hilda says.

"I'm fine. We're almost done."

"I can call Ken. He just went by." Hilda's shadow darkens the strip of light beneath the door.

"No need. Really, Hilda. Everything's fine." She hangs up but holds on to the phone. The last person on earth she wants in here is Ken, and have the shameful, sordid story revealed, especially now, flushed into the mess her life has become. And the thought of Chloe and Drew hearing any of this sickens her. Imagine, their mother involved in an assault, or maybe worse, no matter how long ago or how young she was. They have enough to deal with, as it is.

"Why are you doing this to me?" he whispers, eyes still shaded. "It's wrong. It's so wrong." His shoulders narrow as his chest rises, falls, and she remembers exactly this, the sudden fury, his utter desperation, and its powerful effect on a seventeen-year-old.

"I think you better go now," she says, steeling herself for his next outburst.

"I hate getting upset. You have no idea. The way it makes me feel," he gasps, peering at her in such a contortion of rage and despair it might seem comical if she weren't so scared. "My head's pounding. I can hardly see. I can't think straight."

"I'll call someone. They'll bring you downstairs." Hand trembling, she picks up the phone.

And with that, he opens the door and is gone.

Hilda rushes in, shocked by the mess on the floor. "What happened?"

"Short fuse. No big deal." The papers she's picking up tremble in her hands. Hilda asks who he was. Just some guy, Nora says. He wanted a job. She can tell that Hilda is biting her tongue.

They work together in silence, getting everything back on the desk.

"There was something really wrong with him," Hilda finally says.

"Yeah, no kidding."

"No, I mean it. Just talking to me, he was way too intense. On the edge."

"Like a few people around here. Maybe I should hire him. See what happens."

"No. I mean disturbed. Like, psychotic. I could tell."

"Thanks for letting him in then." Trying to make light of it, her brittle laughter thins into shrillness.

"I never will again, believe me."

Dr. Martelli listens thoughtfully in his oxblood red leather chair as she describes her shock upon learning of the affair. Or the relationship, as Ken keeps calling it. In this, their second session, Dr. Martelli seems determined to let them set their own pace tonight. If Ken wants to dissect his prickly relationship with his brother as he did in their last meeting, well, that's just fine. One thing is certain, Nora has no intention of delving into her own angst-ridden adolescence. Whenever she tries to steer the discussion back to their marriage, Ken will veer off course, and once again she'll be wondering why she's even here. She doesn't know which surprises her more, his utter self-involvement or her blindness to it. Bad enough she has so little patience with this whole process and less hope that it can help, but now her focus and confidence have been completely undermined by Eddie Hawkins. She can't think straight. More than a distraction, he's a growing threat.

Every time he comes Hilda says she's not in her office. Last week he told Hilda that he and Nora have been working on a very important deal and now time is running out. Each visit leaves Nora even more confused about his motives. And now frightened. Tuesday he angrily accused Hilda of lying, asked her what she was so afraid of. Best not to think about him. Not here, anyway. But it's like trying to close a door on smoke; some always seeps in.

"I always trusted Ken. I did," she is telling the pleasant-faced therapist. He has a kind smile, a melancholy weariness she finds touching. She feels sorry for him, almost apologetic for going on like this about herself. How does he stand it? she wonders. Imagine sitting here eight, ten hours a day enduring this spew of human weakness. For that's what it is, what it comes down to in the end, doesn't it? Frailty. Weakness, all this complaining, on and on, this airing out of dirty linen. Strong people don't ask for help; they solve their own problems, she was raised that way. Amazing, how much Ken seems to enjoy this. So typical, always involving others, asking for help his sincerest expression of friendship. He is happiest in a crowd, friends, total strangers, it doesn't matter. He enjoys the mix, the scrum of bringing new people together. Being a good friend matters every bit as much as being admired by his friends. And yet there have been more than a few times through the years when a seemingly innocuous comment or joke has ended a friendship. And once breached, for Ken, there's no return.

When they were first married, his unflagging enthusiasm seemed shallow and immature. There always had to be someone else tagging along, no matter where they went or what they did. Even on their rare dinners out alone Ken would manage, one way or another, to chat up someone at length, the busboy, the couple at the next table. It used to hurt her feelings, but over time she came to understand his incessant approval seeking as part of his charm. His very boyish charm. Hard to be upset with someone who truly cares and, in return, wants only the same.

"I don't know, maybe I didn't want to know. I keep asking myself that now. I wonder. Maybe I was afraid. You know, if I put two and two together enough times, then maybe I'd have to do something." She takes a deep breath and grinds her heel into the rug with an inner groan. What the hell is she talking about? Just talking, that's all. Stating the obvious. Why? To do her part. To make it more than just Ken's endless entanglement of guilt and regret. He doesn't seem to know what he's trying to say. He's just admitted he's not even sure what he wants anymore. With that, she interrupts to clarify her intentions here: to heal and put their life back together. He glances at Dr. Martelli. One thing seems obvious: Ken's desire for therapy has far more to do with himself than with her. "Well, anyway," she says with a searching sigh. "I guess this is what we have to do, isn't it? Work this all out so we can move on." Neither man speaks. They study her. Intently. As if expecting the real truth to come spilling out. Entrails. Her secrets. What? Eddie Hawkins? A chill passes through her. That was something else. A strange new problem. One has nothing to do with the other. With this. "Well? Is anyone going to say anything? Or are we just going to sit here looking at one another?" She smiles, hard though to make it seem like banter when her voice is so tinny with annoyance.

"What about it, Ken?" the doctor asks, as if coaxing him. "Anything you want to add here?"

"I don't know, it's hard." He shrugs.

Nora stares at him. Hard? she almost screams. Try being me, Ken. And *then* see how goddamn hard it is. Instead, she coolly asks, "So, what do you think, Doctor? Are we heading in the right direction here? Ken and I, are we making any headway?"

The doctor shifts in his creaky chair, waits a moment, then speaks with a certain chagrined reluctance. As if he knows more than can be said. Far, far more. As if in this warm, cluttered office there is an unseen presence. "I don't know that *headway*'s quite the right word. There's a kind of energy here," he says, countersawing his hands between the two of them, "but it's contained, I think. Held back, perhaps. Does that make any sense?" Eyebrows raised, he looks from one to the other.

She grips the chair arms to keep from jumping up and leaving. She resents being talked down to, being made to feel childish and insignificant.

Ken speaks up, with sudden relish. "It's funny. I keep thinking there's some one thing, if only I can put my finger on it. You know, to figure this all out. It's like there's Nora, but then there's everything before that. You know what I mean, like . . . like I never got past certain things. Like, what I was saying about my brother last time. Him living in the same house. The same business, all the same people, it's not the way you do things nowadays. People don't get stuck in a place, in a job, in time. Not anymore."

Strangely fascinating, this eager baring of his heart. Where's he going with this? Stuck in a marriage? Stuck in immaturity? It's the most he's ever admitted.

"That's such a . . . a relic, such a throwback. On the one hand, I look at my brother and I say, Jesus, what kind of life is that? And then I think, well, wait a minute, I'm doing the same thing, right? Only maybe I'm an even sicker son of a bitch than he is. I mean, what the hell're we doing? What're we afraid of?

"Like when I first met Nora. She was working at the paper, and she just seemed so different from everyone else. Refreshing, you know what I mean? No bullshit, the real deal, it was like I could tell her anything and not have to worry about a hidden agenda. She was always upfront with me. About everything. Especially about what an asshole I could be."

Everyone laughs. His self-effacing humor. Reminded why she loves him, Nora pats his leg, smiling.

"Even my mom and dad," he continues, "they saw it right away, too. Like some kind of energy had come into the family. New blood. Renewal, you know what I mean? Like . . . like, raising the bar. Not only smart as hell, but she made you think twice before you said something, because she'd damn well take you up on it. She had these . . . these deep values. And she did not suffer fools lightly. Which meant my whole family. They were scared of her. It was hard. I mean, after a century of bullshit, they've got someone like Nora sitting at Christmas dinner telling the emperor he's naked as a jaybird."

"What're you saying, Ken?" Shocked, she can't remember ever offending his parents, especially not his father. "Your dad was like a second father to me. And he knew that. I told him that. Many times."

"I know. But that's not my point. He didn't know how to take you. He and my mother, they were from a whole different species, they—"

"What on earth do your parents have to do with you and Robin? I'm sorry, but I don't get it."

"See? Just cut to the chase," Ken informs Dr. Martelli with a rueful sigh. "Once again."

Nora taps her fingers on the chair arm, chews the inside of her mouth to shreds.

"It might help here, Ken, if you can give us some sense of where you're headed, pull it together a little more. Not just your disappointment, but your family's, the whole dynamic after that summer," Dr. Martelli says.

That summer? So, this is a prearranged script, she realizes. Only problem is, as usual, Ken is all over the place, off-message, getting ahead of himself, forgetting the doctor's coaching, missing the prompts.

Ken is describing the summer after he graduated from college. He naturally expected to come home and work for the *Chronicle* as Oliver had done after graduating. But his father had other ideas for his younger, less motivated son. He wanted to take him out of his element. "I figured I'd throw him to the lions, then use what was left," he said once of Ken's job in a Chicago paper's business office that he'd arranged through a friend. Ken would later describe the job as mind-numbing, a stint that made easily palatable Oliver's becoming publisher of the *Chronicle*. A master stroke on Mr. Hammond's part, Nora has always thought.

"Anyway, Robin and I'd been going together all that time, ever since junior high school, really. So, naturally, I'm thinking she's part of the package, too. The future, Franklin, FairWinds, the *Chronicle*. I'd call and she'd say how nice Bob was, taking her to a club or a movie, stuff like that, you know, places she wouldn't want to go alone. And I'm thinking, jeez, what a good buddy, taking care of Robin till I get back.

Then I come home and the two of them're in deep, and I'm trying to pretend not to care: like, oh, well, what the hell, what're you gonna do. I mean, my two best friends. We grew up together. But I'll tell ya, it took me a long time to get over it." His voice hoarsens. "A real long time."

Silence. How long before someone speaks, she wonders, barely able to breathe in his wounded air. She's stunned. With all their troubles, this still saddens him?

The doctor's chair creaks. "But did you? Did you get over it?" He adjusts his glasses, and it's all she can do to keep from laughing— hysterically. What parallel life has she been living all this time?

"I thought I did." Ken glances at her. "And that's part of what I meant by renewal, and your being such a breath of fresh air. Your energy. I really needed that then. To take my mind off it all." With his smile, she feels the top of her head getting ready to explode. All these years, his palliative. Nothing more.

"I can't believe I'm doing this. Sitting here through your Miss Lonelyheart's confession. Do it in your own session then. Not when I'm here, for godsake."

"No! I just want you to know, that's all. So you'll understand," he implores.

She turns to him. "You can't be serious." But he is, she sees. Perfectly, pathetically, brokenheartedly serious.

CHAPTER · 11

"Will you please chew with your mouth shut?" Chloe growls.

"I can't. My nose is too stuffed," Drew growls back.

"Like I really need the details." She shades her eyes.

"See?" He puts the napkin to his nose, making a dry, honking sound as he tries to blow. "I have to breathe through my mouth."

"You are so gross."

"Yeah, right." He stares at her.

They are eating dinner late tonight. Ken's favorite, pork chops and sauerkraut, so Nora tried to wait. But then he called and said they should start without him. His meeting is running late. Actually, his brother's meeting in Boston, so he drove Oliver in. Uneasiness in crowds is chief among Oliver's quirks, but driving in city traffic is right up there. How many other times has Ken used Oliver as an excuse? She can barely swallow. Is this another lie? Is he seeing her again? Excusing herself, she goes into the bathroom and turns on the exhaust fan. She dials her brother-in-law's number. Holding her breath, she counts the rings. If Oliver does answer, she'll call Ken and tell him not to bother coming home. This all-pervading suspicion, like living on quicksand. Better to end it. Better for everyone.

"Hi, Oll, it's me, Nora," she says when his answering machine comes on. "Give me a call. Just a quick question, that's all."

She sits back down. Instead of being relieved, she keeps expecting the phone to ring. Just because he didn't answer doesn't mean he's in

Boston with Ken. Oliver hates talking on the phone and Ken knows that. He has to take calls at the paper, but at home he'll just let the phone ring.

Drew is trying to blow his nose again. The cut on his cheek has healed, leaving only a hairline scar. Nora notices the rash of pimples on his face and neck. The worst ones are on his forehead, like hard red boils. She wonders if his prescription has run out. He needs a haircut and his sweatshirt is stained. Is her unhappiness blinding her to everything around her, she who has always had little patience with people who let their troubles consume their lives?

"Will you stop that? Please?" Chloe begs with a long sigh.

"Drew has a cold," Nora says sharply. The last thing she needs right now is their arguing. "He can't help it."

"Well, he can go in the other room and do it, can't he?" Chloe says.

"Maybe you should, Drew. If it's bothering your sister," she says. Has their bickering gotten worse lately or is she just more sensitive to it? Stress fractures. Hairline cracks, all the little breaks. Before the big one.

"Everything bothers her," Drew mutters.

"Well, at least I don't go around having fights with people. Brawls, I should say," Chloe sniffs.

Drew keeps chewing, his gaze heavy with warning. "So how come you got early dismissal today? Where'd you go?"

Chloe's face drains of color. Nora puts down her fork. She asks Chloe what time she was dismissed. Chloe isn't sure, maybe around one or two, she thinks. No, it was morning, eleven, it said on the sign-out sheet, Drew explains. Why? Nora asks. Where did she go? And how, without a note?

Finally, Chloe admits forging Nora's signature on the dismissal note. But it wasn't just to skip. It was for a good reason. Jen had a doctor's appointment and she didn't want to go alone.

"So why didn't her mother take her?" Nora asks.

"Because . . . she couldn't," Chloe says with a meaningful stare at her mother.

"Yeah, she probably forged her note, too," Drew scoffs.

"What's wrong with Jen, is she sick?" Nora asks. Jen is Chloe's best friend. This year, anyway.

Chloe's eyes widen. She sighs in exasperation.

"Well?"

"I'd rather not talk about it right now," Chloe says in that up-talking, singsong cadence Nora can't stand.

All right then, Nora says. If Drew will excuse them for a moment, they'll go into the den where Chloe can speak privately. The minute the door closes, Chloe explains that Jen was scared she had cancer. She had this weird mole that kept getting bigger. They're going to run some tests. Why wouldn't she tell her mother? Nora asks.

"Because of where it is." She gestures to her groin. "She's embarrassed. You know how Jen is."

"You're lying to me."

"See! I knew you'd say that. I can't tell you anything!"

Nora opens the phone book. "I'm calling Jen's mother."

"No! Jen'll never speak to me again. You'll get Mrs. Carnes all upset and then she'll hate me."

"A risk I'll have to take, then." She runs her finger down the column of numbers. "Or do you just want to tell me the truth? You were with Max, weren't you?"

Chloe weeps and begs her mother's forgiveness. It's true. He's going away for a three-month work-study in Costa Rica and she wanted to see him one last time before his flight. "I'm sorry, Mom. I'm so sorry."

"Don't you know what you do when you lie, Chloe? My trust . . . you break my heart," she says, fighting tears. *Especially after what your father's done to me,* she aches to say, hungry for her daughter's love and understanding.

"I know and I'm sorry," Chloe cries, "but . . . but I'm gonna miss him so much. It hurts just to think about it."

So much for my feelings, Nora thinks, wiping her eyes, relieved in a way. No matter what disaster is going on with her parents, Chloe's life is still firmly on its normal track, with teenage tunnel vision obscuring all but her own troubles. As it should be, Nora thinks, though it doesn't make her feel any better. Just more alone. On the outside, looking in—at her own life.

It's late afternoon and she's just returning to the office after a two-hour wrangle with Duncan Turner, president of Franklin Memorial Hospital. His cooperation is crucial to the success of the *Medical* supplement. Because they've served together on so many civic and charitable committees and because the supplement will be a great public relations venue for the hospital she expected their meeting to be brief, a formality, if not a courtesy call. But as it turns out, Duncan is a punctilious control-monger, at least in matters concerning the hospital. He is insisting on final approval of every article. Her suggestion that they interview someone from housekeeping was met with surprising disdain. Janitors and cleaning ladies, apparently not the image President Turner wants out there. Doctors, department heads, he'll decide and send her the names. Oh yes, and nurses, he agreed when she mentioned them. She hadn't realized the extent of his vanity when it concerns his public persona. She'll have to be careful.

"That guy. Hawkins. He was just here again," Hilda says the minute Nora comes through the door. "I told him you weren't here, but he said you keep calling, telling him to come in. He said he'd try the house."

"The house!" she cries, then tries to hide her alarm. "God, he's a pest. I don't even know what he wants," she says, dialing the home number on the way into her office and closing the door with her hip. No answer. She tries Chloe's number. No answer. Dials Drew's. Not having heard anything of Eddie in a week, she'd convinced herself that he'd tired of his sick little game and moved on.

"Hey, Mom!" Drew answers breathlessly on the sixth ring. "In the driveway," he says when she asks where he is.

"Doing what?"

"Basketball," he grunts, and in the background comes the running thunkthunkthunk of a ball being dribbled.

"That's nice." She's glad. Even though his cold is better, he's been so unhappy these last few weeks, leaving the house only for school. Because he's turned them down so often lately, his friends have stopped calling. "But don't forget about your ribs. You don't want to aggravate anything."

"I won't."

Hearing a voice, she hunches over her desk. "Who's that? I just heard someone. Who is it?"

"That guy you know. Mr. Hawkins. We're shooting some—"

"You let him in the house?"

"No. I got off the bus, and he—"

"Put him on the phone!"

"But, Mom, we're—"

"Put him on the phone! Now, Drew!"

"She wants to talk to you," she hears Drew say. *She,* not *my mother,* but *she,* as if they've been discussing her.

"Nora!" Eddie Hawkins croons in her ear. "I've been waiting for you."

"I'm only going to say this once. You get out of there, right now! Because I'm calling the police."

"I wouldn't do that. Not a good idea. Too many questions."

"I'm on my way. I'm almost there," she says, hurrying out past Hilda who steps back so quickly she must have been listening at the door.

"Hey, take your time," he oozes. "Don't rush on my account. Please."

As soon as she gets out of the car, she tells Drew to go inside, she has to talk to Mr. Hawkins for a minute.

"That's okay. I'll just keep shooting," Drew says, dribbling then spinning with a quick jump shot.

"Yeah!" Eddie pumps his fist. "Nothin' but net!"

"No, Drew. Now. Inside. This is . . . business."

"I'll come back some other time, Drew." Eddie pats the glowering boy's back. "Work on our three-point shots."

Drew kicks the basketball out of his way, just hard enough to let her know he's upset. Last night he and his sister had another terrible

argument. Chloe is still mad at him for telling on her. And unbeliev-
ably, Ken sided with Chloe. His first loyalty should always be to his
family, he told Drew. Drew's muttered retort got him sent to his room
for the night. As soon as the side door closes, Nora demands to know
what Eddie thinks he's doing, coming to her home, talking to her son.
Instead of answering, he asks if they can go inside, he's freezing. The
back of his jacket flaps in the wind. He blows into his cupped hands.

"Trying to intimidate me is one thing. But I won't have you stalk-
ing my—"

"One-on-one it's called." He grins.

"Look, Eddie, whatever you think happened to you because of—"

"Whatever I think!" His laugh is a bitter bray. "It's not what I think.
It's what happened, goddamnit! That's what this is about. Not what I
fucking *think* happened."

"All right then." She speaks slowly, acutely aware of his wringing
hands. "Because of what happened. That's why you're here. And I'm
sorry. I'm sorry for whatever you've gone through. But that was
twenty-six years ago. I don't know what you want from me. You said it
was to protect me, well, I appreciate that, in one way, but . . . you were
trying to rob him. I mean, that's . . . that's what really happened."

"What *really* happened was you split the fucker's skull in two. And
then you took off running. And who ends up in shackles? Poor Eddie.
The poor sick bastard tryna help him."

"No." Horrified, she can only shake her head. "No. That's not
true."

"It's not? Jesus Christ, then one of us is awfully damn messed up,"
he says, tapping his temple. "And it sure as hell ain't me."

For days afterward, she forces herself to remember that night. Some
details she has forgotten. The truck driver's name. Tom, all she remembers. He seemed so much older, as did most adults then, especially men, all of that murky universe of inconsequential, middle-age
people. The company name on his truck: red lettering? On the cab
door or on the side of the trailer? Did he ever say what freight he was

carrying, where he'd been, where he was going? Probably. She remembers him talking a lot. A nice man. Soft-spoken in spite of his gruff manner. But what did he actually tell her? Did she listen or even care beyond diesel fumes and the sobering horror of the bloody scene she was fleeing? She was so sick to her stomach he had to keep pulling off the highway to let her out. Strange, the things she does remember, prickly weeds at her ankles as she dry-heaved in the gravel, then climbing back up into the big rig's rumble, like his voice, a regretful, damning drone. They drove a long time before he suggested she call home.

"No. I can't." She couldn't face the shame of even talking to her mother much less having to stand in her stern presence. Once again, she had failed her mother, soiled her father's memory. All she wanted was to die.

"Sooner or later you're gonna have to," he said.

"Why? Why can't I stay with you?" she asked, holding her sides.

"Hey! I got kids your age."

"A ride, that's all I meant."

He finally talked her into letting him call her mother. He did most of the talking. It was some comfort, hearing him assure her mother she was fine . . . a little frazzled maybe, but none the worse for wear.

"Things kids do . . . Yeah, I know . . . Been through it with my own." Did he say that? Or is she filling in the blanks, sanitizing the story, because the truth is so foul? Maybe he wasn't kind and paternal. Maybe he came on to her up there in the dimly lit cab, rubbing his hand on her thigh, making her even more sick to her stomach. How long was she with him? Through that night, anyway. She remembers waking up with a start when he pulled off the highway, blinded for a moment by the sun's glare, then seeing all the other trucks in the parking lot. Noisy and bright inside the bustling diner, every stool filled, a shock after the quiet of the night's cloistered cab. The smell of coffee and bacon. Cigarettes. They didn't sit at the counter. In a booth: that, she remembers. She wouldn't look at him. He seemed uneasy watching her eat. Or maybe with his scrutiny she was uneasy, ashamed. Scrambled eggs and coffee. Limp toast. Why that detail, why thin toast on a greasy white plate and not the name of the town or if there'd been a pipe in her hand, but her lip was cut, which had to have been the blood caked under her nails, willing it to be the only blood, hers, as she stared into the filmy restroom mirror with a wad of wet paper towels pressed against her swollen mouth, while the knob rattled and turned, until finally, he banged on the locked door, shouting for her to come out. He knew she was in a bad way, but he was on a tight schedule, six deliveries to make. There was a pay phone, he said. She'd tell him the number but only if he talked first. When he finally handed her the receiver she began to cry.

"Mom." For a moment all she could say. "I'm sorry. I'm so sorry," she surely must have said. Sorry for everything, she meant. All the lies and disappointment. And poor Mr. Blanchard, though she couldn't say it then.

"Just come home. Please. Please, come home." That, she remembers with the same urgent clarity of her mother's voice. Dusk when he dropped her at the bus station. Her mother wired money ahead for the ticket. And for food along the way. A few days after she got home, her mother insisted she write him a thank-you note. Imagine the etiquette of a proper thank-you note from a fugitive, fleeing a crime scene. Her stomach turned writing it. She was too ashamed to tell her mother much of anything. Just that Eddie Hawkins had turned out to be a lot different than she'd first thought. And that there'd been a fight. In his call, Tom had alluded to it, so she had to.

"Did he hurt you?" her mother asked.

"No." She cried.

"Should I make an appointment with Dr. Reisman?" Might she be pregnant?

"No!" She didn't think so.

Her mother must have mailed the thank-you note. Where to, though? It was never mentioned again.

And so it's always the same. Hazy, unfocused. She'd been so young, and certainly intoxicated, drinking all day in the brutally hot car. In needing to forget, had the details slipped away? Or been altered to suit her conscience? Secrets, dreamed so many times, the dream is now both defense and barrier. Her head pushed down, the car door opening; then Eddie shoves him back, the man swings the pipe, and Eddie knocks it away. But now whose hand wields it? Eddie's? Or hers? No. No. She wasn't capable of such an act. Not then or now.

Edward Hawkins, she types, eyes burning wide on the screen, breath held. Nothing. None of the Edward or Eddie Hawkinses match. The Nevada prison system has one Hawkins. Francis. Eighteen years for armed robbery—wrong age, though. He is thirty-three now, so Francis Hawkins would have been seven then. If she only knew the name of the town where they stopped then she could check local police records. Arrests that night, injury reports. Murder. Phil, Eddie said, but she needs more than that.

The roadhouse seemed to be in the middle of the desert. They'd driven for hours, and for most of the time if she hadn't been asleep, she hadn't been especially awake either, fuzzy in the illusion of love and being loved. Certainly not observant.

Clayborne Hotel, she types into Google. Lake George. One of the last big wooden hotels, built at the turn of the twentieth century. Too expensive to renovate, torn down years ago. A water park in its place. Pee parks, Ken always called them whenever the children teased to be taken. That's what she's remembering now over the keyboard, the dank smell of urine in the old floorboards when she scrubbed the toilets clean. Even if the Clayborne still existed there'd be no record of any Eddie Hawkins ever working there. She seems to remember New York plates on his car. Her fingers fly over the keyboard. Reporter's instinct, knowing where to dig. Yale. Census records. Hawkins, a few names. No Eddies. California. His supposed elderly uncle. Probate records. Nothing.

Carol," she says too quickly, too urgently, when her sister answers the phone. And as always Carol's response is distant, reserved, tentative in her fear that something might be expected of her. Seventeen-year-old Nora might have run away for a week, but it was cautious, serious

Carol, the mature RN, who hadn't been able to get away from home fast enough, marrying right after nursing school and moving to California.

A few years later, when Nora was in college, she asked Carol if she could come spend spring break with her and Les. Carol said their apartment was small, but Nora offered to sleep on the couch or on the floor even, she was dying to see the new babies. The twins were six months old and Nora and her mother had only seen pictures of them. When they were born, Mrs. Trimble had planned on flying out to San Diego so she could help Carol for the first ten days. They might both be nurses, but Carol was still a new mother, and twins were an entirely different matter. Then, at the last minute, late, the night before her flight, the phone rang. Les informed his mother-in-law it would be better if she didn't come. He and Carol had decided what they really needed was time alone to bond with the babies.

"What's her problem?" Nora asked her disappointed mother after hearing the litany of Carol's reasons why spring break wasn't a good time for her to come.

"Selfishness mainly." Her mother's answer shocked Nora. It was the first negative word she'd ever heard uttered about her sister. But if Carol had cut her family ties, her mother only blamed herself. Through the years she would regret having expected too much of her older daughter after her husband's sudden death. Carol should have been out having fun instead of being burdened with so much responsibility. With Mrs. Trimble's abrupt return to teaching, she needed Carol to be at the house when Nora got home from school. She needed Carol to drive Nora to Girl Scout meetings and tennis lessons, then home again, often skipping her own extracurricular activities. She needed Carol to start dinner so that by the time she got there they wouldn't have to eat too late. Carol was expected to work her way through UMass, waitressing nights and weekends. And then, as soon as Carol could, days after graduation, she was gone, clear across the country with bright but humorless Les, one of only three men in their nursing class.

"They're doing well," Carol says now when Nora asks about the twins, the niece and nephew she barely knows. Allison is at Caltech starting on her master's and Jacob is taking some time off to paint.

"For his art," Carol said the last time she and Nora talked. Jacob dropped out of college three years ago, but Carol continues to make it sound as if it has only just happened.

"That's wonderful," Nora says. "And Les, how's he doing?"

There's a pause.

"Actually, I've been meaning to call. I . . . Well, Les and I, we've come to a . . . an agreement."

"Oh?"

"We don't live together anymore."

"Oh. Well, that's not good. I mean . . . well, what does that mean? Are you separated or divorced or—"

"He's moved. Closer to the hospital. So now his commute's only half what it was. Twenty-six minutes to be exact."

"And you're okay with that?"

"As okay as I can be," Carol says with a fluttery lilt, helpless wings in a downward spiral.

"What happened?"

"The usual. Midlife crisis and all that." Her voice cracks.

"Carol. I'm so sorry." You're not the only one, she wants to say but doesn't. Let there be one person in her life who doesn't know she's been betrayed, one person whose vision of her holds, one person not thinking "poor thing" whenever they talk.

"It's so strange. I mean it's not as if he's with someone else. He's just . . . he just wants to be alone."

"Maybe he's just trying to work something out." His sexuality, Nora thinks, immediately ashamed of the malice in her heart. While Les has never been unkind to her, he's never been kind either. Only disinterested. Remote. The few times she and her mother did visit, he'd get up from the table and watch television.

"If it was another woman, that I could understand. Or make some sense of. But this is just pure rejection. Of me. Me, he doesn't want to be with," Carol sobs.

"Oh, Care. I wish I was there so I could give you a great big hug right now."

"I'm all right." Carol pauses to blow her nose. "I'm fine," she insists. "It's just the way everything's changing. It's hard. You wake up one morning and everything's different."

Not so different, Nora thinks. Les hasn't changed, only Carol's illusions have. Like her own.

"I don't even make the bed anymore," Carol says. "I mean, what's the point? It's just me. I haven't run the dishwasher in days. And I look terrible. God forbid Les should walk in now. My color hasn't been done in months. You should see my roots. I canceled the papers, magazines, it's all so depressing. And now I even hate Republicans. I mean, imagine, after all these years, but it's like there's something in the air. A pall over everything, like a toxic cloud. You know what I mean? Deadness. Something." Her voice breaks. "It's just so hard."

"Maybe you should see someone, Carol. A therapist, someone you could talk to," she says with a twinge of hypocrisy.

"Could you come, Nora? We wouldn't have to go anywhere, just sit by the pool and talk. I'd really like that."

"I can't, Carol. I wish I could, but I can't. Things're just so . . . so up in the air right now. So busy." Busy trying to hold her own life together. Busy trying to stave off the looming storm that is Eddie Hawkins.

"That's right. I'm sorry, I wasn't even thinking of your job."

"It's not just that."

"You were so smart to go back to work. I wish I had. I should have, but I didn't want it to be like Mom. I wanted to be there for the kids, and for Les. But all I did was make him carry the whole load, and now look what I'm left with. Nothing!"

"That's not true." Nora can't think of a way to steer the conversation back, twenty-six years.

"I've been thinking of taking a trip."

"You should. Get your mind off things."

"Maybe I'll come see you." Carol poses it as a question. A timid one.

"That would be . . . nice." Great idea, she should have said. Or wonderful. Or when, soon, I hope. Instead she is asking her sister if she remembers anything of that long-ago night when she called her frantic mother, needing help to get home.

"Well, yeah, that Mom was beside herself. Out of her mind. For an entire week she just sat by the phone."

"I know. God, when I think of it, how upset she must have been. But did she ever say anything? You know, details like, where I ended up. What state I was in."

"You mean you don't even know?"

"It's just that I'm having a hard time remembering."

"What were you, on drugs or something?"

Nora bristles with her sister's scorn. Obviously Carol finds this conversation therapeutic, restorative to be back on old footing, good sister–bad sister.

"So you don't know? Mom never said?"

"She was a wreck. I mean, you and everything else that was screwy in her life."

"Poor Mom."

"There I was, three and a half months pregnant, but once again it was 'Oh, Carol, please. I need your help.' I flew home. Don't you remember?"

Nora squirms. Yes, now she does. How could she have forgotten? The first of Carol's many miscarriages, and it happened the very day Nora arrived on the bus. Her poor, poor mother, Nora keeps thinking. She never should have called Carol. The psyche protects itself by forgetting. The last thing she wants to remember is the pain she caused her mother, alone and having to deal with one daughter a runaway, the other losing her first pregnancy.

"I never should've gone. Les kept telling me," Carol is saying. "But it was all such a mess. That whole thing with you and what's-his-name, that teacher, and him coming on to Mom. No wonder you ran away. I mean, God, what was she thinking? He was closer in age to you than her, that's what happened!"

"That was a real hard time for Mom." Nora cringes with the memory. Mr. Blanchard, her handsome, young English teacher.

Carol laughs. "I'll say, dating a pervert."

"He wasn't a pervert."

"Oh, really? Then what was that whole trashy mess all about? All the screaming and crying?"

Wincing, she holds her head. "Do you mind, Carol? I really don't feel like talking about all that. I mean, why? What's the point?"

"You're the one that brought it up, asking me what state you ended up in, for godsake!"

"I'm sorry, but you're confusing things. You weren't there when it happened, the teacher, I mean."

"No, I'm just the one you kept calling night after night, remember? Crying, sobbing into the phone, telling me how you were going to kill yourself if Mom said anything to him. And then she'd call and tell me how it was her mandated duty, her professional responsibility. My God, do you have any idea what that was like for me, all that turmoil and long-distance wailing, sometimes in the middle of the night even? And there I am, taking my temp every two hours, trying to get pregnant, and having to put up with that. Finally Les just put down his foot. 'That's it,' he said, 'no more. It's about time your mother and sister solved their own problems and stopped using you as their personal wrestling mat.'"

"I'm sorry, Carol. I am, but that was an awfully long time ago. And besides, you're mixing up two totally different things."

"No, Nora. I'm just being honest. Not like you and Mom, all your little secrets, then expecting me to come pick up the pieces. And don't think I—"

"I can't hear you," she lies. "You're breaking up, Carol." She holds the phone at arm's length while her sister rages on. She hangs up and the phone rings seconds later. She won't answer.

In the days that follow, memory and regret lodge in her heart like a wide, thick blade that constantly aches. Eddie Hawkins has become the provenance of all sorrow and fear, the pain of her marriage. Her mother's loneliness. Her sister's bitterness. If only she'd never met him. If only he'd go away.

CHAPTER 12

Oliver is in the hospital. He and Annette had just been seated for dinner at the Renwood Club when the numbness hit. The waiter was handing them menus, but Oliver could only stare across the table at Annette, unable to lift his arm. When he tried to speak his garbled words made no sense. Nora is in the emergency room lobby. She has been on the phone for the last fifteen minutes, trying to track down Ken, but no one has seen him. His cell phone must still be off because the voice mail cue starts with the first ring. The lobby door flies open and Stephen rushes in. She tells him the little she knows. Annette has come out twice to brief her. Oliver's CAT scan showed there wasn't any bleeding, so the doctors are giving him tPA to break up any other clots.

"I knew this would happen. These weird pains he's been getting. Like tingling in his arms and legs. And here." Stephen touches his neck, the carotid artery. "I told him, do something. Don't just sit there. But he's a mess. The man's a mess. An absolute mess. He and his brother, they just stay mired."

Mired? Her marriage, is that what he means? But this isn't the time to lash back. With distress, Stephen's emotional volatility rages. He and Oliver are not only first cousins born weeks apart, but they were raised almost as brothers. Stephen's mother and Oliver's mother were identical twins who did everything together until Stephen's mother died of a burst appendix when he was twelve. With his own father long divorced and remarried, Stephen was brought up by his aunt

Addie and uncle James, Oliver and Ken's parents. When he was seventeen he had a nervous breakdown and was hospitalized for months. After years of therapy and, more recently, antidepressants and a long relationship with unflappable Donald, he is far more stable and happy.

"If anything happens to him," Stephen declares, shaking his fist. "I don't know. I don't know what I'll do."

"Oh, Stephen, I know." She holds his hand in hers. As exasperating as she has found his snarly pettiness through the years, it is impossible to stay mad for long. She has grown deeply fond of him in spite of his early coldness to her, all part of his unbreachable loyalty to family. His first allegiance was to Robin, "Kenny's little friend," he used to call her. Being that much older, Stephen had known Robin since she was a child. But Nora and Stephen quickly found common ground, the death of a parent in their early adolescence. "But we mustn't think like that," she says to soothe him now as he fears the loss of one of his two closest living relatives. "The EMTs got him here right away. And there's so much more they can do now."

"I blame myself," Stephen says with a gasp, covering his mouth for a moment to compose himself. "Why didn't I do something? Why did I just let it happen?" His ragged whisper echoes past confidences. His beautiful mother's sudden death occurred when he was away at summer camp. He hadn't wanted to go, but his mother made him. Boys' activities, the rough-and-tumble of life in a tent, frogs, bugs, latrines, he needed more of that, she felt, all the things he detested. Make him stronger, toughen him up, especially with his uninterested father on the opposite coast. Stephen would always regret not standing his ground, refusing to go. If only he'd been there, he might have come to her aid, alerted someone, saved her in time. His obsessive caution is a joke in the family, though understandable.

"You didn't let it happen. It's not your fault. You know Oliver. He's—"

"Intractable!" Stephen cries, and two elderly women look up, startled. "But so what? When you see the ship going down, you don't just stand there, do you? No! You damn well do something! You save the people you love!"

Yes, and a chill goes through her. You do. No matter what it takes, or how.

Stephen's cell phone is ringing. It's Donald. Stephen moves nearer the door to tell him what has happened and where he is. Stephen's voice rises. "Let someone else cover! This is where you're needed!"

Flipping open her own phone, Nora walks out to the alcove lined with vending machines. This time, Chloe answers. No, she doesn't know where her father is. She just got in from SAT tutoring and heard her mother's message on the machine. She asks how Uncle Oliver is, grows quiet when Nora says she's not really sure. It sounds like a stroke, though no one's actually said the word yet.

"A stroke," Chloe repeats, and Nora hears the fear in her voice. "But he's going to be all right, isn't he?" she asks, like her father, needing the positive spin, even if it means being lied to. A cheerful outlook is its own strength, Ken said once when Nora complained about his lack of concern, or at least the appearance of it, during the delivery drivers' strike at the paper when Ken had been quoted as saying the stoppage was more about union politics than wages and worker dissatisfaction.

"That's bullshit," Nora said.

"Which makes the world go round and round and round," he laughed, his silken humor and silken life unmarred by want or pain. Until me, she thinks. Is that it? Am I the slub, the chosen flaw? Robin may have married within their circle, but he would choose a woman totally different. An outsider.

"I don't know. If it's a massive enough bleed, there could be paralysis. Or it could even be fatal," she says, hating herself. She's not even sure what she's talking about, but *she's* here, Ken's not, and Chloe should know that. "Could you call around, Chloe, try and find Dad? Tell him something's happened to his brother." The unspoken message: His brother. In time of need your father's nowhere to be found. Cruel to do to her, but the child should see. In betraying their mother he betrays them all.

"Where? Who? I don't know who to call."

"Everyone. Wherever you think he might be."

"But haven't you?"

"Some places. Maybe you can . . . maybe you can call some others."

"Okay." Chloe's voice is small, uneasy with the mission.

"What's Drew doing?" In her rush out of the house she forgot to tell him exactly where she was going, only that Uncle Oliver was sick.

"Watching television."

"He's supposed to be working on his term paper."

"I'll make him turn it off. But Mom . . . do I have to call the Gendrons?"

Nora listens to her daughter's breathing. "Why? You think he's there?"

In the silence, she can feel Chloe's cringe. "I don't know."

"No. That's fine. I'm sure we'll find him. Sooner or later."

Nora and Stephen huddle in the corner. This is as far away as they can get from the coughing. Holding his head, the haggard young man opposite them leans over his knees and moans, then is wracked by a barrage of violent sneezes. Stephen covers his nose and mouth.

"This is ridiculous," he says behind his hand. "Imagine subjecting healthy people to this."

"You can wait outside, if you want. I'll come get you," she says.

"Where the hell's Kenny?"

"I told you. I've been calling. I know there was a meeting with Al Bailey, the new school superintendent, and then—"

He looks at his watch. "Nine thirty at night, what kind of meeting's that?" he says so snidely that she has to take a deep breath.

"I don't know, Stephen. Do you?"

"I thought it was over. Isn't it? What the hell's he thinking?" he asks when she doesn't answer right away.

"He's trying. We both are. It's . . . it's hard."

"Just so you know, I talked to him. I did. I told him he was an ass, an absolute fool, putting everything on the line like that. And for what? She's a disaster. Everything she touches turns to shit. And that's from someone who likes her, you know that. But you don't—"

Along with everyone else in the waiting room, they both look up as Annette rushes through the swinging double doors. Even with the profusion of tears running down her smooth brown cheeks, she looks stunning, regal in her flowing red caftan.

"Oh my God," Stephen gasps, and Nora throws her arms around him. To protect him from the news they both fear.

"He's going to be all right. They just told me." Annette drags a chair closer to face them. Nora hands her a tissue. "I'm sorry," she says, blowing her nose. "I was fine and then they told me, and then I just lost it. I'm so relieved. He's talking. Still a little funny but at least some things you can understand." She needs to get right back to him.

Hugging her, they assure her they'll continue waiting, but the minute she's out of sight Stephen erupts.

"How about that little walk-on? The bitch."

"Stephen! She's relieved. Imagine what she's just been through."

"Goddamn drama queen. If she loves him so damn much, then why not marry him? That's what I'd like to know."

"It's Oliver. He's just . . . he's perfectly content, he's never going to change anything in his life."

"Is that what you think?" His head draws back and his eyes narrow with caustic amusement. "Do you really?"

It is Annette who is perfectly content with her life, Stephen declares. She enjoys the prestige of being Oliver Hammond's social companion without having to endure him as a husband. She's got a boyfriend in Boston. "Her young stud," Stephen sputters. "Oh, I know, she's just, quote, *mentoring* him, but in Jamaica for two weeks? I mean, come on, what's that all about?"

"Maybe it was some kind of, you know, artist colony thing."

"Yeah, right. Well, Delia Lord stayed in the same hotel and nobody was doing any painting that she could see."

"Delia Lord! She's vicious, you know that," Nora whispers, relieved for the moment to be caught in one of Stephen's acid riffs.

"Big boobs and tons of money, though. And she likes you," he whispers back, making her laugh. He has more female friends than anyone she knows, man or woman, or even Ken. That any of them confide in Stephen always amazes her. His sustenance is the folly of others. Only his cousins escape his gossip, except when he discusses them with Nora. And she's no fool; she knows how swiftly eviscerated she would be if Ken were to leave her. From time to time even Donald suffers the sting of Stephen's venom. His weight is a problem between them. They used to play racquetball, tennis, and ski together until surgery following an almost fatal automobile accident left Donald with chronic back pain.

"Nora!"

They jump up guiltily. Giddy with relief, neither one had seen Ken enter. The beauty of Stephen has always been, as Kay once so perfectly observed, his very contagious streak of "junior-highness."

The three of them join Annette at Oliver's bedside. Gray-faced and propped against pillows, every time he tries to speak the wrong words come out. He has just asked Ken for his "fender."

"Sure," Ken says, looking around with a pained smile. "Let's see. Fender. Where's the fender? I don't see it."

Annette searches through the toiletry items in the drawer of the raised tray table. She holds up a disposable razor and Oliver turns away. Then, she opens the narrow locker door next to the bathroom. Stephen raises his eyebrows at Nora. A man of limited patience in the best of circumstances, Oliver is becoming more agitated.

"Fender," he repeats. "There."

"Where?" Ken asks.

Oliver looks down at his frozen right arm, his clawed hand. "Fuck!" he says, and no one speaks. They have never heard him utter such a word. "The times! Go . . . see . . . the the the . . . the times!" He strains forward with a despairing groan. Drool seeps from the corner of his crooked mouth. The right side of his deeply wrinkled face is slack and the eye droops.

"New York? The *Times*?" Annette asks.

Looking around, Nora realizes what he wants. The fender. The *finder*. His BlackBerry on the nightstand.

He grunts and shakes his head as she tries to give it to him. He wants Ken to take it. "On!" he directs, watching closely, anxiously, until Ken gets it going. "Day! Day!"

"Which day? Today? Today's Thursday," Ken says.

"No!" Oliver lifts his left hand. "More. One. The one."

"The next day?" Annette asks. "Tomorrow?" She sighs with fatigue.

"Morning!" Oliver says.

A look of helplessness befalls Ken with the realization of what this means, what Oliver needs, what he is asking. Ordering: Ken to take over for him.

"Ed. board, ten thirty. Jannerby at one," Ken reads, scrolling through Oliver's schedule. "Hugh Delaney . . . Chris Ramiriz." An annoyed, put-upon child, he looks up and rolls his eyes with a heavy sigh, like Drew whenever he's asked to clean his room or set the table. This, Nora knows, is the very last thing on earth Ken wants to be doing right now. "Hell," he says with a dismissive flip of his hand. "Every one of these can wait, Oll. You'll be up and at 'em in no time, you'll see." Grinning, Ken pats his unmoving arm.

"No!" Oliver erupts in spittle-foaming, thick-tongued protest. "You! You do the . . . the flings!" His left arm thrashes into the bed rail. "You!"

"All right! I'll do the flings!" Ken says, but when no one smiles or speaks in the strained silence, he looks back sheepishly, leaning close so Oliver can see the BlackBerry. "Here. Okay, the ed. board, now what's up with that? Who knows? Who should I call? Who's best, Goldman?"

Oliver nods and Ken points to the next item on the small bright screen. Annette slips from the room in search of coffee, somehow more dispirited, Nora thinks, than relieved. Even though he's not supposed to be using his cell phone in this part of the hospital, Stephen is checking his messages. Watching the two brothers struggle to communicate, Nora is touched, encouraged by Ken's tenderness. He would never abandon his brother. Or her. Certainly never his children. He can be careless and immature but is incapable of deliberate cruelty. They've turned a corner somehow. These deepening responsibilities will make him a stronger, better man, she thinks, while a part of her, albeit a shrinking part, rattles the bars, demanding to know if she's this desperate, that even her brother-in-law's stroke must be turned to her own advantage?

▪ ▪ ▪

I know," Ken agrees when they get home. Of course he should have
called her when he knew he was running late. "But after the meeting
with Bailey I ran into this guy. An energy consultant. He's been everywhere. The last year mostly in Iraq. Interesting, his take on the whole
thing. The worst thing we can do right now, he said, is pull out. That's
what the sheiks want—"

"Sheiks? You mean mullahs? Sorry," she adds with his quick
glance. "You're probably right." One of the biggest surprises in therapy
was Ken's admission of often feeling undermined by her easy criticism
and "steely" self-assurance. Steely? More like Swiss cheese, thanks to
you, she wanted to say, but didn't. Couldn't, not from this high wire,
anyway, though she has been trying to be more positive. Supportive,
even when the effort chafes.

According to the consultant, there's a deeply entrenched Iraqi un-
derground. It's all about money. Politics and religion are just smoke
screens, Ken declares, because oil is everyone's bottom line. Sunnis,
Shiites, whoever controls the oil flow can bring the free world to its
knees.

"Which is why we're there," Nora says, again too quickly, though
not snidely, she hopes. She and Ken are so often at odds politically that
they long ago declared these kinds of discussions off-limits. Some be-
liefs, though, are knee-jerk, hard to contain. "What's our smoke
screen? Democracy?"

"I wish you could've heard this guy. He makes a lot of sense." Ken
climbs into bed and turns off the light. He is usually the more accom-
modating one during these discussions, while she will push and jab,
keeping the scuffle going to make her point. But now with so much
passion dulled, it's hard to get inflamed over world events. Even this
brief exchange drains her. There are two Noras, the one who reacted
deeply to injustice and cruelty, and this new one with barely enough
energy to face her own problems. Now, everything seems fragile. Su-
perficial. So different from what she once believed. And took for
granted. She hardly knows who she is most days, much less who lies

beside her in bed, this man, husband and stranger. It's like discovering that the tranquil path she has traveled for years has been, and always will be, loaded with land mines. But she has to keep moving. She wants her husband back. Even if it can never be the same. Seeing Oliver tonight makes her realize how uncertain the future is. For all of them.

"Poor Ollie," she says, gropingly through the dark, a poking cane in search of familiar terrain. "It broke my heart seeing him like that, trying to talk."

"I know, but let's not overreact," Ken sighs. "It's probably only temporary. You'll see. These things always seem worse in the beginning."

She's not so sure, but his boyish optimism floods her with warmth. More than anything, she needs to hope again. She wants to be held. She slides her hand close, fingertips aching for his. He yawns, turns on his side, curling away from her. She doesn't blame him. So far, she has rejected his every plea for forgiveness.

"Stephen was beside himself," she says through the darkness, needing to talk, at least. Even more than physical intimacy she feels the loss of this, their emotional intimacy. The easy rhythm that is the closeness of best friends, together almost twenty years.

"Just more of Stephen watching out for Stephen," Ken says, and she turns her head on the pillow.

"That's an odd thing to say. Stephen and Ollie, they're almost as close as you two are."

"He doesn't know his place, that's all." Face against the pillow, his voice is drowsily muffled.

"What do you mean?" she asks too quickly, recalling Stephen's chiding him.

"Nothing really. I don't know, I'm just tired, I guess."

So here it comes, 'round again, with the button pushed, this cycle of racing thoughts. Suspicion. Every word and detail probed for meaning. He resents her distrust, but it's not her fault. He did this, foisted this paranoia on her, destroyed her peace of mind. Robbed her of trust. Biting her lip, she stares up at the half circle of light reflected on the ceiling from the floodlight mounted in the peak of the eave above their window. On timers, this first of the four will go off at twelve, another at twelve thirty, the next at one, then one thirty, an orchestration of vigilance to convince intruders that, inside, someone is up, awake, and very methodically on the half hour dousing each light on a long trek to bed. They only arm the security system when they go away on vacation. Installing it was Ken's idea. He'd grown up with one at Fair-Winds. As children, his parents had themselves been traumatized by reports of the Lindbergh baby kidnapping, then years later, in the fifties, by the abduction and murder of little Bobby Greenlease. And look, Nora thinks, the very worst thing that can happen to a family has come from within.

"Long day, huh?"

He yawns again. "Long meeting. And Bailey, he never shuts up."

"Maybe you can sleep a little later in the morning." Saying it primes the old tenderness and concern.

"Not with Ollie's list, I can't."

"Anything I can help with?" She squeezes the back of his neck, the rigid muscle in his shoulder, and suddenly remembers a day last summer: she and Robin at the club, stretched out on the bright yellow chaise lounges by the kiddy pool, laughing as Lyra splashed them, then Ken joining them, hot and dusty, just off the course, and surprisingly irritable, complaining about his lousy game, his sore back, and Robin hopped up and began kneading his shoulders, while he leaned forward on the edge of the chaise, groaning with pleasure. And naïve Nora, stupid Nora, looking on, grinning foolishly, not suspicious in the least; pleased, in fact. Delighted. Such dear friends, weren't they all? Their children, as close as cousins. And how like a sister Robin seemed, the exuberant, approving sister she'd never had in caustic Carol. Don't feel like cooking, call up Robin and Bob, and they'd all meet at Ginzu, to watch the Japanese chef catching eggs in his toque and juggling knives while he prepared their dinner on the flaming stovetop, with Clay's and Drew's wisecracks making everyone laugh while Chloe fussed over Lyra, always braiding her hair, teaching her new songs. And deep down, Nora's juvenile pleasure in being the envied object of the most popular girl's attention. If you were going to invite the Gendrons, you *had* to invite the Hammonds, everyone knew that. Such fun couples, so close they finish each other's sentences. And all the while . . . all the while . . . no, can't think like this as she inches closer, slowly, so he won't know she's doing it. His rejection would destroy her.

"I'll be all right." Silence. "But thanks," he adds in a drifting, ragged voice.

"So where'd you run into that guy? The other one." *Don't fall asleep. Talk to me. Please, the way we used to. About anything. For hours into the night. Fill this emptiness, this stark aloneness. This secret well.*

"Hmm?"

"The energy guy, where'd you run into him?" Her knee grazes his leg, and she feels him tense up.

"At this place. I forget the name. Dive, really. God, after Bailey, all I wanted was one beer in silence."

"What's his name? The energy guy."

"Ed."

"Ed what?"

"Hawkins. I think that's what he said."

"What did he want?" She can't move. Or breathe.

"Just to talk. He's only been back a couple weeks . . . well . . . anyway—" His voice fades, and her fingernails gouge her arms.

CHAPTER 13

Escape. Work, the last outpost of control. Safe at her desk since early morning, hours before Hilda, she is outlining articles for the *Holiday* supplement. Won't come out until November. Far enough away to keep her mind off Eddie Hawkins and not knowing anymore which is more real, that night in the desert or her memory of it. If hers is the only valid version, then what is his? The truth, or a lie? Only one can be right. And yet, however it happened, that is exactly the way she has always remembered it. Something violent happened in that car, a crime that stands as its own immutable reality, however inaccessible now with the passage of time. So in the end, the relative truth of both their versions may be the one undeniable fact here. One victim, two killers.

Eddie's meeting with Ken has dissolved any hope she had of getting past this. No matter how delusional or cunning he is, the force of his twisted tale taints everything. What else is false? Has it all been her own chimeric creation, the good wife, good family, her own decency? *Because I'm so weak and scared, this poison seeps into my life, and there's no stopping it without destroying everything. My poor mother, even she had to suffer. My God, here I go again. I can't think straight.* She's told Hilda that if he comes again, she'll see him. And this time she'll be ready.

She forces herself to thumb through previous supplements. This year instead of one or two cooking pages they will publish a booklet-sized insert of holiday recipes from local cooks. Hilda has spent the last few days calling and e-mailing local clubs and church groups, requesting recipes. The response is surprising, if not a little overwhelming. It suddenly occurs to Nora that all the recipes will have to be tested. In the past it was easy finding staff willing to try out the eight or ten they ran, but now there'll be twenty or twenty-five. And who will do that? She makes a quick note to discuss it with Hilda who loves to cook. It would mean overtime, and, of course, the paper would reimburse her for ingredients. *Check Xmas supp $ with O.* she scribbles on another note, sticks both Post-its to her monitor.

Her own attention to detail along with the brilliance of Oliver's overview has made them an effective team. But now with Ken in charge, things are already different. He means well and he is certainly trying to do his best to run the paper in his brother's absence, but his casual approach makes her uneasy. "No big deal": Ken's mantra. If he said it once at the last editorial meeting he said it easily a dozen times. She was probably being overly sensitive, but couldn't help noticing the bemused glances and raised eyebrows around the table whenever he spoke. Everything has always been a big deal to Oliver. No detail escapes his scrutiny. Typos infuriate him, but factual errors are completely unacceptable. Having to run corrections enrages him. He likens it to hanging one's dirty underpants out on the line for everyone to see. An overstatement, she knows. Honest mistakes come with the pressure of getting a story written for deadline-driven editors, but Oliver's old-fashioned ethics are the bedrock of the paper's integrity. Because he involves himself in every department and in all the big local stories, reporters don't even try to do favors, quashing or burying stories, or tweaking facts to make someone look, usually not even better, but less offensive. Until his stroke he was still complaining about Ken trying to soft-pedal the CraneCopley scandal. Oliver has his own prejudices and failings, but truth has always been sacred to him. His private life might be untidy, his domestic situation bewildering, but no one can question his professional probity. And now, how ironic, how cruel, after a lifetime devoted to the precision of language, to be deprived of it, she thinks, seeing her message button flash red.

"Yes," Hilda answers, guardedly, as if to a question, though none has been asked. "There's someone here. Mr. Hawkins."

"Yes. Send him in."

His suit is linty and rumpled. His shirt is wrinkled. The door closes in a draft of stale clothes and sweaty cologne. She's strangely relieved. He's here. The storm having hit is not the gale she feared. Just ordinary, as if it's already spun itself out. A fading turbulence. He seems older, and weary. It was a week and a half ago that Ken mentioned meeting him. Every day since she glances back over her shoulder before getting into her car, steels herself when the phone rings. Last night Drew and Chloe were studying for midterms. Around ten o'clock they decided to order pizza. The doorbell rang a while later, startling Nora from a deep sleep. Certain it was him she jumped out of bed and flew down the hallway. All she could see over the railing was Chloe and, in the doorway, a shadowy man.

"Get away from him! Don't let him in!" With her screams, Drew ran in from the kitchen and Ken burst out of the bedroom.

"Mom!" Chloe shouted, holding out the pizza box. "It's pizza, that's all. It's just pizza."

Ken led her back to bed. "See," he teased, opening the closet door and then lifting the bed skirt. "No bogeyman."

Without being asked, Eddie sits down. "Sorry about your brother-in-law. How is he?"

"Better, thank you." She won't be unnerved. Glancing at him, she opens her bottom drawer. She slides out the large envelope and slips it, unseen, onto her lap. Every move has been planned. She knows what must be done. She knows she never hit that drunken man. It was Eddie wielding the pipe, just as it is his brazen bandying of the outrageous lie, repeating the same facts with enough conviction that makes her doubt herself. If she has learned nothing else in her newspaper experience, it is how easily facts can be distorted to change the story. Truth is an absolute, but with tentacles. As long as there are multiple viewpoints, there can be no one true story. Memory abrades the jagged edges, fills in the holes. Her truth of events that night may have been clouded by alcohol, fear, and abhorrence. But his is the twisted connivance of a desperate man. A liar, and an unstable one.

She has to protect her family, fragile as it is right now. She can't call the police. What would she say, that an unwelcome ghost from her past keeps showing up? That she wants him gotten rid of? The only crime is the one he accuses her of. And how on earth can she defend herself after all this time? Far better to make it worth a con man's while by giving him what he really wants. Before, when she offered money he became enraged, so she needs to wend her way to that point. In an interview her surest tool was always empathy. And the unspoken suggestion of friendship.

"You're still here." She tries to smile, but his grin is disturbing. Greasy somehow, exuding a film into the air between them.

"You sound surprised." He picks up the paperweight. "Or disappointed, I'm not sure which."

"It can be pretty dull around here. You're probably used to a lot more—"

"Oh, there's a lot here. A lot going on." His mouth is less smile than slow, gum-chewing trap of his jaw. "You just have to know where to look."

"Yes. Well, I suppose that's true anywhere, isn't it?"

He shrugs. "Pretty much." He rubs his thumb over the convex glass, the knuckle whitening with pressure. "But you, you got your finger on the pulse, right?" With a gesture, the sweep of his hand reduces everything to insignificance. The deep red and blue Persian carpet, the antique console and alabaster lamps, Annette's oil paintings, props to authenticate her false life. "Can't get much more informed than a newspaper, right?"

"There's a lot we don't know." Her desk drawer rattles as she jams her knees up into the bottom of it.

"Yeah?" He chuckles. "Well, that makes sense. I mean, who's gonna come running in with their own dirty, little secrets, right?"

Blackmail. She's relieved. At least they're headed in the same direction. *That* she can deal with. Her fifteen thousand and ten thousand more from Ken, who thinks it's to help poor, abandoned Carol pay her bills. "You'd be surprised, Eddie." Forces herself to say the name, just old acquaintances catching up, bridging the gap of lost time. "Sometimes people need to. They need to bare their souls. Getting it all out can be a great relief." Purgative, she almost adds.

"You think so." Staring, he pushes his tongue through his gum, makes a little pop, then removes the green wad from his mouth, and sticks it up under her desk. "Well then, that makes everything a hell of a lot easier." He's studying her. "See, one night I'm in this bar." He grimaces. "Real skunky, you know, not the kind of place I'd—"

"Expect to meet my husband?"

He grins. "Yeah. Exactly."

"You didn't run into him, though, did you?" she says coolly so he'll know she's not quite the easy mark he thinks. "You followed him there. You wanted to meet him. No. What you wanted was for me to know you'd met him."

"Actually? I was thinking of it. But the girlfriend, hey, I wasn't expecting that."

Dullness descends. Mental jet lag, this odd detachment, like suddenly finding herself in another time zone. Trying to think straight, groping through fog. All his promises. The night of Oliver's stroke. More lies. He'd been with *her*.

"You got yourself a situation, huh? You know"—again, his raspy chuckle—"I'm sitting there, watching, and I'm thinking, what the hell's your problem, buddy? Someone like Nora, and you're out skanking around? I don't get it." He shakes his head. "You deserve better than that."

His concern is loathsome. He's despicable, and so is she, lowering herself to his level. Once again. But this time she has no choice. Her hand shakes as she places the envelope on the desk. *My God, all this money.* It should be going to a better cause, Sojourn House, the food bank, anyone, but what does it even matter anymore? Ken and Robin are still together. Her life is a lie. Here. It's for him, she explains, keeping to her script. Knows her lines. Rote to sustain her until reason returns, and calm. She understands how difficult it's been for him all these years, and how in need of help he must be. This way, it'll be a fresh start—

"A fresh start?" The paperweight lands with a chilling thump.

If he goes away and never comes back. But she's afraid to say it.

"So it's okay? It's all right? You don't give a shit about anyone, do you?" Squinting, he stares at her.

She coughs to fill the void in this bizarre dialogue. Again, slowly, tries to restate her offer. He needs help, which she is in a position to provide.

"So, that's it?" He shrugs.

"Whatever happened that night is—"

"What? Shit? Because shit happens, right? So, what do you care?"

"Of course, I care. I've never forgotten. I remember everything, every detail."

He looks surprised, flattered. "Yeah. Me, too. I still dream about it. About you. Our song, remember?" He wets his lips in a kind of kiss, starts singing the words, then, seeing her cringe back in her chair, whispers, "It's just you were so young. So fresh and soft and—"

"Stop it! Please," she whispers with a horrified glance at the door, praying the shadow underneath isn't Hilda's.

He laughs. "Smart, that's all I was gonna say. And classy. You still are." He wiggles his fingers. "Different from her, the girlfriend. Quite a looker though, gotta give him that."

"Here." She touches the envelope.

"What's that?"

"Cash."

He smiles. "How much?"

She writes on her *Chronicle* notepad and gives him the sheet: *$25,000.* "Should take care of it, I would think," she says almost lightly, in case Hilda is listening.

"Take care of what?" he asks folding the paper into his pocket. "You finally gonna hire me? Give me a job?" He laughs. "To do what? Get rid of hubby?"

"This has nothing to do with him."

"Really? You don't matter? He can go do whatever the hell he wants?" He leans over the desk, leering. "Oh! I get it." He rubs his thumb and forefinger together. "The girlfriend. Yeah. Okay. Her name's Robin. Robin Gendron, right?" he says.

"That's not important. She doesn't matter."

"Oh? Maybe you oughta tell hubby that."

"I told you, this isn't about him."

"Yeah, just between you and me, right? But then what?"

"I'm sure you'll find something, some other place to start over." Sickened by its touch, she pushes the envelope closer. "Here. It's yours. Take it."

Laughing, he waves it between them. "Gotcha! For all the pain and suffering. Cold, hard cash, just make sure the door don't hitcha in your ass on the way out, Eddie."

"I really should get back to work now," she says with a stern glance. That's all, she will later recall. A glance.

He gets up, but continues to stand over her. He keeps slapping the envelope on the edge of her desk. "Must be nice being rich. Buy anything you want, huh? Little problem comes your way, just stuff an envelope full of cash and close your eyes."

The door closes softly. Quietly. She covers her mouth and sits there, trying not to gag.

Carol has called back. She wants to come out and stay with Nora. She needs to get away, she says. Nora was right. It's not good being alone, all this thinking, obsessing on the past. But whether Nora wants to hear it or not, every single thing she said the other day is true. And being older, she would know, certainly more than Nora. Everyone tried to talk to Mom, even the cousins. After Nora ran away she finally came to her senses, thank God. This time Nora refuses to argue with her sister. Her decision to work at the lake that summer was to get as far away as she could from her guilt every time she looked at her mother. And running away with Eddie Hawkins was in no way connected to Mr. Blanchard.

"Things're a little crazy here right now," Nora tells her, doesn't say why. She'll get back to her in a few weeks. Hopefully, they can settle on a date then.

The worst sin is vanity," her mother would say whenever she or Carol fretted over some personal problem. Self-absorption, because it got in the way of so much else, kindness, charity, love. And the truth. "If you're busy helping other people, then you don't have time for petty problems."

If only she had her mother's strength. Never complaining. Trying hard to be a good teacher and conscientious mother, who put her daughters first, then her students, her only luxury, meeting her unmarried cousins in the city for lunch once a month. She keeps thinking how alone her mother must have felt when Nora's father died. Was it this same emptiness, she wonders, emptying the dryer in the laundry room. Her father died loving her mother, so at least she had that. Even without the physical presence the memory of love can be a source of strength, a comfort like prayer. Nora has a husband, but not his love, though he would probably deny that. Mired, Stephen said. She is an obligation. But Ken is a man of his word. He will do right by her. It's the way he was raised, the way his father managed all his affairs. Sadly, this is her assurance now, she thinks, folding the warm towels.

She is remembering her own father's funeral, all the outfits she tried on before choosing the red sailor dress, the brass buttons with anchors, white piping and blue stars on the square bib over her shoulders. "Aye, matey," her father had saluted, the last time she wore it. She remembers being confused by her mother's reaction, shocked, grabbing her arm, hissing, because the Boston cousins were downstairs waiting with Carol, "What're you doing? Take it off! You look ridiculous!"

Stung, she tried to explain. "But Daddy likes me to wear this."

"It's not appropriate. Take it off."

"No!"

It was the first time her mother ever slapped her. She closes her eyes against the memory of the next, years later. Still can't bear remembering. She's forgotten what she did end up wearing to the funeral but remembers the burning heat that day, the brilliant sunshine, and the eerie displacement, her sense of being caught in another dimension, a discordant reality as if the car she'd been in had come to a wrenching stop, though trees and houses and people continued to blur past the windows. Grief had exposed an acute sentience. Death had made her too alive, too receptive, every nerve quickening with sensation. She remembers the sting of holy water on her smarting cheek with the priest's blessing and the painfully horsey gulp of Carol's sobs during "Amazing Grace." She still remembers the dissonant skirl of birds chirping as the family shuffled after the flag-draped casket out of the small, crowded church, her dizziness in the sudden blinding glare, then at the quiet gravesite her knees buckling with the wormy smell of hot dirt. And afterward the noisy, smoky gathering, the party they called a mercy meal, saying it under her breath, *mercy, mercy, mercy meal,* like a prayer, a plea, over and over through the knotty pine–paneled VFW hall, pausing by her father's poker buddies shocked by his sudden death, but seeking solace in the old stories, their beery, heads-back laughter with each tale told, then, finally, on to the old woman gesturing from a table, her father's testy aunt Louise, raising her fork of macaroni salad to ask what those little green flecks were, onions or celery, because she couldn't eat onions, they made her throw up, and why on earth did people have to put onions in everything anyway when all they did was agitate your insides and sour the mayonnaise. And how good that was to hear, what a relief for the young girl at the mercy meal to be snagged back among the living.

Life was tough, so you squared your shoulders and kept putting one foot in front of the other. Only high honors and Girls' State for Marina Trimble's daughters. Scholarships through school. Work hard, study hard, protect the little that's left. Her mother had been promoted to assistant English department head at the high school. Nora was sixteen, the late spring night when Mr. Blanchard came by the house to take her mother out to dinner. Everything about it was shocking to Nora. He seemed so young compared to her mother. The idea of her mother's wanting to be with a man, even four years after her father's death, was reprehensible, as much a violation of her father's memory, as a threat. She couldn't stop thinking of the flesh of the most vital and sacred person in her life touching another man's, even just his hand brushing hers. Worse though, and equally as inappropriate as the red dress, was her mother's dating someone from Nora's delicately balanced universe, the shy new English teacher, who quoted Emily Dickinson, "Hope is the thing with feathers / That perches in the soul" while her own heart ached for his attention.

"He flirts with all the girls," she told her mother the next morning. Actually, it was the girls who giggled about Mr. Blanchard's curly hair, long eyelashes, and quiet voice, the bolder among them clamoring for extra help. And then, when that didn't work, the lie, telling her mother that some senior girls were thinking of going to the principal because of things Mr. Blanchard had said to them. And done.

What things? her mother demanded, and Nora can still see the arch of her mother's long neck, feel her breath, caught, waiting. Things, Nora said, watching, gauging the impact of her words. You know, suggestive. It seemed minutes before her mother finally turned.

"I've been a teacher long enough to know the way a student's imagination can work."

"It's not imagination," Nora protested. "It's true. He's always bumping up against girls."

"That can happen. Innocently enough. He's a very nice person, and, as a matter of fact, I'll probably go out with him again. A rumor's an ugly thing, Nora," her mother said, her face reddening, whether with anger or doubt, but the quick tremble saying her daughter's name was lure enough to send Nora in for the kill.

"All right then, I'll tell you. He . . . he—"

"He what?"

"Rubbed against me. You know," she said with a squeamish gesture, low, down there.

"When? What on earth are you talking about?"

"A couple weeks ago. I stayed after. My Emily Dickinson report, he said to. For extra help."

"And?"

"It was awful," she said, bursting into tears because without solid ground underfoot there was no turning back. It was a lie already too nasty to retrieve, too shameful to admit. "And even now, every time I think about it I don't know what to do. It's so embarrassing. It's humiliating. You can't say anything. Please. Promise me you won't." Her mother's wounded eyes told her that this could not be the end of it. Mr. Blanchard would have to be confronted. He had violated not only his student's trust but hers as well, his fellow teacher, his department's assistant head, the lonely woman he'd taken to dinner and so desperately kissed in the car, in the late evening shadows with Nora watching from her bedroom window.

Only her threats of running away, then of suicide, some made in repeated, frantic, whispered phone calls in the middle of the night to Carol, stopped her mother from the inquisition, the school board hearing the matter deserved. Yes, Carol agreed with her mother, the man was a pervert and deserved to be fired, but at what cost—Nora's emotional well-being? Instead, a second-year contract was denied softspoken, bewildered Mr. Blanchard, who left that June and would have been such a fine friend, lover, partner for her mother, whose quiet life spiraled in on itself. She taught, saw Nora through school, a brief career, and marriage, retired, took the train into the city once a month for lunch with the last of the spinster cousins, then died in her sleep, in her cold bed, alone. Nora buries her face in the warm fragrant towel. Guilt, one more reason to hate herself. No clarity with the well disturbed. Only sediment. Particles. Can't tell anyone, can only pray he's gone, Eddie Hawkins, the roused beast of an unpunished deed, while in the next room her children laugh, playing cards with their father, the liar, as she stands here surrounded by their underpants and shirts, folding three more facecloths, sea-foam green, from the master bath, a room she hates with its pale green tile, the gold flecks ruining everything. How could she not have noticed, not have known? It was the last room done, and something was wrong, she just didn't know what then, two years ago, insisting that he help her choose fixtures, deal with the surly plumber, go horseback riding, climb Mt. Monadnock with the children, anything that they could do together.

Telling her not to be so paranoid. Of course he wasn't upset with her. Tired, that was all. Just tired. How ridiculous. He wasn't growing distant. Didn't she know how much she hurt him when she said things like that? The sea-foam facecloths and tile, proof of her inadequacy, like her marriage, interfering in her mother's life, running away. The next shirt from the dryer, his, the liar's. Softly old and worn, his favorite T-shirt. It's from the club. Some tournament. FAIRWINDS 2000 in pale blue stitching. The seam is frayed. One more wash and it'll tear. She tosses it into the mending basket, then takes it out. Why does she care? Or does she want him to need this shirt as proof of something enduring between them, her way of feeling needed? Valued. Cooking his favorite food. Tonight, stuffed chicken breasts and garlic mashed potatoes. Pathetic, this groveling, this being a woman, mother, wife, trying to hold everything together, she thinks with a tug on the sleeve, this fury of pulling, ripping, tearing to pieces. Rags. And he won't even notice. A storm of little consequence, lint and bits of thread drifting onto the counter. He won't even know. Only she will. The keeper of rags.

"Rummy!" Ken shouts, and Chloe squeals in protest at his going out so soon. Drew's complaint is indistinct. How can they still love him? she thinks bitterly, but humiliated by her own complicity for leaving the deck of cards on the dinner table, bait, like the T-shirt and his ancient loafers she has the cobbler stitch and reheel every six months, so she can stake him down, securing whatever she can grasp, the little she has of him.

He swears he hasn't been seeing Robin. He was only with her the night of Oliver's stroke because of Bob's accident. Bob had been on his way home when he hit a patch of ice, going too fast. His car skidded into a private school van stopped at a red light. There were eight children inside. Thank God, no one was seriously hurt, mostly just bruises, but a real wakeup call. Bob wasn't drunk, but he'd been drinking earlier, so he panicked and didn't stop. A witness wrote down his plate number. By the time the police came to the house, Bob's brothers were already driving him to the usual rehab hospital in New Hampshire. A glass of cabernet and a bad reaction to a sleeping medication, or so the brothers claimed. Robin called Ken, begging him to keep it out of the paper. His job at CraneCopley was in jeopardy as it was. The reporter Ken spoke to omitted the incident from the *Chronicle*'s police log.

"Poor guy," Ken said. "It was the least I could do."

"No," she couldn't help saying. "The least you could do is stay away from his wife."

She doesn't believe his lies, but what she needs is to believe in him. Whether a shift in the wind or galvanic realignment, something is different. Something has changed. He seems, if not happier, certainly calmer. Of course, Nora can't help wondering if it's Bob's absence that buoys his spirits, but in any event, the effect on the children has been immediate and gratifying. Once again, Chloe and her dad are buddies. Drew's bitterness and anger seem to be easing. Tonight at dinner Chloe told them that her girlfriend Luz's little sister wants to ask Drew to the Sophomore Spring Mixer.

"But don't worry," Chloe said when Drew groaned. "I told her you already have a girlfriend."

"Who? Who'd you say?" Drew asked, and Nora tensed, expecting an outburst.

"You know. Aimée," Chloe said, pursing her lips for full Gallic effect.

"Jhell-ee-no," Drew said, his exaggerated pronunciation making them laugh.

Aimée Gelineau was an old family joke, a kindergarten classmate Drew had declared his love for, then wept when her family returned to Quebec. Even at such a young age he'd been heartbroken. She wishes he had a real Aimée Gelineau in his life, at least one person to be close to. Tonight is the first time in weeks she's heard him laugh.

CHAPTER · 14

Nothing is as soothing as the sound of Robin's voice. Eddie can listen for hours. Nothing gets her down. Not the chaos of Lyra's toys all over the floor or the chicken bones in greasy napkins and the half-filled takeout boxes still on the coffee table, not even the collection agency call. Another maxed-out credit card, she explains, hanging up, one more mess of Bob's left behind. It's so hard now, having to watch every penny, buying store brands when, before, she'd just grab whatever she wanted off the shelf, not having a clue what anything cost. Of course, she can't just blame him, she sees that now, how spoiled they both were, taking everything for granted. That's the problem growing up with money: hard times came and they just kept on spending; it's so confusing, such a helpless feeling, not having control anymore of the most basic things in life, which is why she always reads the price tags to Lyra. She may be only three, but Robin wants her to know the value of things and not feel entitled. And having to scrape by makes Robin appreciate life even more. She wakes up every morning, knowing what a gift each new day is. It really is.

Yes, and for him, too. Especially now that he's flush. He's never had this much money in his pocket. Tonight, he brought dinner over: KFC. The simplest things delight her.

The past is like a dream, she is saying, and once a dream is over, it's gone, right? What's important is living in the moment. This, the right here and now, she declares with such intensity that as he sinks into her blue gaze he knows he'd do anything for her, anything. It's taken her years to see this, she says. Her mother worries that she may be over-medicated. Instead of just drifting along on Prozac and Xanax, she should be talking to someone, a counselor. The very suspicious Mrs. Shawcross called her daughter a little while ago with the name of a therapist her hairdresser recommended.

"She says I'm just existing, not dealing with anything, but that's okay. As long as my children are happy and I'm here with them, what more do I need?"

"What's she want you to do?" he asks, uneasily.

"Oh, just love my husband," she says with a forced lilt. Her daughter sits at her feet, watching television.

"What else?"

"Live happily ever after." She sighs.

"Yeah?"

"It's kinda way past that now."

He met her mother a few days ago when he stopped by with two boxes of cookies. He had remembered Robin's saying money was so tight right now with Bob in the hospital and no more sick time, that she could barely afford treats for the children.

"Aren't you sweet!" Robin said, patting his cheek through the doorway.

Suddenly Mrs. Shawcross appeared, her narrowed eyes cued to the distrust in his.

He and Robin were quick friends. Two old souls, she likes to say. His head spins listening, trying to keep up. He blinks. Sparks in her voice, veering from topic to topic. His heart races. Images flash into mind, churning thoughts, twisted metal and broken glass, goose feathers red with blood, the black arch of a penciled eyebrow. No way, he keeps thinking. Not this time.

Trusting, she holds nothing back. Her truth is childlike in its raw purity. Not like nervous Nora, all that money and still can't have what she wants. She doesn't stand a chance. No wonder, he thinks, hating the two men. Robin is talking about her husband's drinking. This time when he gets out he'll stay sober, swears he will. Still thinks he can, she says with a sigh.

"He doesn't deserve you," he snaps, resenting her concern for the weak bastard.

"It's not just him. Poor Bob, he doesn't want to hear it, and I can't say it."

"What? Say what?" His fidgety fingers twist and turn.

She stares at him. "It's such a mess."

"So do something about it." Hard to hide his impatience. Just an old friend, she said when he asked who Hammond was, the guy in the bar that night.

"I know. I have to. I know that." She looks down a moment, troubled.

"Can I help? What can I do?"

"No. Same thing, it's me." She sighs. "Just gotta get my act together, that's all."

Lyra changes the channel and they sit quietly for a while, watching another cartoon. Robin seems lost in thought. She often does this, the half smile, staring as if she is suddenly somewhere else, or wants to be. She has three cats and loves to go barefoot. The largest, the gray and white cat, jumps onto the couch and settles between them, purring. Cat hair floats through the air, and he holds his breath, trying not to move. The slightest disturbance, an opening door, sets it adrift. When he leaves, his clothes are covered. The tail flips back and forth, whipping up more hair. He picks a strand from his mouth. Cats don't like him, he says.

"Here." She takes his hand and places it on the cat's back. The purring stops.

"Smoky!" Lyra cries, startled as the cat springs past her head and runs from the room.

"He's scared because you are," Robin chides with a pouty look. "He can tell."

He never had a pet, it was all he could do taking care of himself, he snaps back. He feels accused. Judged. He takes deep breaths. Can barely look at her for fear of losing it. He should leave, but doesn't. Can't. His scalp shrinks on his skull. The frantic cartoon voices pitch higher, shriller, faster. He can't think straight. Can't stand being turned on like this.

"Not having a mother, I can't imagine it." Her eyes fill up, blind to his agitation.

"Your mother, she doesn't like me."

"It's not you," she says, with a shrug, and leans closer. "It's me. My judgment. Or lack thereof," she laughs.

"Meaning me, right?"

"No!" She laughs. "Eddie! Why would you say that?" She touches his arm. "Eddie?"

"I can tell, that's all."

What began as rejection ends the way it must, whenever the quest is meaningful. It is an obsession and he accepts it as such, not a flaw or illness to be defeated with padlocks and pills, but a strength. All he seeks in this jangled universe are connections. While others lose their way, puzzling over randomness, he easily recognizes patterns, link-ages, preordained paths only the few, the gifted, ever find. Through perseverance.

Robin thinks their meeting happenstance. Serendipitous, she de-clares again. Her blonde hair is pulled loosely back. Stray wisps frame her face. Like a teenager with her turned-up nose and legs tucked under her. An athletic teenager. She is running again and works out every morning in her friend's home gym. Her slender fingers sift ab-sently through her daughter's fine, pale hair. Lyra wears silky pink Cinderella pajamas and sits on the floor in front of her mother. The child is beautiful. She was there when he found her mother. On the playground. Easy enough. Everyone in town knows Robin Gendron. He watched from the car a few times, watched her hang from the monkey bars to make the little girl laugh. Even in the bitter cold she wore sandals and a bulky sweater, no coat. She dresses Lyra the same way. Skirts, bare legs, that day, a thin red cotton jacket. They're never cold. And never apart, she tells him. Clay is another matter. Sports or out with friends, her son is seldom here. It bothers her, but she tries to understand. It's his age, rebellion, part of growing up. He won't listen to anyone. Bob's no help. Clay can't stand his father's drinking. In a way, it's almost like not having one, a father he respects, anyway. That's when she wishes he doesn't come back. Bob, she means. He barely speaks to Lyra. Her sweet baby girl.

There is something on television now about 9/11. Black smoke pouring from the Twin Towers. All those poor people killed, it makes her cry. Every time she thinks of it, the husbands who never came home, the babies who'll never know their daddies. Even though she can't afford it, she sent a hundred dollars to the Republican Party. She doesn't like the war in Iraq, but Americans should stick together and support their president through these dangerous times, don't you think? she asks him. Everything ends with asking, caring what he thinks. Really? Don't you? she adds. Yes, he replies. Of course, he agrees, thinks so, if only just to continue watching her hypnotic mouth and the little pink dart of her tongue. George Bush, he's a good man in a crazy world, she insists as if arguing with an unseen presence. He's caught in a situation beyond his control. Some things just take time, that's all, time to work themselves out. Poor George, he reminds her of someone, she says, an old friend, decent, upbeat, misunderstood. Sighing, she stares at the flashing screen.

"Scattered!" she announces. "That's what my mother called me. All over the place. Because I told her about last night. Valerie."

Valerie is the old crone she met in the supermarket. They were in the same checkout line, chatting easily, the way people do with Robin. "That looks good," Robin remarked of the old woman's Lean Cuisine Oriental chicken and rice, moving along the black mat. The old woman said Robin should try it sometime. It was delicious and going to be her dinner that night. Naturally, Robin insisted she come home with her instead, for spaghetti and meatballs. Eddie arrived at the tail end of dinner, annoyed to find someone else there, invited, instead of him. Robin's eyes were red. She had already had three good cries, hearing about Valerie's husband's long and painful ordeal with cancer, then the funeral nobody came to, not even his own four children who weren't hers, though she'd helped raise the last one, a girl with a club foot. Granted, he'd been a hard man to live with, demanding. "But for no one to come. To not even care how I'm doing," Valerie said, shaking her head. "I'm not over it yet."

"Well, we care," Robin said, putting her arm over the stout woman's blocky shoulders. "We care very much, Valerie."

And as much as he didn't want to, he found himself offered up to drive Valerie home. Everything about her repulsed him. The yellow tennis balls jammed onto the legs of her walker, the way her teeth clicked, the food stains on her pink nylon shirt, the unwashed sourness of her clothes. He enjoyed her glassy-eyed fear in the mirror when he wouldn't answer her. Why should he talk, she was lucky to be getting a ride home. In her rush to get out of his car, her grocery bag spilled open. Cans rolled along the slushy sidewalk in front of her building in the elderly housing project. She was still picking them up as he drove away. I'm sorry, he'll say if it comes up. Wish I'd known. She's lucky he didn't shove her stinking carcass out of his car, which bothers him that he's still driving it, that is. Shouldn't be so careless. He's had it too long. Mostly, he keeps it in a secluded spot behind the Monserrat, the seedy motel off the highway. Again last night the morose manager put a note under his door telling him to park out front. The back lot is for deliveries. He knows he should get another car, one that can't be traced, but he likes the heated seats and Bose speakers, now even the Céline Dion CD. One more hassle in a life of hassles. Eddie's getting tired of hassles.

They are watching *SpongeBob SquarePants*. When it's over Lyra has to go to bed, Robin says on her way into the kitchen.

"You mind your mother now," he warns quietly, but the child ignores him. She and her mother share a private universe. Even her brother is excluded. Clay plays varsity basketball and tonight's an away game in Abbeyton. He wanted his mother to go, but she said it was too late for Lyra, who is still up. The boy isn't home much, but when he is he's sullen and rude. Yesterday Robin made him apologize when he muttered, "Yeah, right," after Eddie talked about playing pro basketball in Greece years ago. Like his grandmother, the boy is a distraction. But a minor one as long as Eddie has plenty of money and the company of a beautiful woman.

With the barrage of popping comes the smell of hot buttery popcorn. He hasn't felt this content in years. From here he watches her moving around the kitchen. She removes the steaming bag from the microwave. She empties it into a large red and white striped bowl, then carries it into the family room. She sits back down and pats the other cushion for Lyra to climb onto so they can share the popcorn. Lyra giggles every time a squid hiccups. Robin laughs too and nuzzles the top of the child's head. Robin knows all the characters' names. As the credits roll mother and daughter sing the theme song.

Agitated, Eddie checks his watch. Almost nine. Yet another cartoon. Lyra eats her popcorn one kernel at a time. She wipes her nose on her sleeve. Jesus. Her snot is running green. Usually Robin lets her fall asleep down here, then carries her up to bed. Otherwise, she has to lie down with Lyra. A bad habit, Robin admits, but it's the only way she can fall asleep now. He asks how far away Abbeyton is. He'd like some time alone with her. Not too far, she says. Ten or twelve miles. This reminds her of something. She frowns. His brother, she says, did he call him yet? He looks at her. Blankly. A beat. Then remembers. The troubled brother in California, his dead wives. He can't remember his name, though, but it's different this time; he doesn't always have to be on guard. Her easy acceptance and infectious enthusiasm bring out the best in him. She is so positive about everyone and everything, as quick to laugh as she is moved to tears, that he can almost believe he has a brother. He did call, he says, but no one answered.

"Maybe he's in the hospital again," she says.

"Maybe." He slips his arm over the back of the couch, his fingertips so near her shoulder he can feel her heat.

"I don't know," she sighs. "This is Bob's fourth rehab. The problem is, it's always about something else. First, was to keep his job. Then, because of me—my ultimatum: what's it gonna be, drinking or me? Catchy, huh? I like that." She tilts her head from side to side in silent rhythm. "Maybe we could do that, an Al-Anon theme song. Anyway." Sighing, she stares dismally at the television.

Now he remembers. Woody, the invented brother, short for Woodruff. Yeah. Poor Woody, born that way, same as him, too intense.

Sensitive. He knows what people are thinking without them saying a word. Like right now, she wants to tell him something. He can feel it, something important. She has yet to discuss her affair with him. Every time he mentions running into her that night with Hammond, she goes silent. For all her openness, that is the one subject off limits.

Lyra sneezes and snuggles closer to her mother. Robin pulls a tattered plaid throw from the arm of the couch and covers her with it. Lyra coughs, a deep, tight cough. "You feel all right, baby?" Robin murmurs, laying her cheek against Lyra's brow.

"My head hurts," Lyra whines, then lies down with her head in her mother's lap, her knees to her chin. She is asleep in minutes.

Smiling, Robin continues stroking her face, her love for this child so intense that he stirs with anger. If she cares too much, what will be left for him? Her kindness to others leaves him feeling bereft, deprived. He offers to carry Lyra upstairs. She's fine right here, Robin says, stroking her forehead.

"No!" he says, and Robin looks at him, startled. "She should be in her own bed. It's so late."

"I know. You're right. It's me. I just love having her near," she says, picking her up. The child's limbs dangle from her mother's arms and her head hangs back, limply. Lifeless, he thinks with a rush, watching her being carried away.

The phone rings. Robin's voice. He stands at the bottom of the stairs, but can't make out what she's saying. It's him. The boyfriend. Ken. He knows by her tone. Tender, intimate, a voice in the dark, in bed, fucking. His throat burns.

She returns, frowning. She thinks Lyra has a temperature but can't bear waking her up. Lyra hates taking medicine. She gags on everything, poor baby. Her voice quavers as she picks up a large plastic dollhouse and carries it across the room. She walks carefully but the furniture inside rattles as she sets it down on the hearth.

"Or maybe it's me. I'm such a bad mother," she sighs, looking back at the stairs.

"No you're not. She's probably not even sick. She looked fine to me." He doesn't want her back down here.

"I don't know, it's just everything lately, it's all so . . . so messed up."
Face flushed, she takes a deep breath. "I just wish he wouldn't call me
like that," she whispers, then drops down in the opposite chair. "It gets
me so upset."

"Tell him not to. Tell him it's over, you're done. You don't need
that," he says angrily, remembering the first time he saw her. For days,
he'd been telling himself he should be on his way. No sense pressing
his luck, the car was a real liability, the license plate, anyway, but for
some reason he couldn't seem to get going. He had begun following
Hammond. His initial curiosity turning to fascination, an almost
physical attraction, less to the man than to all that he is, all that he pos-
sesses, his own newspaper, an amazing house, someone like Nora. His
car alone cost eighty-nine thousand dollars. One person shouldn't
have all that, he thought, growing angrier as he tailed Hammond from
the paper down a road to Robin's silver minivan idling by a snow-
covered soccer field. From a distance he saw Hammond park behind
her and climb into the minivan. Fifteen or twenty minutes later,
Hammond got back into his own car, then followed her to the bar.
Eddie ambled in after them and watched for a while from the corner. On his way to the men's room, he paused by their table and the
minute she looked up, he knew. He understood why he'd come all this
way and what he had to do. He could tell Hammond was annoyed, but
he kept talking. Anything. Whatever came into his head. Just to see her
smile and hear her voice. Funny how things work out, the connections.

"It's not that easy." She shakes her head in a struggle not to cry. The
corners of her sweet lips are wet. She rubs her nose with the back of her
hand. "Every time, it's the same thing, how sorry he is, how much he
misses us . . . and last night . . . how . . . he had this . . . this dream of
himself and Lyra, and she was standing there with her arms out. And
she was calling him, he said. 'Daddy, Daddy,' she kept calling, and he
kept trying, but he couldn't get to her."

Her husband, he realizes. Bob, not Hammond.

"He wants us to be a family again," she says, drying her eyes with
the hem of her shirt. "But we can't, and I don't know how to tell him."

I'll take care of it, he wants to say. Leave it to me. I'll blow the fucker's brains out. Make it look like suicide. An accident, whatever she wants. Push him over a cliff. Easy, no problem. Whatever she needs, because what he needs, all he wants is right here. He gets up and squats in front of her. "Don't cry." He touches the side of her face. "Everything's going to be all right. You'll see."

She presses her hand over his. "Oh, Eddie. I shouldn't do this to you. Or to any of my friends, but you're all so sweet."

He resents being lumped in with her many friends. Too many. Her phone rings constantly. How is she doing? What does she need? All she has to do is call, they assure her. What about Nora? he suddenly wants to ask. Women can be so vile. Wet and weeping. Does she ever care how Nora feels?

"I'm so blessed." She pats the top of his head as if he were a child. "Sometimes it feels like I've known you forever."

"Maybe we have," he says, and she smiles.

"Don't you just wish you could wake up one morning and be twelve again?"

"No!" Those were the worst years, every moment scrutinized by counselors. One after another, shift after shift, whoever's case he happened to be that month. Crazy Eddie. *Why, why, why,* the constant question, when he hadn't even known the little girl. It wasn't as if he'd thought it through or anything. But suddenly, there she'd been, in the way. Sticky red grime melting down her fist and arm. Dirty face, holes in her sneakers, and ripped panties, what he remembers—and her blank stare up from the parched, rust-colored weeds. *Indian paintbrush,* that's what it said in the police report. *In the way,* they'd ask again, *now what does that mean, why, when all she was doing was walking along, eating the Cherry Freeze she'd just bought from the ice-cream truck, so how was she in the way?* He was sorry. How many times did he have to say it? *A hundred thousand times, and it still won't bring her back.* So stop asking then. Accept the fact. Even at twelve he knew that, knew it better than most. Some things just happen. *Let's see,* each new one would mutter, turning the page, fascinated, that's what they were, by him, especially the women. *To look at you . . . how could you . . . it doesn't make sense.* Well, there you go, wasn't that the whole point, change what you can, and when you can't, know when to move on. *Let's see . . . in the way, you said. In your way? Blocking you?* No. She was there, just there, that's all. *You don't even care, do you, Eddie?*

"The road not taken. You know that saying? I think of it all the time. Things I'd do different. Choices I'd make."

"Like what?" he asks softly, yielding to another of her confidences.

The telephone rings. Glancing at the caller ID number, she gets up quickly. She answers it in the kitchen. He wanders over to the book-case, pretending to read the titles. He takes down a book and opens it. The words are a blur. From around the corner her voice is breathless, expectant; not the husband, he can tell.

"I got it . . . I did . . . It's enough . . . Thank you. But that's not why I called . . . I know . . . I'm sorry . . . But I'm having a hard time . . . It's just, I . . . I know, but I miss you . . . I miss you so much . . . I know, but when . . . He could be like that forever . . . It's like I've stopped living . . ."

Suddenly, screaming from above. Running feet, the shrieking child on the staircase. "Mommy! Mommy!" she howls, then freezes, staring down at him in terror.

"Lyra, it's okay, baby. It's okay. Mommy's here. Here I am." She rushes past and scoops up the child. She sits on a step, rocking the girl in her tight embrace while he swallows against the bile searing his throat. He doesn't want to hate her like this. But it's as much a reflex as flinching from a blow. The good and the bad, love, hate, they always end the same—with this deadening reminder that innocence is false. An alluring snare, another trap set in his way.

CHAPTER·15

Nora and Ken are on their way up to bed. Everything seems natural enough about their end-of-day routine. And yet there is this sting in the air, a kind of static charging their nearness with expectation, all that remains unspoken, unasked, making each acutely aware of the other. Lately at bedtime, one usually lingers behind, so the other can get under the covers first, lessening any occasion of intimacy with the awkwardness of their parallel, though bleakly separate lives. Tonight, as Ken turns out the lights and Nora locks the doors, she has been telling him about lunch today with Stephen. They were at Bollio's, and who did they run into but Annette and Thomas. Thomas? Ken asks. Thomas: from the gallery, she reminds him, her hopeful mood snagging on the memory of that difficult night. But it's a brief stab, lasting only a moment, because they have to move on, and if this is to work, she has to. Maybe even more than he does. Anyway, Stephen was absolutely beside himself to see Annette with a man. Since his cousin's stroke, Stephen's devotion has begun to border on the obsessive. He was making such a nuisance of himself at the rehab hospital, visiting at least once a day, pestering doctors and criticizing therapists, that Oliver begged Ken to tell him to stop coming so often. Ken hated to, but he did, and, now, just as he told his brother would happen, Stephen is terribly hurt. Devastated. And he blames Ken for his banishment, not Oliver.

"I'm surprised he asked you out to lunch," Ken calls in to her.

"Actually, I asked him," Nora calls back from the kitchen where she is pouring detergent into the dishwasher. She forgot to run it earlier. "It's the *Medical* supplement, I need his help."

"Still, I'm surprised he went. Under the circumstances," Ken says from the doorway. Your being my wife, he means. And this easy avowal of their union floods her with warmth. "He's such a head case."

"Ah, but he's our head case, isn't he?" she says, and, of all things, winks as she closes the dishwasher.

"I guess," he sighs.

It's been a pleasant evening, the first in months that they talked so much, even after dinner was over. With prodding, Chloe finally read them a few interesting passages from Max's long e-mails. That prompted Nora's recollection of her first newspaper assignment. It was supposed to be a short piece about an addition on the waste treatment plant, but with all her research and a four-hour interview with the plant manager, the story ended up being ten pages long. A term paper, her editor said, dropping it into the wastebasket. Which editor, Drew asked, scowling, thinking she meant the *Chronicle.* It was the *Lyndbury Weekly,* she was quick to tell him. The chip on Drew's shoulder swells with the least little thing. He seems so watchful lately, guarded. He was quiet tonight, but at least he stayed at the table with them. He seemed surprised when Ken suggested it was time for the next generation to start working at the paper. As what, Drew asked, uneasily. I don't know, you tell me, Ken said. Last year when he'd asked if there was something he could do there, Ken told him to go ask his uncle. Drew tried in his shy, halting way, only to have Oliver cut him off, saying he was too young, to come back in his senior year, adding, when he was a little more aggressive. Drew had been hurt. Ken's angry confrontation with his brother had surprised Nora, but Oliver was adamant. Drew just wasn't old enough. Having to babysit the publishers' nephew and son was hardly the message he wanted the staff to get. The paper might be a family-owned business, but it is no sinecure. A curious declaration, it still seems, with Oliver, Ken, Stephen, as well as herself there.

"Maybe something on sports," Drew said.

Ken smiled. "You know what they say, if you can't do it, you can at least write about it."

She kicked him under the table, but it was too late. "That's just a corny old newspaper thing, Drew. Dad didn't mean you. Obviously."

"Obviously," Drew muttered as he left the table.

"C'mon, Drew, lighten up, will you?" Ken stared after him.

Three weeks, and not a word from Eddie. With him gone she's starting to feel more like her old self again. She can think straight. She sleeps better so her concentration is more focused. She's calmer, more patient, not as quick to blow up over petty mistakes. Her own confidence along with Ken's efforts at the paper convince her they've turned a corner. He's far more organized and attentive to detail. So serious, Hilda observed the other day, adding that she'd never seen him frown until now. Some days he seems drained by the burden of it all, tense, as if he doesn't dare let up. He tries to please her, and yet she notices how easily stressed he's become. An almost constant look of concern has replaced his quick grin. His blood pressure reading is high for the first time in his life: not such a bad thing, in her guilty estimation. Instead of ribbon-cutting parties and frivolous chairmanships in which his most trying duty is the wording of plaques, he's been harnessed into the thankless reality of personnel disputes, local politics, the never-ending morass of community problems, and the public expectation of him as moral arbiter. More than capable, he's just never had the chance. And never wanted it.

Ahead of her on the stairs, his weary sigh stirs a tenderness, an ache she hasn't felt in a long time. She reaches for his hand on the railing then hesitates. She remembers loving him once. Loving him for all that he was and wasn't. Loving him simply for being lovable. For caring and being such fun to be with. For the warmth, the light he throws entering a room, the way it bounces off mirrors and window glass and glows on people's faces. For his complete and sincere acceptance of everyone, including herself, who hasn't always been the easiest person to deal with. Her hand grazes his and her eyes sting with longing. He's hers and she wants him back. She needs both his love and to love him again.

"Oh," he says, glancing back. "I keep meaning to tell you. The Brannigans, I ran into Reed the other day. Their party, St. Patrick's Day, they want us to come."

"No. No, I don't want to."

"We always go. Every year. And we always have a great time."

"No."

"Why?"

"You know why." Laura Brannigan is Robin's tennis partner.

"I don't see the point."

"You don't? You really don't?"

"What am I supposed to do, stop living?"

"Ken!" she whispers, pausing on the step, stunned. "Don't you know how uncomfortable I'd feel? Think about it."

"Well that's your problem, then, isn't it?" he says, with a hatefulness she hasn't heard before.

"No!" she hisses, trying to be quiet. The children are in their rooms but still awake. "It's yours, because you did this. You're the one! You did this to me!"

Trembling, he starts back down the stairs. "I don't know how the hell much more of this I can take," he shouts.

"What does that mean? What're you saying? What're you, threatening me?" she demands, following him. He stalks outside, slamming the door in her face.

Drew charges into the kitchen in his boxers and T-shirt.

"Let him go!" he explodes, fists clenched. "If that's what he wants, the bastard. No-good son of a bitch. Let him go live with them, his other family. Who the fuck cares!"

She feels dizzy. Moments ago, such peace, to this. Her chest hurts. Her head is pounding. *His other family.*

By the time Ken returns, an hour later, a tearful, shivering Chloe has finally left Nora's room, where she's been begging her mother not to break up their family. Daddy is sorry for his mistakes; she knows, because he told her so himself.

"When?" Nora asked, stunned. "When did he tell you that?"

"I don't know, a while ago."

"No, Chloe. When? You tell me when! Exactly when."

"Last summer. I think." Chloe cringed with the guilt of her secret.

"Last summer? He told you? He . . . what? Just came out with it?"

"I asked him. I had a feeling. So I asked him."

What about me? You knew for months and never said anything. Why? Your own mother, why didn't you tell me? she wanted to ask, but couldn't, seeing her daughter's misery.

"He wants us to still be a family, that's all he cares about, Mom, please. Please," Chloe sobbed.

Her daughter's message is clear, keeping them whole is up to Nora. It all rests on her. All her responsibility and, somehow, her fault should the marriage end. So, even they knew before she did, her own children, conspirators in their silence, their conflicted loyalty. And that, for her, is unforgivable. His last betrayal. The rupture is complete. Deadening, and oddly painless. Ken doesn't come upstairs. He sleeps in the study. She hears Drew's door open, the creak of floorboards. She slips out of bed and listens from the top of the stairs. She can barely hear them. Ken seems to be repeating a litany of denials.

"I don't believe you," Drew keeps saying. Then, finally: "You're a liar!"

You all are, she realizes. Every one of you.

They're too loose, Nora thinks, turning the rings on her finger. Hard to keep weight on without an appetite.

"The baby's better," the young woman says, coming into the conference room and sitting down. "One of those GI things."

Nora looks up blankly. And then remembers. Their last visit ended when one of the staff knocked on the door with Alice's feverish child in her arms. Father Grewley is worried about Alice. Something's going on with her, he said in his call.

"That's good," Nora says. She can't remember if it's a boy or girl. Like so much else, pointless to ask, and besides, as if entering a confessional, the young woman needs no prodding. She knows why she's here, to recount what misery has brought her to Sojourn House. If she wants their help, this is the price she pays, the shocking, painful truth, no secrets, no privacy or pride, her story repeated so many times now, the facts by rote, to caseworkers, therapists, mentors, volunteers, potential donors, that it might as well be someone else's. Emotionless. Worn down until there's nothing left, Nora thinks, twirling her rings easily over the first knuckle, then down again. She shouldn't wear them like this, she's going to lose them, as if it matters, as if anyone cares.

"Every time, it was money," the young woman says, and Nora glances up. Is that a dig? She means her, doesn't she, the platinum-set diamond rings, the cashmere sweater set, and alligator purse. Of course she does. She's thinking how she could pay two or three months' rent with what that purse alone cost.

Nora moves the purse onto the floor next to her tapping foot. Can't stop fidgeting. Hard to concentrate. Or even sit still. She feels like she's going to climb out of her own prickly skin. Anxiety, the doctor said, but the medicine makes her even more tired. Weak-willed. Instead of relying on pills, she needs to deal with this herself. Strength and determination, the way her mother held it all together. One step at a time. Doing her best, all she can do, her best, her very pathetic best. At home she goes through the motions. Easier this way. Three hang-ups the other night. Eddie is still in the area. Kay swears she saw him leaving Stop and Shop with a cart full of groceries. Why does that bother her, and who is this mysterious Eddie, Kay keeps asking. Things are as tense at work as at home. Oliver is making progress in physical therapy, but no one dares tell him about problems at the paper. Ken and Stephen had a terrible row during Friday's editorial meeting. Stephen had just found out that Ken covered up Bob Gendron's accident. Even though it happened weeks ago, he wants it reported. Old news or not, Stephen railed, it's fair journalism. The *Chronicle* has never lowered its standards, and it won't start now, no matter whose personal interests are at stake. Stephen has always been critical of Ken's lackadaisical approach to the family business, but now to have Ken in charge is more than he can stand, even if it means a crack in Oliver's carefully managed family façade. Details of the shouting match have filtered down through the staff. Their quick glances gleam with schadenfreude, but she finds it too hard to care. Can't muster the energy. She doesn't look a bit healthy, Hilda told her today. Skin and bones, circles under her eyes. What is it? Kay kept asking through lunch. Work, was all she'd say. What about Ken, Kay asked uneasily, how were things on that front? Better, she lied. Kay wants the miserable details so she can gloat. She was always jealous of Robin and Nora's friendship. So, there's no one left for Nora to tell how lost she feels and, on top of everything now, how paralyzed by Eddie's nearness. She couldn't even tell her sister. She aches for Carol, not this distant, troubled woman, though, who keeps calling with new twisted memories, but the Carol of old who helped her grow up. Robin, she thinks with a stab of painful longing, lost to her, the one person she would have gone to. That's why, why it's so hard, more than the loss of friendship, it's a death almost, the loss of such intimacy. *Because I loved her, too,* Nora thinks, and the realization stuns her.

The room is hot, airless with the young woman's voice, its gloom of resignation, a numbing cant. *She doesn't like me. She doesn't want to be here either but has to, has to do this, has to bare her soul for any bleeding heart with money to give,* Nora thinks.

She squirms. In the best of times she's uneasy here. The wall color is jarring, an orangey pink that reminds her of raw salmon, and the furniture, a clash of donations. The one-armed navy blue couch is half of a sectional. There are two chairs, one, bright yellow with white stripes, the other, a mauve velour wingback. The scented burning candle on the scratched glass coffee table barely masks the musty horsehair upholstery. Each of the three conference rooms is like this, the goal being the comfort and security of home, or at least the young priest's vision of home.

"Maybe if we were rich, none of this would've happened."

Nora glances at the folder. Alice. She always forgets her name. No storybook Alice, hers the wan pallor of drawn curtains and bolted doors. Her faded blonde hair sprouts a good inch of new brown growth. With every sound her small dark eyes scan the perimeter, as if for shelter. Footsteps, murmurous voices, the clang of a water pipe, all threats. Posttraumatic stress syndrome, which for some abused women can last for years, according to Father Grewley's informational packet.

Nora is here as part of his mentoring program. Months ago when he first asked, she said she couldn't. She was too busy with the paper and her family. This is the last thing on earth she should be doing now, but this time Father Grewley persisted. In the beginning he had more volunteers than he needed, but too many would come once or twice, then call at the last minute to say they couldn't keep their appointments. He finds it bewildering that the same people who believe enough in the mission to give money won't give as generously of their time. It's difficult, Nora tried to explain last time he called. They might not show it, but most people have so many of their own problems, it's hard taking on someone else's. She meant herself.

"Nobody knows that better than me," Father Grewley said so tersely she knew he felt slighted. But he doesn't understand, not really. Because he is so sincerely and totally driven, Sojourn House is his whole life, an extension of himself. A danger, but that's what great projects require, hubris and zeal.

"And I'm sure some people feel way in over their heads, Father Tom. I mean, that's what I keep thinking. I'm no counselor. I don't have any training for this." When what she wanted to say was, How can I help another wounded woman when I can't even help myself?

"Living, that's all it takes!" the priest exclaimed. "All your wisdom and experience, that's what our ladies need. Someone they can talk to. It's more than counseling. We've got therapists, but it's that woman-to-woman thing. Girlfriends. A pal. Most of them don't know how to reach out anymore. Confide. Ask for help. Or tell the truth. It's been shamed and beaten out of them. A friend, Nora, that's all I'm asking. A once-a-week friend." She can't even confide in her own friend, but here she is, going through the motions.

Alice is showing her a picture of her family. Three children, two boys and baby girl, husband, herself, all in bathrobes, in front of a Christmas tree.

"That's the most lights we ever had. Twenty-six strings," she says.

"Lovely," Nora says of the somber children.

"Every year I buy a few more," Alice says.

Nora looks up, puzzled.

"The kids like them to blink, but Luke says they use more electricity that way. Off and on, all the stopping and starting."

"Oh. Really. I didn't know that. Pretty tree, though," she says weakly, fighting impatience, struggling to seem interested in the suddenly animated description of her painted dough ornaments, glittery stars sprinkled with raw sugar and reindeer with red jelly bean noses, and the popcorn-and-cranberry garland she and the kids strung with clear fishing line, Luke's, but she didn't dare tell him, and, see, that angel at the top, they made that, too, with cotton balls and tin foil, and, for wings, netting stiff with hair spray. "Really?" Nora pretends to study the picture, thoughts racing with memories of Robin's rum-soaked fruitcakes and personalized gingerbread men, and, every year, the hand-painted glass ornaments dated and signed with her cute robin logo, each card and letter stamped with the little brown red-breasted bird on stick legs, and did they exchange gifts these last three Christmases, Robin and Ken, or was it four, she wonders, this suspicion, new among the constellation of clues and betrayals to be probed, and no matter how distant, the pain, like light from a long-ago star, is just as vivid, even now, trying to retrieve details of their dinner together the Christmas before last, recalling only how happy they all were, or seemed, or thought they were, two of them, anyway, the fool and the cuckold, the other two wishing it could be just them . . .

The now dismal rote continues, "A few minutes later, he dragged the tree outside and put all the kids' presents in trash bags."

Nora blinks, looks at the photograph. Luke, the bland-faced man in the plaid bathrobe, slightly built, hair cropped like a marine. Everyone in the picture has red eyes, but with Alice's story his seems a baleful glare. Money, she says again. Pressure. Weeks go by with everything fine, then the least little thing makes him snap. He even made pan-cakes for them all that morning, but that was part of it, Alice says. Instead of the regular syrup she'd bought real Vermont maple syrup, because it was Christmas. Just a small bottle. On sale, she explains as if still needing to justify her goading error, but it made him so mad. He couldn't stop talking about it. Grumbling. Couldn't get over wasting his hard-earned money on real Vermont maple syrup, 100 percent pure, he read from the label in a voice shrill with disbelief. And for lit-tle kids, the baby, as if they'd even know the difference or had the slightest appreciation of anything, anyway. Anger building, he insisted the younger boy, Cam, stay at the table and finish his pancakes, bloated with the precious syrup, while the rest of the family left to open pres-ents. From the other room she could hear her little boy's sobbing gags as he tried to eat, and it tore her apart. Not only was Cam missing his presents, but he hated soggy food, which was her fault for having poured too much syrup on his plate, her fault for even having bought the expensive syrup. She waited until her husband started opening one of his own gifts, the Rubbermaid tackle box and fancy lures he'd wanted, and then she slipped away to check on Cam. Shh, she ges-tured to the child, as she stuffed his pancake into her mouth. She had just swallowed, when her husband came into the kitchen. He de-manded to know if she had eaten it. No, she said, with her son star-ing into his syrupy plate. He insisted on smelling her breath, but of course, they'd all had the syrup. He checked the garbage can. He turned on the light over the sink and peered into the disposal, sniffing to make sure.

"So then we went in, and took the family picture, and Cam starts opening his presents. And Luke's got that look. Watching. Like he gets when he's fishing, you know, waiting for the tug on the line. Just wait-ing, I could tell. And then Cam opened his Power Ranger. He loves Power Rangers. I'd gotten him two, the red and the blue. I knew he wanted the blue, but he didn't know, he opened the red one first. And all he said was, 'Oh, I wanted the Blue Ranger,' the way kids do. And that was it for Luke. It was like he got what he wanted, finally, exactly what he'd been waiting for. He started running around like a crazy man, all out of breath, panting and picking up presents, grabbing them right of the boys' hands, even the baby, and of course they're crying and begging him not to. 'Ungrateful little bastards,' he's screaming. 'Bring it back. Just bring it all back.' I tried to get him to calm down, but that's when he hit me."

Stop, Nora wants to say, unable to hear any more. Her eyes ache with the pressure of tears against the vision of such cruelty. A father bullying his children, babies really, five, four, and two, on childhood's most magical day, the holiday she and Ken delighted in bringing to life with Santa Claus's boot tracks in the backyard snow, alongside the trail into the woods of chewed carrot tops the reindeer had dropped. Maybe Alice and Luke also set cookies and milk out, leaving the crumbs and streaked glass as proof not only of Santa's existence but of some deeper, more enduring benevolence as well. And maybe at dawn they also crept from bed and waited, breathless, at the bottom of the stairs, jingling an old strap of sleigh bells to wake the children. Maybe they did too, in the hope it would work, the hope that maybe, once again, for a time however fleeting, if even just a day, the power of myth and ritual might be enough to subdue the darkness.

"We were supposed to go to my mom's for Christmas dinner, but how could I, with my eye all swolled up and the kids so upset. So I called and said we were all coming down with something. And of course, my mom, she's so disappointed. My brother's up from Texas and my sister and her kids're there. 'That's all right,' she keeps saying. 'Come anyway, honey. We'll take care of you.' And the whole time, my husband, Luke, he's right there by the phone, listening, scared to death I'm gonna say something, and he writes on a piece of paper and holds it up. 'Tell her we got the flu and everyone's throwing up.' " She laughs. "He was scared they'd come by and see my eye and the hole he punched in the wall." She shudders. "And my poor little kids all huddled together, staring at the TV like zombies."

"Oh!" Nora gasps, this eruption of grief, like a violent seizure. She alternates between crying and apologizing to Alice, who keeps apologizing back and trying to console her.

"I didn't mean to make you feel so bad," Alice says, coming quickly to sit beside her. Her arm over Nora's shoulder exudes the harsh smell of days' old sweat, which not only repulses her, but seems to stimulate some primitive gland, making everything more intense, and clear. No matter what Ken's been, he's never been a bad father, never harmed or abandoned his children. And may still be with her only because of them. She cries harder.

"It's not you. It's everything. It's all . . . all so hard," she sobs into her hands.

"I know." Alice leans her head into Nora's. "And you're nice to listen, to even care. Most people don't want to know. Pretending's easier. That way, no one has to do anything, including me." Her voice drops. "And then maybe next Christmas'll be better because I'd never make that mistake again. You know, real maple syrup. Or pancakes even, putting that kind of pressure on him, that's the way your thinking goes. Or maybe we wouldn't have presents; well, just his, anyway. Because that's what always happened. I didn't even know it, but, after a while, everything was about him. Trying to keep him from getting upset."

Nora looks up, ashamed. She meant herself, her own problems. "How're the children doing?" she asks, blowing her nose.

"Better. You know kids, they never stop loving Mommy and Daddy, no matter what happens," Alice says, wearily.

Nora nods. That's right, they don't. And for that she must be glad, relieved her own still have that security, at least. And Ken was always a great dad, especially when they were younger, going to all their games and coaching their soccer teams. Sometimes he'd be the only father with all the mothers on class trips. She remembers the huge tent he set up in the backyard so he and the kids could "camp out" on Saturday nights, and all the hours he spent in the basement teaching Drew to play pool when he didn't make the majors in Little League, a far bigger disappointment for Ken than for Drew. She smiles a little, remembering the white super-stretch limo Ken hired to take Chloe and her friends and their dads to the middle school father-daughter dance.

"But that's the difference now," Alice is saying, "having it all out in the open. No more secrets. No more lies."

"What do you mean?" Nora asks, and Alice shrugs. "You're not going back, are you?"

Alice's eyes dart away. "I need to give it one more chance." Her voice falls flat again, emotionless. "I owe them that much, my kids, I mean."

"But what about you, what do you owe yourself?"

Alice merely looks at her, with probably the same impenetrable blankness that meets her husband's anger. "You don't understand," she begins, then pauses. Whatever she wants to say is too difficult. "I don't mean this the way it's gonna sound, but it's not the same for me. I don't have choices. Not if I want to be home taking care of my kids, anyway." She smiles but with pinched resolve.

Nora asks when she's leaving Sojourn House. Luke is picking them up tomorrow, Alice says, then asks her not to say anything to Father Grewley. She plans on telling him tonight. "Here, then." Nora takes a business card from her purse and writes on the back. "That's my number at home. You call me, it doesn't matter when or about what. I'd like us to . . . to stay in touch." To be friends, she wishes she had said.

"Okay." Alice nods, reading the card. "That'll be nice."

CHAPTER · 16

The cold, windy night glows with moonlight. Every space in the parking lot is taken; even the side streets are lined with cars. Their brisk, two-block walk to the school makes Nora realize how long it's been since they have walked anywhere together. Ken is telling her about Oliver. Another two or three weeks of intensive therapy, and he's hoping to be discharged.

"Did you tell him I want to come in?" she asks, hurrying after him up the granite steps. It is open house at Franklin High and they're late.

"He still doesn't want visitors." He holds open the wide oak door. "Just family." He means himself and Stephen. She tries not to feel hurt. Maybe she's just grasping at straws, but things have seemed better lately. She's been trying hard to keep her eye on the big picture instead of looking for slights all the time.

The minute they're inside, the PA system announces the start of the first period. Nora checks the schedules. They'll go to Drew's class, then, second period, to Chloe's.

"Hello, parents!" Chloe greets them with breezy relief as they come around the corner. Like Chloe, the hall monitors tonight are all student council members. She has been waiting anxiously for them, Nora can tell. These last few days she's noticed a growing uneasiness between Chloe and her father. His efforts to please her only seem to distress her. Nora can't quite put her finger on it, but Chloe is extremely sensitive whenever he's home and, for one so preoccupied with her own existence, noticeably watchful. When Chloe left tonight Ken still wasn't home from the rehab hospital. Chloe was concerned he wouldn't make it back from Boston in time. Of course he will, Nora assured her. Has he ever missed anything of yours, she asked, and Chloe didn't answer. Her silence said it all, the vulnerability her daughter was feeling for the first time in her secure and happy existence: because, throughout his affair, his other life, he had always managed to be where he was needed, to show up. Being an attentive and dutiful father isn't any kind of guarantee. He can do all the right things and still tear the family apart. The realization that things aren't always what they seem is a hard enough part of growing up, but deeply painful for so trusting and sunny-natured a child as Chloe.

He's trying, Nora keeps wanting to tell her daughter, but to say it would suggest so much more than she has energy for right now. Better that he just keeps proving himself, by being who he is. In last weekend's snowstorm he brought his car, then Nora's, to the cheerleaders' car wash, which ended $370 short of their goal for new uniforms. Here, Ken said, writing out a check to make up the difference. No, Chloe said. She didn't want him to do that. But Ken insisted. Until last night the mud room walls were stacked high with donations of canned goods, which Ken and Chloe loaded into the car and delivered to the St. Francis Harvest Pantry, because Chloe is chairman of the student council's food drive. He's proud that she volunteers once a week at the city's Boys and Girls Club where she and two of her friends give cheerleading lessons. The drama club is probably Chloe's favorite activity. She has been in every annual school play since freshman year. This spring they're putting on *Our Town,* and Chloe got the part she wanted, Emily. While most of Nora's high school activities were strategically chosen to impress college admissions directors, Chloe genuinely loves being part of the school community. Her grades might be lackluster but not her spirit. And in this, like so much else, she is her father's daughter.

Drew's first class is history. Mr. Carteil is giving a brief overview of his curriculum and expectations. Ken and Nora slip into back-row seats. A few parents raise their hands: Why is the class average so low?

they ask. Why doesn't Mr. Carteil scale those tests everyone does poorly on? And why so many papers, four in a term, when no other freshman teacher assigns that many? "Because I'm trying to educate your children, not mollycoddle them," the old teacher wearily replies. The bell rings. End of period. Parents file out, grumbling.

"Consumers," Ken whispers to Nora, as they wait their turn with the teacher. "And they're not getting their tax money's worth."

"Right," she says uneasily, scanning the stream of familiar faces moving along the corridor to second period classes. She dreads running into Robin. Probably inevitable, though. But thank goodness Drew and Clay aren't in any of the same classes. She wonders if Chloe is worried she'll have to escort Mrs. Gendron to a classroom with everyone watching, knowing.

When it's their turn, Mr. Carteil tells them that Drew's test scores have certainly improved and he's been getting his work in on time. But Mr. Carteil is still concerned. Drew acts indifferent, almost sullen. He never volunteers, which is frustrating because Drew is certainly getting the material. Lately he's even fallen asleep in class a few times.

"Well, he's not staying up too late, I know that," Nora says. She is disappointed. Having closely tracked his grades, she expected a glowing report.

"It's a boy thing." Ken shrugs. "They can fall asleep at the drop of a hat. I used to do the same thing. Even fell asleep once during a soccer game. On the bench! They all left me, they thought it was so—"

"Excuse me," Mr. Carteil interrupts. "But the next class is coming in and I'd rather say this privately. Do you think Drew might be depressed? I'm no doctor, of course, but that's what I keep thinking."

She and Ken barely make it to Chloe's class on time. American Literature. The teacher is Mrs. Klein, a petite young woman in a long black skirt. Instead of taking parents' questions, she delivers an abbreviated lecture, similar to the one their children heard today. *The Scarlet Letter.* The irony is not lost on Nora, though she barely listens. All she can think about is Drew. Mr. Carteil is right. Her son is depressed, and she's been too blindsided by her own problems to recognize it. She

knows by Ken's drawn face that he's feeling the mess he's made of
everything. When the bell rings, Mrs. Klein stations herself at the door
and hands each parent a note, telling how their child is doing.

*I am pleased with Chloe's effort and know she will continue to do bet-
ter. She is a lovely girl and always a delightful student to have in class.*

Chloe is waiting in the corridor. She promised Nora at dinner that
she was going to be very pleased by her teachers' comments. Her expectant smile fades. "What's wrong? What'd she say?"

Nothing's wrong, Nora assures her. See? She holds out the note.
It's Drew, that's all. Just something Mr. Carteil said. What? Chloe
asks. What did he say? Nothing they'll talk about here, Nora says as
quietly as possible with the passing din. Is he in trouble, Chloe asks,
and in her daughter's persistence Nora hears more of the dread that
comes when a child's sense of well-being has been compromised. First,
her father. Who next? Her brother? The third period bell rings. Biol-
ogy, Ken says, leaning close and peering at the schedule. Room 202,
where's that? In this wing? Yes, Chloe tells him, but he seems confused. He points to the schedule and asks again.

With Robin's mother heading their way, Ken is desperate to avoid
eye contact.

"Hello, Chloe," Emily Shawcross says, adding with the briefest of
regal nods, "Nora . . . Ken." His face reddens. She is a silver-haired
version of her daughter, beautiful, vibrant, yet somehow managing in
her tight-lipped anger to be if not gracious, then civilized. Before anyone can (or would) ask, she explains that she is here tonight in place of
Robin, because Lyra is still very sick. In the strained silence each hopes
the other will speak.

"With what?" Nora asks, as if their meeting is all so perfectly normal, cordial as ever. There is the need not only to shield her family
from these curious glances, however real or imagined, but out of
respect for Emily. After Nora's mother died, Robin announced she
would be sharing her mother with Nora. Delighted with her new role,
Emily always remembered Nora on birthdays and at Christmas. Com-
paring gifts with accusations of maternal favoritism was a running
joke between the younger women. If Emily made cookies for Robin's

family, then Nora would pretend to be hurt until she got a batch. And the truth is, Nora often felt closer to Emily than she ever had to her own mother. Even in this awkward moment, affection stirs, however tempered by regret now, and sadness. Emily was colorful and warm, always forgiving. But that was then, Nora thinks, seeing her eyes lock on Ken's as she answers.

"Dehydration," Emily says, almost bitterly, as if this might somehow be his fault. "The hospital wants to keep her another day, poor baby."

"Oh, no!" Chloe says, her concern reminding Nora that Chloe is Lyra's godmother.

"They've all had the flu, but it took its toll on the little one." Emily's glance shoots to Ken. "The way things do." The lines deepen around her red lips.

"Poor thing," Chloe says with an empathetic pout that the older woman looks away from. "I hope she feels better."

"Yes," Nora says. "That's so . . ." For a moment, her thoughts blur guiltily. In just a few months she has forgotten so much about the pretty child they were all so fond of. "So young to be in the hospital."

"It certainly is," Emily declares.

"I'm sure she'll be fine," Ken assures the child's grandmother who can no longer hide her disgust.

"You think so?" she hisses, clutching her grandson's class schedule against her chest. "Do you?"

With the loudspeaker's announcement, Mrs. Shawcross turns, hurries toward the stairs. I loved her, Nora thinks. And loved Robin, too. I did.

"Tell her I said hi," Chloe calls weakly.

With that, the pain he has caused registers on Ken's face. Nora knows what he's thinking, first his son's longest friendship, and now, even this ruined, his daughter's relationship with her godchild. The christening party, typical of Robin's gatherings. More people than her house could hold so there was an enormous white tent in the backyard. Catered by Molo's, with a three-piece band and one hundred pink balloons, the party had been great fun but a bewildering extravagance.

Bob had been out of work through much of Robin's difficult pregnancy, the last three weeks of which she had spent in bed. Their finances had become so strained that Bob's retired parents had even lent them money. But Nora couldn't help admiring Robin's determination that Lyra's birth be a celebration of beauty and joy. It had been a true epiphany, Robin confided once. Just when her life with Bob had gotten as hopeless as a marriage gets, she had turned to God. Send me a sign, she said she pleaded in every prayer. Show me the way. And then Lyra was conceived. Her new beginning. *Pregnant, and embarking on her affair.*

"How many more classes?" Ken asks, loosening his tie, on their way into Chloe's physics lab. The room is cold, but sweat runs down his face. Almost panting, he seems short of breath.

"Two more after this." She asks if he's all right.

He nods stiffly as he sits down. His lips are gray.

"You don't look good. Maybe you should go home."

"I'm okay," he whispers across the aisle.

The teacher, young and frazzled, rushes into the room with an armload of notebooks and loose papers. Apologizing for being late, he begins scribbling formulas on the board. This is what his students are learning now.

"I need some water," Ken whispers. "I'll be right back."

Nora watches him gesture weakly to the teacher on his way out the door. For the first time, she pities him. Now he knows, she thinks with a quick wave at Deb Brioni who cranes her neck, trying to see back from the front row. Nora smiles, letting her know, We're going to be fine. We'll get through this.

The frantic cartoon voices grind away at Eddie's nerves. The hospital television is mounted overhead. He slouches in the corner, watching, waiting for the little bitch's eyes to close. A moment ago when he reached for the remote on the bed her cunning eyes shot open. Robin is down at the hospitality shop buying another frozen yogurt. The kid rarely eats a meal, lives on sweets and snacks. Robin has slept here the last two nights. In order to see her he must sit here hour after hour kowtowing to this brat. She enjoys her power, especially over him. A whimper and her mother comes running. Down the hall a child is screaming. It feels like a knife cutting through him. He gets up and closes the door. His unappreciated purple Mylar balloon bobs against the ceiling. Waste of money that was. Five bucks, and she ignores it. On purpose. To put him in his place. Because her mother made such a big thing of him buying it for her. Knowing they'll talk of other things when she sleeps, she struggles to stay awake, to be the center of her mother's attention. The hell with it, he snatches the remote.

"How about a movie?" he asks, aiming it.

"No!" She holds up her hand. "I like this."

"You shouldn't be watching crap all the time. Your brain'll rot." He changes the channel. CNN. A car bomb has exploded in an open-air market in Baghdad. Mangled bodies strewn everywhere.

"No it won't," she gasps, staring up at the gruesome scene. The camera zooms in on a small, dead thing. On her back, limbs splayed, lies a little, dark-haired girl surrounded by tumbled fruit.

"Yes it will. See, that's why you're sick, it's already started. Pretty soon pieces of your brain'll start leaking out your eyes and your nose." The old storm of rage and absurdity surges through him. He doesn't even care, so why bother trying to reason with this brat. But it's her fear, her cowering, that exhilarates him. He leans over her, his hard-on rubbing against the bed. "Little by little, then it starts coming out your mouth and you choke." Holding his throat, he pretends to gag.

"Where's Mommy?" She cringes into the pillows.

"I don't know." He looks around and laughs. "You keep making her get things for you. Maybe she got sick of it and left."

"Where? Where'd she go?"

"On a trip maybe, someplace far away. Maybe there, that place." He points to the television, to the close-up of a grief-stricken old woman in black. Kneeling, arms beseechingly wide, she wails into the camera. He turns the volume up high, higher, until her eerie keening fills the room.

Limp again. This time it's her. He can't stand the kid, it's reached that point. Too demanding. Whining and spoiled. Pampered little princess with ribbons in her hair, propped against the pillows, surrounded by her new stuffed animals and books. Barely looked at his get-well balloon, only thanked him with Robin's coaxing. When's my Daddy coming, she keeps asking her mother and, every time she says it, stares at him. Shut up little bitch, he wants to yell. She knows how to push her mother's buttons. All he wants is to be alone with Robin, impossible with two kids and her mother always nosing around. And the husband, he keeps calling. Every night, bawling, begging her forgiveness. He's coming home soon and everything'll be different, she'll see. Yeah, right, Bob. Real different; she won't even be here, asshole, he wants to grab the phone and say. Meanwhile, he's running out of time. He knows what she'll say so he can't ask. A vacation, he keeps telling her. Money's not a problem. She needs to get away. Someplace warm. Just the two of them. She thinks he means her and the brat.

Her pillows fall on the floor. Inconsolable, Lyra is curled on her side with the blanket over her head. Her shoulders convulse with her sobs.

"Don't cry." He picks up a pillow and stands by the bed. Wouldn't take long for a kid. Not as long as Bevvie, drugged-out whore but strong as a man. Strangling finally did the trick. Made him sick to his stomach, though, all the gagging and gurgling. Lisa, now that was quick, surprising with such a meaty gullet.

"Excuse me," comes a voice from behind. "Is this room three twenty-four? I'm looking for . . . oh! I remember you." Ken Hammond looks confused.

"Hey! Sure!" Eddie holds out his hand, says his name. "Robin'll be right back."

"Uncle Ken!" Lyra cries, throwing back the blanket.

"Lyrrie." Ken Hammond sits on the edge of the bed and hugs her. "Poor sweet baby," he croons into her hair. "I didn't know you were sick. I just found out. Your granana told me."

"I got the flu," the child whimpers, staring up at Eddie now, triumphantly, taunting him, he knows, as he tries to tamp down his fury. At her. At this preppie asshole Hammond in his open-neck blue shirt and brass-buttoned blazer. "I kept throwing up. On the couch and Mommy's bed," Lyra is telling him.

"I know. But I bet you feel better now, right?" Hammond holds her at arm's length to look at her. With her solemn nod, he pulls her back into his embrace. Her eyes dart between the two men.

"It got in my hair and Clay called me barf head," she complains, pouting.

"Well, that's not very nice, but then again, if it got in your hair, maybe you kinda were?"

"No!" she protests, giggling when he tickles her. "Did you bring me a present?" she asks.

"No," he says regretfully. "I was in too much of a hurry. I wanted to see you. But I will," he promises and she grins up at him.

He might as well not even be here, so taken are they with one another. He hates this, hates being reduced to insignificance. Especially by self-centered losers like them.

"Tell me what to get," Hammond says. "Something you really, really want."

"My Pony. One with pink hair."

"Oh, honey," Hammond groans. "I don't think so. Where would Mummy put a horse?"

"Not a real one," she laughs. "A little toy horse." She holds her hands together to show the size.

"Oh boy!" Hammond smacks the side of his head. "You had me worried for a minute there. I was trying to figure out how I was ever going to sneak a real horse not only into the hospital, but onto the elevator, then down the hallway, past all the doctors and nurses, and into this little room."

Giggling helplessly through Hammond's scenario, she keeps trying to pry open his fist. When she does, she finds four quarters inside.

"So, what're you doing here?" Hammond asks, holding up his other fist now, which she grabs. "I didn't know you and Robin even knew each other."

"We didn't. Not then, anyway. But now we do." Eddie smiles knowingly.

Hammond's gaze flickers. "Well, yeah. Small city, one way or another you end up knowing everybody." He opens his fist and Lyra seizes the five-dollar bill crumpled in it.

"Yeah. She's great. She's . . . great."

"Oh, Ken!" Robin squeals through the opening door. She is carrying three frozen yogurt cones in a cardboard box. "What're you doing here?" she asks, pleased, but Hammond, Eddie enjoys seeing, is offended.

"What am I doing here? What do you think?" His smile is strained.

"Oh, I know, but . . ."

"Your *mother* told me."

"I know, but you said not to—"

"Obviously not when it's something like this." His eyes dart to Lyra who sits cross-legged against her pillows. She reaches for the cone from which Robin is distractedly peeling the paper wrapper.

"Here, baby." Robin hands it to her.

"Eddie scared me," Lyra says, licking it.

"What?" Eddie does a double-take, but only the brat is looking at him.

"He said you weren't coming back. Never."

Nora is waiting in the study when Ken gets home. Nothing wrong at FairWinds, but he looks terrible. They were leaving the high school when he checked his phone messages. Oliver's alarm had gone off earlier. Everything seemed to be secure, the security company said, but Ken said he'd better check the house, just to be sure. She offered to go with him, but he thought she should go home, particularly in light of what Mr. Carteil had said. Ironically enough, Drew had the History Channel on when she came in. She sat down next to him and put her hand over his.

Together they watched the bombing of London. She found the old footage hypnotic and eerily calming, high-pitched air raid sirens, terrified people running through the streets as searchlights crisscrossed the night sky, for a moment putting her own troubles into perspective.

"Is everything all right?" she finally asked.

"Yeah," he said with a shrug, staring at the screen. He slipped his hand out from under hers. "Some lady called. Alice something. She left her number." He dug the slip of paper from his pocket, but Nora just put it on the table. Her son was her first priority.

She told him she was concerned, that it was perfectly understandable for him to feel depressed about what had happened between his parents, but it was vital that he talk about it.

"Okay." Another shrug.

"You're not happy, are you?"

"I'm okay."

"No, you're not, Drew. It's so obvious. You're holding it all in, and that's not right."

"Why? What am I supposed to do?" he growled, thumping the cushion with his fist.

She was relieved by his anger. "Just tell me what's going on, what you're thinking, what you're feeling." Bombs dropping from the sky, explosions of light and dust. She turned off the television.

He was chewing the side of his thumbnail.

"Like right now, what're you thinking about? Please, Drew, tell me." She moved closer and tried to put her arm around him, but he leaned forward, almost cringing from her. "It's me, isn't it? The way I've been lately. My moods . . . I know . . . It can't be easy not knowing who you're waking up to in the morning, Attila the Hun or this strange lady who looks like your mother but doesn't act like her anymore."

"You're not strange." His voice cracked.

"Oh, Drew. Honey. I love you so much. Please don't worry. Everything's going to be all right. Really. It is." Realizing that he was crying, she tried again to hug him, but he pulled away. "Sometimes it's hard to talk about your problems. I know. I was the same way. I still am. But I try, and that's all I'm asking you to do. Please, Drew?"

"I'm going up now," he said, quickly standing.

"Drew! I'll make an appointment. Someone you can talk to. At least that—"

"No, don't!"

Trying to get every word right, she has been recounting this conversation for Ken, but he seems distracted, impatient for her to finish. "But I'm going to anyway." She means finding a therapist for Drew. "He's all bottled up inside. He needs to get it out."

"He'll be all right." Ken checks his watch for the third time.

"No, I can tell. He needs to talk to someone."

"He's a kid. He's moody. He'll get over it."

"I don't know. I'm worried. I think we should call someone."

"Let's not go down that route yet," Ken says, opening the study door. "We don't need another Stephen in the family, do we?"

"That's a strange thing to say," she calls after him, "when you're seeing someone yourself every week."

He turns back, glaring, then seems to realize what she means. "I'll talk to him. Okay?" he adds, his coldness a deft and sudden scalpel. She can't do this anymore.

"No! It's not okay! We need more than that."

"What? What do you want me to do?" He looks almost frantic.

"No, you tell me! What do *you* want to do?"

"I'm trying, Nora. You know I am."

"Trying what? To save our marriage? Or are you just putting in your time here? Because that's what it feels like."

"Just so you know," he says with a bitter hiss. "You're not the only one hurting."

"Actually, I'm getting better at that, the hurting. And the anger. No, what's really messing me up now's all up here," she says, tapping her temple. "Because I don't get it. I still don't know what happened. I really, really don't. What did I do wrong, Ken? And don't keep saying nothing!" she warns because he's shaking his head and won't look at her. "That's just too insulting! I tried to be a good wife. And I think I was—most of the time. Wasn't I? I loved you. How did I hurt you? What was it about me you didn't want, that you couldn't stand anymore? When we made love? Was I—"

"No." He rubs his face with both hands. "Don't—"

"Don't what? Don't be honest? Don't tell you how much I still love you? And how sorry I am for my part in this? I know sometimes you think I'm cold—"

"Nora—"

"No. Listen. Please! I *need* you to listen. The thing is, deep down, I never felt good enough—for you or the kids—or anyone. And I think that's what happened. That's the problem, isn't it? Because I hold everything in and I shouldn't, but it's hard for me. I'm so afraid of losing anyone that I just shut down. It's safer that way. Even now, there's so much I need to tell you, things I've never said before—to anyone. And I . . . I still can't. But I want to, Ken. I have to. But I need your help. Because, lately . . . I can't even think straight. And it scares me. It really does."

He puts his hands on her shoulders, but can barely meet her gaze. "You don't deserve any of this."

"Why?"

"Because," he finally whispers. "You're one of the finest people I've ever known."

She closes her eyes and forces herself to stand there.

CHAPTER·17

"Finally," Nora says. She and Kay are having dinner at Chesley's. In the past few weeks Kay has left the same message with every call: "I miss you. Call me and we'll meet for lunch or dinner or something. Please." Nora would want to, but as with most obligations lately, she never seems to follow through.

Kay pours more wine, Nora's second glass. Nora almost feels relaxed. She's missed the intimacy of this, having someone to talk to, another woman. Lately, her conversations are all work-related or with the family. She's either trying hard to be happy or trying hard not to be hurt, angry, suspicious. At least with Kay she can be herself. Their long friendship has been a haven, the one safe place she can let down her hair without fear of betrayal or judgment. All their ups and downs, they've shared a lot through the years, though most of the rough spots have been Kay's, she realizes. Poor Kay, she hasn't had an easy life at times, not compared to her own. *Until now, anyway.*

"When you didn't call, I began to wonder," Kay says.

As Kay speaks, Nora's smile freezes with a sudden deadening chill. *So why didn't you tell me about the affair? Because you enjoyed it, enjoyed watching my so-called perfect life being undermined; admit it, you did, didn't you? Like the rest of them, gloating behind your false concern. Oh, poor Nora, you must be so devastated, all the while thinking, so, the fairy tale's finally over.* She traces her finger around the top of her glass. She can't think like this, can't keep letting herself be consumed by bitterness and fear. And dread, the worm in her soul. On her way here tonight she made up her mind to tell Kay about Eddie Hawkins. She needs to confide in *someone,* tell how the man screamed, begging for the savage blows to stop and what did she do? Nothing. She ran. As bad as him, as guilty, blood money to make him go away, her life in turmoil, in the end it all comes home to roost, the bad you do, the pain you cause, the lies you tell, came her mother's warning as she sat up with a start at two in the morning, wind howling, security lights on. Ken wasn't in bed. Hearing voices, she ran downstairs, convinced Eddie Hawkins was in the house, but it was only the television. Unable to sleep, Ken had gone downstairs.

"Tell you the truth," Kay confesses, "I was afraid you were mad at me."

"Of course not." Nora manages a weak smile.

"We've been friends for so long, that sometimes—"

"It's okay," she interrupts. "It's just me, that's all. You know how I get." She shrugs. "Awfully hung up on things."

"That's only natural. Of course. Especially when something bad happens. It changes everything, our whole perspective. All of a sudden it's a different life. Or seems like one, anyway."

"I know. The worst is always being so suspicious. Of everything. Even now with you . . . I mean, here you are being so kind, and the whole time my head's filled with all these . . . these dark thoughts."

"About me?" Kay says with a little gasp.

Nora nods. "Part of me's a little crazy. Gets scary sometimes."

"Why? Is it Ken? Did he—"

"Have you ever thought about something so much, tried so hard to figure out exactly what happened, gone over and over it so many times that after a while you're not sure of anything anymore?"

"What do you mean?" Kay stiffens back in her chair.

"I've never told anyone this before, but lately I get so scared. I think I'm . . . I mean . . . do you think I could hurt someone? Really hurt them? I mean, physically. Hit them. Smash their face in."

"No! Not in a million years. You're not like that. Why?" Kay leans closer. "Are you afraid that you might?"

"That maybe I did."

"To who?" Kay looks shocked.

"That's the thing, I don't even know, it's all such a mess."

"What is?"

"This dream, I keep having it." Wide-eyed, she shakes her head. Can't bring herself to say it, to make Kay a permanent reminder of her shame. She looks down.

"Hey." Kay pats her hand. "It's going to be okay. Really."

"There's just so much going on." She takes a long sip of wine. It's been a rough week, she explains so that Kay will stop looking at her like this, as if she's a crazy woman who must be humored, while she blathers on how work is taking its toll on Ken. Not only looks terrible, but now he's not sleeping well. The last two nights he barely slept at all. Maybe he should take something, Kay suggests. When that happened to her a couple years ago, all it took was a prescription for a few months to get her sleep back to normal.

Normal, Nora thinks, leaning back as the waitress serves their entrees, swordfish for each. Normal has a whole new meaning now. Normal is what other people have.

"Actually," Kay says, cutting an asparagus spear, "I haven't been sleeping too well myself lately."

"Work?" She drinks more wine.

Kay shrugs.

"Lousy market, huh?"

"Try dead! Yesterday my phone never even rang. Not once. Not one single time."

"Yes it did!" Nora says with a forced smile and a glance at the wine bucket. Her glass is empty, but she doesn't want to seem as anxious as she feels. "What about my call?" Kay has barely touched her first glass. Nora's nightly wine with dinner has become two glasses, filled to the brim. Three. Nothing wrong with a little numbing, she told Ken the other night when he asked if she realized she was pouring her fourth, the end of the bottle. And what could he say? Nothing. Just look away. Strange how his sense of defeat excites her. Makes her want him, loving and hating him more. Twisted and sick. But she needs to see his pain, to know she's not the only one hurting. She even enjoys his problems at the paper. He's in way over his head and for the first time in his life he needs her.

"You're right. And I appreciate that, Nor, I do. It's just lately, I don't know, I feel so, well, kind of, overwhelmed."

Stunned, for a moment she's not sure what to say. In many ways Kay has always reminded her of her mother, resilient, unmarked by life's blows. Self-possessed, the kind of woman men feel comfortable with. Maybe too comfortable, Kay has complained in recent years. There have been a few relationships, the longest, two years with a New York City stockbroker. According to Kay, the timing wasn't right. He was a great guy, but newly divorced, paying huge alimony and wary of marriage. Faithfully alternating his weekends between his teenage children and flying up to see Kay began to take its toll. He begged her to move in with him, but all her years of hard work were beginning to pay off. She finally had her own agency. She wasn't about to give it up and then have to start all over again if things didn't work out, especially with a young child to consider. Her agency is now one of the biggest in town. She is the devoted mother of brilliant Louis, now in his second year of medical school. Kay's is a much respected voice in town government and community affairs. At the moment, though, she seems weary, hesitant, a ghost of herself.

Another month like this, she is saying, and she'll have to close her office and run things from the house. Nora says she didn't realize real estate was that bad. It's not just the business, Kay admits. Her mother's Alzheimer's has worsened to the point that her needs can't be met by the nursing home she's in now. Hillside in Bellham has much better treatment, more specialized, but it's expensive. Far beyond her mother's resources, but Kay is determined to find a way. Nora's thoughts drift to her own mother. Dying suddenly. Too soon, Emily Shawcross said from behind while Robin kneeled at the bier, her arm around Nora. After Ken, Nora had next called Kay with the devastating news, and then Robin. But it was Robin who arrived first at the house. Robin who took the children while she and Ken drove to Colchester to make the funeral arrangements. Robin who filled the freezer with meals for the week ahead. Robin, indispensable, irresistible

Robin, the only living person to whom she ever told the truth about Mr. Blanchard and the vicious lie that drove him from her mother's life. "You were scared, honey, that's all, scared of losing your mom, too," Robin crooned into her ear, hugging and rocking her at the same time.

"Louis wants to take the rest of the term off to help."

"Who?" Nora asks, pouring more wine, just a half glass. "Your mother?"

"No, me." Kay's dark eyes shine. She puts down her fork and takes a deep breath. "Nora," she whispers. "I had a lump. It's malignant." She touches a spot above her left breast. "It's out now, but . . . my lymph nodes, they're . . . it's pretty well spread, the cancer." She takes deep breaths.

"What can I do? Please, Kay. Anything." Nora is devastated.

Kay shakes her head and tries to smile.

"You've got to let me. Please. Let me help you."

"I will. I'm okay now. But I will. Chemo starts next week. Monday."

"Then I'll drive you. Both ways, and that way I can wait there with you."

"Thanks, hon. But you know me. Ever efficient. All arrangements made. Rides, wigs, best to keep busy. Same with Mom, all her details. Which reminds me." She removes a pamphlet from her purse. "My big chance." She points to a frosted blonde wig styled in a pageboy. "What do you think?"

"Yes! Go for it." Nora's tears blur the picture.

"Deep down, there's always been a blonde in me. Crazy Kiki. Time to set her free, don't you think?"

Nora nods. "Kiki. Yeah, you're going to be all right. The two of you, I can tell. You are," she insists.

"Well, we're sure as hell gonna try," Kay says, dabbing her eyes with her napkin.

Also crying, Nora gestures to the waitress for the check. People watch, bewildered, as the sniffling women leave the dining room.

"You know what they're thinking, don't you?" Kay whispers as they put on their coats. "That we just broke up or something."

"Oh God! That's all I need," Nora groans, opening the door. She trips on the step and Kay grabs her arm. "This is bad," Nora laughs, leaning against her. "This is so bad."

"So what. Who cares? We're entitled," Kay says, guiding her through the parking lot.

"Tonight, anyway," Nora says, and starts crying all over again.

Kay's car is closer, so Nora gets in with her. They sit for a long time, talking, crying, laughing.

"I keep thinking how simple life seemed, and all the time . . ." Her voice drifts off. Sighing, she stares out the window.

"We thought we were happy. At least we had that."

"No!" Nora looks at her. "What kind of life is that?"

"There's always something," Kay says. "We just don't know what or when or where, but it's there."

Waiting. Somewhere. Her eyes widen. How stupid of her. What was she thinking? The minute Eddie runs out of money he'll be back for more. She should have told Ken immediately. She still can, and will. Yes, soon, when things are more settled. She crosses her arms, hugging herself.

"I know," she says quietly. "You're right, and that's what I keep trying to tell myself: that this is it. Right here. Now. In the moment, that's how we have to live."

"Well, maybe. If you're a cat or a dog." Kay sniffs, ever the realist.

"Or Robin Gendron," Nora says, and they laugh.

"Which reminds me," Kay says. "Guess who I saw again last week. Downtown. Coming out of the craft shop. Robin, and that friend of yours. That guy."

Nora has no idea who she means.

"That time, the one we had lunch with. Remember?"

She manages to nod.

"Robin's latest admirer. Or, should I say, victim. From the looks of him."

Nora's heart is racing. Even in here she feels it, foul, invasive, the poisonous seepage. Why with her, with Robin? She has to do something, but what? Go to the police, admit how she paid him to go away, and how he's not holding up his end of the agreement now. If there ever was an agreement. Did he ever even say he'd leave? She only assumed he was after money. What else could he possibly want? She never should have given him a cent. What was she thinking? Blackmail, she set herself up for it. Seeing how easily the money came, of course he'll want more. But why Robin?

She takes the long way home, turns slowly onto Dellmere Drive. Every light appears to be on inside the Gendrons'. No cars in front, just Clay's fallen bike, its icy pedal frozen into the lawn. Careless. Like his mother. Irresponsible. Like his father. Things just tossed aside, unvalued. Their one disagreement came when Nora told Robin she was too easy on Clay, letting him come and go as he pleased, never picking up after himself. The only way children learn self-discipline is from their parents. Even saying it, she knew she was out of line, but isn't that what close friends were for?

"Kids learn a lot from their parents, Nora, good and bad, but I'll tell you one thing Clay's not. He's not afraid of anything or anyone. He's just a happy-go-lucky kid," Robin said, message clear: her son was a lot better off than sensitive Drew, so easily hurt, quick to cry, fearful.

The next few days pass in a blur. Her concern for her friend keeps getting lost in her confusion about Eddie and Robin. It doesn't make sense. It must have been someone else Kay saw. He's gone. He must be or she would have heard from him again. Early evening, and she and Ken are on their way in to Boston to see Oliver. The ride is strained. With the heavy downpour, cars creep bumper to bumper. Nora stares into the watery red glare of taillights. Ken is as tense as she is. Their brief attempts at conversation have fizzled into silence. She feels a perverse need to be with him, even when he doesn't want her to. Like now. Something's wrong. She's never seen him so edgy, so irritable.

"C'mon! Damn it!" He blows the horn. Directional flashing, the car ahead straddles both lanes. "Jesus!" He hits the horn again and Nora cringes with the long blare.

"What's the point?"

"It's taking forever." He hunches over the wheel.

"Are we in a hurry?"

He doesn't answer. Even leaving the house, he seemed rushed. She needed to talk to Drew, but Ken insisted she wait until they get home.

Coming in was her idea. At first he said no, reminding her that Oliver doesn't want visitors, but she persisted. She and Ken seem farther apart than ever. They need to be alone together. That's the problem. Or maybe it's her. This constant dread, waiting for the ax to fall. She's always tense, jumpy.

And now, even more worried, about Drew. This is the second day in a row he's missed school. Headache and sick stomach, he claimed. He said he was in bed all day, sleeping, but when she got home from work she could tell he'd been downstairs playing video games, and his bed looked the way it had this morning. A mess, but the exact same mess. Right before they left tonight, she was loading the dishwasher when she noticed a shot glass on the top rack. She sniffed, but couldn't smell anything. She hurried into the pantry, fruitlessly checking the liquor cabinet. Even if something was missing she wouldn't know. Ken might, but the last thing she wants is another confrontation between them. Drew makes no effort to hide his scorn for his father. The least little thing and Ken just glares at him. When she went upstairs, to see if she could smell alcohol on Drew, he was taking a shower. A wet shot glass doesn't mean anything. He was probably just fooling around, the way kids do, shots of orange juice, soda, something like that. And besides, wasn't Chloe about this age when she was caught drinking? Yes, but at a party, with a bunch of friends. Not alone, on a school day, in an empty house.

"Ken, we've got to do something about Drew. He's so unhappy."

"He's a moody kid. He feeds off all this . . . this—"

"Feeds? Feeds off what, Ken? Your lies? The pain he feels? The confusion, all the mixed messages through the years? Can't you see the fallout here? It's not just us. It's our kids. We gave them a good start, a good life, and suddenly everything's at risk. Of course they're going to be messed up. Especially Drew!"

"And you play right into it, you know that, don't you?"

"What're you talking about?"

"These things happen, Nora. I'm not saying it's right, but all this misery, all this guilt all the time!" He slaps on the directional. "I mean, he's not the only kid with a screwed-up family."

"You mean Clay, don't you?"

"Oh, Jesus," he groans.

"You've always compared them. Always. And don't think for a moment that's lost on Drew."

"You can't let anything go, can you? You just can't."

"No. Not when it comes to my children. Because that's sacred ground. To me, anyway."

They drive the rest of the way in cold silence. When they arrive at the rehab hospital, Oliver isn't in bed, but in a chair with a blanket over his legs. He is freshly shaved and his wiry hair has been trimmed closer than she's ever seen it. He's lost weight and his color is good. Except for his drooping right eye you might not think anything had happened to him.

"Oliver!" Determined to be cheery, she kisses his cheek and holds out her arms, then knows instantly not to. Fond as they've always been of each other, theirs was never a hugging relationship and won't be now. No matter his troubles. And seeing his clenched jaw, she's afraid he's angry she's here.

In his struggle to communicate Oliver hardly seems to notice her. This must be what Ken meant after his last visit. Perseveration, he called it. Once his brother gets something in his head, he can't seem to get past it. He gets stuck on a topic and won't let it go. Wasn't he always like that, in a way, Nora said, but sitting here now, observing, she understands.

A week's worth of *Chronicles* is piled in Ken's lap. With one eye still seeing double, Oliver can't read for very long. So Ken has been reading aloud excerpts from various articles. Particularly, stories about the election, the two openings on the city council. One of the candidates is Helen McNally, Oliver's old nemesis in local politics. Nora winces as Ken plods on, unaware of the irony here. She can see it in Oliver's trembling lips. For weeks now the *Chronicle* has had McNally under their microscope. This isn't the way Oliver runs the paper. This isn't even Ken's doing, but Joe Creel's, the managing editor. With Oliver gone, Creel runs what he wants, one less task for Ken.

"Get this," Ken says, shaking the paper for emphasis. "Records show that over the past four years McNally has accumulated nine hundred and eighty-five dollars' worth of unpaid parking tickets," he reads.

What the article doesn't report is that McNally paid those tickets last summer. Stop, she wants to tell Ken. In trying to impress his brother, he's making him feel more helpless. Oliver grunts and gestures with his good hand but can't articulate his thoughts. Something about Stephen, it seems. Ken continues reading.

"No!" Oliver says with a thump on the tray table. "Don't! We don't . . ."

"What? We don't what?" Ken looks over the paper, concerned.

"Read . . . the . . . read," Oliver says, shaking his head. "The point . . . it's no . . ."

"You're tired. Want me to stop? I don't blame you. Getting a little sick of hearing my own voice," Ken says, with that chipper nod she knows drives Oliver crazy.

"No!" Oliver says in disgust, his face purple. "You don't know." Every word is a struggle. "You . . . you never know. You don't care. That's . . . that's how. Why," he adds, and his head sags in defeat.

"Oliver," she says, but he still won't look at her.

"I told her . . . not to . . . you . . . don't . . . not to bring . . . her."

"Aw, c'mon." Ken reaches to pat his brother's shoulder. "Don't make Nora—"

"Don't! Don't . . . touch me," Oliver shouts, and Ken looks stunned. The corners of Oliver's mouth glisten with foamy spittle. His chest rises and falls with agitated breathing. He rocks in his chair. Like a cornered child.

"Oliver?" she says quietly, slipping into the old role, conduit between them. "I'm sorry. Do you want me to leave? I know, I shouldn't have come. But I wanted to see you."

"Well . . . here." Oliver tries to hold out his good arm, even that clearly an effort. "For your . . . your . . . pressure." Again, in his eyes that flash of panic, to have lost his language, to be unable to express himself the way he wants to, the way he used to, in all his sardonic incisiveness. She manages a weak smile. If she speaks she knows she'll cry, but his resentful stare turns to his brother.

Stephen stopped in this morning, Oliver finally manages to get them to understand. "On his way to . . . fly . . ." He shakes his fist, frustrated.

"Fly. Hey, that's good. Fly, his flight. See, we're getting good at this," Ken says as if Oliver's grimacing struggle isn't happening. "It's just going to take time, Oll, that's all. Hey," he says, with a tap on the tray table as he gets up. "Want anything? Magazine? Something from the snack bar?" he asks with a look at Nora. She knows how difficult this is for him, but on the other hand, it's hardly some nettlesome board meeting he can slip out of. His frustration is not lost on his brother.

"Stop rooning the paper, that's . . . what!" Oliver shouts after him.

"What?" Ken wheels around in the doorway. "What're you talking about?"

"That . . . that . . . Gendron! Your private . . . you can't . . . roon . . . the pa-per. You can't! No!" Oliver bellows.

Ken's face reddens, but his lips are thin and white. Through his mangled speech, Oliver accuses his brother of not listening, always taking the easy way out, never caring about anyone or anything, not the paper or his family, just himself. "You . . . roon . . . everything. Always!"

"Stop it, Oliver!" she says, pointing at him. "Just stop it right now. Your brother is trying so hard to help you and help the paper and do the right thing for everyone. And I know how hard this is for you, what you're going through, but don't do this. *Don't* take it out on Ken."

"We don't do that! We don't hide . . . things!" Oliver shouts in a burst of clarity as she heads toward the door.

"Oh, yes we do, Oliver. All of us. All the time," she says, then leaves.

"For you! For you! For you!" His bellowing follows her down the hallway. She is still shaking when Ken comes out to the car.

"I'm sorry. I shouldn't have done that." She feels terrible. Poor

Oliver, an easy target for her own frustrations, she tries to explain. "But Stephen, I mean, why is he doing that? Especially now, running to Oliver whenever anything happens. Why doesn't he come to you if he's got a complaint?"

"He did. I told him to go fuck himself!"

Shocked, she stares at the sweep of the wipers and doesn't say anything for a moment.

"Why?"

"Because . . . because everywhere I turn, I'm . . ." He hits the wheel.

"What? Trapped?"

He glances over, then looks back at the puddled road ahead.

"That's it, isn't it? Isn't it?"

"Things, they just keep piling up, that's all."

"What things? Me? The children? The paper?"

"I'm an ass, okay, I always knew that, but I never figured I'd be this much of a screwup." His voice breaks.

"What're you talking about? Of course this isn't going to be easy. It's going to take time, Ken. And probably a lot longer than either one of us thinks. Especially now with Oliver sick and you having to take on all this new responsibility. But in the end we'll both be so much stronger. I know we will." She squeezes the back of his neck. The muscles are rigid, unyielding. "Okay?" she says, but he drives in silence. "We have to be able to talk, Ken. Especially when everything's so . . . so connected. The children, our work, the—"

"You tell me then. Who's Eddie Hawkins? Who is he?"

"What do you mean?" Her ears ring as if from a blow.

"That guy I met. The night of Oliver's stroke. I told you about him. He said he knows you."

"Not really. I mean, I did. Years ago. Summer of my junior year. The job I had. Lake George? The hotel there, remember? I know I've told you." Eyes wide, she sighs. "God, what was that? Twenty-five, twenty-six, years ago."

"He's seen you. He's talked to you. Just recently. He told me. You caught up on old times, he said. Some trip you took. The two of you. Together."

"He *said* that? Oh, for godsakes!"

"Nora. What's going on?"

"I don't know. Nothing! He was just some guy, that's all. I was seventeen. If that."

"No. I mean now." The way he says it scares her. "Why the secrecy?"

"There's no secrecy." The road blurs.

"Then why didn't you say anything? That night. I told you his name. You—"

"What're you getting at, Ken? What're you trying to say? I mean, with everything that's been going on . . . all the turmoil . . . half the time I'm lucky if I can remember my own goddamn name!"

She stares out the side window. So it's true. Money won't stop him. He wants more. That's what he's doing, and Ken knows. She can tell. He's waiting for her to tell him.

"All right," she says when he pulls into their driveway. "He's strange, that's why. That's why I didn't say anything."

"What do you mean, strange?"

"I don't know . . . like, the way he showed up. I mean, after all these years."

"What's wrong with that? It happens." With his scrutiny, she feels steadied by his concern, reassured. She's not alone in this.

"Because . . . because I can't stand him. And I couldn't then, and he knows it." She hugs herself, shivering. Even this guarded admission floods her with relief. "And . . . and him running into you like that, it gave me the creeps." Her teeth chatter. "And now what, he shows up again? He comes to you?"

CHAPTER · 18

From its beginning, Sojourn House has gotten by with two residential dishwashers, both donated. Now, with one broken and costing too much to repair, it seems time, Father Grewley says from the head of the conference table, to invest in a large, commercial-grade dishwasher.

It is 7:45 p.m. and this was a hastily convened meeting. With eight women and ten children currently sheltered here, kitchen efficiency is paramount, the priest continues. Nora nods. She is trying to pay attention, any problem a distraction from her own. She digs in her purse for a tissue. Pretending to wipe her nose, she's really trying to block the heavy smell of alcohol and musky perfume. It's coming from Letitia Crane, who sits beside her, lips pursed, twiddling her thumbs, alert for any point she can seize, then sermonize to death. As CraneCopley and Lyndell sink deeper into litigation and investigation, Letitia has become a most contentious presence at these meetings. Ever since the omission of her name from the House letterhead nothing escapes her boozy scrutiny. And yet, Nora thinks, aren't she and Letitia clinging to the same life raft here?

Father Grewley passes the pamphlet around. A brand-new, heavy-duty Exlon dishwasher for only a thousand dollars. The wholesaler has agreed to free installation and removal of the old appliances. All Father Grewley needs now is the board's approval. He looks exhausted. He was up all night. One of the House children, a five-year-old boy, had to be rushed to the emergency room, with a raging fever.

"Sure . . . sure . . . sounds good . . . great . . . aye . . . ," each member offers around the table.

"Of course!" Nora says, pained by her exaggerated brightness. Everything feels forced, false, really. She shouldn't even be here. Not the caliber of person they need. Or deserve. Especially tonight.

"Excuse me," Letitia says rather loudly. Hers is the last vote. "But I think there's an even bigger issue here." She poses it as a question.

"And what might that be?" Chris Arrellio asks. The only male on the board, he makes little effort to hide his impatience with her nit-picking.

"Communal spirit?" Letitia squints at him. "And so, here we are, once again, missing an opportunity to teach these women how to help themselves."

Papers crinkle. Feet scrape under the table. No one speaks until Betsy Gleason's natural sweetness wafts through the mute censure.

"How, Letitia? In what way?"

Chris Arrellio gives a deep sigh in his suede bomber jacket. His car wash franchise has made him wealthy, but he wears his rough-edged, self-made persona with pride. Here it comes: no bs, cut to the chase. Any minute now, Nora thinks, this time welcoming it. His smirk doesn't deter Letitia. She's already off and running.

"Instead of always giving them free this and free that, isn't the best lesson of all self-reliance? By doing everything for them, aren't we just victimizing them more? Don't you see, they should be part of the solution. Instead of an expensive new dishwasher, *they* should be pitching in, helping out. Washing their *own* dirty dishes, for godsakes. I mean, what's—"

A light tap rattles the door. One of the new counselors, Dale Morgan, hurries in and whispers to Father Grewley. Excusing himself, he leaves quickly. In his absence, dissension crabs its way around the table. Surprisingly, Letitia has a compatriot, Krenna, the wizened German woman who never opens her mouth but now agrees that maybe we do do too much. Maybe we kill their spirit. Maybe that's what these women need, to learn how to fight back.

Fight back, Nora thinks, closing her eyes. *How? And with what, when we're barely holding on.* Tonight at dinner, Drew and Ken's sullen standoff escalated from Drew's mumbling and not passing the butter when Chloe asked and Ken's demanding that he be more respectful of his sister to Drew's bolting from the table, shouting, "Go to hell. Go to fucking hell, all of you, for all I care!" before slamming the door.

"Let him go!" Ken yelled as she started into the breezeway. "I can't take it anymore. I'm sick of it. He wants to brood, he can go do it somewhere else."

"No, Ken," she said, her tone and look putting him on notice that the day it came to that, the choice would be easy. *He* would leave. Not her son.

"But Mom, he's always like that," Chloe implored from the table. "You should see him in school. I mean, it's so embarrassing. He's always alone. He won't sit with anyone. He doesn't even talk to people. It's, like, weird."

"Well, then maybe *you* should sit with him and talk with him. You're his sister. Maybe that's all he needs, a little attention from you. From someone!" she declared, her voice ragged and trembling.

"Mom!" Chloe cried, jumping up from the table. "That's not fair, and you know it!" She threw down her napkin and ran upstairs.

"She's right," Nora said, more to herself than to Ken who stared into his untouched dinner. "It isn't fair. It really isn't."

"Nora?" Father Grewley gestures through the opening door. Could she give him a hand with something? Her legs wobble. Drew. Something's happened. When she left he still wasn't home.

"It's Alice," he says as they hurry along the corridor to his office. "Her neighbor just brought her in. She's in a bad way. He really did a job on her this time."

Alice sits in shadows, her face in her hands. The neighbor, Roz, is a wrinkled, shrewd-eyed woman with long gray hair. She apologizes in a raspy voice for turning off the overhead light, but it was hurting Alice's eyes. Roz wanted to bring her to the hospital, but Alice refused. She's afraid they'll call the police on Luke and, besides, Roz adds, Alice doesn't have any insurance. Father Grewley asks where the children are. Roz's husband is bringing them to Alice's mother. Is this what she wants? he leans close to ask Alice, who shrugs. Her head bobs, a battered weight on its thin stem.

"Poor thing. She don't know what she wants," the neighbor whispers to Nora, who tries to hold her breath against the reek of cigarette smoke in the woman's clothes, jeans, and a hooded Patriots sweatshirt. "She thinks she's miscarrying. I don't know, maybe that's why. Like, this is the last thing she needs now."

The only available space is on the third floor. A dark, chilly room, its angled attic ceilings are still stained from last winter's ice dams. A frayed braided rug lies molded into the rippled contours of the gray floorboards. But there is a pretty stenciled chest of drawers and an old mahogany double bed with a frilly yellow duvet. And this room has its own attached bathroom; only a few do. Nora waits outside on the landing. Maizie Dennehy is in with Alice. Maizie is one of four nurses they can call on day or night whenever an emergency comes in. Father Grewley leaves the room energized. He will return to the meeting with new resolve. Alice's plight confirms their mission. Before he starts downstairs, he whispers to Nora that if Letitia is so at odds with Sojourn House's purpose, then she must resign for the good of the board. And so must *she,* Nora realizes ashamedly. So overwhelmed by her own troubles, she forgot to call Alice back. Her concern has become a charade. All she really cares about is her family.

Maizie comes out and closes the door. "She may be miscarrying, but at least nothing's broken," she says. A stocky woman, she is a pretty, perky blonde. Even now she manages to smile. Given a choice, the guests always want Maizie. "Terrible bruising. Mostly he slapped her. Every time she'd try to get up he'd start on her again. It's almost like he knew. Nothing that would send her to the hospital. After a while, they get pretty savvy."

For a moment Nora isn't sure who Maizie means, abused or abuser. Both, she decides, entering the room, and herself as well, here again, victim of her own mistakes. Eddie's bad penny, because on it goes. On and on. Pain and cruelty. Everywhere. To think she once considered herself somehow apart from all this. A spectator. Helper. But in the end, what is the difference between her and any of them?

Alice is sitting up in bed. The ice pack for her face is in her lap. Her head turns from the gleam of entering light, from Nora.

"I'm sorry," Nora says. "Is there anything I can do?"

"No." Emptiness. A door closing on an abandoned house. Hope smothered. Love. Children, every youthful dream snuffed out with its utterance. *No.* Nothing.

"Things will get better. You're strong. I know you don't think you are right now, but you'll see. You'll find out. Your strength will come from your children, Alice. That's what he keeps trying to beat out of you. But he can't. Because you're not going to let him, are you? Ever again."

"I wish I was dead."

"No, you don't. You don't mean that." She leans on the bed and Alice winces. "You have everything to live for. You do."

"Not anymore," Alice says with a slow, almost foolish smile. "I'm pregnant. That's why it happened. He's so mad. He said I did it on purpose. To trick him. Because I didn't know what else to do with my pathetic life."

"That's ridiculous! Of—"

"No, it's true. He's right. I did. All I wanted was for us to be a family, to be happy," she bawls, sobbing into the duvet. "Each one, that's all I ever wanted."

Nora lets her cry. She wants to hold her but can't. Robin would, so easily and naturally, she knows. She remembers Robin's tears the day she told her she was pregnant with Lyra, sobbing because she didn't want to be and had even called an abortion clinic but then had decided that it was a sign, because maybe a baby, new life in her troubled house, might change all that had gone wrong in her marriage, Robin had said, bawling, as if at the shallowness of her hope, holding out her arms, shaming Nora with her plea to be held. Still now, Nora wonders, what reserve, what coldness, what emptiness kept her from comforting a woman she had loved. Yes. Loved, with a depth and joy she had never felt for another woman before Robin. And so, how cruel, how heartless, of them for what they did, for using her. And in the end, how predictable. How complicit she was, time after time, in her quick dismissal of the obvious. How easy she made it for them. Because as long as they loved each other, *she* was loved.

"No matter what happens, you've got your children, Alice. You're still a family. All that matters is them. You'll be a better family without him. You will."

Alice buries her bruised face in the bunched-up hem of the bed covering. Nora Trimble Hammond who can't even let food pass her lips under this patched roof sits on the side of the bed. She puts both arms around this broken woman. A child really, she tells herself, waiting for something, goodness, wisdom, some energy to flow between them. She will not pull back, but all she feels is dread.

"There. There, now," she whispers, her hand at the back of this snarled and sweaty hair, days of an unwashed muskiness, she thinks, then realizes it must be the heavy bleed. The smell is blood, sickeningly strong. And familiar. "It's going to be all right. You'll see. I promise," she makes herself say, makes herself sit there, trying not to gag.

A small plane flies overhead. For a moment it drowns out the children's voices. He watches from the corner. The wind gusts and he turtles his chin deeper into his collar. He hates the cold. With the exception of the one child, the others wear hats and mittens. She runs around the carousel, screeching with laughter. Two small girls chase after her. Alone, under the gnarled locust tree, her mother sits at a silvery, weathered picnic table. Her face is hidden by the curled visor of a bright green baseball cap. Black seedpods crunch underfoot as he moves closer. Talking on her cell phone, so deep in conversation, she doesn't look up until he sits down.

"Gotta go." She snaps her phone shut. "I didn't see you coming."

Almost an accusation the way she says it. Still though, he smiles. "You were too busy talking."

"My mother," she says so quickly that he knows she's lying.

"How come you don't take my calls?"

She stands up and looks around, squinting as she watches Lyra swing, belly on the rubber sling, spread-eagled. Like a trapped bug, he thinks. The cricket legs he used to pull out and then the calm he always felt.

"All my messages, you musta got one, anyway."

"It's been so busy. Doctor appointments. Then Clay's . . . he hurt himself. This is Lyra's first day out of the house."

"That's not why."

"It's cold, I know, but she needs this." Shivering in her short denim jacket, she hugs herself, revealing the soft flesh of her waist. "Lyra!" she calls and strides off suddenly, as if something is wrong when all the girl has done is jump off the swing and run to the slide. Instead of climbing the ladder, Lyra is walking up the slide itself. At the top, a younger child sits, waiting her turn. Poised behind her on the ladder, a red-cheeked, curly-haired little girl with glasses grins and waits her turn. Lyra laughs. She enjoys being in the way, holding things up, he thinks as he follows Robin. She tells Lyra to get off the slide so the two other girls can come down.

"That's Jane!" Lyra points up at the petite, blue-eyed child, unlike Lyra, so stiffly bundled in her quilted snowsuit that her legs stick out in front of her. "And Mary, that's her sister." The two waiting children smile down at Lyra. "C'mon, Janie-Jane!" Lyra laughs, daring, taunting, teasing like her mother. Just as Robin reaches to take her daughter off the high metal slide, the child, Jane, loses her grip and hurtles down on her slick nylon bottom, boots first, into Lyra, knocking her back onto the frozen ground. Quickly next, comes Mary, landing on both of them.

Eddie chuckles. Brat. She had that coming.

Lyra wails and Robin is helping up the crying girls. Their mother runs over from the sand box where she's been gathering up their toys.

"Janie!" the woman calls. The smaller girl's nose is bleeding. Her sister hugs her.

Should have been the other one, he thinks. Lyra, the troublemaker.

"I'm sorry," Robin says. "Lyra knows better than to go up the wrong way."

Her tension excites him. He wants the other mother to go at her, attack her, hurt her. She deserves it. A good slap, that's what she needs, right across that full red mouth. His fist clenches as he imagines it hard on her wrist, and her soft, wet face at his, begging forgiveness.

The women apologize, assuring one another it was just one of those things. That's how they'll learn, the hard way, they agree.

Ditto that. The hard way, he thinks, stunned to see her suddenly leaving. Carrying Lyra, she hurries down the street. He calls her name, but she only walks faster. Her car isn't parked in the playground lot, but across the street, behind CVS. Trying to hide it. From him, he knows, easily keeping pace. So close he hears her panting. He waits while she buckles Lyra into her booster seat. Closing the door, she stands with her back against it. Message clear: shielding her kid from him. Raising his hands, he steps back.

"Why? What'd I do?"

"Nothing."

Her weak smile infuriates him.

"I just have to go, that's all." She makes a show of pushing up her sleeve and checking her watch.

The honey brown fuzz on her forearm makes him ache with horniness. More hair than you'd expect on such a beautiful woman, proof of her earthiness, her warmth, all that makes her so desirably real. A creature of flesh and fear, born for a man's pleasure. Submission now in the slow sweep of her gaze. Her soft mouth trembles.

"Please." She steps around him to open her door. She gets into the car.

"Tell me what's wrong," he says, holding the door. She can't close it without hurting his hand.

"Don't do this. Please." She looks up at him as she starts the car.

A woman has left the pharmacy and is getting into the next car. She glances over at them before backing out.

Again, Robin tugs at the door and says she has to go. Why, he demands over the racing engine. He doesn't get it. One minute they're friends, next minute not. Why?

"Everything you told me, all those random things, the space program, your sick brother, and your businesses, but the one thing you never said was, you know Nora."

"Yeah, I know Nora. So?"

"You know what I mean," she says grimly.

"No. I don't. Why's it such a big deal?" He grins, wanting to laugh. Toying with her, he feels giddy, almost silly. And powerful.

"Mommy!" Lyra whines, and kicks the back of her mother's seat. "I have to go potty! Now!"

"I have to go." She shifts into reverse, but he doesn't move. "Please."

"I knew her from a long time ago. Then I ran into her again. That's all. I swear!" He yanks the door open and leans in. "Robin," he says reassuringly. "She doesn't have anything to do with us. Really." Such a look of fear comes over her that he cups his hand on the side of her face. "You're the best thing that's ever happened to me. Believe that."

"Oh my God," she gasps while behind her the little brat's tantrum of kicks and threats to do poop enrages him. Robin leans away from his touch, cringing almost. Her hands shake on the wheel. She inches the car back, until he is forced out of the way. She speeds off.

His skin feels prickly. His eyes hurt. That bitch. It came from her. Why do people do this, always setting obstacles in his way?

Everything enrages him, getting caught next to this wheezy fat man when the light changes to green, the biting wind and honking horns as he darts through traffic to the municipal lot. And now this, the orange ticket flapping under his wiper. He shreds it into tiny pieces, which he flings at the meter. It doesn't make sense, though. She didn't want anyone to know. And all that money, without him even asking. So why would she have said anything? Unless she's been checking, looking back, and now she thinks there's nothing to fear. That she's free of him. Suddenly, he's afraid. What if she wants her money back? Turns it around on him. Extortion. What if she calls the police who've just written a ticket off the other bitch's plate? And here he is in her car. Brandnew, but he should've gotten rid of it. Should've done a lot of things.

▪   ▪   ▪

Years of cigarette smoke have stained the ceiling a dusky yellow. The flat brown carpet smells of dust and mold, the mattress sour with stale pee. He usually sleeps with the window cracked open. But for the last couple of nights the heat's been off. Charlie's been in twice to check the thermostat. He can't fix it and his electrician is out of town, he says with a shrug. Then call another one, Eddie says.

"Easier said than done," Charlie tells him, peering out from his little pig eyes. "I'm just the manager. I gotta use who they say."

"What about the baseboard, the unit?" Eddie suggests.

Grunting, Charlie kneels down and pries off the cover. In a motion, Eddie slips a screwdriver and pliers from Charlie's tool bucket.

"Nothing here," Charlie says, grunting even more as he gets up.

Eddie's no fool. They're trying to freeze him out. And it's Tiff, the girlfriend, Charlie's, the snaggle-toothed beast who cleans. She goes through his stuff, so Eddie won't let her in, and she hates him.

Later that night, as soon as the manager's unit goes dark, he puts on a heavy jacket. Leaves the TV on, volume low, lights on. Shuts the bathroom door, just in case, then slips out, locking the door after him. He drives north, two states up, into Maine. Kittery, little town on the coast. Never been here before, but he likes the narrow, winding streets and old houses, mostly small cottages. He's looking for a car that doesn't appear to get much use. Little noticed. He keeps driving, farther north. Motels and fish shacks. Souvenir shops. Strip malls. And then he spots it, there, next to a sagging red barn, parked close in, on the side, to keep it out of the way of the other old cars in the narrow dirt driveway. Two windowless sheds connect the barn to a small white house. The house is in darkness. He parks down the road, walks back, tools in hand. The first screw spins right off. The second one is rust-frozen so he tries twisting the license plate against it. Suddenly, a light glares from behind and he hits the ground. An old pickup rattles into the driveway. The motor dies, lights next, though no one gets out. He sees the long flare of a cigarette tip over the wheel. The door creaks open and a man slides out. He drops the butt, grinds it under his boot toe. He closes the truck door slowly, then creeps into the house. No lights go on inside. Eddie waits. Then he reaches up, twisting and pulling on the plate until it finally rips free, but the jagged metal corner slices deeply between his thumb and forefinger. Doesn't hurt, though. The sting of cold air at his torn flesh feels good, tells him he's alive, as he runs back to the car with his new plate. Action. Eddie at his best.

CHAPTER 19

This is so nice," Nora says as she pours her second cup of coffee. Ken has assigned someone, Bibbi's daughter, actually, to work on the *Medical* supplement. Jessica Bond is a pleasant enough young woman but easily bewildered. Nora knows she should get into the office early, but it's a rare weekday morning that finds her family together at breakfast. Some peace has been restored, however strained. Drew has apologized for the other night, though he and his father are still barely speaking. By the time she returned from her meeting, Drew was back home. Ken had found him alone at a back table in Starbucks. Nursing a glass of water because he didn't have any money on him: naturally, Ken added with withering scorn. More and more lately, she is alarmed by his harshness toward Drew and their constant tension, as if Ken is the wounded party, as if Drew has somehow harmed him.

Chloe's phone is ringing in her pocket. She checks the number, then runs from the kitchen, grinning.

"Since when do we take calls at the table?" Ken asks, folding the business section next to his cereal bowl. In the past this would have been Nora's censorious line, played to Ken's no-big-deal shrug.

"She didn't. She left," Drew says, jaw clenched, waiting.

Ken ignores him, continues reading. He looks drawn, almost despondent, the way he's been for days. It's the paper, he assures her, particularly his cousin, undermining his authority. On Monday, Stephen called a board meeting without bothering to tell him. She'd never seen Ken so angry or so humiliated. The emotional storms of these last few weeks are finally taking their toll. Strange, though, how those years of his affair still seem their happiest as a family. A kind of mania, really, living as they did in an almost constant state of gusto, exuberance, the house filled with friends, laughter, especially Ken's. Her third child, she often joked. And yet, with his life so tenuously balanced, how could he have been, or even seemed, so carefree, so guiltless? Because he had everything. He did, didn't he? As long as no one pierced the bubble, the illusion of happiness was more than enough.

"Finish up, Drew. You don't want to be late," she says, uneasy with his brooding.

"I'm not the driver. Tell her," he says, nodding toward the other room.

"*Her?*" Ken snaps. "You mean Chloe?"

Drew's snarl is lost as Chloe rushes in to the table, sobbing. Joe Turcotte is dead, she cries. Killed in Iraq, and he's only nineteen. Max just told her. That's terrible, Nora says, unable to place the name. Chloe is devastated. She's not sure, she says when her father asks where he's from. Leesboro, she thinks, but he and Max were friends from camp. They bunked in the same cabin every summer until they were fourteen.

"And now he's dead. Just like that. I can't believe it," she gasps.

"You didn't even know him," Drew mumbles into his coffee.

"That's not the point. That's *so* not the point," Chloe says.

"Such a waste," Ken says with such disgust that for a moment Nora thinks he means Drew.

"Nineteen!" Chloe cries. "He's just two years older than me. I don't get it. Why're we doing this? Why?" she demands as if they know but won't tell her.

"I know, hon." Nora kisses the top of her daughter's head. "It's hard. Especially now when it all seems so pointless."

"Well, maybe all we can do is hope some good comes out of it," Ken says with a long sigh.

"Good!" Chloe cries. "What kind of good's gonna come out of that, a kid dying?"

"That's not what I meant. Obviously." Ken gets up and hugs Chloe.

She stiffens back and Nora remembers how in the middle of the night only Ken could soothe his little girl.

"So what *do* you mean? What kinda good?" Drew is staring at his father.

"There aren't any easy answers, Drew. Maybe we should leave it at that," Ken says.

"Why?" Drew asks with a hint of a smile. "Because that's what the paper wants?"

Ken sighs, regards him for a moment. "The war in Iraq's—"

"No!" Drew protests so venomously that they all shrink back. "It's not a war. It's a lie, just one more lie no one wants to admit."

The silence in the kitchen is thick, suffocating.

When Nora gets to work, she sits in the warm car, listening to the radio. Another helicopter crash near Fallujah, more dead, wounded, maimed, like the rest, nameless for her until Joe Turcotte, a boy asleep on a bunk in a summer cabin, on the fringes of her once-perfect life, hermetically sealed, viewed through glass, as she stares out at the parking lot, alone with her well-guarded secret, its gathering force fed by lies. And, of these, most insidious, all the lies allowed in submission to the greater good. Holding on to her mother. Keeping her marriage together.

After the children left for school she asked Ken to stay, please, just a little while so they could talk, but he couldn't. He had an eight thirty conference call. She's made up her mind. They all have to go to counseling. The family is sinking, fracturing, breaking into pieces. She turns off the radio. Just getting out of the car is an effort. And this briefcase, heavy at her side, why does she carry it? So important, every day, back and forth. As proof she matters? But to whom? For what? And in the end, who cares? Special supplements, filler no one reads, but Oliver insisted. Busywork. Why? Give her something to do? Make her feel important, useful in her meaningless life? No. Not true, not as long as she has her children. And Joe Turcotte—his mother, what's left for her now? She swallows against the lump in her throat.

"Hey!" someone shouts, and she turns with a gasp to see Eddie Hawkins, a strip of soiled gauze dangling from his hand. Scabby shaving nicks dot his chin.

"I gotta ask you something." Agitated, he shifts from foot to foot. "Robin Gendron, she and I, we . . . we're friends, you know. Good friends. Really good. Then all of a sudden, I don't know . . . it's, like, whoom!"

She cringes from the sudden slice of his bandaged hand by her face.

"Like, somebody said something, you know what I mean?"

"No. I don't know what you're talking about." Determined not to show fear, she stares at him. He's panting.

"You said something. About me. You told her, right?"

"Of course not."

"Don't mess with me, okay? There's too much . . . I got too much . . . I'm not gonna put up with it. With this shit, you got that?"

"What do you want? I don't understand. Why're you still here?"

His explosive laughter is like wild gunfire going off all around her. "I'll tell you what I fucking want. I want you and your fag husband to mind your own goddamn business, that's what the fuck I want." He jabs her shoulder. "Robin and me, we don't need this . . . this shit, get what I'm saying? You keep away from her, the two of you. You got that?"

His face is twisted with hatred. There's no reasoning with him. She never should have given him anything. She should have told Ken from the start, instead of thinking money would take care of it.

"I'm not putting up with it! No more! That's it!"

She hugs her briefcase and watches him lurch through the rows, muttering, his hand over the cars' roofs stabbing the air.

"Oh my God, oh my God," she whispers.

Nora!" Father Grewley calls with delight, bounding down the stairs. "Funny, I was just thinking of you. Did you get Alice's thank-you note?"

"I did, yes. It was lovely." Last week Father Grewley called and asked her to go to court with Alice for a restraining order against her husband. He said he had offered, but Alice really wanted Nora there with her. Horrified by the prospect, the visibility, the involvement, no, she couldn't: work, she said, the children, just a crazy week. But if there was anything else, anything she could do, please let her know. Oh. Well, yes. Of course. Her own apartment, that made sense. The poor thing. She'd be only too glad to pay the security deposit, first and last month's rent. Which, knowing Father Grewley, was probably the real reason for his call.

"I'll go get her, she's upstairs. She'll be thrilled to see you."

"No!" she says too quickly. "I wish I could, but I'm . . . on my way to work."

"Well, just so you know, you and your husband, what you're doing for Alice, it's more than kind, more than generous, it's amazing. Absolutely unbelievable. She's a new person. Totally energized. She's going to look at one more apartment before she decides. She said she doesn't want you paying too much. And!" He clasps his hands at his chin. "We may even have a job for her. Part time. Office work. At one of Chris Arrellio's car washes."

Nora squirms. She's often seen him do this. Like klieg lights on a pebble, his profuse gratitude so far exceeds the giving, it somehow manages to diminish its worth. It's his very effective way of stroking donors' egos while making them eager, hungry to do more.

He is wearing jeans and a plaid shirt. He's been moving some donated furniture into the back wing of the House. An additional family room for the guests. Her idea, he reminds her: not true, though, just his net cast wider.

She apologizes for not calling first, but she needs to talk to him. He's pretty sure he knows why, he says, but not to worry, it's been taken care of. Letitia Crane is leaving the board.

"Just not the right fit, that's all I said, and amazingly enough, she agreed!" He pats his chest, rolls his eyes with relief.

A half hour later, she is still talking. Rather than have the desk between them, he has pulled his chair next to hers. Everything spills out:

the shock of Ken's affair and its fallout on her fragile family, still together, though the pressure is building, especially now with the intrusion of Eddie Hawkins into the mess her life has become, and the fear
she feels, this anxiety, this nightmarish paralysis, knowing something
bad is going to happen if she doesn't make the right decisions, but not
having a clue what to do, because there's nothing she can do, nothing
she can change. It was all so long ago it doesn't even seem real sometimes, which is the dichotomy she's been living, two separate planes,
the everyday, physical reality of her family's needs and this looming
blackness of the past. She didn't do anything that night in the desert,
she couldn't have hurt that man, and yet something did happen, something terrible, she's always known that. Even with her uncertainty
about the man's injuries, the priest merely nods. She was so young, his
only comment. If he's the least bit shocked he hides it well. He can't
afford to be too candid. After all, the Hammond name is valuable to
him. She goes to the edge, draws back, can't say the word *murder,* can't
admit buying a scumbag's silence. She describes the dreams, waking
up in a cold sweat, seeing that battered face, and that's when it's most
real, the feel, the smell, the sounds, but all she can do is run. Just keep
running. Still. It's all she does, she says quietly.

"What do you mean?"

"I've lived my whole life trying to keep one step ahead of what I
really am."

"And what's that?"

She stares at him. "A cold, selfish bitch and a liar."

"That's not what I see."

She shakes her head, laughs a little. "Yeah. I'm pretty good at it."
Even saying it, knows he sees what he needs to see. She can't blame
him, a practical cleric, safe in his church. She should leave.

"You think you're the only one, Nora? We're all hiding something.
Every one of us. It's human nature. But if we're at all decent, we're trying to make the best of who we are. Some ways, that's the hardest
struggle of all."

"But I'm losing the battle."

"No. You're just fighting the wrong fight. All you're seeing inside is sin, when it's your own goodness you should be looking for. Acknowledging. Celebrating."

"You don't understand," she sighs.

"Yes, I do. Because I've seen it. The way you were with Alice. That meant so much to her. You have no idea. The giving of yourself, you gave her confidence. That someone like you would . . . would take the time." *Someone like you.* His fervid praise angers her.

"Want to know the truth?" Instead of lowering her gaze, she lifts her head, stares, watching, baiting him. She can't believe what's coming out of her mouth. She's not sure who she's trying to hurt more, herself or him. "I couldn't stand the smell of her. I can't even eat here, have you ever noticed that? I can't stand the meetings, I can barely sit through them. Everyone's talking, and all I'm hearing is phoniness, self-promotion, all their networking, one more rung up the ladder, and I'm thinking to myself, what the hell am I doing here? And then I think, because I'm just like them. I am. That's why."

"No," he says softly, then sits for a few moments in stillness. "Do you know how many times a day I ask myself that exact same question? And how inadequate I feel? Not just to the need, the task, but to my own expectations. But that's okay! Because that's living an examined life, Nora. An authentic life. Being alive in spirit. Being completely and honestly real. Questioning everything you do. But what can happen, though, is you end up turning that same harsh spotlight on everyone around you. And that's not right. It's not fair." Whether real or feigned, his anguish drains her as he compares his own shameful failure of spirit. His disgust with the women's self-pitying paralysis, his irritation with their poorly behaved children, his own prideful impatience when he senses self-important board members wondering what character deficit hounded him into the priesthood instead of into their more valid world of commerce and success. And, of course, the food: he doesn't like it either.

"Not so much," he adds, smiling.

She appreciates the attempt, but his confession, his well-intentioned descent to her level, only adds to the guilt. There's nothing he can do or say to help. Nothing she hasn't already considered. He's still talking. She wants to go but can't leave him thinking he hasn't helped. She thanks him and says she feels much better now.

"But what are you going to do?" he asks when she stands up.

"Keep at it," said with a flash of Nora Trimble Hammond's brightest smile. "Keep slogging away."

"I mean that fellow. Eddie Hawkins."

"Oh, nothing. One of these days, I'm sure he'll be gone."

"You said you're afraid of him. What if he is crazy?"

"Strange. That's a better word. Weird. I guess that's really what it is."

"You're sure?" He frowns. "I got a lotta people I can call." With his attempt at menace, he seems only more virtuous. Innocent.

His hand hurts as he rings the doorbell again. Third time here today. Yesterday, in her mailbox he left a pair of red leather gloves and a note: *Stay warm. Stay close. Love, Eddie.* He walks back out to the street and checks. Still there. He scoops up mud and smears the painted stick bird. Bitch. After all he's done. Groceries, errands, presents, and she can't even pick up the phone, come to the door, or bother bringing his gift inside.

"Robin!" He keeps banging the brass knocker. He leans over the railing and looks in the window. There's a light on, probably from the kitchen. His shoes sink into the squishy lawn as he walks around the back of the house, and now his feet are wet. Two days of rising temperatures have warmed the frozen ground to mush. He peers through the curtained door glass. Stove light on. Cupboard doors open. Soup bowls, box of Ritz crackers, and naked Barbie dolls on the table. Overflowing laundry basket on a chair. Usual countertop clutter, dishes, candles, art supplies, an open photo album, next to the sink, a floppy aloe plant and a bag of soil.

His hand throbs with every knock. Again, he calls her name. Can't go back to the motel. Last night, they changed his lock while he was out looking for Robin. There'd been a complaint, or so they said,

Charlie and the snaggle-toothed beast. His TV was on too loud so when he didn't come to the door, they had no choice but to let themselves in. Anyway, he and Charlie had words. Then the beast had to go and put in her two cents. Next thing he knew they were in a shoving match, when Charlie pulled out a gun and ordered him to clear out his things and leave before he called the cops.

"Robin!" He pounds on the door. Tries the knob and it turns. Now that he's inside, he hears the vacuum cleaner. He follows the sound to the family room, watches from the doorway. She's wearing a red running bra and baggy black gym shorts. Barefoot. Long strands of hair obscure her face in her struggle to maneuver the vacuum under an end table. Sofa and chair cushions are piled in the corner. A can of furniture polish and rags are on the mantel. The television has been pulled out from the wall. His heart swells. He forgives her. She didn't hear the phone or him at the door, how could she? Reaching down, he yanks out the plug, and she turns with a shriek.

"Robin."

"What're you doing?" she demands, arm across her chest.

"The back door." He tells her it was partway open. "These last couple days, every time I come no one answers. I was worried, that's all."

"Well, you shouldn't have been. We're fine. Thank you, but now I have to finish this." She reels in the long black cord. "If you don't mind."

He grins. "No. Course not, go ahead." He sits on the sofa, and then feels foolish, angry that he's been set up. With no cushions, it's like sitting on a kid's chair, low and covered with crumbs and Lego blocks. And stuck under his leg, a leather card holder. He peers down at it. The gold monogram, RAG. Robert Gendron. A for Asshole. "I can wait."

"That's not what I meant," she says.

"Mom!" Clay calls from upstairs.

"You have to go, Eddie. Please."

He stares up in a rage of humiliation. The position she's putting him in, making him beg like this. Her fat white cat jumps with a thud onto the sofa back, sits purring behind his head.

"It's just that I've got so much to do." Her voice drops, and he's pleased. Good. She knows he's mad. "Everything's happening at once," she says.

"Mom! Mom, I need you! Come here, quick!" Clay calls, and she drops the cord and runs up the stairs.

He looks through the holder, removes three credit cards and Gendron's license. As he slips them into his pocket, the cat suddenly hisses. Startled, he swings back with a hard swipe, knocking the cat, meowing, onto the floor. Hurts to get up. His neck aches. The place he stayed last night had a lousy mattress, but warm, at least, and farther out of town. Just in case Charlie did call the cops. For good measure he'd tossed a few lit matchbooks into the motel Dumpster. He plugs in the cord now and starts to vacuum. The Oriental runner is covered with cat hair. He changes the attachment and is dragging the nozzle over one section of carpet at a time, when the vacuum shuts off.

"Don't do that. Please." She's wearing a shirt now.

"See." He points to the cleaned section. "Took me two seconds. Let me finish. You can do something else."

Again, she says no. She's very busy, and he really has to go. Clay is in a lot of pain upstairs with a broken ankle and her mother will be dropping Lyra off soon, so she needs to get as much done now as she can.

"So let me help." Kills his neck, but he starts pushing the television back against the wall. "All the more reason."

No. Leave it where it is, she tells him. It doesn't work, so she's getting a new one. All right then, he says, he'll bring it out to the trash. Obviously, Clay can't, and it's too heavy for her to carry.

"No! It's fine where it is. For now." Agitated, she's making no sense at all.

"You're upset with me. Why?" He's trying to be patient, but it's hard. She's hiding something, he can tell. "Why?" he demands, but too harshly. Her head snaps back, her eyes widen. He can't help smiling. Good, exactly what she needs. Shake her up a little, give him the upper hand instead of walking on eggshells all the time. "What the hell've I done to deserve this? I've been a good friend. A damn good friend, and you know I have, right? Right?" he asks, his face so close he inhales the stale coffee from her shallow breath.

When she nods, he clenches her wrist, not to hurt her, but to keep from hurting her.

"So why're we fighting like this?" His voice breaks. "What happened?"

"Nothing."

"People lie. You know that. You know they do."

Again, she nods, tries to back away. "You're bleeding." She lifts her hand. On her wrist, a bracelet of blood, his. He laughs. Her face is a mask. Part of her allure, her plan, but he's on to her, and now, she knows he is.

"We're the same, aren't we?"

"The bandage. I can fix that."

Even her kindness is sensual, born of desire, caring so she'll be cared for, wanting as much as she gives. He watches from the kitchen table while she washes her hands, scrubbing hard at her wrist, which only amuses him. His eyes are heavy, waiting. He imagines pressing against her round, perfect ass, though his yearning is less for sex than relief from this pressure in his skull, throbbing behind his eyeballs, needing her cries of pain, agony, fear, begging him to stop, to let her go.

She cuts a strip of adhesive tape. "There." She presses it over the loose gauze, then darts to the back door, opens it. He has to leave, she says from outside, but he doesn't budge. So, it was just a ruse, a way to get herself, then him, out of the house. Her mother will be here soon, any minute, she says. And then he understands. All right. Okay. That's why. The old bitch, always on Robin's case for something, dusty table-tops, clutter on the stairs, piles of laundry, unpaid bills, dirty litter boxes, broken window blinds. Him.

"Thank you," he says, grazing past her shoulder when every bone in his body aches to hold her.

▪ ▪ ▪

It is with studious deliberation that he moves from set to set. Takes his time. Squints, backs off, peering from different angles. Price tags don't matter, he assures the Best Buy salesman, it's quality he's after, the best picture, simple as that. Then he wants a plasma, he's told. This one here, the forty-inch SONY. Yeah, plasma, because that's what this surge in his veins is, a transfusion, pure, new blood rousing him as he counts out the bills. Still plenty left. Always been careful with money. Never was that important, not like it is for the rest of the world. His frugality used to amuse Helen, the old bitch. Cheapo, she called him. But it was always about getting by with the basics, the little he needed. The less he wanted, the more she bought for him. Now, it's the same with Robin. Only in reverse. Pleasing her is all that matters.

With every bump and turn the box teeters. The television takes up the whole backseat. He drives slowly, easing down on the brake. It wasn't just to save on the delivery charge but seeing her open it. The thought of her pleasure fills him with excitement. Knowing how the simplest things delight her, he imagines her squeal when she sees it.

"Damn." Yellow Volkswagen in the driveway. Her mother's. "Bitch." He keeps driving. Struggles to stay calm: no rush, he's got all the time in the world. A half hour later, she's finally gone. He pulls in, close to the house. He eases the cumbersome box from the car, shuffles onto the porch, leans an elbow into the bell.

"Surprise!" he says with the opening door.

Clay balances on one crutch. His left foot is in a cast. "My mother's not here." Before he can close the door, Eddie manages to wedge a corner of the box into the opening. When's she coming back? The boy plays dumb, doesn't know where she went or if she's with his grandmother. Did she take Lyra? The boy says he's not sure, then decides she must've, yeah, she did.

Even better then. This way Clay can help and it'll be a complete surprise, Eddie says. He's already pushing the box through the tiled entryway into the family room.

"A new television," Eddie says as he rips sealing tape from the flap.

"Plasma!" Clay says, hobbling around to read the side of the box.

"Yeah. A forty-inch. Top of the line."

"Sweet." Clay watches.

"Got a knife?" he grunts, stymied by the tightly packed Styrofoam. Irritated, panic rising.

"No. Not on me." Clay's sarcasm angers him.

Kneeling, he glances up. "Just get me one, okay?"

Clay seems to be gone for a long time.

"Hey! What's the holdup? I'm waiting!" he yells, propping the box upright. Hearing footsteps from the kitchen, he calls back over his shoulder. "Took you long enough. Where the hell'd you go?"

"I don't want that," Robin says in the doorway. She's wearing a fuzzy pink bathrobe with a red towel turbanned around her head.

"It's for you. And the kids." Even from here he can smell her freshly washed nakedness.

"No. Absolutely not."

"But I bought it for you."

"I can't accept it."

"Can't accept it. What the hell're you talking about? Your TV's broken. It's a TV, that's all."

"No! I don't want it. Take it out of here. Please."

"You need it!"

"No, I don't. We're . . . we're getting one. A new one. It's coming to-morrow," she says, clutching the front of her robe.

He feels foolish, used. The rich boyfriend, that's what this is about. "Hammond's buying his way back in, huh? What the hell's wrong with you? Don't you get it? He's just using you, that's all."

"What I do or don't do is my business, not yours."

"Yes it is!" he yells. Bad move, he knows from her stricken look. "Because I'm your friend," he quickly adds, mind racing. "I worry about you. Here all alone, you and the kids. That's all."

"Well, don't." She speaks so coldly, snidely, that he wants to slap her. "Bob's coming home tonight, so we'll be fine."

Insulted, he speeds off with the television in the open box teetering behind him, angrier with its every thump against the seat. He doesn't believe her. Lying bitch. Got what she needed, then threw him out. Like he's nothing. To her or anyone.

Nora underlines another mistake in the copy, the third time Franklin Memorial Hospital's president is referred to as its superintendent.

"I'm sorry," Jessica Bond says. She keeps biting her lip. This is her first postcollege job after backpacking around Europe for a year. Her writing is terrible, but she is Bibbi and Hank Bond's daughter, credentials enough for Ken. After her abysmally juvenile middle school science fair story for the local page, Ken begged Nora to take her on. Just until he can find a place for her. Ordinarily, she would have refused, but this is one less struggle she needs right now, especially with Ken. And especially here at the paper. It's painfully apparent that the staff, with Stephen's instigation, has little faith in Ken's management skills. Yesterday Clement, the city editor, threatened to quit when Ken killed another CraneCopley story. Stephen called in a rage late last night, demanding that the three of them meet this afternoon. She knows how that will go. Stephen will get indignant, angry, or depressed, and Ken will pretend to appease them while continuing to do exactly what he wants.

"It's that way all the way through." Turning the page, she highlights *superintendent* four more times.

"I thought that's what it was."

"It didn't occur to you to check?"

"I know."

"But you didn't. Why?"

"I know," Jessica sighs.

Nora catches the young woman rolling her eyes. "Am I annoying you?"

"No! God, no!"

Nora looks at her pretty face. "Working at the paper, whose idea was it?"

"Mine." But her flat tone says it all. She doesn't want to be here, or at least not working for Nora.

"This is the real world, Jess. Your parents might have helped you get the job, but it's up to you to keep it. Right now, there are probably fifty résumés up in personnel, all perfectly willing, desperate even, to do exactly this. Anything. Whatever grunt work is available."

"I know." Her resigned sigh skims the surface, depthless, easily bored like her mother, who must have been thrilled to make their boat available whenever it was needed by Ken and Robin, whom they'd known forever, because, after all, she overheard Bibbi say once, "Poor Kenny, all he wants is to be happy," little knowing it was an indictment of her.

"No, you don't. You don't have a clue. You think this is what comes next, don't you? You don't really want to work, you just want a position, something to tell people you do. Well, I'm sorry, Jess, but I have neither the time nor the patience to be holding your—"

A great sob erupts from Jessica. "You're firing me?"

"That's not what I said." What she meant, though.

"It's, just . . . I have a hard time with details," Jessica gasps through her tears. "A really hard time."

"You do?" Nora says with a glance at the marked-up copy, her sarcasm going right over Jessica's head.

"The thing is, I have these, like, issues." Her nose is running, but she makes no effort to wipe it. "Didn't Kenny tell you?"

Kenny. He's not sleeping with *her* now, is he? she wonders, pushing the tissue box across the desk. That'll be next, won't it? Younger women, daughters of their friends, friends of Chloe's. No. She's got to keep her head on straight. Tonight is their first family counseling session. She had a hard time talking Ken into it. Maybe this is why— Jessica Bond. "Issues. What kind of issues?"

"Learning problems. Like, disabilities?" she says.

"I'm sorry, Jess, I didn't know that." Suspicion bleeds into guilt. For being such a bitch. For taking out her own problems on someone so vulnerable, and so annoying. Typical of Ken, dumping this on her, instead of being frank with Jessica.

"Basically, I'm just not . . . not . . . very good at anything," she bawls. The red light on her phone flashes.

"Oh. Oh, hon," Nora says, ignoring it as she comes around the desk and puts her hand on Jessica's shoulder. "Come on, now. Look, don't worry. We'll work this out. There's—"

Hilda buzzes her. Nora grabs the phone. "Leave it on voice mail. I can't—"

"But it's the high school," Hilda says in a rush. "Drew's sick and they need to speak to someone right away."

Since when does it take two parents to pick up a sick kid?" Ken asks as they rush down the corridor.

"I know," she says in a low voice as two reporters go by.

"I'm meeting Stephen and Clem in twenty minutes."

"Call and reschedule." She's racing toward the door.

"Why do I have to go? I don't get it." He holds open the door for her.

"Because he's drunk," she blurts. Outside now, she's finally able to repeat what the school nurse said. "He fell asleep in math, and when the teacher couldn't wake him up, he realized what it was."

Drew is waiting in the nurse's office. Slumped, chin on his chest, he doesn't acknowledge their presence. Even with the window open the office reeks of booze.

"Hey, Ken," the school nurse says, grinning.

Drew looks up, but Ken only nods. Apparently, Linda Raymond and Ken know each other, though Nora has only ever met her here before. Until Nora put her foot down, menstrual cramps had often been Chloe's ploy when she was unprepared for a test.

"What're you doing?" Ken demands, and Drew closes his eyes.

"I put down flu," Linda Raymond says. "Better than being suspended."

"Thanks, Linda. I appreciate that," Ken says.

"Least I can do." And with her brief shrug Nora knows a favor is being repaid, a job, maybe, or buried story. Connections, everywhere. Tentacles.

Leaving quickly is impossible. Drew is too unsteady. Their

shameful procession moves slowly, between them a child they dare not let walk alone down corridors, stairs, through the heavy school doors, locked against intruders, mayhem, harm to their treasured children.

"Sorry," he mumbles, staggering into Nora as they emerge into dazzling sunshine. Birds are singing. A girl and a boy pass them, carrying a narrow wooden bench.

"Hey! Where you going with that . . . that . . . thing you got," Drew mutters with a foolish snigger.

The girl and boy hurry by and don't say anything. Behind them come more students carrying benches. One girl is a friend of Chloe's.

"What're you doin'?" Drew calls, coming to an abrupt teetering stop, but they pull him grimly along. "Hey!" he protests, struggling against their grip.

"Be quiet," Ken says through clenched teeth.

"I'm just tryna—"

"Stop it. You're just making it worse," Nora hisses. The departure bell rings and students stream past them. This is the first time she's ever been ashamed of her own child.

They're finally at the car, but Drew balks, refusing to get in. He needs his books, he insists. They're in his locker and he has to go get them. Chloe will get them, Nora assures him. No, she doesn't know his combination, Drew protests, jerking free of their grasp. Then she'll call Chloe and he can give it to her, she says, fumbling in her purse for her cell phone, as if the books matter in the least, trapped as they are now in this bizarre scenario. Students move through the rows of parked cars. They keep glancing back.

"Get in the car!" Ken orders.

"No! First I gotta go—"

"Shut up!" Ken forces him down into the backseat.

Nora scrambles in beside him. As soon as they turn onto the road he falls asleep. She struggles to fasten his seat belt, but he's sitting on part of it. Pull over, she tells Ken, so she can buckle him in.

"Just forget it," Ken calls back. He keeps driving.

"No!" Their eyes meet in the rearview mirror, and she is devastated by what she sees: more than disgust, more than anger. Hateful despair.

She clicks the seat belt into place. Not another word passes. They ride home in silence. They can't get Drew out of the car. He won't be roused no matter how often she calls his name or jostles his arms. Ken waits by the open door. "Drew, Drew, come on, now, wake up, we're home. Come on. Let's get inside. Please, Drew," she begs.

With the twitch of a smile, his eyes flutter, then close, as if surrendering to a glorious dream.

"Come on!" Ken barks as he drags out Drew's legs. He grabs his arms, yanks him onto his feet. "Let's go. Walk, goddamn it!" he orders as Drew reels into the back of the car, then doubles over, retching.

"He's going to be sick!" she cries, enraged to see her son so brutally handled.

"Good!" Ken says, dragging him up the walk, along the length of picket fence, architectural ornament, artifice, keeping nothing in or nothing out, for here it was, all damage done, the worst of it, to her child. And already she is deciding their next course of action, therapy, private school, a trip, a long family trip. Far away from all this anger and resentment, even as Ken gets him inside and is forcing him down onto the kitchen chair, yes, reschedule tonight's session, the family counselor, she'll call now, soon as they get Drew to bed, but Ken is insisting he has to stay awake. They don't know what he's been drinking, or how much. Alcohol poisoning. Can't let him pass out. Keep him conscious, he says, wringing a dishtowel under cold running water. Torture, she thinks, looking on. The boy needs to sleep, and all Ken wants is to teach him a lesson.

He wraps the cold wet towel around Drew's neck. Drew's head snaps up, his eyes bulge with shock. Ken is wetting another towel. The side door flies open. Chloe hurries in.

"What happened?" Friends told her. Jay and Maddie. Some kids said he'd been drinking vodka all day, from a spring water bottle. Mr. LaPlante brought him to the nurse.

With Drew's deep groans, Nora takes the towel off his neck. His eyes roll and he sags over the table.

"Ken!" she cries.

"He's passing out!" Chloe screams. "Do something!" Chloe lifts her brother's head. She shouts his name, begging him to wake up. "Please, please, Drewie!"

And he does. Looks up and laughs, as if they are little again, conspiratorial in this fuss. Drool trickles down his chin, but he keeps grinning. Chloe asks if he wants some water. He doesn't answer, so she gets it anyway. His eyes keep closing. Ken tries to pat his face with the wet towel. Recoiling, Drew's head jerks back.

"Hold still!" Ken orders, pressing the dripping cloth against his temple.

Muttering, Drew bats his father's hand away. But Ken persists. Nora remains at her son's side, arms folded, in this strange suspension. Looking down at them, at herself, with surreal curiosity and the realization, the acceptance, that the dream is past, all of it a dream, because only *this* is real. And would forever be this way.

"Here." Chloe offers the water glass.

Drew refuses, so she holds it to his lips, and he strikes out in panic, in confusion, knocking the water from Chloe's hand. The glass explodes on the tile floor in a burst of gleaming splinters. Drew struggles to stand up.

"Sit down!" Ken yells, forcing him back onto the chair.

Propelled into action, Nora grabs a mop, and Chloe is unrolling long furls of paper toweling onto the floor.

"I said, sit down!" With Ken's shout, Drew lunges at his father. Ken shoves him back, away from him, again, again, ducking his blows, leaning, not wanting to hurt him. But Drew persists, in his drunken clumsiness, staggering against the refrigerator, now, the narrow table display of Delft plates that teeter, but Chloe steadies them in time.

"Fuck you! I hate you, you fucking asshole!" Drew bellows and sobs, but Ken gets behind him, arms around his son in a bear hug that only makes him cry out more. Sobbing, Chloe begs her father not to hurt him. Ken grunts with his fierce grip, afraid to let go, his own face grim, sick-looking, as afraid as Nora is, of what he will do, not to them, or to anything in this room or house, but to himself because he is frantic, beyond their reach.

"Calm down, just calm down," Ken begs.

"Listen to your father," Nora pleads, stroking his pinioned arms and bony shoulders, his face. "Please. Please, Drew. It's all right. Dad's just trying to help you, that's all."

"No, he's not!" Drew yells, laughing, in his struggle. Tears and snot streak his face. "He wants me to shut up, that's what he wants. Shut up! Shut up, Drew, you fucking little freak! You just forget everything. Cuz you don't know, you don't know what the hell you're talking about, you freakin', fuckin' little freak."

"Stop. Please stop." Ken's face presses against Drew's head, and something inside Nora is breaking off, piece by piece.

"It's a secret. His dirty little secret—"

"Don't," Ken groans at his son's ear. "Don't. Don't—"

"Stop it, Drew! Stop it!" Chloe screams, pounding her fists on the table as Drew shouts over her.

"Ask him who Lyra's father is. Go ahead, Mom. Ask him." The words pour out as if he can hold them in no longer. "Because it's not Mr. Gendron. It's him. That's who it is, it's him."

Chloe is sobbing into her hands, not with the shock of revelation, Nora realizes, but with pent-up anguish over what must happen now. Ken's arms fall away from Drew, who looks around in panting, stunned surprise. Relieved, finally, of this, their last secret. For a moment she thinks she's having a heart attack. She can't breathe. Or move or speak. And yet, this calm voice—hers.

"Leave, Ken. Please. Just leave."

CHAPTER·20

Apparently, Ken has found refuge in the huge, run-down home of his privileged childhood. So far, he hasn't called, but Oliver does from rehab. He asks if she and the children are all right. Whatever they need. His voice breaks. His speech has improved, yet when he tries explaining that he just got off the phone with Ken, he says he's just gotten off the john with Ken at FairWinds. She's not to worry, he says again. He's told his doctors he wants to be discharged. As soon as he gets home, he'll take care of everything. Everything his asinine brother is hell-bent on destroying. The paper, Stephen, but especially her and the children.

"You and the kids, Nora, that's the most important thing," he gasps.

She's shocked, hearing him trying not to cry. He's never been sentimental or the least bit emotional with her.

"I feel so damn guilty. I should've said something. But I didn't know about that, their having a kid, I swear I didn't. I didn't!" he cries. "He never said that. Then, after that night, you at the house, after, I told him. I was sick of him, I said, sick of his bullshit, all his phony, goddamn, phony . . . phony . . ."

Her eyes close with his painful struggle for words. "Oh, Ollie, I know. I know. It's not your fault. In a million years, it's not."

When Stephen arrives later in the day, she pretends to be surprised and pleased. He pretends to be sorry, embarrassed for just dropping in on her like this. But he wanted to tell her in person, and privately, that if there's anything she needs, anything he can do, whatever it is, he'll be there for her. Anytime, day or night. Anything, he says, squeezing her hands, peering into her eyes with his usual withering intensity. Time to call a lawyer, she thinks, already knowing his mission, to put out another fire. As Oliver's most trusted envoy, he's surely been sent with a generous offer. She'll be well taken care of as long as she goes quietly, doesn't put up a fight, doesn't embarrass anyone. Without asking, she opens the liquor cabinet: whisky neat, as always. How lovely, she looks, absolutely lovely, especially in that sweater, he says with a sigh of relief as he follows her into the study, drink in hand. With such dark hair and fair skin, she should always wear violet. And black, too, he's always admired her in black. His mother used to wear a lot of black. He remembers that, he says, settling into the oversized leather chair by the stone hearth. She sits in the smaller chair, awaiting the terms.

"I used to think it was my father's abandonment. You know, that she felt like a widow or something. And so I asked her once. I told her I thought she'd feel so much happier if she'd only wear bright colors. 'But I am happy,' she said. 'And I'm sorry, to break the news to you, Stephen, but, you see, men prefer me in black,' " he explains, in a breathy imitation of his mother. His exuberant laughter is always unsettling, a surprise from such an ascetic.

They pick their way round the minefield. Pleasantries first: Chloe and Drew are doing well. And though she doesn't say so, they seem almost relieved. It's only now that they're older, Stephen admits, that he enjoys them. Not that they weren't always very well behaved, he says, but he's just never known how to talk to little ones. Well, anyway, he sighs, thank goodness for the warmer weather and longer daylight. Actually, this has been his best winter yet. Well, his least depressed one, that is. Light therapy, an hour every morning, it's been amazing, the difference.

The usual coughing, sniffling mess, he replies when she asks how Donald is. Red-nosed, wadded tissues everywhere. Allergies. As soon as the trees start to bud, his misery commences, from now until November. Of course, two farty old Labs in the bedroom don't help. They discuss various treatments, Stephen's new car, another Audi, the paper's dwindling ad revenue, ever-shrinking circulation, her dismissal of Jessica Bond, which delights him. Right now she's doing something on the entertainment page, but if it were up to him, he'd fire the ditz. Simple as that. One more nail in the coffin. Well deserved and long overdue. "And the next head to roll, his princess in circulation," he says with a lift of his glass, and it's a moment before she realizes he means Sheila Nedderman, Ken's old paddle tennis partner. Typical of Stephen, needing to put a vile spin on Ken's kindness. Desperate for a job after her divorce, Sheila pestered Ken for months. The calls came night and day.

"His princess? Oh, come on, Stephen, please. That's not even funny."

"I know. I never did understand the attraction. The big poufy hair, oooh!" He cringes. "But a hound's a hound. Or so they say."

"Stephen!" She looks at him. "I don't want to do that. I'm not going to start looking under every rock. I mean, after all, the children. He's their father. I'm trying to respect that. It's hard, but I have to."

His mouth puckers. He is incapable of hiding his feelings. Part of the reason he was never a practicing lawyer, or heterosexual, he confided once.

"Such noble sentiment, my dear. Stay vigilant, though, and protect thyself."

"I know, but—"

"No! No buts. Protection, that's the most important thing here. From this point on it's all about"—he rubs his fingers together—"who gets what."

"Yes, and Ken and I will—"

"Ken's an ass. Start with that and the rest'll be easy."

"Stephen," she warns, looking toward the door: her children.

"Nora," he says, in the same intonation. "This is more than a marriage on the rocks. It's not just you and Ken, it's Oliver and me, it's the paper."

"Well, those are things Ken and I have to work out. I know it's complicated, and I appreciate Oliver's concern, but it's not going to be like that. Believe me."

Stephen finishes his drink and sits back, his lean face grooved in shadows. He begins by saying that he doesn't want to hurt her. He's here because there are things she has to know, certain facts that Oliver is unable to articulate. Three years ago Ken asked his brother to buy out his share in the paper. He wanted to get a divorce and marry Robin, and he needed money to support the two families. Oliver refused, so Ken took the same offer to Stephen, who also turned him down. A few weeks later, Ken returned with another proposal. Or threat, as Oliver saw it. If they wouldn't buy him out, then he intended to file a lawsuit contesting their father's trust that prevented him from selling his share to anyone but his brother or cousin. Oliver laughed him out of the office and then called Robin Gendron to tell her in no uncertain terms what he thought of her. This caused a breach between the brothers for months. It was right around that time that Nora returned to work at the paper. A good move, Stephen says, because it forced the brothers to at least be civil to each other. And also because Oliver was counting on her presence to keep Ken on the straight and narrow. But Ken persisted in wanting to be bought out. It was Stephen who finally got them to agree that at the end of two years a sale would be negotiated. In the meantime, though, Ken had to do the right thing: a promise Oliver thought Ken had kept.

"What do you mean, a promise?" Nora asks. She feels short of breath.

"That he'd stay with you."

Stephen's voice plays like a recording, deaf, blind, heedless.

"Oliver figured by that time he'd be over Robin, that it'd be just one more affair."

"One more?"

"Oh, come on, Nora." He leans closer, his sibilant whisper, little whips lashing her face. "You can't be serious."

Stop it! she wants to scream. Why are you telling me this? It's too much. I can't do this anymore.

"Oh my God, you are, aren't you? I can't believe this. Some kind of detective! Where do I start? I mean, it'd be quicker telling who he didn't f—" He catches himself.

She stares as he lists the affairs, wondering how many times this practiced little riff's been recited at parties, all the friends, women at the paper, names she's never heard before. Bibbi Bond. "Annette even. One time she was here doing the kids' portraits and he came on to her. Kay, your friend. She finally had to sic Oliver on him. But what'd she expect? I mean, she let it go—"

"Don't." She holds out her hands. "Please."

"Well, probably won't make you feel any better, but that kind of crap's been over for a while now."

Because through the years of Ken's forced union with Nora, he stayed faithful to Robin by not sleeping with other women. Actually, the ideal arrangement, Stephen says, for spineless Kenny who couldn't bear confrontations. His family was intact and he still had Robin, who had little choice except to wait it out. But it was becoming an increasingly expensive arrangement for Ken with Bob's chronic unemployment. At the end of the two years, Robin wanted out of limbo. She began putting pressure on him. Back he went to Oliver with the same proposal, still never mentioning the child. However, with profits at the paper slipping, his brother managed to put him off, for almost another year. Apparently, though, Robin had had enough. She didn't care about money or shares in the paper, and if Ken still couldn't bring himself to tell his wife, then she would.

"And then came the stroke, so what could Ken do, he had no choice but step up to the plate. Brilliant move, though, the detective." He winks at her. "Because that's when Kenny's dark little world started spinning out of control. Finally, somebody had to do something."

Everything makes sense now. And nothing does. So much that never will. The phone rings. She's afraid to answer. Afraid of Eddie Hawkins, afraid of friends, neighbors, her own sister, who keeps leaving messages: she really wants to come visit, why won't Nora call, is something wrong? There is, isn't there? In her bathrobe for days, blinds drawn, sleeping while the children are in school, claiming she has the flu, she can barely go through the motions when they get home. Chloe steeps bay leaves in mugs of broth, carries up dry toast points. Her miasma ends this afternoon with Drew and Chloe, arguing. She runs downstairs to find him screaming at his sister. Over nothing, really. Chloe told him to stop complaining he was out of clean underwear and wash his own damn clothes. He punched the laundry room door, stands there now holding his hand. He can't stop crying. Chloe is hysterical. Get away, he warns them both. Leave him alone. Just leave him alone. She won't, she can't, she says, holding him.

An examined life, Father Gendron said. How could she have been so blind for so long? That her own children knew the truth about Lyra devastates her, not because they kept it from her. She understands their reluctance to see her hurt and, probably, even more compelling, their fear of breaking up the family. But what she can never forgive Ken for is the painful weight of their guilty burden, entangling them in his secret. It tears her apart now as Drew finally tells her how he found out.

"Ask your dad. Go ahead, ask him," Clay growled in his ear, pummeling his own shame and rage into his childhood friend, who didn't believe him.

Days later, Drew confided in Chloe. She said he was crazy. Clay Gendron was sick, a liar, she declared, a sadistic asshole. Of course, it wasn't true. It couldn't be, she insisted. Whatever had happened between Dad and Mrs. Gendron (Chloe no longer calls her Robin) was bad enough, but there was no way Dad was Lyra's father. It had been the night Nora went out with Kay that Drew finally confronted Ken, with Chloe looking on in disbelief. Ken refused to answer his son. He didn't admit or deny it.

"This is not a conversation I'm going to have with either of you. Now or ever again," he said coldly before walking out of the room.

"Then it's true! It must be!" Chloe cried on her father's heels, all the way up the stairs. "It is, isn't it?"

The click of his bedroom door lock was all the answer she got, or needed.

"I can't believe this. I can't believe this is happening," she sobbed on the landing. Her father never opened the door. Drew came up and calmed her down. It would be their secret. Their mother had been hurt enough.

On Saturday Nora is clearing out closets, a catharsis of almost manic energy. She can take care of everything, her children, herself, and doesn't need anyone. It's a relief to be getting rid of it, all the excess. And yet, she's quickly tiring. It's not the physical effort that's so draining, but this mind-racing intensity that makes her realize how close she is to the edge because there's nothing she can do to make things right, but, my God, she has to do something, has to keep moving, keep busy. Staggering under armloads of winter coats and jackets, hers and the children's, she carries them out to the garage, piles them into the back of her car. This afternoon she will bring them to the dry cleaner. Next, she jams Ken's coats and jackets into two jumbo trash bags, drags them into a corner of the garage, along with the other bags of his wrinkled clothes. Vindictive and juvenile, but better than putting them curbside for trash pickup, which she had actually considered. So far, she has managed to avoid him at the paper. Thursday and Friday she called in sick.

Beyond that, she's done little else, except try to keep busy around the house while staying as close to Chloe and Drew as they'll allow. Pain has been their bond these last few months. At least now with the truth, they seem more themselves, still wounded, but softer somehow. Almost more real, as if they've returned from the land of betrayal with a deeper appreciation of each other.

Dinnertime: their bright voices and quick laughter, the music blasting from Chloe's iPod, like stuffing holes in a dam with newspaper, a flimsy effort, but right now all they can manage. The fragrance of duck sauce and garlicky chicken wings fills the warm kitchen. The two shopping bags on the counter contain enough food to feed three families, Nora declares as she removes the steaming hot containers. Now she is the permissive parent. If Chloe wants pipa tofu she should go ahead and order it, even though she is the only one who likes it. And Drew can get whatever he feels like and, for once, won't have to share with the rest of the family. Small triumph saying it, emphasis on *family*. Because that's who they are now. Stronger without him. Better. And who does she think she's fooling? Them. She has to.

"My Lord," she says, prying off the lids. "Six appetizers. What were we thinking?"

"We weren't. That's the point, isn't it?" Chloe says, and with her quick glance at her brother, Nora knows she's trying to ignore his grunting as he gnaws teriyaki steak off the skewer.

Soothed by the familiarity of their hungry pleasure, Nora enjoys watching them eat. Sustenance. The comfort of simple rituals. What fine children, especially Chloe, who even as a baby seemed to know what came next, what needed to be done, even when Nora, in her overcautious, by-the-book mothering, didn't. She was always so forgiving and caring, especially with her sensitive little brother. Drew's misfortune, Nora thinks, is to be too much like herself, tentative, wary, afraid to take a chance, always waiting for the other shoe to drop.

"Here, Mom." Chloe passes her the container of Szechuan shrimp. "But, careful, it's spicy." She and her father love spicy food.

"I can handle it." One bite and Nora's eyes water and her nose runs. She reaches for her water glass and Chloe tries to smile, has to look away.

Twenty minutes later Drew pushes back from the table with a groan and a soft belch. Chloe gets up, rinses her plate in the sink. Otherwise, she'll just keep on stuffing herself, she calls back over the running water. A small bone cracks as Nora bites into another chicken wing, not from hunger, just to feel normal again. Drew lines up the cookies, breaks them open, his father's way, in their cellophane wrappers. He is reading their fortunes to them when the doorbell rings.

Nora freezes. No. Please. Not Eddie Hawkins. Not now. Not here. Drew looks at her, but his concern springs from hope, like the expectation in Chloe's voice. Their father. They want him back. Just as Alice said, children will endure and forgive anything to be with their parents.

"I'll get it!" Chloe flies into the front hall, hurries back. "It's Mr. Gendron." She grimaces, gesturing toward the shadows.

"Nora." His doleful intonation holds her name in the dark hallway like a long-tolling bell. She turns on the overhead light. He's lost weight. He looks dingy, inconsequential, a thing too often and carelessly handled. Because his nose and eyes are so red, she assumes he's been drinking, until he speaks, and she realizes he's crying. He keeps wiping his eyes, but the pity she feels is for herself and her children.

"This is a mess. It's all a mess. Robin, she . . . she wants a divorce. At first I didn't believe her. She was always saying things like that, warnings so I wouldn't drink, so I'd stop. But now I know. It's true. It—"

"Bob. The study." She follows him in, leaves the door open. Of course Chloe and Drew are listening. And why shouldn't they? Let them decide for themselves. They still don't know about all the other women, but sooner or later they will. She knows they shouldn't hate their father, and yet she wants them to, wants to be all that they have. Selfish as it is, in their pain she finds strength. And solace. And some slight triumph, however thin and cheaply veneered. They need her and love her, now more than ever. And their dear father, once so revered, deserves their anger and resentment, every scathing bit of it. But in the end, whose will be the bigger price to pay? The deeper loss? She gets up and closes the door.

Bob sits, knees wide, sobbing into his hands. His beige V-neck sweater is stained and baggy, his pant cuffs frayed. He wears old, dirty sneakers. The stitching on the right one is torn. Compared with Ken, he always looked messy. Robin used to joke that even new clothes looked secondhand on Bob. Nora always felt tolerated by him, easily dismissed and overlooked. Ken's wife and Robin's friend, but to him always the outsider. She had no history, didn't really get them. Together they could still be children while she was the menacing grown-up, watching them trifle their lives away. Suddenly, she despises him, a snobbish, shallow weakling.

"I can't believe it. She's changing Lyra's birth certificate. She wants Ken's name on it." He rubs his eyes. "The way she said it, like, now all the rest is details."

"Which it probably is," she says coldly. He's yet to say he's devastated, sad, disappointed, or even doubtful that he's not Lyra's father. She remembers Robin's complaining about his lack of enthusiasm. About the pregnancy, she wonders, or the child herself? Has he known all along? She can't bring herself to ask.

"It's all my fault. I know it is," he weeps. "I just kept fucking everything up. Everything. She kept telling me, 'I can't live like this,' but, I don't know, I just couldn't get a handle on things. I tried, but then I'd . . . I'd just . . . and now . . . now it's all gone. Everything." Face in his hands, he hunches over his knees and can't stop his wheezy sobbing.

"Don't," she says, fighting tears now. "Don't blame yourself. Please, Bob." She throws up her hands. "They didn't care about us. And we just made it easier for them, that's all."

He looks up. Odd, the way he peers at her, more bewildered than distraught, or even angry.

"It's not just Robin." He chokes on her name.

"No. I know." Sympathy stanched by his knee-jerk defense, she is amazed that he continues to make excuses for Robin. Pathetic. He expects her to blame Ken, not his dear wife.

"It's Ken. He's like my brother. I can't remember a time not knowing him. All my life . . . we were . . . we were inseparable."

In her disbelief, she can only stare at him.

"What am I going to do, Nora?" he pleads. "I don't know what to do."

She doesn't answer and instead pats his hand. For without Robin and Ken to love and resent, what will he do? How to justify anything now, sobriety, drunkenness? They've been his whole life, his two lode stars, brilliant but blinding in their complete attraction to one another. They've loved and coddled, and used him.

Eddie has been trying to see Robin for days. She won't answer the phone or come to the door, why? he pleads, rushing alongside her mother to the house.

"See!" He holds out a fistful of money. "I just want to help her, that's all. I gotta tell her what's going on. Before something happens."

The old bitch flips open her cell phone, to call 911, she warns.

So he's back in the car. His whole world has collapsed. He knows he should leave, just go before it's too late, but that's the problem. Knows he should, but can't, because that's exactly what he needs: something to happen. It's this feeling, like she's stuck in his brain, and he can't get past it until she's out. It's always this way, only this time, worse. This time he's scared. Because he's getting old, because his head's so messed up. It always hurts. He can't even eat. He's not thinking straight. Usually comes on fast, suddenly, the black rage and he strikes. And then it's over.

But this time he's consumed. This time he can't do what needs to be done and move on. Nothing's logical this time. The pieces don't fit. Hasn't slept in days. Maybe he's dying, or maybe he's already dead, and this is all hell is, fog. Confusion, he thinks, waiting at the corner, waiting, and, sure enough, she passes him. Again, he follows her along this same route. To the outskirts of town. Past the country club. Wrought-iron gates and high shrubs. Hidden driveways, one huge house after another. At the weathered sign, she turns. FairWinds. Up the long, bumpy road. But he parks down below on the street and waits. Two hours she's been in there, same as yesterday. He gets out, trudges up the rutted road, to a sheltering grove of hemlock trees. He brushes pine needles off the pitch-blackened granite bench, then sits down. He stares up at the brick mansion. Slate roofs, porticoes and balconies, French doors, stone urns gray with weeds, and he feels runty and insignificant, unwanted, never good enough, always scrambling after scraps, the little he's ever had, while she's in there, inside with him. Fucking Hammond and she wouldn't even let him touch her. Making him the fool. Taunting him. Daring him to. It's her fault. How many more chances does she deserve? One—he'll give her one.

His eyes open with the racing engine. Her silver minivan flashes by. Asleep for only a minute, and he's missed her. He runs down to his car. With every corner and bump the big box thumps against the back of the seat, reminding him what an ass she's making of him. But not anymore. No, why should he? When it's done, he'll leave. But maybe she'll listen, and he won't have to. He's tired. There she is. He drives so close behind he can see her face in the side mirror. Good, she's scared. She stops at the red light and he lets his bumper goose hers with the slightest tap. Again. When the light changes she turns suddenly, so does he.

"Give me a chance!" he yells. "One last chance!" That's all he wants, that's all, but she pulls her car, tires screeching, into the police station parking lot, so he keeps driving with the television in its box thump-thumping away.

CHAPTER 21

It's a rainy Sunday morning. The call comes at nine as Kay said it would in last night's message. Nine on the dot as if she's been staring at the clock, hand on the phone, counting down the seconds. Nora lets it ring. The machine clicks on.

"Nora! Call me, please. Please? Why haven't I heard from you? I keep leaving messages. I'm very worried. Something's wrong, I know it is . . . You're not mad at me, are you?"

This time Nora snatches up the phone. Kay sounds tired, weak, but so far she hasn't been sick, she says. Her hair started falling out after her second chemo treatment so she's had the rest shaved off. She wants Nora to come by and see her in her new wig. Nora says she'll try, she's just not sure when. There's no hiding the coldness she feels. Not even anger, just disinterest.

"Are you all right?" Kay finally asks.

"I'm fine."

"No, you're not. I can tell. I know you too well."

"I guess that's the mistake we both made, isn't it?" Nora laughs. She can't help it.

"What do you mean? Tell me. Please, Nora. Please," Kay gasps.

No, she decides in the long silence. She can't do this. What's the point? But then it erupts, her spew of accusation flattening Kay's denial. It wasn't like that. No, she never . . . it never . . . he didn't . . . there wasn't . . . nothing like that . . . once, just a stupidly weak and silly thing . . . met him for dinner, that was all, then felt so horrible she actually got up from the table and called a cab to take her home. He kept calling. It went on for weeks, until she finally asked Oliver to tell him to stop. Afterward, Nora won't remember the words, just the same pangs of fear she felt as a child wanting to see, but scared of leaning too far as she dropped stone after stone to the bottom of the deep well behind the house where her mother and the Boston cousins gabbed inside, smoking cigarettes, then said they didn't, hadn't, wouldn't ever, even though her mother reeked of it, her one vice.

In the afternoon the rain still falls. Nora and the children are driving home from the elegant Sea Cliff Manor in Salem, where they used to go as a family on special occasions. Today, after brunch they walked on the storm-scoured beach, in a show of good-natured hardiness, skimming rocks off the waves, scavenging for sea glass, pretending not to mind the cold as they plowed headlong into the raw, drenching wind. And now, still clinging to the tatters of family unity, they stifle yawns and endure the half-hour ride back, shivering in sodden clothes, with glazed eyes and strained conversation. Chloe sits beside her, staring out the window. In the backseat Drew pulls out one earbud of his iPod. He says he's freezing. Nora turns the heat higher. He's not the only one in the car, Chloe mutters, repositioning the vents; she's getting a headache.

Pretending to be happy takes enormous energy. For all their quick smiles, they often seem weary, drained, trying to protect what's left. She remembers one of her first interviews with an exhausted but plucky family, parents and children, working through the night to sandbag their besieged home against rising spring floodwaters. No human effort was going to stop the river's crest, but still, they had to do something, they said. And do it together. Nora notices how at night now Drew finds reasons to stay downstairs with her until she goes to bed. After that he'll study in his room for hours. Chloe got A's on her last two tests, American Lit and math. Her room is perfectly neat.

Yesterday she did all the laundry. She starts dinner now without being asked, usually because Nora is sleeping, which is how she spends her days.

Max is such a jerk, Chloe announced last night, as she ripped up his nine-page e-mail, her final and ultimate rejection: dropping the pieces into the trash instead of the recycling bin. It was an article he'd written about his experiences in Costa Rica. He asked if she'd please get her father to publish it. "Work on him—the way you do," he wrote, as if she were some bimbo, she said, equally infuriated by his next request. Would she also find out about job openings at the paper this summer, maybe set up an interview for him next month. Otherwise he'll have to spend the entire vacation working at his uncle's sawmill in Maine. When he comes home, she's breaking up with him.

"Not because of what's going on. I mean, your father and me," Nora said, resenting Ken even more: the emotional fallout souring even his children's relationships.

"No, that's not it," Chloe insisted, but Nora knows that's part of it. Chloe wants to be valued for who she is, rather than as someone's meal ticket into the family business. As she drives she can't help wondering if Ken ever thought that of her. But then, he had been a most avid pursuer, managing to get her assigned to him, which she soon discovered meant being at his beck and call, phoning at all hours just to talk, wondering what she was doing, she must have a lot of down time not knowing anyone in Franklin, then showing up at her apartment on Friday nights with Chinese food and ridiculously expensive bottles of wine, flowers on her birthday, party invitations, dinner invitations, finally wearing down her qualms about getting involved with someone so different from herself, easygoing, carefree, always after a good time, and one of the kindest, sweetest men she'd ever known.

By the time they get home Drew's teeth are chattering. Cold and wet, they scramble out of the car, peeling off their wet things as they run inside. She forgot to turn the heat up before they left so the house feels damp and chilly. Hearing the quick thud of pipes up in Drew's bathroom, she smiles. One way to get the boy into the shower. In the family room she searches everywhere for the remote for the gas logs, finally finds it wedged between the sofa cushions. The house is messy, has been ever since Ken left, especially here and in the kitchen where most of their time is spent. Soda cans, coffee mugs, magazines, newspapers, cast-off sweaters and jackets, it doesn't bother her anymore; if anything, it seems a validation of some hard-earned ownership, like strips of ribbon and pieces of string birds leave in their nests. She even canceled the cleaning lady these last few weeks, couldn't bear the intrusion. All that matters is being with her children. Her compulsive neatness has given way to this newfound negligence, and it's liberating, if not a little crazy. But so what? She's entitled to a touch of madness. Instead of a nervous breakdown, she has rings in the toilet bowls and dust kitties in all the corners. If he doesn't care, why should she? Because it's the dailiness, all the work, effort, and attention to detail, that keep people together. Duty, responsibility, values they once shared. She aims the remote at the fireplace and the gas logs ignite with a bursting whoosh of flames that always startles her. She is remembering her mother's pronouncement of their neighbors, the Kemptons' run-down, weed-choked house around the corner from them. "Marriage on the rocks." Surface blight, the first sign. Or message, the harm that's been done. Pain made visible. Evidence of how fast they're sinking.

She's on her way into the kitchen to light those logs next when she realizes she forgot to close the garage door. So what, who cares, she decides with perverse pleasure. Turning, she notices the blinking light on the answering machine. Four messages, the first, snappishly frantic, is from Carol, saying she just got off the phone with Ken. She's been so worried, not hearing anything from Nora that she finally called the paper Friday and left a message for him. He just got back to her this morning, and what he had to say was shocking. "Absolutely shocking. What on earth is going on there? It's one thing not to be upfront with me, but an out-and-out lie? How could you—" With a little cry Nora deletes Carol's querulous voice mid-rebuke. Once again she's met her sister's very low expectations. The next three messages are all from Ken. Each the same, terse, urgent. "Nora, call me." Not once asking for his children, or wondering how they're doing, or do they need anything, just *call me.* "Sure. When hell freezes over, that's when," she hisses, jamming the erase button so hard the machine slides off the little blue table. "Selfish bastard!" she mutters, picking it up from the floor.

"Maybe something's wrong," Chloe says from the doorway, and for a split second it's all Nora can do to keep from spitting back, *Maybe? Maybe* something's wrong?

"Don't be so concerned about your father. I'm sure he's doing just fine." Without us, she almost says, but seeing Chloe's pinched face, doesn't.

"Can I call him? Is that all right? Do you mind?" Chloe asks in a small voice, and Nora realizes she's trying not to cry.

"Oh, honey. Come here," she says, pulling her close. Of course she can call him, anytime she wants, anytime she needs to, and she certainly doesn't have to ask permission or apologize. "He's your father, that's the most important thing. And it has nothing to do with whatever's going on between us."

Chloe nods, limp in Nora's embrace. "It's just I . . . I miss him . . . I miss him so much it hurts," she whimpers.

"I know. Of course you do. He's been a good father." *If nothing else.*

"No!" Chloe sobs. "If he was, then none of this would've happened, and we'd still be—" The ringing phone cuts her off. "It's Dad," she says, checking the number. She stares back desperately, a grown child needing assurance that all the myths in her life are really true.

"Well, then answer it. Of course." She starts up the stairs.

"Hi, Dad." The anticipation in Chloe's voice follows Nora down the hallway. She's trying to sound natural, as if her father might only be away on a business trip. "I know. We just got in . . . the beach . . . well, first, we had brunch at the Sea Cliff Manor, which was great, and then we . . . Oh, okay. Mom!" Chloe calls up and Nora leans over the railing. "Dad wants to talk to you."

. . . *the thing with feathers / That perches in the soul* . . . Nora sits on the edge of her bed, phone pressed to her ear, eyes closed. He wants to come home, she thinks in a swell of irrational elation, in spite of everything, wanting him back, desperately, hungrily. That explains the terse message, the urgency, the coldness. He doesn't want to get the children's hopes up. Or his own. He's finally realizing his family is too important, they've been together too long for it to end this way. If he really wanted to be with Robin and Lyra, he would have done it long before this. He feels responsible, trapped. Trapped by Robin. Tricked, the same way Robin used her, manipulating everyone and everything to get what she wants. Never has she despised another human being as much. And that includes Stephen and his vicious version of events, claiming Ken stayed with her out of loyalty to the family business, because of some far-fetched, byzantine promise supposedly exacted by poor Oliver, who can barely string a sentence together, much less recall details of a conversation he had three years ago. No, that's just more of Stephen's vindictive pettiness. Somehow, they'll get through this. They will.

"I've got it," she tells Chloe. "You can hang up now." She thinks she hears a click, can't be sure. She takes a deep breath. "Yes, what is it?" Coldly, to hide her relief.

"Listen to me. Listen to every word I say." The hateful sting of his rage burns like lye in her ear. Interrupting, she tells Chloe again to hang up the phone. She already did, he growls, his last words about his child before launching into a diatribe so bizarre that she freezes, listening with a rising hysteria and confusion that border on giddiness. At first, his bitter demand that she call off her private investigator strikes her as pathetically funny, a sick joke, until she realizes that must be what Stephen meant by her "detective." Stephen, pretending to be her confidant and playing both sides. And if she doesn't, Ken's crazed rant continues, then he'll be forced to take matters into his own hands. Which, given the delicate nature of the circumstances, he's reluctant to do, since making this a police matter will only embarrass everyone concerned.

"Imagine! Embarrassing us!" she says, pressing down on the top of her throbbing head. "As if it could be any worse." She can't help laughing. A police matter! So, it's all starting to catch up with him, that rampant paranoia that always seems to affect the most guilty. Finally. Now it's his turn to twist in the wind. His turn to panic, his turn to feel watched and judged. Humiliated.

"You hired him, Nora, now you get rid of him."

"I don't know what you're talking about."

"Of course you do. You not only hired him, you set him up to come on to Robin, and how sick is that?"

"You can't be serious." She swallows hard. "That's crazy."

"I'll say it's crazy. *He's* crazy, and that's why, that's why you hired him. To hunt down Robin. To harass her, to scare her and the children, and not just them, but her mother. Emily, I mean, of all people. You've got to do something, you'd better. And if you won't, then goddamnit, I will."

"I haven't hired anyone to do anything!" she shouts back.

"You paid him! I already know that!"

"No! That's not—"

"The money for your sister, but poor Carol, she never got it, though, did she? Not a penny of it, because it was for him. You had to pay him!"

"What're you . . . you . . . Eddie Hawkins?" she stammers. "Is that who you mean? He's not an investigator. I told you before, he's just someone . . . I don't even know who he is, really, or what he does. He's just . . . just this guy. It was the picture in *Newsweek*. He looked me up. That's all. I never hired him to do anything. And that's the truth."

"Nora, I've got proof. You withdrew money. You paid him! Thousands of dollars. He told Emily. He even tried giving it to her. He was irrational, he—"

"You're the one that's irrational!" she screams, then hangs up. Her heart is beating too fast. She sits on the edge of the bed, rocking back and forth. He's jealous, and he wants her to get rid of his rival. He better get used to it, because that's what his life will be like with Robin. Adorable Robin, pretending to care, probably doing everything in her power to make Eddie worship her, so what did she expect, always toying with people, a sickness really, her toxic need to be the center of everyone's universe. Well, once again, she's made her own careless bed and now she can damn well lie in it. They both can, for all she cares. And besides, there's nothing she can do. After all that's hap-

pened she doesn't even care anymore who he tells, and who would
ever believe him?

She keeps trying to undo the same button on her damp shirt, but
can't. Her hands shake violently, her fingers limp and gripless. She
tries the next button, same thing, same shameful panic, frantic to get
out of the red sailor dress because they're all down there waiting, waiting to see what she'll do, but she won't give them that, the satisfaction
of seeing her hurting, seeing her cry. If she does, then it will all be real.
He will be gone, he is gone, leaving her trapped in her own wet skin, so
cold she can't stop shivering, and nobody cares. Nobody at all, which is
the hardest reality to face, so afraid of being alone, being left behind,
that in begging her mother's forgiveness for running away she had to
confess everything, quitting her job, wasting the money she'd earned,
drinking and sleeping with Eddie Hawkins, but couldn't bring herself
to tell about the man with the mutilated face, and so perhaps to make
up for that gaping omission, to at least come close to decency, and
because her mother still hadn't moved, censorious in her abiding silence, she finally blurted out what she needed to be the worst, most
damnable secret, admitting that the poor banished teacher had never
touched her, never come near her or anyone else, and she welcomed
the outraged cry that came with her slap, the hard, knuckled slap, that
resplit her still-healing lip and finally dulled her shame.

"That's so disgusting," her mother said. "How could you have done
that? How?"

Finally, she grabs her collar and rips open the shirt, buttons flying
across the floor.

Sobbing, she changes into dry clothes, then suddenly begins slamming her closet door, banging it shut, again and again and again, and
now she feels horrible, ashamed, for losing it like this, for being so out
of control with her children downstairs. Chloe and Drew don't deserve
any of this. "Calm down, calm down, just calm down," she keeps gasping as she wraps her rain-soaked clothes in a towel to take down to
the laundry room, but then doesn't move, can't, instead just stands
here, teeth chattering, trembling in the middle of her tranquil ivory

bedroom with the gray-tinted tray ceiling, hugging the damp towel to her chest because it's not her fault, none of it is, but this is what they want, what they've all been expecting. Damn them, all of them just waiting for this to happen, the crack in the façade, well, get ready, because here it comes, everybody, one hurtling stone to start the landslide, needing her to fail so they can absolve him of everything, poor, dear Kenny, all he ever wanted was to be happy, in spite of her, the witch, the cold, lying bitch, she never deserved him, no wonder he chased every woman in sight. "No wonder!" she screams, hurling the bundled towel against the wall. "No wonder!"

The rain helps, harder for anyone to see who's driving, especially with the wipers beating back and forth on high. So far every cruiser's gone right by. The car they're looking for is miles away in a mall parking lot, brand-new TV in back, keys in the ignition, some lucky bastard's just for the taking. Now, he's got a rental. Had to use Gendron's Master-Card, the only one they didn't reject, but still, he's not kidding himself, once the hunt's on it's only a matter of time. He drives by her house again, no sign of life, no car. Not at Hammond's either. He knows where her mother lives, pale green house way up top this steep hill. Only her mother's Volkswagen is in the driveway. Robin's car might be in the garage, though. Slows down, can't tell unless he gets out. No sense chancing that. As he drives by he stares up at the bedroom window she pointed out once. At night she could see all the lit-up houses below. She said she used to pretend she was a princess looking down on her kingdom—still does, that's the problem. Looking down on *him,* now that she doesn't need him anymore. He parks at the bottom of the street, next to a blue mailbox, under a large tree, just starting to show its pale green buds. The rainy murk lulls him into drowsiness. His eyes close. He turns the radio on and tries to keep the beat on the steering wheel so he won't doze off.

Doesn't have long to wait. Sure enough, the side door opens. Robin and Lyra hurry down the porch steps. Robin carries a frilly pink umbrella and the girl is wearing a red raincoat. She puts the girl into the backseat of her mother's car, then gets behind the wheel. Perfect. Easy quarry, that bright yellow Rabbit. When she drives by he leans over as if he's looking for something on the floor. Eases out, keeping his distance, lets other cars get between them. A mile into town she turns into the drugstore lot, and he grins. Faster than he thought. But as she pulls behind the store he realizes it's a drive-through pharmacy, so he backs into a parking spot, slides low on the seat. She hands cash out the window to the unseen clerk, receives her white prescription bag. Again, he follows at a distance, then loses her when she turns too quickly.

"Goddamnit," he mutters, doubling back. She's pulled into a busy strip mall that has a supermarket, a furniture store, a McDonald's, and five smaller stores. The lot is filled with cars, so she drives around until she finds an empty spot at the far end of a row. He waits, two rows behind, watching her lift Lyra out of the car. She opens the umbrella, then kisses the top of the girl's head, which enrages him. He starts to open his door and just then she calls out, waving to a man and woman in hooded yellow raincoats, pushing a loaded grocery cart toward her. She knows everybody. They embrace, talk animatedly a moment, then continue on to their car, which is too near hers for him to safely make his move. Holding Lyra's hand, she heads toward a children's shoe store. He knows by the spring in her step, the way she keeps looking down, that she's laughing with the little bitch. Her guard's down. She could give a shit about him, Eddie, the poor sap who doesn't have a clue why she turned on him. Far as she's concerned, he's as good as gone. He watches her bounce into the store. Better wait, no sense alarming her too soon. He's beginning to feel calmer. From here on, it's all smooth sailing. Whatever he did he'll make it right. Needs to get her alone though so they can talk, that's all he wants. He turns on the radio. Still in the store. Twenty minutes go by. How the hell long does it take to buy shoes? Probably knows everyone in there, too. He sits forward and starts the car. His lucky day. The white Escalade next to the mother's VW is backing out. Another car waits, directional flashing, but he zips into the space. The driver gives an indignant toot. Yeah, right, Eddie could care.

Just in time. She leaves the store, carrying two bags. Same as Aunt

Tina, always crying poor-mouth, but her kids get whatever they want, nothing left for him. Ever. He cracks open his door, watching them hold hands as they skip along, laughing when the girl splashes through a puddle in the new lime green boots she's wearing. So lost are they in their fantasy of happiness neither one notices him. With the girl at her heels, she opens the back door, leans in, flips the bags and her purse onto the seat, then turns, ready to lift her onto the booster seat, but he's made his move, scooping up the little bitch, shoving her into the back of his car.

"Lyra! Lyra!" she screams, pulling on the door, but he's already got the child lock on.

"Shut up! Shut the fuck up!" He grabs Robin's wrist, twisting it up against his chest.

"Don't do this. Please. Please, I beg you," she gasps, looking at him stupidly while inside the little bitch bangs on the window, wailing for her mother. "What is it? Whatever you want—"

"Get in the car! Get in the car!" He opens the passenger door.

She hesitates, then ducks inside. As he runs around the front of the car he sees her frantically hitting door buttons, either to lock them in, or to let Lyra out, but he's too quick, as always in these moments, so swift of mind and deed that it is another self he sees perform, a mastery unhindered by doubt or fear.

"Shut up. Just shut up!" he yells over her screaming demand that he let Lyra out of the car. She didn't do anything. Why is he doing this to an innocent child? Sobbing, the little bitch stands behind her mother, arms locked around her neck, a stranglehold that impedes Robin's flailing attempts to grab the keys from the ignition. He's not going to hurt them, he yells. All he wants is to talk, that's all. "Shut up! Just shut the fuck up!" he barks at Lyra, batting his hand over the back of the seat, a tap really, but she shrieks and that's when he sees Robin's cell phone, grabs it out of her hand. "Jesus Christ!" he yells, peeling out of the busy lot.

As he drives, he keeps trying to explain. He just wants to know what happened. What did he do wrong? One day they're so close and the next, she's ordering him out of her house. Did he ever once do anything to hurt her or her kids? That's what he wants to know.

"I was good to you! I was always so fucking good to you!" he bellows over the steady whack of the wipers and the rain beating on the roof. Her silence frustrates him. A good slap, that'd get her talking. From the corner of his eye he sees something glint. The diamond heart hanging from her thin neck, a gift from Hammond, he thinks, so seized with resentment he can barely see the road. "Is that what I did wrong? I was too good? Too fucking good? Is that it? It is, isn't it? You want to be messed with, don't you? You like it. You like being shit on, right? Knocked around, right? Is that it? That what hubby and the boyfriend do?" He snaps his hand out, just missing her beautiful scared face. She flinches and the little bitch screams. He laughs, can't help it. Frantic as it all seems, their terror is the perfectly clear lens through which he can now see. It magnifies everything, expanding his mind so that he's a calm, lethal force. Now they respect him. He enjoys their bloodless pallor, their shriveled nerves, their inarticulate dread. This is the power he wields over these docile, groveling lambs. "Hey, Mommy likes it," he tells the little bitch through the mirror. "Keeps her on her toes, doesn't it? Maybe that's what I shoulda done. Want me to? Want me to start slapping you around like them? Well, do you? Do you?" he screams at Robin whose hands clasp Lyra's clenched arms. "Do you?"

"No," she says, finally settling down, more reasonable, taking deep breaths as she looks over at him now. "Of course not. I just want you to let us go. I'm sorry you're upset. It's been a bad time, that's all. Everything's been so crazy, if I hurt your feelings, I didn't mean to, really, believe me, I'd never do that."

"Well, you did! You damn well fucking did!"

"I'm sorry. I'm so sorry. And you're right, you were good to us. You were, and I appreciate it. You don't know how much I appreciate it. It just got hard, that's all, I mean, knowing why you were there. It was like . . . like you were spying on me and then running back to her. Everything I said, you—"

"Running back to who?"

"Nora. And once I found out, of course I was upset. I mean, to think she'd actually do that, pay someone, pay you to investigate me."

With a burst of laughter, he reaches out, aching to touch her, but she cringes against the door, which only enrages him, to think that's what happened, that snippy cunt Nora Hammond, trying to poison the well, dump him and the mistress at the same time. He wasn't investigating her or anyone else, he insists. He just liked her, that's all. And the better he got to know her, the more he cared about her. Still does, maybe more than he's ever cared about another human being. His heart swells with the tender truth of this stunning pronouncement and he grins at her. She's confused. Someday they'll have a good laugh about this. Yes. *Someday:* the word amazes him.

"So, will you let us out now. Please?" she begs as he stops at the light. Just then there is a blur of red as a pickup truck pulls alongside. "Help! Help us!" she suddenly screams, banging on her window, but no one can see her through the sheets of heavy rain. As the light turns green, he roars off. This isn't going the way he wants. In the backseat the little bitch whimpers and all he wants is to shut her up. He feels trapped, suffocating in a tumult he can't pass through, or stop. He's been set up. Set up to fail. Once again.

Nora feels a little better after her shower. Dinner is in the oven, marinated chicken thighs and carrots. Tomorrow she'll go back to work. It's the last place she wants to be, but this is ridiculous, letting her life go to pieces around her. She can't keep falling apart. It's not fair to her children. They need her to be strong. She measures a cup and a half of broth into a pan, adds butter, sets it on the burner, needing the rhythm, the most mundane tasks to pull her back into normal living. She is in the pantry looking for the box of wild rice, when the bell rings at the side door, leading in from the garage. Odd, she thinks, quickly closing the cupboard. Only the family ever comes in that way, and Chloe is up in her room, listening to music, and Drew is in the family room, playing a video game. Ken. She hurries to the window, peers through the curtain. She doesn't recognize the dark blue car parked halfway into her garage. Again, the bell rings, this time urgently. When she opens the door Robin Gendron is standing in the breezeway. The last person on earth she wants to see. The unbelievable nerve. If ever she felt like slapping her it's right now.

"What do you want?" She clenches her fists.

"Nora, please," Robin says with a wide-eyed gasp, white-knuckled, ringless hands clasped at her chin. "I need you to come out here. Into the garage. Please!"

"No! You want to say something, say it here." Something in Robin's stare makes her hold the door edge between them. She looks frantic, desperate.

"I can't. Please, Nora, please. I'm begging you," she whispers, tears running down her cheeks. She's hyperventilating. "Please come out here. I need your help. You have no idea—"

"Nora!" The car door opens and Eddie Hawkins's feet swing out onto the garage floor, but he stays in the car. Now with the light on she can see Lyra's face pressed against the rear window, mouth open, crying. "Seems we got a little mixup here, a little misunderstanding," he calls out, the pouring rain and his voice such a boding turbulence through the open garage that for a surreal moment she finds reassurance in that mountain of black plastic trash bags piled in the corner. That's what they've come for, Ken's clothes. Tennis racquets, too, probably. They hang on the far wall over his golf clubs, alongside his skis, downhill and cross-country, his helmets and snowshoes, though not the bright green and orange snowboard, ridiculously expensive, like all of Ken's toys. The first and only time he used it he dislocated his knee. He was going to give it to Clay, an excellent boarder, but she was afraid Drew's feelings would be hurt. Annoyed by her interference, he begrudgingly gave it to Drew, who, as predicted, wasn't interested. Never used it. Ken's bicycles hang on hooks from the rafters. All the things he values most are in here. A good time. His lover, their child.

"He's got Lyra," Robin whispers. "He won't let her go. He made us come."

"Nora," he calls again. "She thinks I'm some kinda detective or something. That I'm working for you, like tryna get dirt on her and the boyfriend. Your fine, upstanding husband!" He laughs. "So tell her. Go ahead!"

Nora stares at him for a moment, then looks back at Robin. "What do you want me to do?"

"Tell her!" Eddie shouts, and she realizes he's staying in the car because as long as he's got Lyra, Robin won't leave. Isn't this what Robin just said? Her brain's not working. Worlds have collided and nothing seems real. She's rooted here, on the outside, looking in.

"Help me. Please help me." Robin's eyes burn into hers.

Like some crazed ringside fanatic, Eddie's insistent demands continue in the background. Threats, warnings, outrage. His menacing voice pitches higher.

"Help you? Help you do what?" she asks, confused and biding for time. What she should do is reach inside the door for the phone—and call who? Ken? To come and rescue them from each other? From Eddie Hawkins?

"Call the police," Robin whispers, barely moving her lips, sending a chill through Nora. She can't do that.

"What? You think I'm just gonna keep sitting here?" With that, he starts the car, pressing down on the gas so that the garage resounds with the acceleration.

"No!" Robin screams, and darts out to stand inside his open door. The only way he can back out is to knock her down in the process. "Don't leave. Please don't leave. Wait. Just wait," she begs, palms outward, trying to soothe him. "I'm talking to her. Nora and me." She points back. "See? We're talking. She's telling me what you said, everything, and now I understand. I . . . I'm sorry for what I said. I didn't mean to hurt your feelings. I mean, you of all people," she says, and he turns off the engine.

She's good, Nora thinks in the silence. Such a good liar. Smooth. But then, of course, she'd have to be, wouldn't she? Because of her openness, deception comes easily. Caring, that's her skill. A hound on the scent, relentless. Frailty, her prey.

"What'd she tell you?" His angular face sharpens with suspicion as he peers up at Robin. Reaching, he touches her hair, combs his fingers into it, an almost tender gesture, and Nora feels Robin's abhorrence, reads in the practiced tilt of her head the strained forbearance necessary to placate a drunken husband. She even tries to smile.

"What you said, that you weren't trying to hurt me or anything." Robin's hands have slipped behind her. Suddenly, there's a click, door buttons unlocking. Robin has managed to yank open the back door, at the same time, screaming for Lyra to get out, get out, but in the split second of the terrified child's hesitation, Eddie has leaped from the car. He lunges at Robin, pinning her against the hood.

"Bitch! You no good, lying cunt bitch."

"Stop it! Stop it! Stop it! Stop it!" Nora cries from the doorway, still only dimly comprehending. Or so it seems. There is the struggle and beside her, cowering, clawing at Nora's long sweater, as if to climb inside with her, this sobbing child in lime green boots. Nora pulls Lyra closer, holds her head to keep her from seeing. Robin is athletic and strong but no match for such crazed, ruthless anger. With every punch her head snaps back. She keeps trying, but she can't escape his viselike weight pinning her against the car. Finally, she brings her knee up into his crotch, but it's a weak, off-balance thrust that only seems to enrage him to new heights of savagery. Staring closely at her now, as if with necessary precision, he grunts as each blow of his fist batters her face, the side of her head. Her mouth and nose are bleeding. When she tries to speak, he roars with an almost childish rage, telling her to shut up, shut up, shut up, over and over and over again, but she keeps trying, even as his hands close around her neck, and Nora's eyes lock on those writhing, tightening fingers that are squeezing all the careless ardor and easy laughter out of her, she who in only wanting to love and be loved has destroyed everything. Robin's mouth sags open and she looks back at Nora in disbelief, shock, because how can any of this be happening? Now, as if in answer, he bangs her head back, smashing it against the car with a series of sickening thuds. Robin's arms hang limply at her sides.

"Mommy! Mommy!" Lyra shrieks. Tearing herself away from

Nora, she bolts to her mother, and her screams seem to feed a last, weak flame in Robin. She lifts her head and in sickening gags tries to say something as if begging Lyra to go away. Screaming at him to let go of her mother, Lyra kicks Eddie's ankles and the backs of his legs, but it's futile. A mere swipe of his arm sends the little girl crashing into the garden cart. Finally released, Robin slides down against the car, her head sagging so far forward it seems connected to her body by only the thinnest wire. Either too badly hurt or too afraid to stand, the little girl scoots on her backside as far as she can get from him, scuttling in between the bags of Ken's clothes, shaking her fists, bawling, "Mommy! Mommy! Mommy!"

"Shut up! I said shut the fuck up, you little bitch," he bellows, advancing on the child, hand raised, warning her to stop unless she wants the same as her mother. Glancing back at Robin, his shadow obscures Lyra, and suddenly Nora knows, having seen it, having dreamed it so many times before, exactly what will follow, and how necessary, how justifiable it seems in this deadening ether of fear and hope.

But a helpless child. No, not her, she would scream, and will later remember, if not shrieking, then the searing rawness in her throat, but in this moment there is only his roar over the child's mewling pleas to leave her alone. Please, please, please, and yet here she stands, again, doing nothing, because there is nothing to do, though the shameful choice is clear, an insidious pact only she can end, as it began. The ceremonial shovel first from the glinting row on the wall is surprisingly heavy. The initial blow lands between his shoulders, does little more than make him glance back. She swings higher, at the back of his head, hits his neck instead, the silver blade's sharp edge slashing deeply. Spurts of blood darken his white collar, and his hands shoot to his head. Turning, his face is monstrous, a festering welter of pain and rage as he comes toward her. An animal, a cornered animal, desperate, beyond feeling or reason, she strikes again, this time slicing his cheek. With a wounded, bowel-deep bellow, he lunges for the shovel, but she hits him, keeps hitting him. Again and again. He staggers a moment then sinks onto the floor, and she stands over him, sobbing with every blow after chopping blow, even though the side of his face is gashed wide. What she wants is for him to look away or close his eyes, but they stay open, their dull knowing stare holding hers. A halo of blood pools out onto the spotless gray concrete. As his torso twitches, his hands and feet spasm because he won't die, won't be silenced no matter how many times she must hit him.

She doesn't remember hanging the blood-streaked shovel back on its hook with the others, but that's where they will find it. She doesn't remember Drew chasing her down the street through the lighter, lifting rain that finally promises spring. She doesn't remember him begging, then insisting, she come back with him. She doesn't remember him crying. All she knows is that right now she has to get away, far, far away. She wants to go home. That's all she wants. Come with him, then. That's where he'll bring her. That's what he does, holding her hand.

There are two ambulances left in the driveway that is cordoned off by yellow tape. Jimmy Lee is out there as well, taking pictures of the house. Her lovely home is teeming with people, some in uniforms, most of them somber strangers, these very busy people, hurrying back and forth, respectfully, quietly as they can. Knees together, hands folded, she sits at her kitchen table, shivering, waiting, knowing it's out there. Where it's always been, dormant, capable of flaring up at any moment, a chancre in her life. Behind her, Ken paces back and forth, talking on the phone. Everyone else speaks in whispers. Her marriage is over, but she is a very lucky woman they want her to know, keep assuring her. Can they get her anything? the policewoman asks. Is there anything anyone can do, yes, explain how such evil can be, because that was her agony of puzzlement, Robin, who would carry spiders and ants outside rather than kill a living thing, even bees, though she was deathly allergic, trapping them in cups against the window glass then sliding cardboard over the opening until she could set them free. A very brave woman, someone else insists, resting a hand on her shoulder, a gesture she's distantly aware of, sees and doesn't feel. Probably saved her own children's lives as well. And who knows how many others. Men's voices. Women's. Excited, yet subdued. Yes. Who knows, she wonders as they hurry by, measuring, taking photographs, finger-prints. Clues, facts to tie it all together. To make sense of the dream. The secrets. Will they know? Will they guess?

"Here you go, Mrs. Hammond," Jimmy Lee says, coming in from the family room with the teal blue afghan that Robin knit for her, once, a long time ago. He arranges it over her shoulders. He heard the call on his scanner.

"Did they take them yet?" she asks, but he doesn't seem to hear. When the policewoman leaves, he looks around, then hands Ken a thick envelope. Found it under the car seat, he says. Must be Mrs. Hammond's. Her stationery, anyway.

"Did they?" she asks. No reply. No need. Details matter now. Yes, of course. She understands, though most are hard to remember. Like waking up with a start and trying to make sense of a nightmare. Who had the shovel first? How did she get it away from him? Is that what he hit her with? He never hit her. Who did, then? She's not sure what they mean. They're confusing her. The coffee in her mug is cold, un-touched. A brown ring stains the porcelain. Bleach, that works. But not on blood.

Ken's pallor is grimly white. His hands tremble, can't even hold the phone still against his ear. He is trying to contact their lawyer. The po-lice detective has agreed to wait before asking any more questions. From the other room now comes a piercing scream, Emily Shawcross crying out, "Oh my God. Oh my God." She has just arrived and they are telling her what has happened, the little they know. No one has yet been able to locate Bob Gendron.

He's not answering his cell phone, his mother told Ken, who's been trying to reach him for the past half hour. The door opens and another police officer comes in from the garage. Frowning, he tears a sheet from his notepad and leans over the table to jot something down. Nora watches his heavy-handed pen, knowing it will leave indentations in the polished cherry wood. But what does it matter, she thinks with dull relief to be this bodiless creature who no longer needs to think or care about anything or anyone. Not even her children who are holed up in

Ken's study with Stephen. The world goes on quite well without her, doesn't it? Interesting, how unnecessary she actually is. Everyone has their job to do. They are very kind. Donald is on his way. To make sure Nora's all right, Ken has just told someone. Her own personal anesthesiologist. To numb her, she hopes. Forever. She only has to sit here. Nothing left to do. They will take care of everything. These most efficient strangers. Outside, someone is smoking. She smells it when the door opens. There's a terrible taste in her mouth.

A woman sits next to her and takes her hand. *Celery, not onions, that's all she has to say.* But it's Kay. Her skin is jaundiced. Her wig is brown. So her hair really did fall out, Nora realizes and tries to look sympathetic but instead is grinning, she sees by her reflection in Kay's glasses.

"Here, honey." Kay is holding a glass of water to her lips. "Take a few sips."

"Where's Robin?" she whispers.

"They've already taken her."

"Where's Lyra?"

"With an EMT. But Emily's going in."

Going where, she wonders, doesn't ask. "Robin's dead."

"No, but she's in a pretty bad way."

"It's all my fault," Nora tells her.

"Of course it's not."

"Okay, good. Good. That's what we'll do," Ken says before he hangs up the phone. He pulls a chair out from the table and leans in close to the two women. Bruce Levant is on his way from Lincoln. He doesn't want Nora speaking to anyone until he gets there. Just sit tight.

"She's upset. She thinks it's her fault," Kay whispers, and Nora averts her head from the foul breath.

"Take it easy," Ken says, and she knows that cautionary tone.

"Everything's going to be all right. You'll see," Kay says, and tries to hug her.

"No," Nora says, pulling away, and Ken glances at Kay. He says he'll take her into his study. There's too much commotion in here. People passing through, most of them out of curiosity, he says, that's what's upsetting her. He asks Kay if she minds going on ahead and telling Chloe and Drew to wait upstairs. Their mother needs to be alone right now. Yes, of course, Kay says, hurrying off, glad to have a mission. He's very accomplished, Nora thinks. Cooler in a crisis than she ever would have guessed. She never appreciated him enough. She wanted to be in charge so he let her think she was.

Stephen closes the study door. She asks where Robin is. She's been brought to the hospital, Ken says. She's in a coma. Swelling on the brain. It was a brutal beating. Savage, Stephen adds, sitting down across from them. Crazy bastard almost killed her. Probably would've if she hadn't stopped him.

"But what the hell happened?" Stephen asks. "I still don't get it. I mean, why here? Who the hell is he?"

"Levant's on his way," Ken says. "We'll let him handle it."

"Handle what? Jesus, Kenny, she . . . there's a dead man out there. Nothing wrong with getting your ducks a little lined up."

"Ducks?" Ken snaps.

"I'm sorry, but you know what I mean."

Their discussion doesn't seem to involve her, though the details are important, Stephen is saying. He keeps looking at her. Damage control, she thinks as he fires off questions they need to anticipate if this is to come out right in the end—the way it should for good people. The script matters if they are to go on being decent people. The dead man, was he an intruder? Was he breaking in? What were Robin and Lyra doing here? Why the savage attack on Robin? Not to offend Ken, he's only playing devil's advocate here, but there must have been some kind of prior relationship for a crime of such passion. Was the guy . . . well, was he an old boyfriend or something? No, Ken answers bitterly. He blames her, she realizes. And well he should. Poor Robin, poor all of them, caught in such a mess. She can't stop seeing Robin's last look of bewilderment. Now Stephen is asking her exactly what happened.

"I hit him. I killed him."

She knew right away he was dead, so yes, the details are important. She understands that. She has to remember. Everything, but it's very confusing with the taste of cocktail onions, cherries, rum, and bile souring her bloody mouth, the reek of his sweaty crotch as he shoves down her head. The empty stare. Her silence alarms them. They need her to talk, the right words to frame the story. Spin.

"Nora," Stephen says, touching her hand. "You're the only person, the only adult, anyway, who knows exactly what happened. That's why we have to set the record straight now. The important thing is not to let anyone put words in your mouth. If they ask you something and you're not sure, just say that. You don't remember, that's all you have to say. And if it comes back to you later, fine, we fill in the blanks then."

We have to set the record straight? *We* fill in the blanks? But how can they unless she tells them about that night? "I'm trying to remember."

"Good," Stephen says. "That's all anyone can ask. And if you can't, that's okay, too."

"I didn't have to keep hitting him like that," she says to no one in particular, because this is vital, the most important thing. "It was more than him, it was everything else I wanted dead. It was me. Always being afraid of doing the wrong thing. People knowing the truth about me. It's my fault. It is. I did a terrible thing." She sees by Ken's cold stare that he already knows. And has for a long time.

"Nora!" Stephen says. "You had no choice. I mean, my God, there you were watching a madman attacking a child and her mother, you did exactly what every one of us hopes we would do. Particularly given the very painful relationships in the situation," he adds, though his sting of rebuke seems lost in his cousin's shock.

"What do you mean it's your fault?" Ken asks.

"Because I never did anything. I let it happen. I didn't want to know, did I, Ken? But I must've. How could I not? And then it was the same thing all over again, and that's why. That's why he came. Because there was something in me, something weak and repulsive, and he knew it then, too. I was seventeen. We were somewhere in the desert. It was dark and hot, and I'd been drinking all day in the car. It was so late when we stopped, and there was this man. I didn't even know his name. I still don't."

"Hawkins," Stephen says. "Eddie, right? Or at least that's what they said."

"No, not him. The man . . . there was this man, he was drunk and he . . . pushed my head down." She closes her eyes. Can't look at them. "He thought I was a prostitute. He even paid. Twenty dollars."

"Nora, what in God's name're you talking about?" Ken leans closer.

"I'm telling you what happened, why he came here. Oh God, I'm so tired, I can't think straight."

"Jesus!" Stephen sighs and stares at Ken.

"She's obviously in a state of shock," Ken tells him.

The two cousins confer, speaking quietly, as if she's not in the room. She's not making sense. They think she's hallucinating. No way should she be talking to the police in this condition, Stephen keeps saying. Ken says he needs to talk to her alone before Bruce arrives. Stephen disagrees, thinks a third party is even more necessary now. To take notes, he says and grabs a pen from the desk. Ken insists that he leave. After all, he is still her husband. *Still.* She clings to that.

"My point exactly!" Stephen declares. "You're just way too involved."

"That's it! Get the hell out! Now!" Ken explodes, and Stephen scurries from the room.

Even after the door closes Ken continues to stand there looking down at her. His hands open and close, gesturing helplessly. He's trying to control himself, struggling to find the right words to hold their shattered lives together. Do you see, she wants to ask. Do you finally understand what you've done?

"Nora," he says so softly that she begins to weep. "Before Bruce gets here . . . we need . . . I have to tell them something. You've got to tell me the truth, and I know how horrible this is, how confused you are, but . . . this money." He pats his breast pocket. "You paid him. Why? I don't understand. What exactly was it for? You've got to tell me, no matter how bad it is. Was it for evidence in a divorce?"

She hesitates, rubs her mouth, needing to wipe away this disdainful grin. So, it's still about her. Robin.

"No. I already told you it wasn't. I was afraid of him, afraid of people finding out what had happened, so I gave him money. And the crazy thing is, he didn't even ask for it. I paid him to go away, that's all I wanted. But he didn't. He wouldn't. He was evil, Ken. And the sick thing is I knew he was."

For a moment, he looks down at her, shaking his head. Pity? Contempt? Both. "Yes, you paid him all right. To get rid of Robin, Nora. And it didn't matter how, did it?"

"No! I never . . . I never asked him to do anything but to go away. And that's the truth. I swear it is." But even in this, she can't be certain. In her anger and desperation is that what she really wanted, the unspoken barter, with her silence, her failure to act, allowing it to happen?

He buries his face in his hands for a moment. "I don't think we know what the truth is anymore, do we? Either one of us." His anguish cuts through her numbness.

"You've got to believe me. Please, Ken."

There is a light tap at the door, which Ken ignores. "These are the facts, Nora, chilling as they are." Slapping her would hurt less than his whispered hiss. "You paid him twenty-five thousand dollars and you stood there watching. You let him beat Robin—to death, right? Or at least that's what you thought. And then what? Lyra? Was she supposed to be next? An innocent child?"

"Oh, my God, how can you—"

"But then you stopped him. Why? It wasn't going quite as efficiently as you wanted? Not neat enough for you? Not quick enough? Or did you hear a noise? Were you afraid someone might walk in on it? One of the children? Drew, he was down here, he was in the kitchen, so you had to move fast, didn't you? You had to make sure he'd never tell anyone, didn't you?"

"And you believe that? That I could do something as . . . as hideous as that?"

His cold, hateful eyes are answer enough. "All I know is we have to protect our children. That's the most important thing now."

Now. Yes, of course. Far more so than the truth. She understands.

CHAPTER·22

They still don't believe her. Not really. No one ever comes right out and says so, but when they look away or suddenly stop speaking with her approach, she knows. Like white noise the rumor of her complicity is a hum in the room, constant yet, in recent years, low enough to be endured. She manages, on the surface, to lead a normal life. For all those who do avoid her there are as many sympathizers who insist, given the circumstances, they might have gone out and hired a hit man themselves. Her children love her and they are good young people, which, in the end, is all that really matters. With Chloe and Drew away at school, she lives alone most of the time.

For the last year, Ken and Robin have been renovating FairWinds. After two even more damaging strokes, Oliver has been admitted to a nursing home, with little hope of returning to that enormous old house. An elevator has been installed, primarily for Robin's needs, but for some reason, whether their tenacious optimism or perhaps to salve their consciences, they tell people that it's also for Oliver so that when he does come home, he can have his own wing in the house. They hope to be able to move back in between Thanksgiving and Christmas.

They were married a year ago, before 350 friends and relatives. Typical of Robin, it was a storybook wedding, an amazing fairy tale come true, a happy ending for the childhood sweethearts, kept so long apart, finally marrying, with beautiful Lyra sprinkling pink and white rose petals in her brave mother's halting path down the aisle on Clay's arm. After the ceremony hundreds of pink and white balloons and doves were released from the church steps. Even Bob attended, well into his fourteenth month of sobriety. He sat in a back pew and was the first guest out to embrace both bride and groom in the receiving line. Nora didn't go, of course. The details came from Chloe. The wedding was originally going to be a small, private affair, but how could they possibly limit the guest list when so many people had been so kind, cooking meals for them, driving Robin back and forth to physical therapy appointments, minding Lyra whenever Robin has one of her blinding headaches. The pain, which is so debilitating that even the slightest glimmer of light is unbearable, confines her to bed rest for days at a time behind closed blinds and heavy drapes.

At those unavoidable family occasions when they must be together, such as Chloe's and Drew's graduations, Robin is always gracious, her kindness as natural as ever. Women admire her courage and men want to protect her even more now. Her unspoken forgiveness is painful for Nora. There can be no setting things straight. Life can only run its obdurate course. She still dreams the same dream, still wakes in a cold sweat, afraid of being found out, even though one demon is dead, his known homicides three women and a child but, as it turns out, not that drunken man in the desert roadhouse. The man was robbed and badly beaten, but survived. And his assailant, according to Silver Tellmine police records, was a stranger, a young man they never found. No mention of a teenage girl. Not a word.

Just as in the law she studies, whatever the truth proves in one case may little matter in another. More important than answers in an examined life are the questions. And like flames round the phoenix these continue to sustain her. Why did she pay him? What was she trying to protect? Why did she stand there doing nothing? What did she really want to happen? Evil is contagious. It thrives on blindness and denial, inevitably infecting those who are afraid to speak or act against it.

She no longer works at the *Chronicle,* where Ken, according to Stephen, chafes under the mantle of publisher. Instead, she is a full-time law student nearing the end of her first year. She volunteers twice a week at Sojourn House, one of those nights in the dining room where she simply visits with the families while they eat dinner. She enjoys talking with the children, often taking the smaller ones off to play so their mothers can eat in peace, for a few minutes at least. It saddens her that some of the children are so hard to reach, their wariness having been ground into them at such a young age. Like their mothers, they are often quicker to forgive and accept than they are to trust. The women are always kind to her. And if any have heard the story, they never let on. Their own secrets are burden enough.

About the Author

Mary McGarry Morris is the author of seven novels. She was a National Book Award and PEN/Faulkner finalist for her first novel, *Vanished*. In 1991 her novel *A Dangerous Woman* was chosen by *Time* magazine as one of the "Five Best Novels of the Year" and was made into a motion picture. Her bestselling novel *Songs in Ordinary Time* was an Oprah Book Club selection and a CBS television movie. Also among her critically acclaimed novels are *Fiona Range, A Hole in the Universe,* and *The Lost Mother.* She lives in Massachusetts.

About the Type

This book was set in Elegant Garamond, a transitional serif font. The letterforms are based on Granjon, an oldstyle typeface designed by George William Jones in 1928 for the Mergenthaler Linotype Company.